"The perfect blend of history, faith, and love in all its forms, this tale of second chances and brave choices swept me away. Laura Frantz brings colonial coastal Virginia to life so well, I could almost taste the salty sea breeze. Expertly crafted and elegantly penned, *A Heart Adrift* proves once again why this author ranks among my all-time favorites. Highly recommended for fans of historical fiction."

Jocelyn Green, Christy Award–winning
author of *Shadows of the White City*

"Laura Frantz has a way with story, lacing her books with hope and starlight. *A Heart Adrift* contains a considerable amount of both. It's a sweetly satisfying novel that is as addictive as the chocolates Esmée Shaw creates and Henri Lennox craves. A slow-burn romance aches with longing and the possibility of second chances, but it's the relationship between vastly different sisters that stole my heart: gentle Esmée, who finds all she's ever wanted against the backdrop of crashing waves and an isolated island, and vivacious Eliza, a woman who discovers everything she was always meant to be in the loss of all she thought she was.

"*A Heart Adrift* firmly anchors readers during the stirrings of the hardly remembered French and Indian War. And in the middle of that storm, it shines a light on providential grace and the beauty of redemptive love."

Kimberly Duffy, author of *A Tapestry of Light* and *Every Word Unsaid*

"*A Heart Adrift* is a lush treatise on love lost and found at the intersection of ambition and desire. While Esmée was endearing to me as a woman with agency and intellect, persevering against the rigid constructs of her time period, Henri's passion to forge a life with the woman he loves while danger looms awakened every last one of my romantic sensibilities. Laura Frantz's rich tapestry of history and heroism is destined to dazzle readers of Susanna Kearsley and Diana Gabaldon—all while luring new fans with its intricate plot, delicious pacing, and welcome intrigue. This long-established queen of epic historical fiction is at the height of her game. And I know I speak for many when I happily say I cannot wait to see where she sweeps us away to next!"

Rachel McMillan, author of *The London Restoration* and *The Mozart Code*

A HEART
Adrift

Books by Laura Frantz

The Frontiersman's Daughter

Courting Morrow Little

The Colonel's Lady

The Mistress of Tall Acre

A Moonbow Night

The Lacemaker

A Bound Heart

An Uncommon Woman

Tidewater Bride

A Heart Adrift

The Ballantyne Legacy

Love's Reckoning

Love's Awakening

Love's Fortune

A HEART
Adrift

a novel

LAURA
FRANTZ

Revell
a division of Baker Publishing Group
Grand Rapids, Michigan

Published by Revell
a division of Baker Publishing Group
PO Box 6287, Grand Rapids, MI 49516-6287
www.revellbooks.com

Library of Congress Cataloging-in-Publication Data
Names: Frantz, Laura, author.
Title: A heart adrift : a novel / Laura Frantz.
Description: Grand Rapids, MI : Revell, a division of Baker Publishing Group, [2022]
Identifiers: LCCN 2021018771 | ISBN 9780800734978 (paperback) | ISBN 9780800741020 (casebound) | ISBN 9781493434121 (ebook)
Subjects: GSAFD: Love stories.
Classification: LCC PS3606.R4226 H43 2022 | DDC 813/.6—dc23
LC record available at https://lccn.loc.gov/2021018771

Scripture used in this book, whether quoted or paraphrased by the characters, is from the King James Version of the Bible.

Published in association with Books & Such Literary Management, 52 Mission Circle, Suite 122, PMB 170, Santa Rosa, CA 95409-5370, www.booksandsuch.com.

Baker Publishing Group publications use paper produced from sustainable forestry practices and post-consumer waste whenever possible.

22 23 24 25 26 27 28   7 6 5 4 3 2 1

To my heart sister,
Ginger Graham,
who reached home ahead of me.
I hope heaven has a beautiful library.

Prologue

> Sigh no more, ladies, sigh no more, men were deceivers ever;
> One foot in sea, and one on shore, to one thing constant never.
>
> Shakespeare

Virginia Coast
April 1745

With his back to the coastal wind, Henri Lennox settled his arms around Esmée Shaw, guiding her soft, pale hands with his tanned, callused fingers as they let the long silken line out. The pear-shaped kite caught on a gust, tugging at the string till it threatened to snap.

"Let it fly away from you bit by bit," he told her.

She did so, her laugh a surprised trill as the kite climbed higher. "Shall I let out more line?"

"Slowly, aye. With the right technique, you can even make it dance."

"What?"

"Just give a tug to the string now and again. Like this." He showed her as they gazed upward, the kite zigzagging against the azure sky, its tail a scarlet streak as it soared and dipped.

Wonder laced her tone. "Where did you get such a winsome creation?"

"The East Indies. They've been kite-flying for centuries. We colonials are just coming awake. Our kite lacks but one thing."

"Oh?" She tugged on the line and sent the kite dancing again.

He relaxed his hold on her hands, resting his jaw against her hatless head. She fit neatly beneath his chin, her back warm against his linen-clad chest, the wind riffling her carefully pinned hair like he longed to do with his fingers. He breathed in the telltale rose scent that seemed to imbue every ebony strand. "The kite lacks decoration. Our entwined initials should suit."

"Henri . . . how romantic." Her voice held a touch of teasing. "'Tis something I might fancy, not you."

"You've no idea what keeps me awake long nights at sea."

The afternoon sun sank behind them when it had been in their eyes minutes before. Had it not just been noon? At their feet was an empty basket, the remains of a *piquenique*. The cold meats, cheeses, and fruit had been devoured, even the little comfits molded in the shape of anchors from Shaw's Chocolate shop. Esmée's hat was atop the sand near her discarded shoes. Henri saw Admiral and Mrs. Shaw at a distance, slowly walking the beach with Esmée's younger sister.

He kissed his beloved's soft brow, his hands falling to her tightly cinched waist. "With you, time seems to melt away when I want it to stand still."

"If I could stop the clock, I would." She let out more line, head tipped back as the kite soared higher. "I want to run with it."

"In those petticoats?" Even as he asked it, she darted away from him. Lithe and laughing, she ran full tilt along the shore, a ruffled white wave breaking over her bare feet.

He started after her, stepping over her hat and slippers. The sand slowed him, his boots heavy, but he finally caught up with her. He untangled the kite string from her fingers and led her behind a dune that hid them from any onlookers.

"Henri, will you spoil my merriment?"

"My mind is more on kissing than kites, Esmée."

She caught her breath as he brought the kite string behind his back, out of her reach, while his free arm encircled her. She laid her head upon his chest, her long-lashed eyes closing. Emotion knotted his throat. Did she realize she held his heart? Not just a piece of it. The entire whole of it.

She raised her head, her green eyes soft yet wary. "*Don't*, Henri."

He brushed back a dark tendril of her hair. "Don't kiss you?"

"Don't tell me you're leaving again."

"All right, *ma belle*. I'll just kiss you then." The tender moment was theirs, the future be hanged. He kissed her soundly. Rather, she kissed him, her arms tightening around his neck as if anchoring him to the spot and preventing their parting. Sensations she alone was capable of rousing swam through him, widening eddies of desire shadowed by regret.

"Captain Lennox? Esmée?"

At the sound of the admiral's voice they drew apart, and inexplicably Henri let go of the line. The colorful kite kept soaring, borne on a west wind over the water, seeming to touch the clouds before vanishing from sight.

CHAPTER

York, Virginia
September 1755

Chocolate had been Captain Henri Lennox's one weakness. Was it still?

Pondering it, Esmée wiped cocoa-dusted hands on her apron and stood in the open doorway of the chocolate shop facing York's sail-studded harbor. The noon sun still held a touch of summer, drenching her in buttery yellow light.

A pint of honey-sweetened milk. Two dried Mexican chilies. One cinnamon stick. A crushed vanilla pod. All whisked into a steamy froth with a wooden molinillo.

That was how the captain preferred his chocolate. Though it had been ten years since she'd last seen him, Henri Lennox's memory still chafed like a saltwater rash. Would it always?

Overhead the shop's wooden sign swung noisily on its iron bracket in a contrary coastal wind. *Shaw's Chocolate.* Newly painted and adorned with a silver chocolate pot, it beckoned countless cocoa-craving customers.

At six o'clock, Esmée moved to close the door, trading the briny tang of the sea for the warm, rich scent of cocoa instead.

"Daughter, have you finished Lady Lightfoot's almonds?"

Esmée rounded the worktable as her father emerged from the adjoining coffeehouse that served as his office, his pleasure plain. Upon the long wooden countertop before them was tray after tray of confections. Esmée's favorites were the chocolate almonds, but she'd made several batches of sugared almonds too.

"Fit for the most fastidious matron in all the Tidewater," her father announced after close perusal. "And her annual ball."

Esmée smiled. "I've used cochineal and saffron to color them red and yellow—and spinach and berries for green and blue."

"Vibrant." He tossed a red confection into his mouth. "Delicious."

"I've more to do tomorrow if the weather continues cool, though I'm running short of orange flower water."

He crossed to the large bow-fronted window, taking in the moored vessels like the admiral of old. "We're overdue for a merchant fleet. We've too much illicit Dutch tea and silk handkerchiefs of late."

Was there a beat of regret in his voice? Did he miss his seafaring days? Alarm unfurled like a pirate's black flag inside her. Barnabas Shaw held himself erect, defying the stoop of age, his silver hair hidden beneath a white periwig, his garments tailored to his distinguished frame. He seemed preoccupied of late. A bit on edge. He claimed it was on account of all the bloodshed, but that seemed naught but a bad dream, the conflict on the distant frontier betwixt faraway England, France, and the Indians.

Or was he pondering her mother? Though Eleanor Shaw had been gone three years, it seemed far longer.

Turning, he faced Esmée. "Where is our summons to the ball? I've not had a look at it."

She unearthed a stack of papers beneath the counter, the gilt-edged invitation at the very bottom.

"Read it to me, if you would, as I've misplaced my spectacles."

She held the card aloft in the fading light. "'Pleasure Ball. While we live, let us live. Admiral Barnabas Shaw and Miss Esmée Shaw are requested to attend the ball at Lightfoot Hall on Tuesday, seventh of October current, at seven o'clock p.m.'"

"Your sister is coming from Williamsburg, and we shall go together as a foursome."

"Eliza never misses a frolic." Esmée placed the invitation on a shelf. "She and Quinn are a popular pair. They dance divinely."

"As do you." At last he moved away from the window. "I shall be your proud escort. No doubt you'll not lack dance partners, even at eight and twenty. 'Tis not too late, you know . . ."

Not too late for love, for marriage.

The ongoing lament was now a familiar song. "I've no wish to wed and leave you, Father. An occasional frolic is enough for me. Besides, who would manage the shop? Your other business ventures take all your time. You don't even like chocolate."

He chuckled. "'Twas your mother's preoccupation. But she came by it honestly, being a chocolatier's daughter."

"A preoccupation I am happy to continue." Esmée eyed the almonds for any imperfections. "At least for now. I've none of Eliza's ambitions. I want to live simply. Be of benefit to somebody somewhere."

She reached for the commonplace book stuffed with recipes penned in Mama's faded, scrolling hand. The secrets of the chocolatier's trade. She'd not exchange the old book for a chest of buried treasure . . . or a husband.

Smoothing her soiled apron, Esmée set the chatelaine at her waist clanking. Crafted of sterling silver, it had been her mother's, a practical yet whimsical piece of jewelry she was rarely without.

"Be that as it may"—her father cleared his throat—"you were in love once."

His low words rolled across the empty shop like a rogue wave, swamping and nearly upending her. Schooling her astonishment, she stared at him. "A foolish infatuation I've since recovered from."

"Have you?" He kept his gaze on Water Street. "Or is it more you met a man who's made every would-be suitor of yours unworthy ever since?"

How pithy he could be. How wise. But how wrong he was about this antiquated matter.

"A man who set me aside for the sea." Esmée untied her apron and hung it from a wall peg. "A man who is deemed a respectable privateer in some circles but a pirate prince in others."

He looked at her then, no apology in his weather-beaten features. "I don't mean to nettle you, Daughter. I only mention it because there's been talk that Captain Lennox has returned to the colonies."

Her hands fisted in the folds of her skirt. Though she'd been about to retreat into the kitchen, all such practicalities flew out of her benumbed head.

"The scuttlebutt is he intends to finish the lighthouse on Indigo Island. And I must say I heartily approve. Virginia—Chesapeake Bay—has ne'er needed it so much as now. Guard ships are not enough. We must have a light."

The light that was my idea and he abandoned upon our heated parting.

Her father talked on, unaware of the maelstrom in her head and heart. "No doubt that and his usual business bring him back, owner and part owner of several vessels as he is."

Captain Lennox—Henri—hadn't been home for years, at least not on the streets of York. Last she knew he'd been sailing the trade routes of the Spanish Main, his many exploits printed in the *Virginia Gazette*. Of late he held the record for the fastest sailing time, some 240 miles in less than a day. Exploits she'd dismissed as more fancy than fact. Betimes he seemed more ghost, haunting the coast.

Haunting her.

She'd grown used to thinking him afar off, not hazarding a meeting on some side street in York or even Williamsburg. The very possibility of stumbling across him had her all aflutter, her claimed recovery in question.

"Time for supper." With a jangling of keys, her father locked the front door. "I'll walk up the hill and home with you after I dismiss the indentures."

She hardly heard him, lost as she was in the tattered memories of the past. His footsteps retreated, but his hard words outlasted him.

"You were in love once."

Absently she fiddled with her chatelaine, toying with the ornamental chain with its many pins and clasps. It bore several significant trinkets. A key. Scissors. A watch. A pincushion ball. A needle case. A heart-shaped vinaigrette and another for sweetmeats.

Even a tiny silver lighthouse.

CHAPTER

Henri's homecoming had been as silent and stealthy as he could make it. He'd struck his vessel's colors, emptied her of all crew, and moored the *Relentless* at the island's opposite end, facing the mainland and not the Atlantic. Now, climbing rickety, weathered steps to the stone cottage he once called home, Henri stowed his captaincy as he'd soon stow his tarred garments.

Behind him trod Cyprian, his steward and a native of the Mosquito Coast. Clad in trews and a Monmouth cap, he was still barefoot, as he was when on the deck.

"You needn't shadow me," Henri said over his shoulder. "You're as deserving of a pint and freedom as all the rest."

"Aye, sir. But first I must see this pile of sand ye call home—and the light tower ye oft speak of." Cyprian's dark eyes reflected new appreciation. "Are ye lord and master of all the island?"

"Such as it is, aye. But not the ordinary on Indigo's opposite end. That is Mistress Saltonstall's business."

"And who is this woman, sir?"

"The widow of one of my ablest sailors, God rest him," Henri replied, anticipating his next question. "When he died he left her enough prize money to build the ordinary."

"She will not care ye seek yer cottage instead?"

"Nay." Henri reached into the bosom of his shirt and withdrew a coral necklace. "Give her my regards. I'll pay her a visit in time. For now, she'll be hard-pressed to keep up with you henhearted numbskulls."

Cyprian laughed. "We shall drink and eat our fill and tie our hammocks to the trees tonight, then row to the mainland tomorrow?"

"I row to the mainland. You stay and careen the vessel."

"So my role as steward ends? Ye'll be alone tonight? Is that not lonesome?"

"Nay."

Even as he uttered the half-truth, Henri wished it back. How could he explain the pure pleasure of profound solitude after crowded months at sea? The disorienting process of regaining one's equilibrium as well as one's land legs, which were better acquired alone?

They came to the cottage, tarrying outside its locked door. His gaze swept the shore, the sunburnt grasses and sand, till it came to rest on the half-finished light tower rising like a smokeless candle over the beach.

Cyprian's mouth sagged when he saw it. Recovering himself, he gave an admiring whistle. "Ye'll finish the light?"

"It requires a stonemason and a glass top." Henri discarded the longing he felt when he looked at it. In memory it stood taller, needed less work. The keeper's cottage was finished, at least, though it would remain empty till the tower was done.

Would it always remind him of Esmée?

The boxy lines of his cottage—deceptively plain outwardly—were softened in the September gloaming. He unlocked the door, and it creaked open at the push of his hand. As Henri entered, Cyprian all but gaped on the threshold. Fine furnishings. Colorful Turkish carpets. Framed maps. Dutch paintings in gilt frames.

And dust.

A mouse skittered by his booted feet. He'd need a cat. The tiger-striped feline on board the *Relentless* would do.

"Fetch Clementine for me the next time you come round, aye?"

"Shall I bring the wee hammock she sleeps in?"

"Aye."

With a nod, Cyprian continued surveying this treasure chest of stone as Henri passed into the kitchen. His cupboards were bare of all but tinned tea and a few unopened bottles of Madeira, which was mostly for guests, as he drank little but bumboo and brackish water.

What he craved was chocolate.

As Henri poked and prodded his way about the cottage's four rooms, Cyprian grabbed a rag and wiped a Windsor chair clean in the parlor. The hearth bore a blackened log and soured ashes from Henri's homecoming five years before. He'd avoided York and done his business in Norfolk then. But this time he'd lay over longer. Attend to his investments and business ventures. At the very least deliver the letters from fellow seamen to kin on shore.

With a low whistle, Cyprian eyed the shelves that framed the fireplace like bookends. "So many books, sir, and I cannot make out a single word."

"Find someone to school you."

A ready grin. "Someone in petticoats."

With a wry smile, Henri sat down on the dusted chair. When he said no more, Cyprian saluted him and sailed out the open door in the direction of the Flask and Sword with urgency in his rolling gait.

In the utter stillness came the familiar lapping of water against the shore and the odd chorus of cicadas in the surrounding trees. The richly appointed room tilted and spun and finally settled. Henri fought to stay awake.

He was too weary to shed his sea-tainted garments. Too weary to quench his thirst. Too weary to even shut the door on the encroaching night. His head tilted forward, his bristled jaw nearly resting on his chest. His clasped hands, never far from the pistol at his middle, relaxed. He drifted . . . dreamed. In time his own snoring jarred him awake.

Or was it something else?

He blinked the sleep from his eyes. Tried to focus on a cobwebbed corner. Someone seemed a part of the velvety shadows now filling every crevice and cubbyhole, a rebuke in her unforgettable forest-green eyes.

Esmée Shaw.

That sent him to his feet. He slammed the door, locked it, and passed into his bedchamber with a prayer on his lips rather than a barely squelched epithet.

Let the words of my mouth and the meditation of my heart be acceptable in Thy sight, O Lord, my strength and my redeemer.

Within the confines of the Williamsburg milliner and mantua-maker, Esmée watched her sister turn slowly about in her new gown. A great quantity of silk and silver thread had been expended, every extravagance granted. Eliza Shaw Cheverton—Lady Drysdale—was everything Esmée was not. The wife of a leading Virginia official. Social. Beautiful. Daring. Queenly in height. And as round as five months of pregnancy could make her.

Eliza pirouetted despite the baby's bulk. "What say you about the color, Sister?"

Esmée caught her bottom lip between her teeth. "'Tis . . . eye-catching."

"Blindingly orange, you mean." Eliza's blue eyes glittered. "Like a pumpkin."

"'Tis an appropriate color for autumn. You'll make a striking entrance."

"I do believe the length needs altering." Mouth puckered with pins, Mistress Bell knelt and began fussing with the hem.

Eliza put a hand to her tawny hair, a mass of unpowdered curls. "You should see my towering wig, powdered to perfection and boasting a ship or two."

Eyes rounding, Esmée tried to envision such an elaborate coiffure. Eliza had a knack for influencing fashion with her shocking style. "You jest."

"Father will be amused." Taking out her new lace-tipped fan, Eliza stirred the heated air. "I do hope Lady Lightfoot's ball is on a cool night. Rainy, even. I can't imagine dancing in such heat, especially with two to consider."

"As your elder sister"—Esmée's gaze traveled to her sister's expanding middle—"I caution you against dancing at all." Even as she said it, she knew her hopes defied conventions. Gentry or no, women were rarely slowed by pregnancy, continuing to go and do till they became too uncomfortable. Eliza showed no signs of slowing her pace.

"Nonsense. Tell me again which of Mama's gowns you'll be wearing?"

"The saffron silk."

"Surely *you* jest." Eliza's distaste led to a theatrical shudder.

"The fabric is still lush, though the lace is yellowed with age."

"Old as it is, I'm surprised it's not moth-eaten." Eliza took command as she always did in such matters. "As for the lace, a misfortune easily remedied. I spied an exquisite length of blond Mechlin in the back room."

"Indeed." Mistress Bell finished her pinning. "I've also an exceptional Brussels lace."

Lips pursed, Eliza studied Esmée. "I suppose you'll go wigless and natural again. But 'tis just as well. 'Twould take a whole hogshead of powder to coat that black head of yours." Her fan fluttered harder. "What about jewels?"

Esmée brought a hand to her bare throat. "Mama's pearls."

"Pearls are passé. Father's emeralds pair well with so yellow a gown."

The largest emerald was big as a hen's egg. "Pearls are always my preference," Esmée said. Elegant. Unassuming. "As for Father's jewels, you know what will be said . . ."

"Ill-gotten gain," Eliza whispered dramatically, then gave a wicked laugh. "Let them whisper what they will. Father is beyond reproach—"

Esmée put a finger to her lips as Mistress Bell reentered the room, hands full of blue cards wrapped with lace. For a few minutes, her worries were pushed aside as she perused the offerings, finally deciding on the Mechlin bobbin lace, which Eliza insisted on paying for.

The fitting finished, Eliza hurried her down Nassau Street to their townhouse. If Esmée ever rued anything about her younger sister, it was Eliza's infernal rush.

"Look at the maples turning the very hue of my ball gown—and yours." Esmée slowed her pace, brittle leaves rustling underfoot. "Williamsburg is glorious in the fall."

Eliza turned her face skyward as a maple leaf drifted down. "Glorious indeed, and a wee bit more refined than York. All those jacks and rogues along the waterfront! I do wonder why you dally there when Quinn and I have opened our home to you. You could have a splendid season here . . . go husband hunting."

"But the chocolate shop—"

"Turn the shopkeeping over to the servants," Eliza told her. "Promise me you'll come and stay once the baby arrives, at least briefly."

"I know precious little about infants, but I'll be glad to help you if I can. Father may well come too. He's counting down till his first grandchild."

"I wonder if he will come. He was always at sea when we were small. I don't know how Mama managed it. Writing letters perpetually to some port that were rarely answered."

"Not a port. Ascension Island. I found an entire box of letters sealed with red wax from Father after Mama died, remember. All lovingly perused."

Sadness shaded Eliza's finely molded features. "Would that we had Mama instead."

They turned down a brick walkway that led past a grand magnolia tree to the Cheverton townhouse. A butler in livery opened the door before they'd set foot on the first step, greeting them and then sending to the kitchen for tea at Eliza's request.

Esmée left her lace purchase and straw hat in the foyer and followed Eliza into a newly refurbished parlor of Egyptian blue overlooking the rear garden. They sat, and a tea table between them was soon laid with the latest creamware tea service.

Eliza was unusually subdued. "Father's last exploits were the death of Mama."

Esmée didn't care to dwell on it. Many years had passed since they fled the pirate's den of Rhode Island, exchanging Block Island for York's sandy shores. Something nefarious had sent them south, with Father's northern enemies determined to lay him low. Escaping their net, he'd begun anew in Virginia, a respected admiral turned shipbuilder, merchant, tax assessor, and founding member of Grace Church.

Not the scourge of merchant vessels sailing the trade routes of the Spanish Main.

"Do you ever wonder why Father turned to privateering after so illustrious a naval career?" Eliza whispered.

Tea was brought, delaying Esmée's answer.

"Hyson or imperial?" her sister asked.

"Hyson with cream, please." Esmée looked out the window, where the last summer irises bent beneath the rising wind. The tea's delicate fragrance, usually soothing, failed to relieve. "Father's very lifeblood is salt water."

Eliza leaned in conspiratorially. "Speaking of maritime matters, there's tittle-tattle floating about that a certain sea captain has returned to Virginia."

Esmée felt a slight tremor as she lifted her cup. "Father said the same."

"Does that upset you? Your hand is shaking." Eliza's concern only elevated Esmée's unease. "I thought perhaps after so many years, you'd all but yawn at the mention of his name."

Yawn? Rather, yowl. "Henri Lennox remains a conundrum, then and now."

"Who is the captain anyway?" Eliza mused. "Respected privateer . . . or pirate?"

Esmée lifted her shoulders in a slight shrug. "'Tis ever been a puzzle separating pirates from privateers. People have a terrible thirst for gossip and believe the worst."

"I'll not align with his enemies and call him a pirate but rather a respected privateer and former commissioned officer of the Royal Navy." Eliza's hand slipped to her middle as if her maternity stays were laced too tightly. "Tell me again why you two parted. The details escape me after so long. All I can remember is the both of you being absolutely besotted."

Besotted. The word, once sweet, now seemed laughable.

"He chose the sea—his captaincy and ship—over me." Esmée took a silver spoon and stirred sugar into her cup. "And I could not conscience being left behind on shore."

"No doubt our family history has some bearing on your very messy parting. With Father away at sea so much, we hardly knew him. Mama was more widow. We seemed rather fatherless except we never lacked a thing. Even now, deeply involved in colonial maritime affairs, he is a riddle, always on the go and remarkably closemouthed."

Esmée knew firsthand her father's long silences—rife with unspoken regrets, she'd often thought—and the surprising recent words he did utter.

"You were in love once."

Even now, a sennight later, the words clung to her like pitch.

Desperate for a distraction, Esmée looked about the lovely parlor still smelling of fresh milk paint. Eliza's redecorating had no end. "I fear Father is missing Mama more rather than less as time goes by. Lately he seems especially restless. Preoccupied."

Eliza's alarmed eyes pinned her over the rim of her Sevres cup. "'Tis almost October, the month Mama passed. Surely that is the reason."

Was it?

Esmée forced a smile, more undone by Eliza's rare discomfiture than Father's moods. "Perhaps the Lightfoot pleasure ball is just the antidote for us all."

CHAPTER *three*

Henri rowed the five miles from Indigo Island to the mainland in under an hour, spurred on by seas so flat and smooth they resembled an opal. Such becalmed waters were usually a hindrance, stranding ships and starving crews nearer the equator. The doldrums were the bane of Atlantic sailors. But here off Virginia's coast, all was in his favor, though he wished for a light wind, if only to allay the late September sun beating at his back and dampening his linen shirt.

A sack of letters lay in the jolly boat's bottom, brought over eight thousand miles from Ascension Island to loved ones throughout Virginia. Since his own familial ties were so meagre, he'd had no letters to post. The lonesome lack sharpened his resolve to keep the tenuous ties of his fellow mariners intact.

Looking over his shoulder, he squinted beneath the brim of his cocked hat as York's sprawling façade took shape. His mental map of the thriving town was largely intact. Little had changed other than an array of new warehouses as befitted a port town. Water Street still boasted a staggering assortment of taverns and rum shops and bawdy houses, as plenteous as the ships glutting the harbor. On the cliff above, handsome, genteel homes looked down like disgruntled parishioners on the sinning street.

His gaze hung on one. The Shaw residence. He'd last ducked beneath the door's lintel at the age of five and twenty. Esmée was younger, a vision of midnight hair, eyes green as a Montserrat forest, and a smile that had once stood him still. What had ten years wrought? Likely she'd wed. Given her parents grandchildren.

His mind reached back to a memory long blocked, the day he and Esmée had first met. The *Relentless* had moored at Block Island, a stronghold of privateers, pirates, and assorted mariners in Rhode Island. He rarely sailed so far north, but unexpected business had taken him there.

Three young women had been walking the beach, a fragile April sun breaking through after a fearsome winter. They were shelling, bare of foot, skirts lifted above their ankles. Their lilting voices carried over the water as the *Relentless* docked, drawing the attention of his affection-starved crew. He'd rebuked them for gawking but was hard-pressed to rein himself in and follow his own admonishment.

And then, that very eve, he'd found himself at a supper party hosted by the prominent Williams family. In Esmée walked, her smile wide, her pale green gown beguiling. Henri was taken aback by her warmth, her genuineness. She was flushed by the sun, as curvaceous and inviting as tropical fruit.

"Captain Lennox," their hostess queried, "have you met Miss Esmée Shaw?"

Henri gave the requisite bow while Esmée curtsied prettily, hands clasped at her slim waist.

"The privateer?" she asked, her long-lashed gaze holding his. "Henri Lennox?"

Ahn-ree. Her French was perfect. Few pronounced his forename well. That alone left him half-smitten. "Should I bow out now?"

"Never fear." Her face dimpled into a laugh. "I don't believe half what the papers print."

"The truth is never so colorful, nay." He clasped his hands behind his back and struck a non-piratical pose. "You are the daughter of the renowned Admiral Shaw of Rhode Island."

"Soon to be situated in fair Virginia."

He regarded her closely. *What?*

"Father won't stray far from the sea. He's purchased a townhouse in the port town of York. We'll be opening a chocolate shop and coffeehouse on Water Street."

"Not far from my home off the Virginia capes."

Her expression was unsurprised. "You own an island, 'tis said."

"Indigo Island, aye."

"How did you come by it?"

"As payment of a debt owed me."

"Do you know its history?"

He smiled, enjoying their banter. "Perhaps the better question is, do you?"

"Father told me a ship heavily laden with indigo from Porto Bello foundered there in a storm a hundred years ago." Her eyes sparkled. "I should like to see your island."

Such bold words bordered on coquetry. But her eyes held such guileless interest he was charmed. "Indigo Island's shells are the finest I've seen beyond Hispaniola, the pearl of the Caribbean."

"You saw me shelling today as you docked." She extended her fan, its leaves painted with a ship, the edges lace tipped. "A handsome vessel you command, Captain Lennox."

The rest of their conversation was a pleasurable blur. If not for his unusual foray north, would they have ever met?

Shoving his musings aside and returning to the present, Henri pulled harder at the oars, then beached the jolly on a little-used stretch of white sand north of town. His senior-most crew had come ashore the day before, the rest careening the vessel and biding their time at Mistress Saltonstall's ordinary. His own day was a blank slate once he'd taken care of the post, the hours to fill as he willed.

By noon he'd walked the length and breadth of town, dined on York River oysters, and purchased supplies for Indigo Island. Word was spreading he'd returned, and by three o'clock, he'd been invited to a function that necessitated a visit to a tailor and some serious second thoughts.

Steeling his resolve, he entered the spacious shop of Brambly and Boone to find half a dozen tailors at a worktable before the large front window. September's waning light streamed over breeches and coats and waistcoats in various stages of construction. No shoddy cloth here.

"Good afternoon, sir." A small, bespectacled man emerged from a back room and gave a little bow. "Richard Boone, sir."

"Henri Lennox." He removed his hat, aware of his dishabille after a morning's row and a day about town. "I've come for a suit of clothes fit for a pleasure ball."

Respect smote the man's close-set eyes. "Ah, Lady Lightfoot's, no doubt, though there's a great deal of entertainment to be had in Williamsburg as well." He went to a glass case and retrieved paper ribbons with which to measure Henri. "Lennox, did you say? Captain Lennox of the *Relentless*?"

"The same," Henri replied, aware of every eye at the worktable now upon him.

"Honored, Captain. I promise you a suit of clothes that befits your rank and station. A quality wool broadcloth woven to a rich finish, perhaps. Our seamstress shall sew your shirt." Boone took a wheezing breath. "Have you any preferences, sir?"

"No pleated ruffles or other frippery," Henri said as the measuring ribbon stretched from his shoulder to his wrist.

"Mother-of-pearl buttons and a stock of the best linen, adorned at the end with fringe or knots, is my recommendation." Boone stood back and surveyed him. "Should I summon a wigmaker, sir?"

"No need." Wigs and powder were as unwelcome as ruffles and lace. The sea had stripped him to the barest essentials, including dress. While many good men on shore suffered want, others smothered themselves in velvet and silver thread. He'd not be among them. "But a shoemaker is in order."

"Consider it done." Boone's scrutiny shifted to Henri's booted feet. "Silver buckles and black leather seem in order as well."

"Agreed."

"We'll have your garments ready in two days' time. Will you be lodging at the Swan like so many watermen?"

"Nay. The Royal Oake on Church Street."

"Of course. A gentleman's establishment. Would you like your purchases delivered there, sir?"

"Obliged, aye."

"And will this be on credit, Captain? Or otherwise?"

"Spanish silver dollars."

"Ah." The sudden smile on the tailor's face promised a handsome suit indeed. Coin was always hard to come by in the colonies. "Very well, sir."

The Royal Oake's dining room boasted a table for twenty, and a dizzying array of dishes promised no one would emerge hungry. While the other lodgers lingered at table, Henri sought the silence of the parlor, where a case clock's ticking reminded him that time was all too fleeting. On a side table was a stack of Virginia newspapers from as far back as summer to the present day. He reached for the latest, the ink smudged from repeated perusals. Best familiarize himself with local matters, at least, before braving the ball and being asked his opinion on colonial politics or the ferocious fighting on the frontier.

"A gentleman cannot possibly ponder current events without a pipe." His hostess, Charlotte Oake, a comely widow who operated the inn with her aging father-in-law, held out not only a handsome filled pipe but a light. The pipe's clay bowl bore a Scottish unicorn on one side and an English lion on the other.

Pleasure warmed his words. "Your hospitality is unsurpassed."

"Bull's-eye tobacco." She smiled as she lit the pipe, and fragrant smoke purled between them. "Only the best for our guests."

At the sound of her father-in-law's voice, she moved away with a beguiling swish of her skirts while Henri returned to the most recent *Virginia Gazette*. International news, most of it disturbing. A plethora of notices for runaway slaves and indentures. And ads—a great many.

Yellow candlelight spread across the page, and his gaze landed on the last thing he wanted to see.

> Sold here. Shaw's Superior Chocolate. Water Street, York. Soconusco, Caracas, and Maracaibo cocoa, the purest in the world. Greatly recommended by several eminent physicians for its lightness on the stomach and its great use in all consumptive cases. Two shillings sixpence per pound.

He set his jaw. His sweet tooth roared.

Pulling the pipe from between his teeth, Henri eyed the door through which his hostess had disappeared. Was there any chocolate to be had in the house?

He'd passed by Shaw's on his afternoon walk through town, the sweet, velvety aroma slowing his pace. He needed a pressed cake or two wrapped in paper and stamped with the Shaw insignia before returning to Indigo Island. 'Twas his one indulgence. Two shillings sixpence per pound exceeded a sailor's daily wage, if not a captain's.

On second thought, mayhap he'd avoid Shaw's altogether and see if there was any chocolate to be had in Williamsburg instead.

CHAPTER

four

Of all the things in the aromatic, tidy kitchen at Shaw's Chocolate, Esmée's favorite was the chocolate stone. Made of white Italian marble and placed at one end of the long worktable, it was the heart of a chocolatier's trade. Heated, the stone began melting the cocoa nibs even before she pressed her rolling pin to the brittle mass. She applied sure, even strokes born of years' experience by her mother's side, and the gritty nibs began to liquefy beneath her hands, releasing the most exquisite fragrance to be had indoors.

Around her the kitchen hummed, the indentured servants at different tasks. Simon was out back, grinding the cocoa at the hopper. Molly was but a few feet away from Esmée, molding a batch of soft, sugared chocolate in tiny tins, while Anna wrapped and stamped bricks of chocolate before carrying them to the storefront for display.

Father preferred Esmée out front. She drew customers as much as the merchandise, he oft said, remembering names and preferences and prior orders. But when her spirit grew troubled, she retreated to the kitchen, losing or at least solacing herself with the work. Within these walls were memories of her beloved mother, warm, rich, and sweet.

Shaw's Chocolate was Mama's doing. Mama's vision. But it was

Esmée's dowry and the place where she invested herself. One of two places where she felt a tie to her mother.

Even now her thoughts of a certain captain and a certain ship and a ball gown that lacked lace trim faded to the far reaches as she poured a waterfall of Maracaibo sugar onto the chocolate stone, then rolled and mixed the mass till all was smooth. Next, she reached for a small tin, extracted orange peel, added it to the mixture, then threw in a dash of vanilla and more sugar. Bittersweet became a more delicately flavored chocolate. With a swipe of her finger she sampled it, waiting a discerning second before her eyes went wide with delight.

Chocolate perfection.

Molly chuckled. "'Tis a wonder, mistress, yer not broad as a bulkhead with all the cocoa butter ye partake."

Smiling, Esmée took another lick. She *had* gained a stone since . . . She forced herself to finish the untimely thought. *Since the captain last saw me.* She took a wooden tool and scraped the melted chocolate into a waiting bowl to cool.

Anna stopped her stamping. "Is it true yer father has ordered a hand mill from Boston, Miss Shaw?"

Nodding, Esmée poured another pound of cocoa nibs onto the stone. "Not only a hand mill but a large grinder that produces one hundred weight of chocolate in six hours."

"I second that!" Simon shouted through the back door.

"Chocolate's becoming the beverage of choice for colonists," Esmée said, "if for no other reason than the crown's infernal tax on tea."

"Glad I am that cocoa sails straight from the Caribbean and England has no say." Molly began picking out the chocolates that didn't pass muster. "I'm drinking so much coffee lately I nearly forget what tea tastes like!"

Esmée ceased her rolling as Josiah poked his head into the kitchen from the shop entrance. "Widow Oake to see you, Miss Shaw."

"Let's trade places then." Esmée handed him the roller, washed her hands, and exchanged her soiled apron for a clean one with a readiness she was far from feeling.

"Good morning, Miss Shaw." The widow's chilly smile seemed no more genuine than paste gems. Beneath her beribboned hat, Charlotte Oake's eyes held no warmth. "I would rather deal with you than the help."

"What do you buy?" Esmée replied, hoping to conclude their business as quickly as possible. Charlotte's maid stood in back of her, wearing a timid smile.

Esmée's gaze flew from the calendar proclaiming it the first of October to the clock Father had taken down. Time seemed to stop when the Oakes appeared. The widow was fond of reminding Esmée she was not among York's founding families but an outsider, an easterner.

Still, Esmée tried to be cordial and fill the lengthy silence. "How goes it at the Royal Oake?"

"All our rooms are full at present." Charlotte moved about the charmingly arranged shop, her gloved hand touching this or that. "I'm in need of chocolate for our table. Certain gentlemen lodgers seem especially fond of such."

As Charlotte passed by a front window, her gown caught the light, the celestial blue silk cascading like a ruffled wave to her elegantly shod feet. From London, likely. Her father-in-law insisted on London-made goods.

Esmée gestured to the recently stocked shelves. "We've a new array of flavors—anise, Ceylon cinnamon, nutmeg, and Madagascar vanilla if you'd like a taste."

"Vanilla, then." When Esmée passed her a sample, Charlotte pursed her lips as if she'd been handed a lemon instead. "I find Shaw's no match for the chocolatiers in New York and Philadelphia."

Esmée bit her lip. She'd never visited the foremost city chocolatiers. Could those goods be that much superior? Though theirs was a humble shop, they did their best to turn out a quality product.

"How do you recommend preparing your hot beverages?" Charlotte asked.

"Hot cocoa? I simply add powdered chocolate and sugar to steamed milk, stirring all the while. Once it's off the fire, whir the milk mixture with a hand mill till frothy."

"Milk, not water?"

"Milk makes for a richer drink."

"I'll take this pewter chocolate pot with the lidded hand mill, then, though I cower at the price." Charlotte passed it to Esmée with a frown. "And five of your best bricks of chocolate." Drifting to the display of other confections, she pointed to a chocolate tart Molly had baked that morning. "And this."

As Esmée wrapped her purchases, she was nearly undone by the widow's scrutiny.

"How is your sister, Lady Drysdale? I rarely see her in York these days."

Though Eliza had been married two years, Esmée oft forgot her sister's formal title. "She is busy with Williamsburg pursuits now that she resides there."

"I'd heard you might open a second chocolate shop in the capital." Charlotte gestured for her maid to take the purchases. "'Tis said your sister has been talking of such. Rather a step down for a titled woman to still be meddling in matters of commerce, is it not?"

The jibe barely skimmed Esmée's conscience. *A second shop?* More indentures. More machinery. More labor. And more cross, inquiring customers like the Oakes. Esmée returned the matter to Eliza's lap.

"My sister shall be happy to enlighten you on the matter if you ask her." Esmée knotted the string binding the purchases and passed them over the counter to the maid.

"Come along, Verity," Charlotte said at last. "We've the chandler to see next."

The petty tension dissolved at the closing of the shop door, which soon jingled open again as other customers entered. Half an hour later Esmée returned to the kitchen to gather chocolate for a delivery while Simon readied the pony cart outside. 'Twas her day to visit the almshouse, following Mama's habit.

Leaving the indentures to mind the shop, Esmée took the reins in hand and sought the end of Water Street heading north, blessedly free of her sister's lofty trappings and title, no lady's maid in pursuit. After the heat of the shop, the afternoon seemed cool, clouds piled as high as meringue and snuffing the sun. The road to the almshouse followed the coast with a sweeping view of the water, thus making it more pleasure than chore. Already the coastal landscape wore the robust mantle of autumn.

She hadn't delivered cocoa since last May, as their season for chocolate making was short in the Southern colonies. Fall to spring was when they plied their trade, their sultry summers devoted to other business.

Out here amid the wind and salt tang of the sea, she felt far more at peace than in some fussy ballroom, yet Lady Lightfoot's assembly loomed, a sennight away. Esmée nearly groaned aloud.

"Not all balls are bad, mind you," Eliza oft said.

Once, Father had escorted them to the governor's palace in Williamsburg, past the imposing forecourt and into the immense rear ballroom that bore double doors with steps leading to an elaborate formal garden. There, like something out of a fairy tale, Eliza captured the attention of Quinn, Lord Drysdale. A felicitous match, Father said, when all the stars aligned and turned a simple Eliza Shaw into a titled lady.

Esmée was content to be the older sister and watch the romantic drama unfold. The congenial, handsome Quinn. The ebullient, beautiful Eliza. His prominent kin scandalized that their rising star of a relative might be tainted by the privateering past of his affianced's admiral father. In the end, rumors were quelled, the wedding commenced, and now Esmée herself was to become an aunt in a few months' time. What would life hand them next?

The pony cart bumped along, hitting a stone or two and churning up dust. The brown ribbon of road unwound ahead of her, little traveled. Father didn't like her traveling alone, but the pistol secured beneath the seat hadn't been used once. Never had she encountered a threat. 'Twas simply a lonesome path to a place most avoided.

Tugging on the reins, she paused on a grassy knoll overlooking tidelands and islands. Indigo Island was the farthest, its rocky shore like a raised shoulder shrugging her away. Somewhere on the island stood the unfinished lighthouse, tall but dark. The plan had been to complete it prior to her and the captain's nuptials. They'd agreed to dismiss custom and wed on the beach, then honeymoon in his cottage. Sunrises and sunsets were said to be spectacular from that speck of land, the quiet and privacy unsurpassed.

Lately she'd heard no more from Father about Captain Lennox's return. A pity he was so seldom home, all that beauty unappreciated. For all she knew he'd already set sail again and she could drop her guard like a hot iron, letting go of her dread at encountering him on every corner.

Snapping the reins, she guided the pony onto the road again. She had little need of the dashing, intriguing Henri Lennox in her life. Her days were full, even if her heart was still adrift. She would not allow herself the tiniest spark of intrigue at his rumored appearance. The captain had not found her worthy then, nor would he now. They were both older and wiser, long past any youthful infatuation.

Another half mile and she rolled into the courtyard before the cluster of brick buildings that made up the almshouse. Two women gathering nuts in their aprons beneath a hickory tree looked up as she passed. In a far yard men chopped firewood and broke stones for road building, while unseen women spun cloth and gardened or worked in the kitchen.

To live here was to punish the poor for being poor, Father said. Elderly outcasts, widows, destitute women, disabled men, and orphaned children led a cheerless existence. Upon the arms of their humble garments was a bit of red cloth marked with a *P*, as they were wards of the parish. This humbling distinction hurt Esmée too. Was it not enough they were here? A hundred untold stories lived in their somber, shrunken faces. Even the children seemed half-alive, deprived of affection and family and life's basic comforts.

Her heart gave a little leap as half a dozen youngsters broke free of their chores and rushed toward her, as taken by her pony as the cocoa she brought. A sharp rebuke by the female trustee stole their joy. Mistress Boles approached, chronically ill-tempered and grasping, followed by the cheerier and slightly younger Miss Grove.

"I've need of helping hands to unload." Esmée oft wondered if the children ever saw any of what she brought. "I've real sweetmeats this time, not dry bricks of cocoa. Come near and I'll give you each a treat as a reward for your labors."

Before the matron could protest, Esmée doled out the best of the bounty—raisins and extra chocolate almonds from Lady Lightfoot's order. Something like daylight spilled into their eager, childish faces, their open hands wrenching Esmée's heart.

"A waste of confections, I daresay," Mistress Boles muttered.

Steeling herself against the rising tide of heartache—and the stench of unwashed bodies and mended garments—Esmée watched Mistress Boles chase the children away. She called after them, "I wish I could bring you a hundredfold more."

"If only every soul in Virginia was as generous as you, we'd be called the poorhouse no longer," Miss Grove told her as the cart was emptied, the goods carried to the kitchen.

Esmée focused on Miss Grove's wavy hair, swept back severely beneath her mobcap. Her yellow dress, though faded, brought a burst of color. "What need have you of blankets and linens?"

"There is never enough, I confess. Your gift of stockings and caps last winter helped a great deal."

"Never enough of those either, once winter sets in. I've been knitting steadily all summer, as has my late mother's sewing society in York."

"I'm heartened to hear it." Miss Grove smiled, her complexion's spiderweb of wrinkles easing. "You'll be pleased to know the children are being schooled twice a week by an itinerant master . . ."

"Because there aren't sufficient funds to maintain one permanently," Esmée finished for her. "Is the schoolmaster fair? Kind?"

"Fair, perhaps. I've yet to meet many who are kind. Most seem overfond of the lash."

Mistress Boles reappeared, ending their honest conversation. She raised dull eyes heavenward. "Surely you'll be wanting to return to York, Miss Shaw. The clouds bode ill."

As does your countenance.

Schooling her dismay, Esmée made ready to leave. "Perhaps you and Miss Grove can make a list of all your needs and give it to me next visit. With prayer and industry, we shall remedy what we can."

A child snuck forward when Mistress Boles turned her back. "Thank'ee, Miss Shaw." Her freckled face softened in a smile. "Come back soon, if ye please. We've so few visitors and need a bit o' cheer."

The matron turned round again. Had she heard? "Shoo!" she shouted, then looked at Esmée again. "Jenny will as soon pick your pocket as give you a sly word."

Esmée knelt down till she was eye level with the scolded girl. "Of course I shall, sweet Jenny. Count on it."

Turning away, Esmée swiped at her eyes with a gloved hand as the wind tugged at the surrounding trees and sent the leaves adance in colorful disarray, adding a touch of whimsy to the disheartening scene. She'd always sensed God's Spirit in the wind. Surely He was near now, comforting society's castoffs, even brushing her damp cheek with an unseen hand.

Wasn't He?

Esmée climbed into the cart and took up the reins again. She waved goodbye, the pony lighter in step as the cart was now empty, though her heart was still burdened. Perhaps Lady Lightfoot's ball would be a good place to begin her almshouse entreaties.

CHAPTER *five*

After a sennight, Henri began to feel as though he resided in York. His tailoring took longer than expected, requiring him to stay on at the Royal Oake, which left no time to return to Indigo Island before Lady Lightfoot's ball. He wasn't overly concerned, as his crew was a well-disciplined lot for the most part. They were deserving of a rest when they weren't at work on the vessel, anticipating the next as-yet-unknown sailing. He'd crossed paths with his quartermaster and ship's carpenter in town. A few of his crew were already selling wares at York's market—Monmouth caps and stockings they knitted. They gave him a hearty greeting, clearly glad to be ashore. Others were taking notice of their return from all quarters.

"Can it be Captain Lennox?" A burly, ham-fisted merchant stopped him midstride, walking stick in hand. "I'd heard you were again in York. Might I have a word with you about a shipping venture I have in mind?"

"Monday, mayhap," Henri put forth. "Where would you like to meet?"

"At Shaw's coffeehouse, none other. Say, two o'clock?"

With a nod, Henri continued his walk. Best get used to Shaw's, the preferred meeting place. Did the admiral hold a grudge over what had happened between him and his daughter?

He lifted his cocked hat to a passing carriage of colorful straw-hatted ladies, their lingering looks reminding him of Esmée again. How odd it felt to be a landsman. Yet the last few sailings had left him feeling that the ship had shrunk or he'd expanded, a grown man regarding everything in miniature.

York seemed more interesting than ever before. His stay had been sweetened with Shaw's cocoa at breakfast, and he'd not even had to darken the door of their shop. Nor had he seen any sign of Esmée anywhere, though he'd caught sight of her father at a distance, coming out of the customhouse on Main Street.

He'd always been fond of the admiral. Ten years had knocked him down a stone or two, but he still bore the erect carriage of a former commander, making him stand out on a bustling, hazardous street. Mistress Shaw he remembered as a force in her own right. Hospitable. A generous benefactress. A shrewd woman of trade.

He wouldn't dwell on their two daughters.

Shutting the door of the inn as quietly as he could still resulted in Widow Oake appearing. She sailed into the narrow hall, sleek as a shallop, as he set one foot on the stair to his rooms.

"Captain Lennox . . ." Her silver eyes held an unspoken invitation. "Father wanted me to tell you all is in hand for your transport to the ball tonight. Our coachman will come round at half past six."

"I'll be ready." He took the second step as a case clock thundered four o'clock. Plenty of time to prepare.

"Are you fond of dancing, Captain?"

Fond was generous. "Nay." He softened his reply with a half-smile. "I'd rather ply shark-infested waters."

She chuckled at his half jest. "Something tells me your attendance at the ball isn't due to your skill at allemandes and minuets."

"If it were, I'd not be invited."

"Might I wheedle *one* country dance out of you in our very own parlor at our next entertainment? A reel or jig?"

He gained another step. He'd seen less persistent pirates. "Mayhap."

Her smile was coy as he departed. Finally upstairs, he paused to admire the elaborate bell system his host had threaded on copper wire from lodgers' rooms down to the servants' quarters. A pull on an embroidered silk cord quickly gained him the hot water he needed. A water closet with a little door opening into the hall allowed a servant to attend to any needs without entering guests' rooms.

Once bathed, shaved, and dressed, he studied himself in the looking glass, something he rarely did aboard ship. All in all, his new suit left him looking like anyone else of genteel status in Virginia.

No doubt at the ball he would see many Virginians he knew and some he didn't.

And others he didn't want to.

"Are you skittish, Sister?"

Skittish? *In spades.*

Esmée locked eyes with Eliza as they finished dressing in their adjoining bedchambers of the York townhouse. Quinn was below with Father, waiting impatiently, probably.

"You seem unnaturally disquieted." Reaching out, Eliza tugged on a tightly coiled curl till it relaxed and draped over Esmée's shoulder.

"You know how I feel about these genteel gatherings." Esmée stared at her sister's elaborate coiffure, a powdered pouf over a foot high crowned with a ship, which had taken over two hours to achieve and left Eliza's lady's maid in tears. Even now the nautical headdress seemed to be listing despite its intricate scaffolding.

Eliza studied her with a canny eye. "So, the pearls win?"

Atop the dressing table an assortment of gems winked up at them in the candlelight, myriad velvet-lined jewelry cases open. Eliza dangled a glittering garnet on a gold chain, then exchanged it for another.

"I rarely wear anything but pearls." Esmée touched her throat where the necklace rested. "As for you, how about this star ruby Father brought Mama from the city of Karur in India?"

"How do you remember all the details?" Eliza fastened the ruby about her neck. "Your fondness for geography, I suppose. Celestial navigation has always been your strong suit."

"As society is yours."

"If you'd been a son, you might well have been a sailor," Eliza teased. "A jack."

With a last look at each other and the looking glass, they put on light silk capes a maid brought and went below. In the coach, the seven-mile distance would be easily managed despite the rutted road. Lady Lightfoot lived halfway between York and Williamsburg in a grand brick mansion named Lightfoot Hall, its ballroom a twin to the governor's palace in the capital, but as she and Dinwiddie were kin, no one made much of the likeness.

Esmée settled back on the upholstered seat, wishing the seven miles were seventy instead. But even that distance would not give her time to compose herself. "Pleasure" balls they were not. Already she was counting the hours till she could peel off her many layers while ruminating about all the things she'd said and done but shouldn't have. Yet she liked Lady Lightfoot. And she did not wish to offend by declining her gracious invitation. As she was not prone to lying, pleading illness didn't suit either. Let the ball be a ruse for raising funds for the almshouse.

Beside her, Eliza sat fussing with the pins in her hair. Her sister's shipwreck of a coiffure only added to Esmée's angst as she watched it barely clear the coach's narrow doorway. The men got in after them warily. Father looked resplendent in admiral attire, and no one could fault Quinn for his wardrobe, respected barrister and member of the governor's council that he was.

"How goes your marine atlas?" Quinn asked Father as he settled beside Eliza.

"A piece of work," Father replied, clearly pleased by the subject. "Charting the Atlantic coast is a tedious process, but if it improves navigation safety, 'tis well worth it."

"I heard the admiralty is hurrying you to finish on account of the French threat."

"Understandably with the enemy coming by sea . . ."

The men continued their talk as Eliza gave a final poke with a pin, and the ship seemed anchored at last. "You are my foil tonight, Sister. Unpowdered and unwigged. Plain pearls and remade gown."

Did Eliza suspect she tried to blend in with the paneling? "All the better."

"Did I mention Quinn's parents gifted me an heirloom tiara upon news of the baby? A shocking assortment of diamonds, Quinn says, that's been in the Cheverton family a century or better. Sadly, my in-laws remain in England but plan to sail unless a declaration of war is decided."

"When shall you wear the tiara?"

"As soon as it—and the heir—arrives."

Esmée took a deep breath, her stays overtight. "What makes you so sure the heir isn't a she?"

"We've only chosen names for a boy, so a boy it must be."

Esmée quelled her eye rolling. "Best ponder daughter's names, as the Almighty might have other designs."

"Quinn has his heart set on a son." Eliza lowered her voice as the men droned on. "I daren't suggest otherwise."

They rounded a curve that marked the last leg of their journey, sending Esmée sliding toward the window. She unclenched her fists from the folds of her gown to find her palms damp beneath her gloves. Her ordeal was at hand. How she wished for some of Eliza's joie de vivre, her ability to glide through whatever life dealt her, smiling and undaunted.

The coach rolled into the forecourt of the Lightfoot mansion behind a line of conveyances as liveried servants sprang into service. Esmée alighted from the coach on her father's arm, then followed Quinn and Eliza into the marbled hall, where a butler waited at the ballroom's entrance to announce them. Biting her lip, she fixed an eye on her sister's coiffure lest she need to right it, rather than the press of people on every side. There seemed an audible gasp at Eliza's entry, which soon subsided as other guests appeared.

Lady Lightfoot was known for her democratic guest list. Among

Virginia's bejeweled gentry were wealthy Scots merchants and other notables of questionable pedigree who'd risen to prominence in the colonies because of their wits and business acumen and advantageous marriages. They had few of the airs and graces of the titled and genteel but were far more interesting, at least to Esmée.

Her father steered her safely to a corner, where old friends greeted them. Eliza and Quinn, ever popular, were moving about, speaking to those they knew and some they didn't. From all appearances, her sister's headdress was staying the course.

"My dear Miss Shaw . . ." Lady Lightfoot's distinct tone cut through the hubbub as she passed in front of Esmée after greeting her father. For a widow of many years, she had retained her agile mind and slim figure. "I believe I spy a long-lost acquaintance of yours." With that, their hostess moved on in a glittering display of silk and feathers, leaving a trail of dread and trepidation in her wake.

Father watched her departure with a lift of his graying brows. "I suppose this means Captain Lennox is at hand."

Esmée scanned the ballroom, dismay leaving her breathless. "In truth, I never expected to see him here. He wasn't one for dancing. Nor did I expect Lady Lightfoot to mention him outright."

"She didn't name him, my dear, though I did detect a certain glint in her eye. Lady Lightfoot has ever been one for a trick or a little matchmaking." He gave Esmée a pained, apologetic half-smile. "Speaking of which . . ." His gaze strayed to the rear doorway, open and leading to the garden. Esmée's did the same.

There stood Henri Lennox, hands clasped behind his back, shoulders squared and expression resolute, looking for all the world like a commander at the helm of a ship in a storm. As if a ball was more a navigational hazard than the high seas.

Esmée took out a hand fan and cooled her face, wishing the painted silk device were the size of a sail and she could hide behind it. Her smothering anxiety was overshadowed by a rush of heartsore remembrance. All the captain's youthful lines had been chipped away into the sculpting of the hardened man he'd become. The jut of his jaw told her so, as did his sun-cast features more sharply chiseled. A face shaped by countless foreign ports and untold destinations. A gloss of black hair caught back with silk ribbon. Eyes of so cold an ocean blue they hurt her.

Ten long years.

She hardly knew him.

CHAPTER

Amid so much finery and so many faces, Henri felt at sea. And when he'd barely rediscovered his land legs, he was expected to dance.

"Captain Lennox! Just the man I was hoping to encounter." Virginia's acting governor gave a formal bow, his wig powder flaking onto the shoulders of his velvet suit. "Lady Lightfoot assured me of your presence tonight but cautioned me against cornering you and denying you an evening's entertainment."

"On the contrary," Henri replied, warming to the official's forthright manner. "Corner away."

"After supper, certainly." Dinwiddie's broad Scots brogue warmed Henri's ears, as did his convivial wink. "I dare not earn the ire of every unmarried miss in the room straightaway."

The dancing commenced, a minuet stepped by the most prestigious and well placed among them, including a stunning young woman in a fanciful wig with a ship perched atop it. Henri's wry amusement faded as recognition kicked in. *Upon my soul . . .*

Eliza Shaw?

The certainty took hold as guests framed him on both sides. His hostess, Lady Lightfoot, was making straight for him.

"Captain Lennox, how utterly dashing you look."

Henri gave a little bow as she tapped his sleeve with her fan.

"I half expected to see you in naval uniform, but of course you are a free agent now and no longer one of His Majesty's officers." She smiled widely, eyes roaming the glittering assembly. "There are a number of young ladies here who are noticeably agog at your presence . . . including Admiral Shaw's daughter, a prior acquaintance of yours, is she not?"

Was Lady Lightfoot jesting? He'd not spied Esmée in the throng, though it was likely she'd be present. Given their acrimonious parting, *agog* was the last word he'd choose. *Aghast*, rather.

Lady Lightfoot moved on, and the young woman to his right smiled up at him. He'd rather partner with a roomful of complete strangers than the estranged Miss Shaw.

"A dance, Miss . . . ?"

"Miss Traverse." The young lady brightened at his forced words.

The minuet ended and a reel that all the Scots present excelled at was struck. Henri found himself caught up in the gaiety, the steps and turns easily recalled, his partner's pleasure tempering his impatience to get on with the evening.

When the dance ended, he excused himself, distracted by a naval officer in uniform who drew him into conversation with two York shipbuilders.

"Tell us about the *Relentless*, Captain Lennox," one gentleman said. "A three-masted ship of the line with seventy-four guns, aye? A gift from the governor of Nevis in the Caribbean for warring with buccaneers and securing shipping lanes in his province?"

His back to the ballroom, Henri spoke with ease about what he knew best, sharing details of his last cruise and the current careening on Indigo Island.

Another gentleman joined in. "You're the talk of all the coffeehouses on the coast, not to mention broadsides and newspapers, with your black jacks and lucrative prizes."

"Is it true you've captured more than thirty enemy ships in a twelvemonth?" an officer asked. "Spanish, mostly, as well as notorious buccaneers?"

"Much of it hearsay," Henri countered. He shied from any praise or applause, though it was preferable to being vilified as a pirate. "As privateer, I simply align with colonial authorities in wanting the lawlessness by sea stopped."

"Well, I for one welcome your return to port amongst us proud Virginians. 'Tis hurricane season, after all."

Henri grimaced as a line began forming. He might be headed straight for a tempest with supper at hand.

The double doors of the dining room swung open. Like with dancing, those of highest rank went first, titled Virginia officials and whatnot, which left the Shaws somewhere in the middle. Quinn and Eliza were far ahead, at the front of the line behind Lady Lightfoot, thus removing one of Esmée's familiar underpinnings. Thankfully, Father was at hand, speaking with a Williamsburg merchant. Behind them was her dear friend Kitty Hart, followed by . . .

Captain Lennox.

Esmée fixed her gaze straight ahead, feeling as wooden as a ship's figurehead. Were his intense eyes boring into her stays-straightened back? Censuring her for sitting out the dancing more than she danced? Finding fault with her for being unpowdered and plain? Her plan to remain in the shadows backfired badly. Instead she'd gained unwanted attention because of her simplicity.

Breathe, lass.

Mightn't the captain have forgotten all about her? Perhaps she'd left so little a dent in his conscience that she was all but invisible now. Certainly he'd had other flirtations since. She certainly couldn't hold a candle to many of the young belles tonight in their whispering silks and winking gemstones.

The line crawled toward the dining room's entrance, supper smells mingling with fragrant beeswax candles. She put a hand to her waist to finger her chatelaine, something she oft did when distressed. But it was a habit of no use to her now, for she wasn't wearing it.

Places were sought, a great shuffling and fuss occurred, and Esmée found herself staring at the one remaining seat.

To the right of Henri Lennox.

All the other places around the immense table were taken, leaving her standing conspicuously. She dared not look at the captain, yet she felt his unease like a stone wall between them. Or was it her own discomfiture? She sat down and looked to her lap, a hammer tapping at her temples and threatening to flip her stomach.

How had they left it at the last? When they'd faced each other that final time in the Shaws' townhouse parlor, their voices rising notch by notch?

"Marry me, Esmée."

"I would, Henri, if not for the sea."

"So the sea is the only obstacle between us."

"It robbed my mother of my father. I would not have it rob me of you."

"You would have me forsake my calling, then."

"Better your calling than your wife."

"Your stated reasons are your refusal, I take it."

She had made no reply. And then, a decade's absence.

Supper's seating arrangement left Henri feeling keelhauled—roped and thrown overboard only to be dragged under the ship's backbone to his doom. So far Esmée hadn't said a word. The long table was wide enough that conversations across it were impossible. He tried to say a few words to the elderly lady to his left who was stone-cold deaf. Esmée seemed in a similar predicament with the gentleman to her right, who was more absorbed by laughter and talk farther down. Awkwardness did not begin to describe the arrangement.

Henri swallowed. Removed all regret and blame from his tone. He stole a look at her. "How does one account for ten lost years, Miss Shaw?"

Esmée's pale hand stilled on her wine glass. The pearl ring she wore unearthed a long-buried memory. "One does not, Captain Lennox. Or, if left no choice, very carefully."

Silence.

He stared at the candelabra in front of him. "By some trick of fate, we have ended up side by side."

"*Fate*, sir?" Mockery curdled her tone. "I don't believe in it."

"Mayhap the Almighty is having a fine jest at our expense." He drummed his fingers lightly atop the damask tablecloth. "To your credit you were never one for theatrics or hysterics. You'll simply soldier on through supper and make the best of it."

"And you, stalwart seaman that you are, shall do the same." She shifted as if uncomfortable in her chair. "Despite the fact we are drawing noticeable attention."

He raised his gaze. No less than half a dozen pairs of eyes were on them. "People have long memories of thwarted love affairs."

"Indeed."

"Well, I for one have a few overdue inquiries," he said, then paused to swallow a sip of wine. "How is your dear mother?"

"Buried."

Nay. Dismayed, he let the news settle. Her terse answer begged details he could not ask about. "My deepest sympathies." He meant it. Eleanor Shaw had been an uncommon woman. A woman ahead of her time, or rather a woman who made good use of the time she'd been given.

"A question for a question," Esmée said as soup was served. "Why have you come ashore?"

He eyed the monogrammed bowl surmounted by the Lightfoot family crest that was set before him. Crab bisque? "I spent the last three years in the Summer Isles. I was beginning to forget Virginia."

To this she made no reply. The lukewarm soup was more enjoyable than their stilted conversation. Only a dozen more courses to go.

"How is your father?" he asked, having spied the admiral earlier in the evening. It was a far safer question.

"Adrift without my mother."

"And your sister?"

"'Tis my turn, Captain."

He wished for a little levity, but she was unsmiling. Intense. Gone was the warmth and approachability that had once marked her. Had she somehow assumed some of her sister's mercurial hauteur? If so, it was a cold, shrewd beauty that left him missing the Esmée of old.

"What of your own Virginia kin?" she asked, turning intelligent eyes on him.

"Deceased. The rest are in Scotland, if you recall. And France. I've none left in the colonies."

Her lengthy pause rattled him. "I'm . . . terribly sorry." She ran a spoon through her soup but made no move to eat it. "To answer your earlier question, my sister is as irrepressible as ever."

Down the long table came Eliza's unmistakable laugh. She was heavier than he remembered. *Enceinte?* And all aglitter from head to toe. In the press of guests he'd not gotten a good look at the bewigged gentleman who'd danced with her. Her husband?

"Your sister was always one to land on her feet," he murmured.

Esmée herself was dressed far more sedately. Her yellow gown seemed rather faded, but the lace draping her bodice and sleeves was exquisite, a foil to her bountiful black hair. And her pearls . . . She'd always preferred them. When in the South Seas he'd oft been reminded of that.

Fish was served along with dishes he later couldn't recall, so intent was he on their forced talk. Esmée pushed her food around her plate while he managed a few forkfuls. Had his presence stolen her appetite? Pale as she was, she resembled the wilting white roses at table's center. Hardly the enchanting creature he'd stored away in memory's darkest corner.

The silence chafed. Whose turn was it now? Though he wanted to convince himself he could navigate this encounter with aplomb, that her hold on him was irretrievably broken, he could not.

CHAPTER

They seemed an island unto themselves. Little eddies of lively conversation on all sides of them made their forced, close proximity all the more painful. The silver fork grew heavy in Esmée's hand. Every bite seemed more difficult to swallow. All at once she felt far from a self-possessed woman of nearly thirty but rather childlike and fragile, throat tight and near tears.

Dear Hermione.

Sorrow made her sag and went unrelieved as supper wore on. Esmée felt blindsided by the news, further thrown off by the captain's stoicism reporting it, as if family were of no more merit than his crew and deserved little mention.

Once she and Hermione looked forward to being sisters-in-law. Eliza had been especially fond of her, though she'd lost touch with her after her rift with the captain. The Lennoxes had lived in a handsome house facing the waterfront in Norfolk back then. His father had been a respected shipbuilder there.

At least her own sister had been spared. Tonight Eliza was shining, her coiffure miraculously intact. She'd not stopped smiling all evening. Didn't her cheeks feel the strain? Father seemed to be enjoying himself too. At home, devoid of Mama, their suppers were quiet affairs. Here he seemed to forget himself, mingling with his fellows, making merry, and toasting this or that.

She took another tasteless bite. Captain Lennox was finally conversing with the woman on his left, the heavily rouged and powdered wife of a port official. Stealing another look at him, she fixed upon the scar above his brow, a thin, pale line she didn't recall. Concern softened her for an unguarded moment. She'd likely never know how it came to be there.

But it was the tattoo inked on his right wrist that most intrigued her. The Jerusalem cross? Five black crosses were etched beneath his silver-buttoned cuff, ever popular with mariners. Some shipboard artist's doing, no doubt. Was the accompanying Latin phrase, *Coram Deo*, also there? *In the presence of God.* Was that how he felt upon the sea in all its magnificence? In the Almighty's very presence?

Fingering her pearls, Esmée tried to strike up a conversation on her right as dessert was served, to no avail. So far, all her efforts on behalf of the almshouse had come to nil, making the evening a complete loss.

A small crystal dish was set before her—blackberry flummery. What she craved was chocolate. Cocoa bolstered, soothed, and satisfied while the flummery was sticky and cloyingly sweet. She darted a discreet look left. Captain Lennox sat back in his chair like lord and master, making no inroads on his dessert. He seemed sunk in thought, and she'd wager it wasn't flummery he was pondering.

Supper was nearly at an end, God be thanked. A two-hour ordeal that would require a fortnight's recovery. She nearly sighed aloud in relief.

As the dancing resumed, Esmée hovered near a partially open window, drawn by a cool breeze. She'd not danced in ages, though she was partial to the English country dances stepped by a number of couples. Once she'd been lauded as graceful, on par with Eliza. A wistful longing tugged at her, dusty memories of their former French dancing master sweet.

Watching couples assemble for a longways dance, she found herself drawn forward at the press of Kitty's gloved hand. Though she'd steered clear of the captain since supper, she could do so no longer. Someone had coerced him onto the ballroom floor. A young woman in shagreen silk waved her fan at him, looking as cunning as a fox in a henhouse.

Esmée's middle twisted, souring what little supper she'd partaken of. As lines formed, the captain stood across from her, not the fan-waving coquette. By accident or design? Accident, she would wager. She tried to smile and be at her dancing best lest anyone apprehend her fluttering nerves, a dozen unwelcome memories assailing her.

Once her dancing best had been with him.

Though he'd claimed to favor supporting the wall, he'd managed dancing admirably back then. And now?

As she thought it, more dancers assembled, and the green-gowned woman nudged her aside as if determined to partner with the captain. Esmée yielded as a flash of irritation gave way to a feeling far more startling. Disappointment? But there was no time to dwell on it. The music prompted them forward, and in time he did indeed become her partner. She placed her fingertips lightly in his upraised palm, more a whisper than a touch, her heart in her throat. Up and down the rows they went as one, dancing figures with all the other couples.

Increasingly breathless, she met his eyes again and again as they matched steps. The dance required it. To look away from one's partner was rude and sure to be noted. Each time their eyes and hands touched she felt a slight shift, an inexplicable thawing. His eyes . . . had they really been so silvery a blue? His face so handsomely weathered?

A tiny flicker of something long dead threatened to rekindle.

The next morning found Esmée at work, Lady Lightfoot's ball a hazy dream. Tying on an apron and toying with her chatelaine, she stood in the still-dark kitchen, breathing in vanilla and orange essence and cinnamon, letting her spirits settle. Everything still felt a bit off. The help weren't due for an hour or so, but evidence of the previous day's labor adorned every available counter and workplace. She'd barely been hungry for her hyson tea and dry toast at breakfast, so now she reached for a shell-shaped sweetmeat, letting its richness melt on her tongue.

But it in no way assuaged the previous night's encounter.

Sighing, she passed through the door into the shop, where the first ribbons of light streamed through the bow-fronted window. The majestic view of the harbor never failed to swell her heart—all those tall-masted brigs, schooners, and ships of the line commanded by stalwart, unflinching men the likes of Henri Lennox.

The stirring spectacle sent her back into the kitchen again, where she grabbed a broom and began sweeping an already pristine floor. She hummed a hymn. Eyed the clock. Perused account books and receipts. She would not wallow in sore memories or the sorry one they'd made last night. Like as not, the captain was still at Lady Lightfoot's. She'd seen the way he'd been sequestered by Virginia's foremost officials at a break in the dancing, then once a cotillion resumed, he had disappeared into an antechamber.

She'd slipped outside into the garden, the moonlit darkness sweetly scented and consoling. Couples strolled about as she hid herself away in a folly at a far corner. Knowing Eliza, Esmée felt her hopes for an early exit fade. Pregnancy had not curbed her sister's high spirits or her nocturnal habits.

They'd finally returned home at three o'clock in the morning, Eliza still chattering like a magpie, Quinn snoring on the seat beside her, and Father as mute and contemplative as a monk. He'd gone into that antechamber with the captain and gentlemen. She'd witnessed it before fleeing to the garden. And the door had not reopened till long after midnight, at which point the men emerged without a hint of whatever had detained them. Nor had Father said a word since. This morning he'd slept well past his usual rising time of five o'clock. Eliza would be abed till noon, though Quinn usually sought out one of the coffeehouses to visit with his York friends.

Opening a sack of cocoa nibs, Esmée inhaled their familiar scent much as she did coffee. The roast was exactly right. Too long over the fire turned the cocoa bitter. Too little heat robbed it of flavor. Those Philadelphia roasters knew what they were about. The nibs had been winnowed free of chaff and were ready for refining.

She poured the entire sack into a large marble mortar while the chocolate stone heated at the hearth. Raising a pestle, she let loose all her angst and began pounding the nibs to dust. An airy brown powder rose and tickled her nose, sending her sneezing into her sleeve.

By the time the shop opened, a sheen of velvety chocolate covered the stone. A lick of her finger left grit on Esmée's tongue. Switching to a different roller, she continued crushing and adding sugar, even a bit of orange essence, Eliza's favorite. She stopped only when Anna came into the kitchen with a package in her arms.

"Miss Shaw, look at what was left on the front step." She held it out to Esmée, who stopped her rolling. "Your name is on the outside."

Esmée wiped her hands on her apron, took the package, and untied the string binding the wrapping paper. *The Complete Confectioner.*

Wonder bloomed. Bound in leather, the long-coveted book held a whiff of new ink. Or was it her imagination? Tentative, she opened it and marveled at the pristine pages unmarred by grease or chocolate. "You saw no one?"

"None, Miss Shaw. 'Twas just sitting by the door alongside a stray cat." Anna sniffed. "I'm surprised it wasn't thieved with all the riffraff on Water Street."

Clutching the book to her bodice, Esmée returned to the shop and perused the chocolate pots and accessories, excited to try a new recipe.

Who might the gift giver be?

CHAPTER

Henri hadn't reckoned on old houses having so many ghosts.

The keys from his father's solicitor hung heavy in his pocket as he unlocked the front door of the Norfolk townhouse on Prince Street. Dust overlaid the once busy entrance hall, running up the elaborately carved balustrade and coating every nick and scratch in a sandy powder, even dimming the crystal brilliance of the chandelier and windows. He shut the door and it echoed. A dismal sound.

Shrugging off the melancholy that had dogged him since coming into the city by coach, he strode across the foyer to the parlor, opening doors and traversing rooms with an eye for change. Paint—the rooms were overdue for it. The carpet was threadbare and nearly colorless with age. Dustcloths hid the furnishings except for an occasional chair leg or table end. But the paintings on the walls, seascapes and oils depicting his ancestors, seemed unchanged. 'Twas a well-built house. A handsome house. A place of many memories, most of them happy.

He climbed the stairs and entered the bedchambers, including his own before he'd gone away to sea. The narrow cot with its plain indigo counterpane . . . had he really lain there? Beneath a window was his writing table, old and scarred in the harsh light piercing the grime of the windowpane. There by the fireplace were knifed notches that marked his growth. He'd gone from a sickly baby to a man full grown at a towering six feet two inches and fourteen stone.

After breathing past the musty smell of unused rooms, he opened a door to the three-tiered portico. Here on the shaded second floor, a scattering of lightweight Windsor chairs and a small game table sat forlorn. He peered over the portico's railing into the walled garden below.

Roses were still abloom, a clash of pinks and oranges and yellows amid the drooping perennials and weeds. Nothing too amiss here that a sennight's work wouldn't mend. The sundial and dry fountain at the garden's heart eased him. Intact. He'd played many an hour around them as a lad. Some things, at least those cast in stone, didn't change.

The servants' quarters in the attic had him bending low not to scrape his head. Even with cocked hat beneath one arm, he still touched the low ceiling. Back down the winding stair he went to the foyer, then exited out a back door to sit on a bench and catch the sun's last rays as they brightened a battered arbor.

He stared at a twisted quince, once a favorite climbing tree. Age made one reflect, he guessed. At five and thirty, what would be said about him that truly mattered if he were to die tomorrow? That he sailed the high seas and was rarely at home.

Better ponder the pasts of those he loved. Memory took him down a hazy path, heart-tuggingly indistinct but painful as a cat-o'-nine-tails nonetheless. His mother had been most at home in the garden. She'd sewn dried lavender into the hems of her petticoats and linens, even concocted lavender lemon water. And Hermione . . . His sister had arranged for a pianoforte on small wheels to be pushed onto the portico in good weather. There were garden parties. Guests. Towering trays of marzipan and endless bowls of punch. His father had presided over all with characteristic good humor. Until that dark day at the docks.

What bitter irony that he'd once teased his father he'd someday go to sea in the very vessels his father constructed. He'd been jesting.

Though he'd long been enamored of shipbuilding, not once had he entertained the notion of sailing.

"By Jove, Son! Will you torment me in my old age with such far-flung notions?" His father had stared at him, his Scots temper roaring. "Am I to see you gone from here for months—years on end? The sea is a fickle mistress. She'll abuse you like Jonah and coerce some behemoth to swallow you and spit you out, only you might never return to us."

His mother bore his playfulness with a smile, her usual French effusiveness undimmed. "You'll be the handsomest jack to ever sail the high seas. 'Captain Lennox' sounds *magnifique*!"

"A privateer you'll be? 'Tis but a rude disguise," his sister teased. "Henri Lennox, buccaneer à la corsair! Will you share your prizes with us poor relations who'll be pining for you at home?"

Then, just shy of his sixteenth birthday, he'd been working late in his father's dockyard when a press-gang overtook him, the certificate of exemption he carried in his pocket of no consequence. Though the lad with him had gotten away, the gang pummeled him into a corner, tore up his paper, then took him aboard the HMS *Victory*.

Fueled by fury as well as ambition, he'd worked his way up from cabin boy to midshipman to officer till he'd used the Royal Navy to gain his own vessel and his own captaincy. And then, much like a courtship, as wooing as a siren's song, the sea had finally won him over. As commander, he'd been freed of rebellious shipmates and overbearing admirals. Freed to chart his course, choose his crew, and sail where he willed. This was what he'd been designed to do, though the Almighty had used an unjust impressment and the Royal Navy to accomplish it.

But now that he was back in Norfolk where it all began, his impressment seemed especially bittersweet. He'd missed much being at sea, not only the sorrows but the joys. If he'd been closer to home, might his parents' and sister's lives have been better? Easier? Might they still live? Their voices echoed in his head and heart, so bruising his eyes stung. It caused a man to reconsider. Who did he have? And who would come after him?

A bird trilled. A few colorful leaves drifted down, reddening his black coat and boots. Near at hand was an unkempt climbing rose. It bespoke . . . Esmée. He hadn't wanted her to intrude. Not even the thought of her. But she'd once been in this garden, making a mighty fuss over this very rose and especially the trellis-in-the-round at the garden's heart. In midsummer it resembled an overflowing flower basket.

His gaze slid to the west corner of the overgrown yew hedge where he'd kissed her. And she'd kissed him back.

"Captain Lennox, might that be you?"

A high, reedy voice trailed over the garden wall. He stood and walked toward the sound, envisioning the ancient lady on the other side. "It is I, Mistress Ludwick."

"Can it be? I've not seen you in an age! Mightn't you humor an old crone and show yourself?"

In moments he was at the iron gate that divided her garden from his. With a sweep of his hat, he bowed and then took in her parchment-paper face, white and lined but much as he remembered.

"How mournful it must be to return to an empty house once so full of life!"

He frowned. "I am wondering whether to sell or occupy."

"Sell? Your dear mother would resurrect herself if she knew!"

"But a man like myself, living here alone . . ." He looked back at the house, allowing himself a rare glib moment. "It begs a family. Life. Laughter."

"Indeed." She pursed her wrinkled lips. "A shame there's no Mistress Lennox or offspring to settle down here. But should you decide to reside in our fair city, that would follow in the blink of an eye, most assuredly, though I thought York had its hold on you. Indigo Island, rather."

"'Tis always wise to explore one's options, aye?" After the debacle at Lady Lightfoot's, Norfolk held unmistakable appeal.

"Don't tell me you're tiring of the sea." She studied him unblinkingly. "Ah, I do believe you are. I see it in your sun-weathered face, those honest eyes of yours."

He smiled at her sharp appraisal. "I'm no longer the wee lad you fed kissing comfits to, but you still know me."

"Of course I do. A man is merely an overgrown boy. You are wanting change. This place suits you. You could raise a family and be a man about town. Here there are no shadows to dodge."

Shadows. Did she suspect him of being a pirate? Or sense his personal safety was in question on the mainland?

"Fare thee well, Captain Lennox." She moved away, her gait slow yet graceful. "I do hope to see you again soon."

CHAPTER *nine*

The shop door jangled shut at noon, and finding herself alone, Esmée drifted toward the Dutch door separating the chocolate shop from the coffeehouse. Shipowners and merchants, politicians and literary men gathered in the spacious, beamed room that hummed with hearsay, headlines, and other matters whatever the season. Newspapers and broadsides were scattered about, the *Virginia Gazette* foremost.

This was how Esmée kept track of the captain after a fashion. Discreetly. Privately. Without involving anyone else. Once the ire of their parting had cooled, she was beset with an insatiable curiosity time could not dim.

How did such a man handle a failed love affair? By wintering in the Caribbean. Intercepting pirate ships preying upon merchant vessels. Testifying at the admiralty court in Boston. Recovering an abandoned Spanish wreck near Madagascar. Trading the aptly named *Bachelor's Delight* for the more enigmatic *Relentless*. If she had a shilling every time she read "Taken by the *Relentless*, Captain Lennox," she'd be a wealthy woman.

And now she knew how he handled a loathsome reunion. Stoically.

Handsomely. With nary a trace of trepidation. As if he'd forgotten all about her and recovered unscathed from their liaison of old.

While she herself was a tangle of tarred rope.

"Sister! Why on earth are you loitering at the coffeehouse door? Father forbids it!"

Eliza stood behind her, winking in merriment. The truth was, Father did forbid it, but Eliza cared not a whit. It was how she'd kept the attention of Quinn, a regular at Shaw's coffeehouse back then. Even now he was at his preferred corner table, one of their male indentures replenishing coffee and chocolate as he and his highborn friends talked taxes and tariffs.

"What is it you're clutching to your chest?" Eliza peered at *The Complete Confectioner* with a sharp eye.

"Anna found it on the shop steps this morn." Esmée had hardly set the book down. "The giver is a mystery."

Eliza's smile curled expectantly. "A secret admirer, perhaps?"

"Secret, aye. Admirer, nay."

"A gift from Captain Lennox is my guess. I saw the two of you at supper. Quite cozy after so long a separation."

"Cozy?" Esmée rolled her eyes. "You're in need of a pair of spectacles. We were simply thrown together quite unexpectedly and spent an excruciating supper, followed by dancing, trying to be polite while wondering what on earth we ever found attractive about each other in the first place."

"Ha! He's still a remarkably gallant devil, you must admit."

"A tattooed devil."

"Most mariners are." Eliza laughed and took the book from her. "I recall you and Mama trying to find this very volume with no success. Till now."

"'Tis so hard to come by, printed in England. The York and Williamsburg booksellers have not been able to obtain a single copy of it."

Eliza paged to the flyleaf with gloved hands. "I do wish he'd signed it. But of course, you might have burnt the book if he had."

"Shush. 'Tis too valuable a tome. I would simply have torn out his signature."

"Hmm. How long has it been since you two were enamored with each other?"

"It matters not. You've already asked me. 'Twas a foolish infatuation."

"I wonder." Eliza seemed to reconsider. "In and out of every foreign port as he is, and for so long, I suppose he has a paramour somewhere. Several, perhaps."

The notion nearly made Esmée squirm. "He made no mention of such."

"Of course he wouldn't confess such intimacies to you, his prior sweetheart. Nor would he ask such of you, being a gentleman of rank. Which begs the question . . . what *did* you two talk about?"

"Really, Eliza. Your interrogation knows no bounds." Esmée took the book back. "Though he did ask about you."

"Did he?" Eliza looked flattered. "How are his Norfolk kin?"

A pang shot through Esmée, arrow-sharp. "All have passed."

Eliza's face crumpled. "Poor Captain Lennox. I only knew of his father's death. 'Twas in the papers a few years ago, but Mama hid it from you."

"What?"

"She knew it might upset you. Unearth the past." Eliza sighed. "But I had no idea about Mrs. Lennox and Hermione. I do recall Hermione wedding a landowner of some merit."

The tightness in Esmée's chest expanded. Might Hermione have died in childbirth? Eliza, for all her fearlessness, had a mortal dread of such. So many failed to survive the ordeal and enjoy motherhood. Esmée's fervent prayer was that her sister be spared.

"I suppose the captain has returned to Indigo Island and I can breathe again," Esmée said. The thought was nettling. Sore. A bittersweet mix of things regretted romantically that would never be righted.

"More's the pity." Eliza went to the shop window and stared out at the teeming harbor. "Farewell, our masterful, commanding Captain Lennox."

Did her sister know something of his whereabouts? An imminent cruise? Quinn had gone into the anteroom with the other officials during the ball. Had the captain already set sail again? Esmée opened her mouth to ask, then closed it. She'd rather bite her tongue in two. What would knowing profit her?

Let the past pass.

"We must make the most of the time we've been given." Eliza spun away from the glass. "I asked Father if he could spare you in the near future. Quinn will be in meetings, as the assembly will soon be in session. Some nonsense over outlawing the importation of slaves."

"Nonsense? I beg to differ."

"*Nonsense* in that such a measure will never pass muster in slave-heavy Virginia." The mettle in Eliza's tone suggested it was a frequent topic of discussion in the Chevertons' townhouse. She softened, her eyes as imploring as a spaniel's. "Come, Esmée. I get frightfully lonesome."

Esmée set the book on the counter. "What of your many friends?"

"None suit like the company of my elder sister."

Before Esmée could reply, a customer entered and ended the matter, inquiring after a new chocolate pot.

"See you soon, Sister." Eliza smiled in farewell. "We shall have a splendid time in Williamsburg."

Beset by a headache, Esmée left the shop and walked uphill toward Main Street, knowing Quinn and Eliza had departed and the townhouse would be quiet. Since Mama had died, Father rarely arrived home till supper at eight o'clock. As usual, Esmée was greeted by their housekeeper, Mrs. Mabrey.

"A headache, you say?" Her lined face grew pinched with concern beneath her beribboned mobcap. "Some thyme tea should do. Shall I bring it to your bedchamber?"

"Father's study, thank you." Esmée removed her straw hat, set it on a foyer table, and moved past the stairwell into her father's bower. Instinctively she reached for his mahogany spyglass, standing at one window and training her sights on Indigo Island. On such a clear day every speck of sand glittered, trees swaying like the grass-skirted women her father told stories about. Somewhere she couldn't see sat the Flask and Sword, the boon of sailors. Captain Lennox was on the back side of the island in the cottage Father had told her about. He'd visited more than once, though not for years.

"Here you go, Miss Shaw."

"Thank you, Mrs. Mabrey."

The tea tray was placed on a small table near at hand, infusing the paneled room with an earthiness that mingled well with Father's pungent tobacco and heady brandy.

The housekeeper shut the door behind her, and Esmée returned to her musings. Sleeplessness pinched her eyes, and the ache gripping her temples throbbed unrelentingly. Returning the spyglass to its lined case, she sat down to her tea, then remembered the scrap of paper in her pocket. She laid it in her lap as she sipped from her cup. Her name, oft misspelled, was written flawlessly in a bold, masculine hand. The bookseller's? Or the giver's?

Despite her headache, a wee thrill couldn't be denied. A little intrigue in her chocolate-laden world was not amiss. Might Eliza be right? Could the giver be the captain?

She took out her old memories of him, sorting through each one like antique buttons in a box before settling on one that shone like glass. 'Twas when he'd whisked her south to meet his Norfolk family. What a fuss had come beforehand as trunks lay open and garments were examined and cast off in favor of something suitable.

"You ken what this means, dear daughter." Mama looked at her, a knowing glint in her eye.

Esmée, caught up in the novelty of a serious suitor, thought little beyond the present moment. "I know not except Captain Lennox wishes to acquaint me with Norfolk."

"'Tis a thoughtful move toward matrimony, if that is what you both want."

Torn between two hats—a straw bonnet with a cluster of silk violets and a beribboned bergère—Esmée turned this way and that before the looking glass. "Has Henri asked Father for my hand?"

"Perhaps he's waiting for his family's reception of you first. No doubt 'twill be as warm as ours of him. His mother is French, remember. I hope you'll say a few words with her in her native tongue."

Esmée had finally decided on the bergère. "How I wish I was as fluent as Eliza."

Now she hardly recalled their coach ride south to the old port town steeped in the tobacco trade. But all the rest seemed near as yesterday. There in the entry hall of a large brick townhouse, Henri had introduced her to his family as if she'd been royalty. Their kind regard of her had been equally memorable.

His mother, expressive and garrulous, took to her at once. She had Henri's ocean-blue eyes, calm as the sea on a summer's day. His father, a giant of a man, was a bit stern, his dark hair unpowdered, his dress Quaker-plain. And his sister, Hermione, as lovely as her name, was blessed with the same blue eyes and coal-black hair, a dimple in her chin.

And now they were all . . . gone. While he'd been away at sea, she guessed. How did the captain come to terms with that? Esmée wrestled with the emotion the dusty memory wrought. It seemed out of place here in this still room years after the fact.

If only the tea would assuage her head *and* her heart. All her carefully stowed feelings, any remaining tenderness toward him, had been hardened by long, barren years. Or so she thought. Seeing him again—his once beloved features, the silky hair she'd run her fingers through, the broad shoulders that seemed a bulwark against the world—made her realize the great void she'd experienced in his absence. Though Eliza and others had tried their hand at matchmaking and a few would-be suitors had come forward, Esmée had spurned them all, politely but firmly. Much to Eliza's dismay.

"My dream is to have children close in age," Eliza had confided. "Cousins are truly one of life's best gifts."

"I may well never marry. Not everyone is called to it. You'd best have as many children as the Lord allows to make up for my lack."

"Well, I shan't stop conspiring." Eliza winked at her brazenly. "'Tis what I do best!"

"Scheming is more like it," Esmée shot back, close to tears and trying to hide it. "Praying gets better results."

But somewhere along the way even she'd stopped praying. Whereas once Captain Lennox's safety and well-being on the seas were first in her heart, she'd jettisoned those petitions. Her fervent prayers went the way of her hopes and became floating wreckage. As the years passed, it hardly seemed to matter.

Hers was a heart adrift.

And the captain's sudden, unexpected return reminded her of all that.

"Daughter, are you unwell? I smell medicinal tea." Her father entered his study, a concerned eye on her as he stowed his walking stick and cocked hat. "'Tis rare I see you home so early in the day."

She forced a smile. "I might ask you the same, Father."

Yawning, he took a seat behind his desk. "One gets little done the day after a ball, I'm afraid."

Esmée poured a second cup of tea. Father disdained the stuff. "Shall I have Mrs. Mabrey bring you some coffee?"

"Nay, I drank my weight in it this morn. A bit of brandy will do." He uncapped the decanter on his desk and poured the amber liquid into a waiting glass. "Though what I crave is your mother's milk punch."

She studied him sympathetically as he drank deeply. "Perhaps we shall make some at Christmastide."

"I saw you standing at the Dutch door earlier, gazing into the coffeehouse." Rebuke was in his tone. The previous eve's late hour had turned him not only tired but testy.

"You know I like to peruse newspapers left by your customers. Since Eliza has invited me to the capital for an extended stay, I must keep current lest I be branded a bumpkin."

"I'll be happy to tell you any pressing news." He leaned back in his chair, gaze drawn to the windows at the screech of gulls. "For instance, Captain Lennox has returned to Indigo—"

"Father! I *need* no telling." Her rare outburst rattled the teacup in her hand, sloshing liquid onto her skirt.

He stared at her, fanning the flame in her face. "Pretend all you like. I'm not your doting father for naught. You've been completely addled since you first heard of his return. I only thought to take the worry from your countenance with news he's left the mainland."

She dabbed at the damp on her skirt with a handkerchief, her headache thundering again. "If my countenance is clouded, 'tis because I'm missing Mama, like you. And truth be told, I'm dreading Williamsburg society, where I am referred to as Lady Drysdale's spinster sister or Captain Lennox's jilted sweetheart."

"Not the respected businesswoman of York and patron of the parish almshouse."

"The former is far more savory." She gave a brittle smile. "Perhaps I shall try my hand at raising support among Eliza's genteel friends. That was my intent at the ball before I was . . . um . . ."

"Unmoored by Captain Lennox's arrival."

Rather, shipwrecked. "What other news should I be aware of?"

"I'm loath to heap more unwelcome reports on you, but there's said to be a large influx of French expelled from Acadia who'll soon be at Virginia's door. Not only that, there's been a dozen more arrivals at the almshouse, yet scarcely room to house them."

Her heart squeezed. "Who is among their number?"

"A drunkard. Two lewd women." Father was nothing if not forthright. "Four abandoned children. A lunatic. One destitute expectant mother. An invalid with no memory. I forget the rest."

"'Tis exactly what troubles me. Out of sight at the almshouse, they are all easily forgotten."

"You've had some success at providing care for the elderly in private homes here in York."

"Only four, sadly. Private benefactors are few."

"Then seek support from the wealthy in Williamsburg with my blessing."

"I'd rather spend time at the almshouse."

He poured a second brandy. "How like your mother you are. 'Twas all her visits to the poor that influenced you, accompanying her as you did. And in the end 'twas the death of her."

His mournful tone hurt her, but he spoke truth. Mama had contracted an illness at the almshouse that had indeed been her demise. As for Father, he was ever generous to the poor, but lodge or visit them he would not do. Yet pounds and pence only went so far. These unfortunates—shunned outcasts—needed to be seen, spoken to, touched.

He returned to the window and took up the spyglass she'd set down. At once she was cast back to the quarterdeck, windward side, where he'd stood as commander of his beloved man-of-war. Even at almost seventy he looked stalwart. Commanding.

"I nearly forgot." The spyglass came down. "Your sister told me to relay you're to see the milliner-mantuamaker ahead of our going to Williamsburg. Something about stripping you of your old gowns and infernal chatelaine and outfitting you in something splendid."

Esmée made a face. "Betimes I feel like the younger sister, not the elder."

He smiled indulgently, the deep, sun-weathered creases in his face softening. "Eliza will have her way."

Esmée smoothed a worn fold of her skirt, its once vibrant pattern faded. While she appreciated her sister's generosity—*extravagance*—it seemed at odds with her almshouse sympathies. She would not look like royalty and go there. Or anywhere.

"You might better benefit your cause if you didn't appear as if you were one step away from the almshouse yourself, my dear."

"I'm hopelessly disinterested in dress, Father." Her sister's ongoing fascination with fashion skimmed past her like a butterfly across a millpond. She felt a mere moth. "I'm guessing Eliza is planning an entire wardrobe for me."

"Your sister is generous to a fault." Her father's levity vanished. "Quinn humors her so, importing all manner of this or that and giving in to her every whim. I fear my grandchild shall be spoilt."

Esmée feared it too. Finishing her tea, she pushed up from the chair and excused herself. "Till supper, Father. I believe I'll go rest in my room."

CHAPTER *ten*

Having had his fill of the mainland, Henri rowed back to the island, standing in the jolly and facing forward, a habit of old watermen who claimed it was less taxing and more navigable. Squinting in the sun's glare, he set his sights on the Flask and Sword, its beleaguered façade begging paint and repairs. A small sloop and dory were docked, both unknown to him. The ordinary never lacked for customers, whatever the season.

Some of his crew sat upon the beach. Others hung in hammocks stretched between wind-whipped trees. Still others toiled on the *Relentless* now beached on the island's bay side. A few waved a hand as Henri drew nearer.

Home.

Only Indigo Island didn't seem much like home, he'd been gone so long. Now it felt unfamiliar. Foreign. Like any seldom seen port or landing place.

He beached the jolly and made for the ordinary, boots sinking into white sand. His men knew his swift stride too well to slow him, other than a hand flung to a forehead as he passed. Into the ordinary he went, seeking his preferred corner by a wide window open to the salt air.

Without asking, Mistress Saltonstall fetched him a dram and set it down with a wide, gap-toothed smile. "Welcome, Captain Lennox, on this bonny October day."

"Obliged." Henri leaned back in his Windsor chair, his tattooed hand encircling the pewter cup. "How is Hermes?"

She seemed pleased he'd remembered the varmint's name. The monkey—a small marmoset from Peru—perched on her shoulder. Baring its teeth, Hermes gave a cackle before traveling to her other shoulder.

She winked. "Ornery as ever and a constant reminder of ye."

He'd gifted her Hermes after sailing to South America five years before. Eccentric as she was, she'd taken to the creature immediately, even teaching it tricks, to the amusement of the watermen who frequented her establishment.

"How goes it at York?" she asked, petting Hermes's long tail. "Norfolk, rather."

"Busy. Crowded." He took a drink. "Full of itself."

She laughed, her wrinkles collapsing in mirth. "Everything Indigo Island isn't."

He took another drink and willed the memory of Esmée away as he'd done a decade or better. Leaving him to his ponderings, Mistress Saltonstall moved on as Cyprian and the ship's drummer appeared, intent on his table.

"Hats off, lads," he said with a slight smile. Their land manners had yet to catch up with them.

They grabbed their caps and sat opposite him, eager as schoolboys.

"Where to next, sir?" they asked in unison.

"I know not." Port Royal was their hope. Or the lucrative Windward Passage between Cuba and Haiti. "How goes the careening?"

Cyprian grimaced. "Full of ship's worms as she is, we'll have to winter over right here." He looked at his tarred breeches. "The masts—or parts of 'em—had to be removed. We've not finished scraping 'er down."

"When that's done, I'll set you to work on the light," Henri said. "A stonemason has been hired and will be here shortly."

Their expressions brightened. This was far preferable to scraping down a worm-ridden vessel, truly. They began to chatter as Henri's gaze stretched beyond them to the ordinary's entrance. His four most trusted men ducked beneath the door's lintel—the Africans Tarbonde and Udo, his sailing master and quartermaster, followed by the Englishmen, sea chaplain Ned Autrey and ship surgeon Alistair Southack.

Hermes screeched at their entrance and fled behind the bar. Henri's two youngest crew followed suit and scurried out a side door, their seats left vacant for their superiors.

"Welcome back, sir," Tarbonde said with a grin, the country marks or tribal scars across his cheeks a perpetual reminder of just how far he was from his Ghanaian home.

More ale was served, but Henri waited till they'd quenched their thirst before satisfying their curiosity about his time on the mainland.

"You were missed," Southack said after a long sip. "Some of the crew respect no man's authority but yours."

"Other than a small tussle or two, all has been the doldrums." Udo took a long drink. "I trust your time in York was eventful since you tarried awhile."

Henri nodded, sharing the high points. "I got my bearings. Attended a ball. Was thrown from a horse."

They chuckled. Horsemanship was not one of his strengths. He'd been too long at sea.

"There's a great deal of war talk," he told them. "I spoke at length with Virginia officials."

"Ah, at last we get to the meat of the matter." Southack leaned in, eyes alive with anticipation.

Henri nodded. But how to condense hours of conversation? "The British are commissioning seamen to prey upon and plunder French ships, thereby cutting supply lines to enemy allies on the frontier."

Udo toyed with his pewter tankard. "Commit acts of freebooting?"

"Aye, all in the name of establishing English dominance on the high seas as well as North America and the Caribbean."

"'Tis a war, aye, or soon will be," Tarbonde said. "A contest over who wins America and other foreign interests."

"And the plunder?" Southack's gaze never left Henri. "If we risk our lives as privateers under an official letter of marque? Are all prizes taken given over to the British government?"

"A great many questions remain unanswered. And I've made no promises as to our involvement." Henri ran a hand over his unshaven face. "Closer to home, Virginia's government is desperate for reinforcements to protect Chesapeake Bay from pirates. This from the lord commissioner for trade and plantations and the secretary of state."

Udo frowned. "When will you learn more, sir?"

Henri looked out the window toward York. "In a sennight I'm to attend a meeting in Williamsburg. A gathering of officials and certain mariners of note, including Admiral Barnabas Shaw."

"Famed commander of the Royal Navy?" Tarbonde queried.

Southack's brow lifted. "Famed commander and former privateer turned pirate."

"Careful." Henri leveled his gaze at the surgeon. "The same has been said of us."

Ned regarded Henri warily. "In that same vein, be watchful of your enemies in the capital and elsewhere who would rejoice to see you brought low." His gaze slid to the Africans. "And slave catchers ashore who would like nothing better than to ensnare bona fide freemen."

The warning led to a sullen silence. Henri had nearly forgotten the high feeling against him among Virginia's planters and politicians. So much falsehood was printed about him by those who opposed him, it turned previously unbiased citizens against him as well. But he was most concerned about the Africans. Many of them were inked with the Jerusalem cross as he was, identifying themselves as his crew in a show of unity and pride.

"Let us talk of more pleasant matters. Like the ball. What I'd give to see a comely petticoat or two." Southack let out a long breath. "I'd gladly suffer a minuet."

Ned nodded. "As would I."

Henri understood. He knew they longed to escape their wooden world and form feminine ties. "'Tis your turn to go ashore. We've no imminent sailing to pursue to keep you from staying as long as you like. Not yet. But once on the mainland, be on your guard."

"Are you sure it's only a meeting you're going to in the capital?" Southack's wink was sly. "I seem to recall Admiral Shaw having several beautiful daughters."

"Only two," Henri corrected. "One is wed."

"Which leaves the second." Southack drummed impatient fingers atop the scarred table.

When Henri said nothing, his sea chaplain filled the silence. "Miss Esmée Shaw? A chocolatier who has a shop along the waterfront, or once did. Last we were in port, Shaw's supplied us with chocolate before we sailed."

"Shaw's will need to resupply us ahead of our next voyage," Udo said. "Six pounds of chocolate per man, much like the officers marching with Braddock's army."

"God rest Braddock's sorry soul," Ned breathed.

They observed a moment of silence for the fallen general. But in truth, the frontier was so far, the war threat felt even further removed.

Southack brightened. "So what is your recommendation for lodgings in York?"

"The Royal Oake should suffice," Henri said. "The bell system is rather extraordinary. And the owner has a very accommodating daughter who may not be able to withstand your charms."

Udo winked. "Though she withstood yours, no doubt, immune to matrimony as you are."

They all laughed soundly, and Tarbonde called for more ale.

Henri regarded them fondly. "If I wed, then I'd have to relax my cardinal rule of prohibiting married men as crew."

"With all due respect, your crew might be better for marrying," Ned replied.

"I'll not separate husbands and wives and families." The rule was ironclad. And it was Esmée who had been behind it.

Talk turned to other matters. But Esmée's memory, repeatedly tossed overboard, stubbornly resurfaced. And now he was no longer here by the open window with a salt breeze caressing his unshaven face. He was at the ball's supper again, seated beside her, a decade of ill feeling between them.

Though time and weather had simply lined him, she was remarkably changed. She'd grown rounder and even more beguiling, as if she'd snuck one too many chocolates in his absence. She was . . . voluptuous. And guarded. No longer the guileless girl he'd left behind.

And now the possessor of a hard-won copy of *The Complete Confectioner*.

CHAPTER

Methinks yer more buccaneer than privateer." Mistress Saltonstall gaped in outright astonishment as Henri shoveled sandy soil back into a deep hole. "Buried treasure, indeed, even if not ill-gotten!"

Dusk was layering Indigo Island in silvery shadows. It was his favorite time of day, be it by land or sea. "Remember this exact location. You're the only soul who knows besides me." His wink was likely lost on her in the gloaming. "And if it goes missing, I'll know who to blame."

"Hoot! I'm no long-gone fool or babbler. Yer stash is safe with me." She dug in her pocket, withdrew a silver ingot, and admired it. "Especially since ye see to the needs of so many and don't hoard yer prizes."

Tossing the shovel aside, Henri began covering the spot with brush, glad to have it done before dark. She lent a hand, dragging fallen pine branches and grapevines to help finish the task. He'd left caches she didn't know about in half a dozen places on the island, carefully marked on a map he had stashed beneath a floorboard in his cottage bedchamber.

Winded, she eyed him. "Tell me again how ye came by such a haul."

Henri straightened to his full height and took the flask she handed him. "A flotilla of Spanish ships wrecked off the coast of Florida in a late summer's gale. A great many pesos were lost and a great many regained, including the silver."

She whistled through gapped teeth. "Is it true what yer quartermaster said—that all them jacks drowned?"

"To the last man, God rest them."

"The Spaniards claiming those alligator-ridden waters are no doubt hotter than Hades over yer haul."

He swiped at his sweaty brow with his sleeve. "None witnessed our recovery of the cargo."

For all their blether claiming Florida, the Spanish had done little to settle it other than found St. Augustine and build an impenetrable stone fort. It was made of seashells, his men had scoffed, yet it had withstood twenty-seven days of cannon fire during the last British attack.

He took a drink. "I'm to return to the mainland and have need of riding instruction as there are so few carriages to be had. Any recommendations?"

"So, yer in need of a fine-blooded horse fit for a gentleman captain." Mistress Saltonstall's gaze held more mirth than he liked. "None better than Jago Wherry. He can be found at the quarter-mile races of a Saturday outside Williamsburg. Or the almshouse when his pockets are empty."

"He's a homeless gambler, then."

"Aye, but he kens horses, and everybody knows it. Tell him Polly sent ye. We were once acquainted in our youth." Born and bred in York, she knew any name Henri put to her. "So ye can't ride, Captain, being boat bound for so long?"

"Riding the waves is the sum of my experience, I'm afraid."

She chuckled and took back the flask.

"That and the horse latitudes," he added.

Her mirth vanished. "All those poor creatures thrown overboard in the windless passages. 'Tis a wonder America has any horses at all."

"Now Virginia abounds with them." He looked toward the fading sunset beyond York's distant lights. "And a great many excellent riders."

"Take care to buy yer mount from the Tayloes, who import the best breeds," she told him. "Then stable yer steed at Grant's on Ballard Street."

"Obliged. What can I bring you when I return from the mainland next?"

"Nary a thing, Captain." She looked sly again, a light in her pale eyes. "Since the rheumatism plagues me so on the island come foul weather, I may winter in York with my widowed sister. She keeps a snug little house on the outskirts. But ye can keep an eye on the Flask and Sword if ye stay on. And Hermes."

Henri opened his mouth to protest, but she'd already turned her back with a cackle and was soon well beyond hearing as she hurried to return to the ordinary before dark. He looked after her with welling dread.

Hermes. And a horse.

He didn't have a good feeling about this.

Esmée might have been royalty for all the attention the milliner-mantuamaker paid her . . . when she had paid her scant attention before.

Eliza must have spent a pretty penny. Madame Suchet was French by birth and styled herself a *marchande de modes*, her mellifluous accent and shop nothing short of sumptuous. Esmée rarely came here save for a length of lace or a pretty fan.

"Your Chinese silk gown is finished, but your cream brocade lacks lace," Madame Suchet said. "Lady Drysdale insists on Dutch linen petticoats and shifts, matching slippers for every gown, clocked silk stockings . . ." She paused as if all the details eluded her. "And a cape of purple broadcloth lined with white silk shag."

Esmée's senses swam as her gaze roamed the rich interior. Fans, gloves, stays, hats, and furbelows she had no name for adorned every available inch of space. Bedazzling. Overwhelming. Suffocating. She took a deep, discreet breath.

"Nothing but the first fashion here in York, with imported cloth arriving daily." Madame Suchet's smile was elusive, the shadows beneath her eyes telling. "I am in a battle royale with the Williamsburg milliner, an Englishwoman. Do you know her?"

Esmée fingered a peacock feather. "Barely."

"Miss Bell may claim the capital, but I am *la dame* of the harbor, all these handsome ships at my beck and call."

"You no doubt created many of the gowns for Lady Lightfoot's ball," Esmée said.

"*Oui*, including Lady Lightfoot's lavender ensemble." With a proud smile she draped the aforementioned cape about Esmée's shoulders. "Winter is coming, and Lady Drysdale wishes you to be warm."

In truth, Eliza wanted her dressed for Williamsburg society more than the weather, and for a sum that pricked Esmée's conscience. Was Quinn agreeable to such an expenditure? Did he even know? Granted, the Chevertons rivaled Virginia's ever-prosperous Byrds, but . . .

"Pish-posh! One would think you were a Philadelphia Quaker with your plain ways," Eliza had scolded recently. "Or indisposed to milliner-mantuamakers."

"Touché!" Esmée teased. "In a word, these ladies of trade furnish everything that sets off our beauty, increases our vanity, and renders us ridiculous, as has been said."

"Sister, you simply *must* stop perusing the coffeehouse papers!"

Esmée returned to the laborious if lovely present. The cape was removed, and a rustling chintz in various hues was draped over her for a final day gown. A fawning assistant helped with pins and suggestions. Esmée stifled a yawn, wishing for a cup of cocoa, as the forenoon was crisp.

"I shall have everything delivered to your residence the day before you leave for Williamsburg," Madame Suchet promised.

Thanking her, Esmée lingered by a display of ribbon near the door.

"You are admiring the silk taffety ribbon, no? How about a yard or two of this Parisian blue or pear green? Scarlet is also gaining ground, though sable is the preferred color." Madame Suchet took up the black and strung it round her own throat. "A ribbon choker necklace is all the rage."

Esmée took out her embroidered pocketbook. She'd not add to Eliza's account. "I'll take three yards of each, including the rose and purple."

Smiling, Madame Suchet bid her adieu and let the shopgirl handle the matter.

At last, purse lighter, Esmée walked uphill toward home. Once there she donned a riding habit, hiding the ribbons in a saddlebag when the groom brought her saddled horse round. Atop Minta and shivering beneath the muted midday sun, she moved past wagons and carts and hawkers going about their noisy business in town.

In minutes she'd gained the coastal road, cantering along its rutted path, pausing once to let her mare water at a creek and sample a patch of seagrass. She savored the seascape, a palette of blues and grays as the sun broke free of scattered clouds.

She'd timed her almshouse visit carefully, hoping the trustees would be elsewhere. Once she arrived, she had her wish. Mistress Boles was absent and Miss Grove was busy with the children. Glad for the lack of supervision, Esmée sat down at a long trestle table in the dining hall with sixteen almshouse women, including the new arrivals Father had mentioned. Quickly she learned their names. Lucy, Hannah, Jane, Arminda. They regarded her with wide-eyed surprise. Gentlewomen didn't oft dine with the destitute. Or were they staring at her riding habit? Eliza called it shabby, outmoded, but even if the green velvet was worn and the feathers limp with age, it was an extravagance they'd rarely beheld.

"Ye picked a good day to sup with us, Miss Shaw," one woman told her. "'Tis meat Monday."

Meat? Esmée glanced at her own plate. Could this paltry bit of bone and gristle be called that? Smiling nevertheless, she wondered how she'd eat a bite. Almshouse men were served before the women, while the children partook in their schoolroom.

"Will ye say grace, Miss Shaw?" came another timid query.

Joining hands, they bowed their heads. Esmée paused, sensing all the unspoken, unmet needs at hand. "Dear Lord, let it be our earnest prayer to serve Thee better day by day as we grow in grace and trust

Thee for our wants in soul and body. For these and all Thy blessings, God's holy name be praised for Christ's sake. Amen."

The shallow bowl of soup ladled out next bore a tiny potato and a sliver of parsnip. Esmée took up her spoon without complaint, aware of half a dozen eyes on her as if awaiting a wince of distaste.

Stale bread reminding her of ship's biscuits—with no butter—rounded out the meagre meal. She thought of the citrus delivered to their very door two days past from a ship newly returned from the Caribbean. These women were alarmingly thin, even the pregnant Alice. Such humble fare was barely enough to keep a bird alive.

"Thank ye for the chocolate ye brought last time," another woman murmured.

A few capped heads bobbed. The most talkative sat across from her. "We've had a bit in hot milk and it's divine. But seems like the trustees take the lion's share. Guess it's their due for puttin' up with the lot o' us."

Esmée managed another disagreeable spoonful. "Is Mistress Boles away often?"

"Her mother's ailin', so she hies to Tobacco Road now and again to tend to her."

They ate in companionable silence, a comment made now and then. Esmée soldiered on, trying to determine what was most needed near at hand. The mother-to-be required far more than the ribbon she'd brought. She'd seen better dressed indentures and slaves. The eldest among them bore sores on her wrinkled cheeks. What bathing facilities did these residents have? Nary a bath in a twelvemonth, it seemed for some. Surely there was no excuse for uncleanliness with the York River at hand.

"Before you return to work," Esmée said, "I beg you, tell me your most pressing want. Shoes? A comb? Pockets? A pinch of tea or a remedy from the York apothecary? A petticoat? Today I've only brought a bit of comely ribbon."

They rushed her at the mention, and when Esmée passed around the taffety ribbons, the women laughed and compared colors, proving poverty and age failed to dent an appreciation for pretty things.

Each woman then confided her most pressing need. Miss Grove returned to help, jotting down each whispered request with stylus and paper. The women left merrier than when she'd arrived, clutching their bit of finery as they returned to their assigned chores, be it garden or washhouse or kitchen.

Miss Grove handed the lengthy list over. "How can you possibly provide all these items, Miss Shaw?"

"I shan't provide them," Esmée said with a confident smile, pocketing the paper. "The Almighty shall."

Miss Grove gave a sigh. "My faith is small, I'm afraid. I've seen a great many broken promises and hearts here."

Esmée squeezed her hand before turning away. "I can assure you every need on the list shall be met, though it may take time."

She left the main building, the wind rising and threatening to unseat her hat. Minta was hobbled beneath a widespread oak wearing a leafy coat as colorful as the biblical Joseph's. Esmée started toward her, the sun in her eyes, before coming to a sudden stop. There, across a wide stretch of meadow, were two men and a handsome bay horse. A nicer mount she'd never seen save from the stables of the Tayloes or Lees.

Yet it wasn't the horse but the rider she lingered upon. Could it be? Only an uncanny resemblance, surely. Wasn't the captain back on his island? If so, his twin swung himself up in the saddle.

And promptly fell off the other side.

Oh, Henri.

Nay. *Captain Lennox.* She wouldn't allow herself the more intimate *Henri.*

Or would she?

If ever she'd wished him a humiliating moment, such played out before her very eyes. To see him so undone when he was usually all mastery and finesse was a shocking sight.

He stood, failed to dust himself off, and tried again. He succeeded on a second try, though he swayed a bit. She held her breath as the portly man on the ground gave some instruction. Jago Wherry? Reins in hand, the captain prodded the bay forward and began a slow, uncertain walk . . . in her direction.

The wind gusted and a shower of crisp leaves ended her gawking, adorning her beaver hat. Brushing them aside, she mounted her mare with great speed and a new appreciation for the riding lessons of her youth. Prodding Minta into motion, she rode toward York's smoke and spires far faster than she'd left them.

CHAPTER *twelve*

Henri's tumble from the saddle was far less jarring than the realization he had an audience. If it had been anyone other than Esmée, he wouldn't have minded. There she stood in a fetching tailored jacket and skirt of the palest green. A jaunty hat with several white feathers crowned her head. He regarded her just long enough for Jago Wherry to take note.

The canny Cornishman gave a chuckle. "'Twas Miss Shaw who caused ye to take a tumble, no doubt."

Henri smiled past his humiliation and turned his back on the comely vision as Esmée fled with far more grace than he was capable of. Reins firmly in hand, he gave up the thought of chasing after her. A far-fetched notion, as she was born to the saddle like any well-bred woman. He'd never catch up with her.

Wherry cleared his throat. "Riding is not so far afield from commanding a ship, aye, sir? Ye must control the direction and speed with great discernment and a minimum of meddling. Ye must let the horse—like the ship—do the work."

"A worthy comparison."

"Yer posture is without fault, but yer a bit stiff." Wherry took a step back. "'Tis all about balance. Ye must learn to think like the creature upon whose back ye sit."

"A tall order."

By hour's end Henri had grown comfortable with this, his third lesson, enough to manage a brisk walk if not a trot. "I believe I can make my way back to Grant's stables."

"Without breaking yer blessed neck, I hope."

"If I do, Trident is yours."

Wherry gave a wheezing laugh and scratched Trident's withers. "Ye learn quick, Captain. And a better horse cannot be had. Spritely but not too spirited. Even tempered. Surefooted."

"And long-suffering with a sea rover like myself."

"Ye have a way with Trident, calm and assured as ye are. That bodes well for ye both."

Henri reached into his waistcoat and withdrew coin enough to pay for Wherry's trouble. "We have a gentleman's agreement, aye? I'll not see my hard-earned cash wagered."

Wherry chuckled. "Come to the races, Captain, and ye might well change yer mind."

"Once I can ride there without cause for shame, I may take you up on it."

They parted, Henri taking the same road that had returned Esmée to town. She'd seemed to appear out of nowhere, as if he'd dreamed her standing there. What was she doing miles from York, and alone at that?

Thirsty and winded, Esmée slowed to a trot as she neared York. With the almshouse women fresh in mind, she spent the next hour visiting various shops to purchase what she could. Intent on the apothecary last, she abruptly changed course, avoiding Charlotte Oake as she came out of the bookbindery next door. Remounting Minta, saddlebags bulging, Esmée quickly considered her options and reined left.

Down an alley she went, intent on Matthews Street. At its end, the

Harts' residence beckoned with acres of fragrant flowers and ripening orchards. For many years, the Harts had imported upwards of hundreds of flowering species from a London nursery to adorn their corner of Virginia. 'Twas a beloved spot since the Shaws had only a small kitchen garden and a few straggling roses now that Mama was gone.

Kitty, her dearest friend, was an able businesswoman in her own right. Her antidote to the popular, male-dominated coffeehouses in the colony was to open a female-dominated tea garden. As usual, Kitty was outside, tending to the last of the season's trumpet flowers and tuberoses.

"Esmée!" Kitty tossed aside a spade, peeled off her soiled gloves, and hurried down a brick walkway to greet her. "Nary a penny is needed!" she joked about the usual entrance fee paid by visitors.

They embraced and passed beneath an arbor's rose-scented shade. Though it was October, the blooms continued lush. Empty wicker chairs called for an extended visit. In summer, musicians were hired to play as visitors strolled the attractive paths over several acres.

"You've been to the almshouse is my guess." Kitty's amber eyes sharpened. "But you seem rather . . . bestirred. Might that have something to do with the passing of a magnificent bay horse just moments ago carrying your captain?"

"*My* captain?" Esmée darted a glance at the road, safely distant. "Most decidedly *not*."

"'Twas what I always called him once upon a time," Kitty said unapologetically as they took their seats.

"We didn't cross paths, not this time. I simply saw him from afar as I left the almshouse."

"You're still recovering from being thrust together at Lady Lightfoot's ball, I suppose." Kitty picked a rose from overhead and brought it to her nose. "What a hullaballoo when the captain strode in! All the women regarding him as if he were Poseidon himself. He has as many admirers as naysayers, you know."

Naysayers was kind. *Enemies* was more accurate. There was no denying Henri had a colorful past. Impressed as a lad by the British navy—a form of white slavery, he'd once said—he'd since caused an uproar among slave-owning Virginians once he became commander of his own vessel.

"You're remembering the brig *Swallow*, as am I," Esmée said, focusing on a cardinal as it winged by with a swoosh of red.

"Captain Lennox was right to intercept it. To burn it." Kitty's voice was low, as they were not alone in the garden. "Would that all of those slavers suffer the same fate."

Only two days out off the coast of Cabinda in Africa, the *Swallow* had been intercepted by the *Relentless* and returned to port. Its cargo of several hundred slaves who were crammed between the hold and deck had been liberated, the ship's crew left on land as their vessel was torched.

Esmée flinched recalling it. "'Twas the utmost irony the ship was bound for Virginia. Thankfully, none could prove it was the captain, with it happening so far from our shores. And he wisely stayed away."

An absence of years Esmée knew all too well. For a time the *Swallow*'s burning had incensed slave owners and ignited a fierce debate on the ills of the trade, but the Middle Passage continued robust. Of all the American colonies, Virginia enslaved the most Africans, and they landed almost daily in dizzying numbers.

"Quakers and free Africans have long been crying out against slavery," Esmée said. "'Tis rumored a large portion of the captain's profiteering prizes help fund those who oppose it."

"And now the renowned Captain Lennox has returned to our shores. Quite courageously too, making so public an appearance at the ball and now about town."

Esmée bit her lip, pondering it all. "Father led me to believe he'd left York. I assumed he'd set sail again. Glad I am I'll soon be at Eliza's in Williamsburg. Perhaps I shall stay longer than planned."

"On account of the dashing captain?" Kitty laughed. "Though you hope to ignore him, why does it appear you are as enamored with him as at first?"

"Enamored?" Esmée shook her head so vehemently it set her hat's feathers dancing. "Do you have any inkling how mortifying it is to keep being reminded of a thwarted love affair at every turn?"

"Ah." Kitty studied her pensively. "What you need is cherry syllabub."

"Cherry?" Esmée brightened. She *was* thirsty. "Grog is more like it. 'Tis stronger."

"Grog? Bah!" Waving a hand, Kitty summoned a servant to bring refreshments. "Foul stuff fit for common sailors."

"Are you calling Captain Lennox common?"

"Hardly! But what is that to you?" Kitty's eyes narrowed with mirth. "Yet you seem all too ready to leap to his defense."

Esmée lapsed into stymied silence.

"I do believe he's even handsomer than I remember. And those eyes of his, serene one minute, then intense as a tropical storm the next—"

"You are no help at all."

Kitty leaned in with a sympathetic purr. "So, he still holds your heart, at least a bit of it."

Did he?

Esmée shook her head in denial. When he'd left long ago, she'd vowed to never let another man affect her so, her heart torn asunder at their impasse.

"Which reminds me . . ." Kitty brought her round with whiplash haste. "I read in yesterday's *Virginia Gazette* an advertisement that might interest you. 'Twas remarkable in its brevity. Simply, 'Wanted: Lighthouse keeper, Indigo Island.'"

Esmée listened, ripples of dismay widening inside her. She'd avoided the papers of late, not wanting to read more about the captain than she must. But now . . . "Have you a copy?"

"I shall ask Father what he did with it before you go. 'Tis all the talk about town. That and the captain's return. Reading it brought back all that you once told me. About your shared plan for the light."

"Once, yes." Surprise gave way to an immediate wounding. A second betrayal. Esmée vowed to return home and remove the little silver lighthouse from her chatelaine once and for all. "Long ago we'd planned to marry on the island and keep the light."

"But it goes back further, does it not? To childhood?"

Dear Kitty. Remembering all the poignant details. "You mean when I was small and Father took me to Massachusetts to see the Boston harbor light. The first of its kind in the colonies. I recall him carrying me up steep steps all the way to the top. Heaven's view, he said. I've never forgotten it."

Ever since, she'd carried that remarkable moment like an ember inside her, stoking it and breathing life into it as the years went by. Father had helped fan that dream. The Chesapeake with its treacherous capes and shifting sandbars needed a similar light, he'd often said.

With a little nod, Kitty placed the wilting rose on the table. "I heard Boston Light recently burned."

Esmée nodded, her dream now ashes too. "Father told me. He keeps in contact with the lightkeeper there."

The syllabub came, a cold, sweet distraction.

"I know the chocolate shop was your mother's dream, not yours," Kitty said. "Yet you've faithfully maintained it, and 'tis quite successful. Successful enough for you to leave it should you want to and simply keep it as your dowry."

"I adore chocolate, but 'tis not what sets my soul on fire," Esmée admitted.

"And the island and lighthouse do?"

How could she answer, having never experienced either? She took another sip, feeling oddly unburdened at their honest talk, knowing Kitty was a safe harbor. "What do you know of the captain's present whereabouts?"

"I have it on good authority that he's lodging at the Royal Oake when in town and that the widow Charlotte is rather smitten. You've not seen him at the shop?"

"He's not so much as darkened the door, though something curious happened the morn after the ball. A cookbook I've long coveted was found on the shop's doorstone. The booksellers here and in Williamsburg haven't been able to import any from London. So I wondered . . ."

"Might Captain Lennox be behind it?" Kitty looked hopeful. Far more hopeful than Esmée felt.

"I don't know what to think. 'Tis a riddle I'll likely never solve. Imagine my brazenly asking him if he'd gifted it to me, only to have him say nay." Esmée chuckled despite herself. "Though I would like to thank whoever it was that was so thoughtful. So generous."

"Why don't you give him a secret gift in return?"

"Nonsense."

"A riding crop, perhaps, now that he's become a horseman. I spied a handsome silver one with a tortoiseshell handle at Christie's store just yesterday."

Dare she?

Kitty pressed forward, clearly smitten with her plan. "Arrange for it to be delivered to the Royal Oake discreetly, as happened at your chocolate shop. Let Charlotte wonder as well. Hoodwink her into believing the captain is taken."

"How . . . bold." Esmée warmed to the plan nevertheless. "Amusing, even."

Kitty laughed, looking like a cat with cream. "'Tis romantic . . . intriguing."

"I pass by Christie's on the way home," Esmée said, still torn. "If the crop is still there, 'twill be his. If not . . ." Might that be her answer? "I'll let you know what transpires. But not a word to anyone, promise me. Not even your dear father."

"'Tis our secret. I'll keep you in my thoughts and prayers." Kitty's expression clouded briefly before her smile resurfaced. "You were never quite the same after Captain Lennox went away years ago. I'd be delighted if the former Esmée Shaw came around again."

CHAPTER
thirteen

Williamsburg in autumn nearly blinded him with color. Accustomed to the muted blues and grays of sea and sky save a brilliant sunset or sunrise aboard ship, Henri rode down Duke of Gloucestershire Street with a raptness that made him half forget his poor horsemanship. Countless oaks and maples rustled like a silk skirt in a brisk wind, sending a torrent of painted leaves swirling down onto dusty cobblestones.

He'd nearly forgotten Publick Times every April and October when the courts were in session, people overflowing every inch of Williamsburg. If he hadn't been invited to stay at the governor's palace, he doubted he'd find a room at one of the inns.

To his right was the Raleigh Tavern with its deep porch fronting the street, the din of crockery and men's voices from the taproom making him almost risk the spectacle of dismounting and tethering Trident to the hitch rail. He swallowed, his throat bone-dry, and gave the Raleigh a last, lingering glance. In one hand he held the reins, in another the mysterious riding crop used to cue his horse at intervals.

Wrapped in brown paper and string, it had been delivered to his lodging house just yesterday ahead of his leaving for Williamsburg.

Charlotte Oake had looked more perplexed than pleased as she presented it to him when he entered the foyer.

"For you, Captain," she'd told him, unsmiling. "A courier from Christie's store said this was to be given to you posthaste."

He took the package, wanting to open it privately, but curiosity got the best of him, so he tore open the paper. "No mention of the giver?"

"None." She gave no sign of leaving till he'd unwrapped it. "Do you have a secret admirer, sir?"

He stared at the crop, a costly piece of work. "One with decidedly good taste, if so."

Was Esmée trying to pay him back for his gifting her a book? Granted, *The Complete Confectioner* had long been in his possession. He'd thought, upon his return to Virginia five years before, to ask her forgiveness and give her the gift. But second thoughts had the tome going around the world with him instead, tucked beneath a stack of sailing manuals in a bookcase, a continual if barbed reminder of their broken tie.

Charlotte's features tightened. "How long will you be in Williamsburg, sir?"

He gave her no firm answer, as he hadn't one. He considered it now as he turned up Palace Green. The governor's brick residence with its ornamental iron gates at the far end was the undisputed crown jewel of the capital, away from the crowds and confusion of Virginia's largest town. He sought the palace's cobbled forecourt, where a groom waited to take his mount to the near stables.

Stiff and slightly saddle sore, Henri climbed stone steps to the palace's front door, gaze rising to the towering lanthorn impaling the October sky. The door opened, and a butler ushered him into a weapon-lined hall that seemed more military fort than palace.

"The governor is upstairs in the middle room with his officials, sir, but will see you in due time. I'll show you to your chamber."

Henri followed the liveried servant down a carpeted hall and up a stair to an enormous bedchamber. Compared to his cramped sea cabin aboard the *Relentless*, it was sumptuous—fit for a prince—and painted as yellow as a finch's wing. The bed linens bore a floral pattern all the rage on land these days. He was most drawn to the comfortable chair near a crackling hearth. Though the day wasn't cold, the room was airy, and night would soon set in with autumn's chill.

Restless, he crossed the thick carpet to one of two windows and pushed aside the ornate drapes. Palace Green stretched before him, his second-floor vantage point giving him a bird's-eye view.

His gaze drifted from the mustering militia to a man playing a fiddle to a bevy of laughing, chatting belles strolling in colorful procession past the palace gates. The ribbons on their wide straw hats fluttered behind them, their elegant skirts teased by the wind, all of them paired in twos but for the lone graceful straggler at the back . . .

Esmée?

He took a second look, gaze darting to the front of the column before returning to the rear again. Esmée followed at a distance, obviously content to keep her own pace. She paused to buy paper flowers from a barefoot young girl selling them on a corner.

Crossing his arms, he allowed himself an unhindered look at her. She was talking to the flower peddler, twirling the paper blossoms in one gloved hand. She'd always been kind. No airs about her. Her sister and entourage were now halfway down the other side of Palace Green as if they'd forgotten all about her. As usual, Eliza was leading the charge, undeterred by her pregnancy or anything else, for that matter. He watched them through the trees till they'd turned a distant corner by Bruton Parish Church.

Was Virginia so infernally small?

He was used to an ocean, and town had him tripping over people. Was it not uncanny that he and Esmée kept crossing paths? First the ball, then near the almshouse, and now this. What next? As she likely didn't associate with Virginia's officials, he doubted they'd move beyond this chance encounter from afar. No mention had been made of a rout or any other form of entertainment, not at the governor's palace, anyway. He could rest easy, mayhap. Finish his business with colonial officials and be gone.

He turned away from the window and sought the hearth, sinking down into the velvet-upholstered chair. A tug on the bell cord gained him something to allay his thirst. In minutes, a footman brought a silver tray and poured him a cup of strong, hot tea. Bohea, from the scent of it. A dram of French brandy rested beside it. Here it was a relief to escape the near constant shadow of Charlotte Oake, even if she did serve Shaw's chocolate.

The book he'd brought—Thomas à Kempis's *The Imitation of Christ*—awaited reading, one quote worth remembering.

Everywhere I have sought peace and not found it, except in a corner with a book.

He stretched out his legs, his boots near the elaborately cast brass andirons, and pondered. Why had the governor called him here? Something to do with the current conflict, no doubt. His gaze traveled to the window again, the sky so blue and the town so peaceful it was hard to believe there was a war nearing official declaration.

Surely Dinwiddie didn't want to make a soldier of him.

CHAPTER *fourteen*

Esmée pressed her paper flowers to her nose in a fit of whimsy. Just ahead were Eliza and her friends, returning to tea at the Cheverton townhouse. They'd had a delightful stroll about town, mindful winter would soon set in with an icy vengeance. The autumn wind was rising, pressing against them as they passed Bruton Parish Church and continued toward Nassau Street. Eliza was laughing, spirits high on so lovely an afternoon.

Esmée warmed to the sound after a fretful two days. Upon her arrival, her sister was complaining of pains and the physic was sent for. With the baby not due till January, any trouble was unwelcome. Still, Eliza had insisted on entertaining friends and walking about and now presiding over tea. She waited on the steps for Esmée to catch up as her guests went over the threshold into the townhouse.

"Sister, how you dally!" Appearing amused and exasperated, Eliza gestured her inside, clearly ready to sit down. "What fuss over paper flowers!"

All six ladies swarmed into the parlor like colorful butterflies, removing hats and gloves before settling around a tea table. Esmée felt like the odd woman out. The present company did not make her feel unwelcome, but neither had they common ground, with their talk of parties and French fashion and the latest gossip to be had.

"What have you in hand there?" Lady Griffin asked her, leaning in and enveloping Esmée in a cloud of toilet water.

"Paper carnations and roses." Esmée held them out so she could see the painstaking care with which they were crafted.

"Clever." On Esmée's other side, Miss Cartwright wrinkled her pale nose. "But I prefer silk flowers from the milliner. Nothing so common as paper."

"Common? 'Tis artistry to me," Esmée replied. "Look at the parts of the flower from stamen to petals, all dyed such lovely hues. The child—Lottie is her name—would make a botanist proud. I asked her for a whole nosegay of them to last me through the winter."

"Well, they shan't wilt, truly," Lady Griffin said with a chuckle, eyes on the refreshments being brought into the room. "Though I fancy they won't retain their color either."

Across the table, the governor's eldest daughter, Rebecca Dinwiddie, took out her fan. "The flowers are lovely, though I'd rather talk chocolate, Miss Shaw. Your sister says you may well open a shop right here in Williamsburg."

Esmée opened her mouth to naysay it once again, then bit her tongue lest it only stir up Eliza's zeal for the plan. Would her sister never let go of the notion?

Eliza simply smiled, pouring tea into prewarmed cups for those who wanted it, making a great show of it with her Wedgwood tea service. The maid stood by with a porcelain chocolate pot new to Esmée, twisting the molinet between her hands to blend the beverage.

"Enough about chocolate," Miss Cartwright said, her color high. "You know what's said."

"Indeed, I do," Lady Griffin replied. "The fair sex is to be particularly careful how they meddle with romances, chocolate, novels, and the like."

"The *Virginia Almanac*, for one." Miss Cartwright's capped head bobbed. "Especially in the spring, as those inflamers are very dangerous."

"My dear sister, which is your preference?" Eliza asked, clearly amused by the conversation. "The very tepid-in-reputation tea? Or the more passionate and provoking hot chocolate?"

Esmée replied unashamedly, "Chocolate, please."

Smiling, Miss Dinwiddie raised her own chocolate cup. "I'm especially partial to Shaw's dark cocoa with orange essence, as is my father."

"Speaking of your father, our respected governor"—Lady Griffin fingered the opal choker about her neck—"do tell us about the next function he and your mother are rumored to be planning."

"Indeed, the new ballroom and supper room will host a splendid assembly this January."

"A holiday ball?" Miss Marriot exclaimed. "Enchanting!"

"Miss Shaw, will you join us, or have you other reasons to stay in York?" Miss Dinwiddie asked.

Another assembly. The frivolous cost of which could feed and clothe the almshouse till next Christmastide. What could Esmée say to this?

Judge not that ye be not judged.

Eliza pouted when Esmée failed to answer. "I shan't attend, for obvious reasons."

A tittering of sympathy went round the circle. Esmée sipped from her cup in silence, glad the conversation had gone another, less inflammatory direction. In the foyer she could hear her father and Quinn about to go out. They'd been summoned to the palace. Some sort of meeting that involved maritime matters. They wouldn't return till after supper, they'd said that morn, which left her and Eliza to their own devices.

"And you, Miss Shaw?" Lady Griffin seemed determined that Esmée answer. "Are you not fond of dancing? I believe I saw you at Lady Lightfoot's ball. And in the company of Captain Lennox, I daresay."

The room stilled. The ladies were looking at her over the rims of their cups. Heat climbed from Esmée's tightly laced stays to her powderless cheekbones. What could she say?

Eliza set her cup down. "My sister and Captain Lennox do not belong in the same sentence. They simply happened to be thrust together at Lady Lightfoot's table and later when dancing."

"Quite a shame, as he is so *very* eligible," Lady Griffin whispered, brows arched as if privy to inside information. "Though his detractors are many."

Esmée's pulse quickened. Feigning disinterest, she took another sip of chocolate. Had she been a fool to send the captain that riding crop? She could not blame Kitty. She'd wanted to do it, had been rather charmed by the suggestion . . . and therein revealed the state of her heart. She was not at all over Henri Lennox. Not one whit. She'd have to be confined to a casket first. How had she convinced herself over the long years that he had no hold on her?

Eliza flashed her dimpled smile and passed the tray of ginger cakes. "Let us talk less of dashing ship captains and more of the coming assembly."

"Have you heard?" Miss Cartwright brightened. "I was at the mantuamaker's just yesterday. She told me of a new fashion influenced by the secret language of flowers. By embroidering one's clothes, one conveys a message." She looked at one of the paper flowers Esmée had placed on the table. "A carnation means 'my heart aches for you.' A rose in bloom signifies love. I say we all embroider our gowns with meaningful flowers for the coming ball."

"You refer to my very colorful friend, Mary Wortley Montagu," Lady Griffin told them with a touch of pride. "She started the craze for a floral love language in England and the continent. It *is* rather amusing to consider which flowers we might choose."

Eliza was clearly smitten with the idea, her expression rapt. "If I could attend, I would buy up all the scarlet thread and smother my gown in bright red roses, which must symbolize passion."

"I would pick a white lily, which symbolizes purity." Miss Dinwiddie reached for another tea cake with a blush. "Father says that at seventeen I'm too young to consider a suitor."

"Bosh! Never too young—or too old!" Lady Griffin retorted, having outlived three husbands. "Love visits us at any age and often quite unexpectedly."

"What would you choose, Miss Marriot?" Esmée asked her. Of all the women present, she was the undisputed beauty, second to

Eliza, with her flawless skin and flaxen hair, and was reputed to have a great many admirers.

"Purple violet, I believe, though I have no inkling what it signifies."

"Daydreaming," Lady Griffin told her. "'Near them the Vi'let glows with odours blest and blooms in more than Tyrian purple drest.' Next time we gather I shall read from some of Lady Montagu's letters. They are quite eloquent."

"Tyrian purple, indeed." Eliza poured another round of tea and chocolate. "I spied silk of that very color at the mantuamaker's the other day. Needs be you ladies begin embroidering straightaway. January is not far off."

"Shall we meet here, then?" Miss Cartwright suggested. "Company always makes needlework more enjoyable. Unless it would tire you too terribly, that is, Lady Drysdale."

Esmée returned her attention to her sister, who'd reached down to pet her enormous Angora cat, Dulcet, that had crept into the parlor on furry white feet. Eliza looked tired. Half-moons rimmed her eyes, and she'd stifled more yawns than Esmée could count.

Straightening, Eliza flashed another smile. "I beg you, come. Embroidery is not my strong suit, but company keeps my mind off my coming confinement."

Did anyone else detect the note of dread in Eliza's voice?

"I'm nearly done with the babe's welcome gift," Esmée said. "I hope you like it." Declining another cup of tea, she reached for her sewing bag and took out her latest handwork. Tea drinking and talk didn't satisfy for long. She must be doing something.

Lady Griffin raised an eyebrow. "What have you there?"

Esmée threaded a needle with practiced ease. "Clouts and pilchers for the almshouse infants."

A quiet nearly as lengthy as that of Captain Lennox's mention ensued. The ladies looked on as she plied her needle.

"Ah, the almshouse." Lady Griffin's tone implied both distaste and indifference. "Overfull of a great many feebleminded as well as fallen women, not to mention beggarly, idle men."

"You might be surprised if you visited. I welcome you to accompany me." Careful to hide the ire she felt lest she hurt her cause, Esmée continued, "There are a great many orphaned children. And infirm elderly with no means or family to support them."

"I've heard conditions are dismal." Miss Cartwright turned troubled eyes on her. "How often are you there, Miss Shaw?"

"Every sennight, usually. More often if there's cause." Esmée raised her gaze and smiled at them in invitation. "If you cannot accompany me, I encourage you to give what you are willing—goods, foodstuffs, coin. Anything at all helps."

"Hearing about orphaned infants makes me melancholy." Eliza put a hand on her burgeoning middle. "Imagine being brought up homeless and even motherless. And then there are the children indentured almost before they are out of pudding caps and leading strings!"

Enlivened by too many cups of sugared tea, Eliza was in full theatrical mode, embarrassing Esmée but perhaps aiding her mission. Rebecca Dinwiddie looked shocked. Was the governor's daughter shielded from such harsh realities? Beside her, the sensitive Miss Cartwright sighed while Miss Marriot took out a handkerchief and dabbed her eyes.

Lady Griffin appeared unmoved. "Is that not how your saintly mother died, Miss Shaw? A malignant fever? Contracting her very death by patronizing the almshouse . . ." She shuddered and closed her eyes. "*Pesthouse* is more like it."

Chafed, Esmée continued stitching, though she had another idea of how best to use her needle. Lady Griffin was in dire need of deflating, her arrogance unchecked. "How hard your heart is, madam. My mother did indeed die from a malignant fever, but she could have gotten the same from the very streets of York or Williamsburg. The Almighty has the final say over life and death. 'Twas simply Mama's time or she would never have contracted it to begin with, pesthouse or no."

The ensuing silence grew strained. Miss Marriot coughed into her handkerchief. Had Esmée stirred a hornet's nest?

"How blithely you say such, Miss Shaw." Lady Griffin's haughty tone was Esmée's final undoing. "The Almighty I worship is a different being altogether, a Creator, certainly, but one who remains apart from His creation, giving us leave to act as we will. Personal responsibility and accountability are foremost."

"You speak of a clockwork universe, not divine Providence." Esmée finished one clout and moved to the next, eyes on her stitches. "If you read less of misguided deists and more of the Bible, we might be spared this futile conversation."

"Ladies, please." Eliza's wide eyes flashed a warning.

Esmée smiled at her, dispelling the tension, or so she hoped.

But Lady Griffin was not finished. "What of the danger to your sister and her unborn child with your frequent forays to the poor?"

Esmée replied, "I am seldom in Williamsburg and am vigilant about my own welfare in York. If I find myself ill, I shut myself off from everyone, especially my sister. No one has cause to worry."

"Glad I am to hear it," Lady Griffin concluded with a chill smile. "As for the almshouse, I suppose a shopkeeping, bluestocking spinster must be passionate about something."

Though the slight stung, it held a pithy truth.

Eliza opened her mouth to leap to her sister's defense, it seemed, then caught Esmée's warning glance and quieted. Only the Almighty could change Lady Griffin's heart. Or her own, for that matter. Biting her lip lest their banter develop into a full-blown row, Esmée drew a relieved breath as talk returned to the ball. But her mind remained on the almshouse and how to better it.

CHAPTER *fifteen*

"Captain Lennox, might I have the pleasure of your accompanying me home for supper tonight?" Quinn said.

Henri pushed up from his chair after two days of meetings in the middle room at the governor's palace, stomach rumbling in answer. "Obliged, Lord Drysdale."

"You've yet to meet my lovely wife. She's quite fond of company and conversation." Quinn, known far and wide for his hospitality, clapped a hand on Henri's shoulder. "And I hope you'll find our new French chef second to none here in Williamsburg, even the governor's own."

After a few more minutes exchanging farewells with a dozen or so officials, they left the governor's residence and began their walk down Palace Green. A late afternoon drizzle had done little in the way of dampening the revelry. Market Square was glistening, numerous stalls and hawkers offering all manner of Virginia goods.

"Fresh air is never more welcome than after being sequestered in the palace or the House of Burgesses," Quinn said with a relieved smile.

"Mind if we stop by the fruit seller?" Henri eyed the booth across the wide street. "Lady Drysdale might enjoy a pineapple or some bounty from the Summer Isles."

"No purchase quite like a gift." Quinn swung his walking stick with élan. "Do I detect a note of wistfulness in your tone? A longing for the Caribbean, Captain?"

"Mayhap. It nearly became home, as I was away from Virginia for so long."

"My family has a sugar plantation in Barbados. Dreadfully hot. Mosquitos as big as dinner plates," Quinn lamented. "I'm due to return soon on necessary business after the birth of my firstborn."

"I prefer Saint Barthélemy with the hidden coves of Anse du Gouverneur and the sandy beaches of Saline." Henri's pleasant tone turned wry. "French buccaneers, iguanas, and *le chocolat.*"

Quinn smiled his amusement. "You speak fluent French, no doubt."

"*Oui.*" Henri shrugged. "*Je peux communiquer de façon simple.*"

"There is nothing simple about you, Captain," Quinn replied as Henri selected two lush pineapples and paid in pieces of eight. "And I can't help but wonder whether you will risk the governor's dangerous proposition or decline and simply sail away to fairer destinations."

"I have some time to consider it, though the sea, sun, and sand are a powerful elixir," Henri confessed, his head still full of the arguments for and against the proposal in the governor's chambers. "At least we all agree something must be done to stop the French by sea lest we be ruled by the French on land."

"Agreed. But at what cost? Your very life, mayhap. And those of your men."

"War is the trade of kings, after all."

"Indeed." Quinn tipped his hat to someone in passing. "I'd much rather speak of our shared opposition of the slave trade."

"'Tis rare to find one with such convictions, especially in slave-heavy Virginia."

"A tragedy I strive to rectify, though I may see little done to abolish it in my lifetime." Quinn turned to him, his ever genial eyes grave. "But at least I can begin making changes on the sugar plantation I mentioned, replacing Africans with indentures."

"You have an air of Granville Sharp and other staunch abolitionists about you."

"I was trained at London's Temple Court with the best of them. And I've been inspired by your past burning of the *Swallow*, an audacious act that gained considerable attention and made a great many men and women consider their stance on the matter. Far more effective than printing a broadside or waxing eloquent about it in the newspapers."

"Nothing remotely eloquent about smelling a vessel before it's sighted. Or men, women, and children chained and lying in filth after only two days at sea." Though it had been eight years since the tragedy, the misery was burned into his memory like an African brand. "I have no words for those who captain such ships or claim human cargo, many of them our fellow Virginians."

"Woefully so." Quinn's eyes flashed. "'Tis a trade of the greatest inhumanity and an affront to God Almighty."

"Yet slavery remains the cornerstone of the British empire clear to the Caribbean."

"You had a taste of slavery yourself, being impressed in the Royal Navy, taken from your home and family and all you held dear."

"It hardly compares to the evil done the Africans, but aye, a small taste. The experience opened my eyes to those held against their will, their God-given rights violated."

They walked in silence for several moments, beyond the busy marketplace. Henri breathed deeply of the autumn air. Fall, despite its melancholy bent, had always been his favorite season.

"I'm a poor host bringing up such dark matters." Quinn quickened his pace, his voice lifting. "Let us dwell on the present instead. You are our honored guest, and I'm certain Cook has prepared something that will tempt your French sensibilities. My wife will entertain us after supper with the harpsichord, and if you choose to stay on, there will even be illuminations on Palace Green after dark."

They turned up Nassau Street with its deep shade and elegant townhouses, the gardens surrounding them still abloom and untouched by frost. A few welcoming lights shone in windows, lifting

Henri's pensive mood. If he refused the governor's offer, he could settle down. Have a wife who might even play the harpsichord. Hire a cook to turn out endless tantalizing dishes. Beget children to chase after. Cultivate landlocked friends like Quinn. It sounded . . . idyllic.

Impossible.

They mounted brick steps to a door opened by a stone-faced butler in livery.

"Good evening, sirs."

The foyer, fragrant with cooking herbs, was dominated by a curving staircase. Hats and coats discarded, they passed into a spacious, blue-paneled parlor. Feminine voices could be heard upstairs, and then came a light tread on the steps. Henri faced the doorway, ready to greet Lady Drysdale, whoever she might be. His acquaintance with Quinn was just a few days old, but they'd found common ground in the governor's oft heated meetings. Henri was impressed with the younger man's sound judgment and thorough knowledge of colonial affairs.

"Quinn, is that you?" The lovely voice heralded the appearance of a young woman in rustling crimson silk, her throat wrapped in rubies.

Henri's mind whirled.

Lady Drysdale née Eliza Shaw?

The wrench in his gut was offset by Eliza's trilling laugh. "Dear husband, have you played a prank on our unsuspecting captain?"

Though she seemed every bit as taken aback as he was, Eliza recovered well. Henri looked down at the pineapples he held, wishing himself back at the governor's palace. Had he judged Quinn wrong? Was this some sort of tawdry prank?

But it was Quinn who appeared the most confused. He shot a glance at Henri, then returned to his wife. "I was unaware Captain Lennox was known to you."

"Well . . ." Eliza flushed the hue of her gown. "Long ago, yes. We retain a great respect for him, of course, though we did not think to cross paths again."

"*We?*" her husband prodded.

A sigh. "My sister and myself. And Father, of course." Eliza swallowed and darted a glance at the foyer. "But mostly Esmée."

Understanding seemed to dawn on his host's face. "Blast!" Quinn blanched. "Forgive me, Captain. At least take back your pineapples—"

"A peace offering," Henri jested, still trying to grasp Eliza's very advantageous marriage to one of Virginia's foremost officials.

Thanking him, she came forward and took the fruit from his outstretched hands. "How did you know pineapples are my preference?"

A sudden movement in the foyer caused all eyes to shift to the doorway. Esmée, of course. Admiral Shaw was just behind her, obviously as delighted as his oldest daughter was not.

"Captain Lennox!" he all but thundered in the distressed silence. "What brings you to our door?"

"Lord Drysdale invited me to"—Henri's gaze hung on Esmée—"to cause a commotion."

They laughed, all but Esmée, whose tentative half-smile didn't reach her eyes. She came toward them, as comely as ever in a shimmering blue gown. He preferred it to her yellow ensemble at the ball. Blue was always eye-catching, mayhap because it reminded him of the sea. The silken fabric seemed like water poured over her, so flattering was the fit, every inch of cloth and lace accentuating her buxom figure.

"Best have it out in the open." Esmée came to stand between her father and Eliza. "Once upon a time Captain Lennox and I had a . . . an understanding."

"Of the romantic sort," Eliza finished with a genuine smile. "But 'tis ancient history, and today dawns anew. This evening, rather."

"Well, I for one don't believe in coincidences or chance meetings," Admiral Shaw said, showing no befuddlement. "When I left the governor's meetings early today, I never expected you'd be our guest. I couldn't be happier."

"Please, come into the dining room as supper is at hand." Eliza gestured toward a candlelit chamber, where a long table already bore steaming dishes. "'Tis much more informal than Lady Lightfoot's ball." She gave a charming wink in Henri's direction. "Though the seating arrangement is exactly the same."

CHAPTER *sixteen*

Esmée sat down, Henri to her left. Across from them was Eliza, while Quinn and Father occupied the ends of the table. For a few seconds, the lovely flowers at table's center caught her eye and softened her dismay. Gotten from Eliza's formal garden in back of the townhouse, the last of summer's roses showed off their cream and scarlet hues, their scent heady.

Also heady was the man beside her. His hair was tousled by the windy walk here, and the faint facial lines, etched by wind and weather, were kinder by candlelight. His tailor, whoever that might be, needed applause. Henri was dressed for town, his dark broadcloth suit as striking as any she'd seen among Virginia gentlemen. She'd always found a well-dressed man appealing right down to his polished, buckled shoes. But more than that, she was impressed with Henri's graciousness and humor moments earlier as they'd navigated another hazardous meeting.

All too aware of him, she placed her serviette in her lap, taking a bit from this or that dish without thinking. Oh, if she could only say amusing things like Eliza, not sit here tongue-tied and awkward and wishing they didn't have so bittersweet a history to overcome.

But if they couldn't be lovers, might they be friends? She daren't hope for more. Her heart wasn't ready for more. Nor, she surmised in the stilted silence between them, was his.

"How fortunate we have French cuisine, Captain Lennox." Eliza's smile hadn't dimmed yet. "Our cook has made a delicious beef ragout that I hope you'll find delectable."

Henri smiled. "I'm sure I shall."

"And what is for dessert?" Quinn asked as a footman began to pour the wine.

"Your favorite apple tart, made with those pippins from the orchard," Eliza told him. "The rest will be pressed for cider."

"Take care to have some fruit set aside for winter. They oft improve with age. Much like fine wine"—Quinn looked up from sampling his beef ragout—"or romance."

Esmée stared at him. Was she being too sensitive, or was his comment meant for her and the captain? Quinn was, in his own way, as shrewd and forthright as Eliza. That he had a recent high regard of Henri there could be no doubt. Something was afoot beyond the usual supper invitation, surely. But what?

"So please inform me, gentlemen, of the happenings behind closed doors at the palace." Eliza posed the question foremost in Esmée's mind. "Or is it hushed?"

"Alas, too private and too dense for polite supper conversation, I'm afraid," Quinn replied, sending a small smile his wife's way and sparing his father-in-law and Henri an answer. "I'd much rather hear about your day."

Eliza set down her fork. "I shan't bore you with all the feminine details so will just say Esmée entertained us by debating deism and a clockwork universe with Lady Griffin." She smiled, a flash of triumph in her eyes. "Esmée won."

"Lady Griffin?" Her father's brow rose. "A rather dangerous sparring partner, is she not?"

Eliza continued, gleeful. "Esmée even invited her to the almshouse."

Quinn broke out in laughter. "Now *that* I would have liked to witness. My own parlor sounds far more riveting than palace chambers, I must say."

Esmée caught Henri's wry smile. Would he think her a shrew? Eccentric in her spinsterhood?

"Open and honest conversation is never amiss when handled civilly," she said quietly, losing what remained of her appetite. "I rather enjoyed meeting the governor's lovely daughter and Eliza's other friends."

"It does you much good to be amongst society, Lady Griffin aside. You are too often at the chocolate shop and almshouse," her father told her. He looked toward Henri. "Speaking of York, I hope you feel free to darken our door on Main Street when you're ashore. Or at least come by the coffeehouse."

"I may come to you injured and in need of a physic, as I've recently taken up riding."

Laughter rippled round the table. His newfound interest in horses intrigued Esmée. A daring endeavor after so long at sea. He fancied the freedom to be had on horseback, no doubt.

"How goes it offshore?" Eliza asked him, ever fascinated by those who lived in the barrier islands. "I hope your crew is well."

"Glad for a lull, most of them, after two years at sea. Having the Flask and Sword at their beck and call makes it even more agreeable." Henri took a sip of wine as a footman whisked his empty plate away. "Repairs are being made to the *Relentless* as we speak."

"If you're not anxious to return," Quinn offered, "why not accompany us to church in the morning?"

Esmée stared at Quinn. Though a dutiful churchgoer, he often napped during lengthy sermons, as did her sister.

Eliza offered her most charming smile. "If we could sweeten the offer with chocolate, Captain, would you agree?"

Would he?

Henri darted a glance at Esmée. Was he seeking her approval? His gaze traveled from her to her sister, leaving her a bit bereft. Once she'd grown lost in those sea-blue eyes, a silvery light in them when he was amused.

"Church?" A softness crept into his tone. "Most welcome after salt-spray services with a sea chaplain."

Would he attend with them, then? The wonder of it washed over her, and she sighed a little too audibly. Henri's intent gaze ricocheted back to her. She forced a smile and looked to her lap.

As soon as supper ended, thinking Henri might excuse himself and leave, Esmée was surprised to find herself seated beside him on the parlor sofa while Eliza played the harpsichord across the room. Her father and Quinn were deep in conversation by the hearth.

Henri leaned back, one arm along the sofa's curving arm. "So, tell me, when did your sister meet Lord Drysdale?"

Esmée was distracted, not by the question but by his nearness. Her full petticoats brushed against his leg and completely covered one of his buckled shoes. The room was cool, but she felt flushed. She needed to do something with her hands, only she didn't have a fan. Nor could she fiddle with her chatelaine, which was upstairs on the dressing table.

"They met a few years ago." Esmée was cast back to their courtship, far smoother than her own had been. "Quinn first spied her when at the York coffeehouse. Eliza was helping Mama in the chocolate shop. But it wasn't till Eliza was riding around Williamsburg in an open carriage that he decided to further their acquaintance. He happened to leave the Raleigh Tavern the precise moment she went by. And so she tossed him the love token she kept in her pocket as the carriage passed. 'Twas engraved with her initials and a heart."

A romantic story, making falling in love seem ridiculously easy. To her credit, Eliza hadn't known who Quinn was, other than a well-dressed gentleman, and couldn't be blamed for the fortune hunting some accused her of later at the governor's ball.

Henri ran a hand over his clean-shaven jaw. "Do you remember how we met?"

His quiet question was nearly lost as Eliza finished a robust Italian concerto, the notes soaring. They clapped, delaying Esmée's answer. Hoping for a quieter piece, she asked Eliza, "Won't you play Bach? *The Well-Tempered Clavier*, perhaps?"

"Why don't you?" Eliza replied good-naturedly. "'Tis your favorite, and you perform it better than I do."

Esmée gave a decided shake of her head. Nothing would tear her away from answering Henri's surprising question. "Please . . . play on."

With a slight lift of her shoulders, Eliza returned to her music.

As she struck the first note, Esmée toyed absently with the lace trim on her sleeve. "I do remember how we met." *Though I've tried to forget.*

Was he recalling finding her shelling on the beach? And later at the supper party? Her lowered gaze caught the slow fisting of his hand where it rested on the sofa, the Jerusalem cross plain.

"Mayhap the end of a matter is more important than the beginning." The gravity in his voice held her, much like the inked tattoo.

"Perhaps," she replied rather vacuously.

What more could she say? And what exactly did he mean? She looked at him in question, the drone of Quinn and her father's conversation and Eliza's quieter playing a thousand miles distant. He was not looking at her but straight ahead as if weighing his words. Charting his course.

"Are you . . . spoken for?" His was a bold query, made bolder by their broken past.

"My heart, you mean?" Her calm reply belied the roiling inside her.

"Aye." His eyes roamed her face as if trying to reconcile a decade's difference and all the events and people that might have come between them.

"I . . . nay." She paused, her need to know overpowering any shyness and turning around the question. "And you?"

"Aye." A curt nod of his tousled head sent her spirits to her shoes. "Betrothed to my ship. My crew. The sea."

Heat stained her face. "I regret saying such."

"You simply stated the truth, Esmée. Though at the time I was unwilling to hear it."

Esmée. Not *Miss Shaw*.

Her stomach flipped. His use of her given name muted the harsh memory somehow. A long-suppressed desire flickered deep inside her. How she wanted to say his name in return and not merely think it.

Captain seemed so formal, keeping him out of reach. *Henri* seemed a leap forward yet held the rusty disuse of years.

She swallowed. Fought to steady her nerves. "I—I am not the woman I was, Henri." Entreaty framed her words. "I regret a great many things."

His gaze cut to her again, held her eyes for a beat longer than propriety deemed necessary. The music had stopped, as had the room's conversation. All eyes were on them, bringing their heartfelt conversation to a sudden, maddening halt. Flushing again, Esmée looked away from him. How much had her family overheard?

From beyond the damask window drapery came a pop and a soaring white light. Through the glass, small rockets left starry streaks against the night sky.

"Glory! The illuminations have begun! We must join the festivities on Palace Green." Eliza led the way into the foyer, pausing to let Quinn fetch her cape against the chill before they exited out the door the butler had opened, Father after them.

Henri took Esmée's own cape in hand. "Is this yours?"

Nodding, she turned her back, letting him drape the purple garment over her shoulders before they followed the others outside. Skittery as he made her, she almost stumbled on the steps. His hand shot out to steady her, cupping her elbow in an endearing—and searing—gesture. Her heart, once aflutter, now began to knock about her chest like a fist on a door.

Woe to her if he didn't feel the same.

Together they walked toward the display, joining countless gaping, guffawing onlookers. The night assumed a kind of magic she'd not felt for so long that it seemed she'd been living in a trance since he left. With him beside her, the heavens glittering above, the mood one of festive jubilation all around, she came awake.

And it shook her to her new calamanco slippers that he might well walk away again.

CHAPTER *seventeen*

Esmée was back in the chocolate shop three days hence, her chance encounter with Henri in Williamsburg seeming naught but a woozy dream. Until she saw him go past on his handsome horse, right down teeming Water Street, looking like he was born to the saddle. Was he still having lessons with Jago Wherry?

With no one else in the front of the shop to witness her befuddlement, she rushed to the bow-fronted window to see him tying up his mount at a hitch rail in front of the coffeehouse. Instantly her hands flew to her hair and cap, a bit untidy after a busy morning. Her apron bore a chocolate stain, so she whisked it off, only to look up again as he spoke with a woman in a wide, beribboned hat. Esmée's heart lurched.

Kitty?

Her friend was her exuberant self, her lithe form clad in lilac silk taffeta, her gloved hands gesticulating as she spoke. And she was . . . gesturing to the chocolate shop. A sudden clatter in the coffeehouse made Esmée jump. Broken cups? One glance at the Dutch door earned her nothing but the sight of a great many men reading papers or conversing amid a great many beverages.

When the shop door pushed open with a jingle of the bell, Esmée made a pretense of arranging chocolate pots and cups before the wide window.

"There you are!" Kitty closed the door, her lady's maid nowhere in evidence. "Be forewarned. You might well have a visitor."

"Captain Lennox?"

"The one and only. Apparently he has business in the coffeehouse." She looked toward the open Dutch door. "One never knows what he might do next. He's carrying that riding crop you gave him—"

"Shhhh," Esmée said, gesturing to the counter. "Would you like a sweet? We've a new batch of anise-flavored chocolates topped with sugared orange rind."

"I'd rather talk gentlemen," Kitty whispered.

"I'd rather *not*," Esmée whispered back with another glance at the door.

"There is no one near enough to eavesdrop. Your indentures must all be in the kitchen, and the coffeehouse is full of commotion." Kitty removed her gloves, still smiling. "Oh, this shop smells divine! No wonder you spend your days making confections."

Esmée held out a tray filled with hardening sweets, a wisp of orange rind atop each. Pippin knots, millefruit biscuits, preserved cherries, and apricot tartlets were Kitty's for the taking.

She chose an apricot tartlet, her eyes closing as she sampled a bite. "I've come to buy a pound or two of cocoa for drinking. With winter coming on, we must have hot chocolate."

"I've a quantity of especially good Caribbean cocoa." Esmée moved to a cupboard where the best was stored. "What with the French trouble by land and sea, our supplies are low."

"Ah, the French. How weary I am of war talk." Kitty watched as Esmée wrapped the whitish cocoa bricks in paper. "Why not visit us this afternoon? Our winter tearoom awaits, freshly painted and warmed by the Franklin stove Father ordered from Philadelphia."

"Sounds cozy." Esmée tied the bundle with string. "But I'm overdue at the almshouse, being away in Williamsburg as I was."

"Of course. I would offer to go with you, but . . ." Kitty wrinkled her nose. "I don't know how you abide the wretched conditions. The sadness."

The sadness. That was the worst of it. Betimes she couldn't bear it. Yet still she must go. "One young woman is nearing her confinement." Esmée checked the watch pinned to her chatelaine. A clock wasn't on the shop wall. Father wanted his customers to forget the time and dwell on confections. "I hope to take her some things that might help with the baby. Clouts and blankets and such." She'd finally gathered all the needs the almshouse women had confided last visit, and she felt a little like a child at Christmas in her desire to deliver them.

With a sigh, Kitty paid for her purchase. "Imagine a babe being born in that place. A ward of the parish, I suppose." She took the wrapped chocolate and started for the door. "Do come by when you can. We've much to talk about, like your churchgoing the past Sabbath with Captain Lennox. *That* has set both Williamsburg and York astir!"

Esmée smiled sheepishly. "How on earth did you come to learn of it?"

"I have a dear aunt who attends Bruton Parish, remember."

"Captain Lennox was Eliza and Quinn's guest, is all."

"I do wonder if that's all there is to the tattle." Kitty cast a final, probing look her way. The shop door jingled anew as she went out. "Farewell, dear friend!"

By the time Esmée left Shaw's Chocolate shortly after two o'clock, Captain Lennox's horse was no longer tethered before the coffeehouse. Something inside her dimmed at the apparent rebuff. Where had he gone?

Her answer came when she rode her mare down the coastal road toward the almshouse.

A figure on horseback in the distance drew nearer in a storm of dust. Jago Wherry? He sat atop Captain Lennox's handsome bay horse, headed back toward York.

"Good afternoon, Miss Shaw." He tipped his battered hat, looking pleased with the world.

"Good afternoon, Mr. Wherry. A fine mount you have there."

"Aye, 'tis not mine, Miss Shaw, but Captain Lennox's. I'm playing the groom and returning Trident to the stable."

Trident. The weapon of Poseidon, god of the sea. Why was she not surprised? She bit her lip before the next burning query escaped her.

Where is the captain?

But Jago, unless inebriated, was known to be close-lipped, and at this moment he was most decidedly sober. She cantered on, aswirl with her most recent encounter with Henri at Eliza's. Used to confining his memory to a small corner of her mind, she could do so no longer. He was back, larger than life, and she could not shake his intriguing questions.

"Do you remember how we met?"

"Are you . . . spoken for?"

Mostly she recalled his enigmatic answers.

"Mayhap the end of a matter is more important than the beginning."

"You simply stated the truth, Esmée. Though at the time I was unwilling to hear it."

He had called her by name, a name he once said he found beautiful and musical. Once he'd even teased her, calling her Esmée Shaw Lennox. She'd penned those very words over and over on scraps of paper when no one was looking, scrolling the *E* and *S* and *L* endlessly before throwing her daydreams into the hearth's fire.

The road before her took a winding turn along the sun-soaked coast. For all her woolgathering, she saw the beach and boat plain. A small jolly was leaving shore, filled to the brim with all sorts of boxes and kegs.

The small hopes she'd begun to cherish fled. He was leaving. Rowing away from her just as he'd sailed away years ago. Bound for Indigo Island and looking for all the world as if he wouldn't be back for some time, perhaps spending the winter there and taking a long-deserved rest after years at sea.

She took refuge behind a bunch of stately sea oats bronzed by autumn and tried to reconcile herself to his going. His coat and cocked hat were off, his sleeves rolled up, the thick muscles of his forearms like knotted cordwood. He plied the oars with an expertise born of experience, his linen shirt rippling like a white flag in the breeze. Gannets and gulls careened overhead as if inspecting his cargo.

Did he carry chocolate?

If he'd come into the shop, she would have given him a supply for his men, as they'd done one cruise. But he'd chosen the coffeehouse instead. That, in some way, seemed a rejection, a slight, even if exceedingly small. And yet the hurt loomed large. Overcome, feeling much like the little girl who'd fallen from an apple tree and had the wind knocked out of her, she bent her head.

Lord, help mend my still-broken heart.

Not feeling fit for company, she finally reined Minta in the direction of York. Till she'd collected herself, the almshouse must wait.

CHAPTER *eighteen*

Henri felt a release as he pulled away from shore and slid into the current. With the governor's meetings behind him and an uncertain future ahead of him, he needed the sanctuary of Indigo Island to weigh his decision. A decision best made away from distractions like a belle in a blue silk gown bearing chocolate. Or anything resembling the bustle and fuss of Tidewater Virginia.

He plied the oars with all his might, the breeze buffeting him, the sun's sliding behind a cloud allowing him to study his launching point. He'd thought it secluded. Private. Just sand and scrub. He blinked and narrowed his eyes. A beat of amusement pulsed inside him and led to an outright grin.

Amid the tall beach grass and sea oats mingled with thick stands of bayberry and wax myrtle was a froth of white ostrich feathers. Just like the ones he'd spied atop Esmée's riding hat. Eliza's doing, likely. Esmée wasn't one for fripperies and seemed to have forgotten the telling feathers that now gave her away. Had she unwittingly followed him here? Passed Jago Wherry on her way to the almshouse? Whatever had transpired, there she was in her befeathered hat, spying on him.

He resisted the urge to wave or raise the spyglass for a closer look. Let her believe she remained out of sight. He turned his head sideways, his rowing rhythmic, his gaze on the infinite blue of the sea instead of the memory of her jade eyes. A man could as easily drown in those depths as the ocean.

Though something deep within urged him to take a second look, he was now safely beyond sight of her. The shoreline receded, Indigo Island at his back. His senses were soon assaulted by the smell of roasting oysters and beach bonfires and crying gulls.

Several of his crew threw up their hands or tossed their hats in the air at his return. He waved and rowed on, past the Flask and Sword where Cyprian was hanging linens out to dry, on toward the back of the island where his cottage rested on its rocky perch. He wanted peace. Solitude. The kind he'd not had in York or Williamsburg.

But he couldn't outrow Esmée.

Thoughts of her trailed him like a leaping dolphin riding the wake of a ship. Twice they'd been thrust together without warning. He'd even accepted Eliza's gracious invitation to attend church. Every head had turned as they'd entered, assuring him the past had not been forgotten as he'd hoped but was being resurrected. Esmée was left to traipse through the eddies of gossip ashore while he sought his island refuge.

He'd gone to Shaw's coffeehouse briefly on a matter of business. The adjoining Dutch door leading to the chocolate shop was a nearly irresistible invitation. But considering his openness with her as they'd sat in the townhouse parlor, distance seemed the wisest path. His own conflicted feelings about her needed unraveling first. She was not the young woman he remembered. Time had turned her into someone else entirely.

Once docked, he secured the mooring lines and began unloading cargo—foodstuffs and necessaries to last till his next trip to the mainland. By the time he'd heaved the last crate to a shed, he heard footsteps. Henri put a padlock on the door and turned to greet whoever it was that intruded on his desire to be alone.

'Twas Cyprian, a steaming kettle in one hand, a linen-wrapped loaf in the other, and a large smile on his deeply tanned face. "Good day to ye, sir."

"Aye, so it is." Henri stomped wet sand from his boots before he went inside the cottage. "What do you bring?"

"Some victuals from Mistress Saltonstall. She said ye'd be powerfully hungry and in no mood to make yer own supper."

Gratitude chased away any inconvenience. "She would be right." Henri took the kettle and set it on the table. Oyster stew, from the smell of it. The chill of late October seemed to call for such.

Cyprian unwrapped a loaf of wheaten bread and gazed upon it as if it were the Mughal emperor's jewels. Was he famished?

"Why don't you take supper with me and tell me what has transpired since I've been away?" Gesturing to a chair, Henri went to a near basin and washed his hands, trying to recall where he last saw utensils.

"Aye, sir. With pleasure." Cyprian set the bread down and took a seat, still smiling. "No butter or cheese, I'm sorry to say."

"Ah, but there is," Henri said over his shoulder as he went to fetch both from the stores he'd brought.

Cyprian lit a candle as the shadows deepened, casting fragile light over what proved to be a delicious supper. The lad talked between bites, allowing Henri to slow down and savor his meal. Mistress Saltonstall was an admirable cook.

"All yer officers are still on the mainland, sir . . . just us small jacks stayin' to keep to task on the ship . . . She's looking spry . . . but there's been some worries what with the weather . . . Old Jacques feels a hurricane in his bones . . . That creature, Hermes, got into some rum and turned lunatic, he did."

Nodding and chuckling, Henri waited till Cyprian fed him the last piece of news with a sound belch.

"Beg pardon, sir." He pushed back his empty bowl with a sated sigh. "Ye've taught me better."

"Belching isn't mutiny, Cyprian." With a wink, Henri brought out a small bag of candied lemon peel gotten from York. "Care for a sweet?"

Cyprian grinned back at him. "Have any chocolate, sir?"

Blast. "Nay. I have none." To his everlasting regret. Hot chocolate sounded good on a chilly eve. "Needs be I send you to the mainland for some before winter sets in."

"Would ye, sir?" Cyprian chewed on the lemon peel, eyes alive with anticipation. "Shaw's chocolate, aye?"

"None other."

"I do wonder, sir, why ye didn't go there yerself."

I nearly did. Henri shrugged. "No milk cow on the island, at least since I was here last. No cause for hot chocolate."

"Needs be we get a cow, then."

"Consult Mistress Saltonstall. She may have one hiding in the woods," Henri replied, thinking of the times they'd weathered a crossing with distressed animals for some menagerie in England. He'd put his foot down after transporting a duke's orangutan and an earl's zebra. All he wanted was a rat-catching cat aboard ship. Or a dog. A sudden meowing assured him the ship's cat, Clementine, was about her business.

Spent, Henri sat down in the Windsor chair facing the cold hearth while Cyprian jumped up, still chewing, and began laying a fire. Soon the cavernous, blackened hole glowed as red-gold as a tropical Maldives sunset, a few sparks flying past the andirons into the room.

"If ye don't mind my asking, sir . . . what's that curiosity on yer windowsill?"

Henri looked to where he'd left the mystery gift. "A riding crop. Something that requires a horse."

"Mayhap we need a horse and a cow, then."

"Nay!" Henri's vehemence sent his steward back a step. "I've no time for farming. Another cruise may be imminent."

"Well, sir, needs be I get back to the Flask and Sword lest ye say otherwise."

Henri looked about, noticing the shine of floorboards and essence of beeswax. "I suppose I have you to thank for making this cobwebbed cottage fit for habitation."

"Aye, Captain. I take my duties seriously whether aboard ship or off it."

"Good night, then. Sleep well."

The lad departed with a grin and the empty kettle.

After the hum of York and Williamsburg, the island seemed especially tranquil. Henri added another log to the fire and stepped outside, looking west toward the mainland. Tonight the sunset was quiet, no splash of spectacular color, no jaw-dropping hues. Lights twinkled from York, a beguiling vision in the gathering darkness.

How did Esmée spend her autumn eves?

She liked books . . . or once did. Endless cups of tea with cream and sugar. Talking by the fire in a favorite chair. Trouncing him at table games. That was the Esmée of old. The woman at the ball and in Eliza's parlor seemed different somehow. Understandably guarded. More than a bit discomfited in his company. Face-to-face with him again, she was even comelier than he remembered, if that was possible.

No doubt she couldn't say the same about him.

He felt a bit old. Achy. He rubbed his perpetually sunburned neck at the back, where his hair tailed from a black silk ribbon over his collar. His muscles were a bit stiff from riding horseback, something he'd begun to enjoy but might never master. He needed to return to the mainland, if only to ride again.

And give the governor and Virginia's officials his answer.

The water lapping against the rocks failed to solace him like usual. Night was filling in all the nooks and crannies of the island, whippoorwills calling among the darkening pines. The hearth's fire crackled at his back through the open door, calling him in from a chill eve that might lead to a black frost. Glad as he was to be back, the island suddenly felt a tad hollow, as did his cottage.

To say nothing of his heart.

CHAPTER *nineteen*

The next day, Esmée arrived at the almshouse at a most inopportune time. Father had advised her against going. There'd been a frost, the ground hard as cast iron, and a bitter wind blew her nearly sideways as she traveled the coastal road. When she neared the spot where she'd watched Henri leave in the jolly, she prodded the gentle Minta into a near gallop as if to bypass the hurt of his leaving.

When she arrived, her gaze hung on the far field where Henri had had his riding lesson. Now crude shelters covered the ground, smoke from fires casting a haze about the camp. The French émigrés Father had told her about? Men, women, and children roamed about, heads bent, dejection about them. An occasional burst of mellifluous French wafted toward her.

No sooner had she hobbled Minta outside the women's quarters than an anguished cry rent the chilly air. Alice?

Last visit she was having ghost pains, the midwife called them. Was her travail now upon her? Within the bricked walls the cries echoed, making Esmée rue she'd not heeded Father.

Summoning help to carry in the items she'd brought for all the women, Esmée pondered leaving. Sheer duty propelled her forward till she stood on the second floor outside the birthing room.

Another cry raised the gooseflesh on her arms. This was what was in store for Eliza. *Heaven help us.* Eliza was not fond of pain or exerting herself. Or untimely interruptions.

Feeling slightly squeamish herself, Esmée uttered a silent prayer for both her sister and Alice. Next came a fragile but piercing howl, which had Mistress Boles calling for broth and bread and fresh linens.

Esmée began unpacking the needful things for Alice. Clouts. Blankets. Feeding cloths. Even a play-pretty or two as the babe grew.

"Miss Shaw." Looking relieved, Miss Grove approached with a bundle. "Mind the babe, please, just till Alice is set to rights. He's a robust little fellow."

The warm, squirming infant was placed in Esmée's outstretched arms. Rosebud pink and oddly wrinkled, the tiny boy blinked up at her in wonder. Did all babies have such blue eyes? She bounced him gently when his mouth puckered, determined to keep him quiet for his exhausted mother's sake. When he threatened to howl again, she caressed his velvety cheek, her voice more a whisper as she sang an old lullaby Mama had sung to Eliza.

"'Hush! The waves are rolling in, white with foam, white with foam. Father toils amid the din, but baby sleeps at home.'"

The babe's father was a soldier, she'd been told, gone to join up with Washington's army in the back country. The young mother hadn't heard from him since and, with no kin of her own, had sought refuge at the almshouse. Their future seemed bleak. Someone once said every child was a promise that God wanted the world to go on. But what a world it was, full of conflict and strife, regret and heartache.

Esmée overheard Miss Grove's kindly question. "What will you name the child, Alice?"

"I'll call him after my father, God rest him. A humble tinsmith but a God-fearing one." The answer came so quiet Esmée nearly missed it. "Alden Reed."

Mistress Boles sailed past Esmée with a terse greeting and a mention she was needed elsewhere.

Esmée entered and approached the bed. Surely Alice wanted to hold her child, at least till a meal was brought. "Little Alden is beautiful, Alice. And in need of his mother."

Alice smiled back at her wanly, perspiration calling out her pockmarked skin, her fair braid tousled like straw. "I'm sorry about all the fuss, Miss Shaw. A lady such as you shouldn't have to put up with such as me."

"Nonsense." Smiling, Esmée laid the baby in the crook of her arm. "He's beautiful. Your father would be proud."

"Aye, that he would be." She looked down at her infant as wondrously as Esmée hoped Eliza would look at hers in time. "And my husband too, when he returns from service."

As the linens were changed and a meal was brought, Esmée took her leave, following Miss Grove out. "I'd best hasten home as the weather is sharp. I just wanted to bring the women's things as promised. They're below in the trustees' office."

Miss Grove clasped her hand in thanks. "I don't know how we'd fare without you."

"'Tis but little. I see now the French refugees have come, and with them more needs."

They passed downstairs into the courtyard, where a lone oak had been spared the men's woodcutting. A few benches were scattered about with a view of the large common garden.

"The French encampment is growing." Arms folded against the chill, Miss Grove looked out on the field, which bore shriveling vines and a few plump pumpkins. "We're in charge of feeding them. The government has promised provisions, but I wonder if any will be forthcoming. Winter always means a lack as it is. The garden's long spent."

"I've heard they're to take the oath of allegiance to King George," Esmée said. "But I thought they might be moved further south to Georgia and the Carolinas." Unable to stomach the sight of so much poverty and all its accompanying ills, she looked toward the York River turned to pewter by thick, hovering clouds, the water adorned with vessels of all descriptions.

"I wish they would move on, though I know 'twill not be any easier elsewhere. A few fights have broken out between the almshouse men and the French. These newcomers are hungry and exhausted. Their spirits are low. Some are in forced isolation because of illness."

Lord, help. These French papists, considered enemies of the crown, weren't even of the same religion. Yet the king expected Virginia to host such a number? And deepen the almshouse woes besides?

"How long must you help them?"

"I cannot say. 'Tis another of the king's edicts that brook no argument." Miss Grove's tone turned entreating. "Might you acquire some meat for us in the meantime? Even bones will do. Something with which to make broth and feed many."

"Of course. I'll speak with the butchers in York."

"And pray, please, that we aren't beset with sickness like last season. With the cold came fevers and every imaginable malady, more than the physic could remedy, if we can even get a physic to come."

"Perhaps a visit to the apothecary would help, to have a supply of medicines beforehand."

Miss Grove's lined face eased only slightly. "'Twould be most welcome, as always."

"You're in no danger of running low on firewood, thankfully." Esmée had seen growing woodpiles deftly stacked all about the property. "Though a coal stove would be warmer, at least in the dining hall."

"We've plenty to warm us, thanks to the men's woodcutting. Coal is a luxury few can afford."

"'Tis never amiss to hope . . . dream." Esmée spoke softly, wanting to lift the discouragement in Miss Grove's beleaguered face. "I've no doubt you're in need of something yourself, carrying the weight of the women and children as you do."

"Mercy, Miss Shaw." The woman's surprise revealed she thought little of herself. A hand went to her hair. "A new cap wouldn't be amiss. This one is so worn it's now threadbare."

Two caps, then. Esmée bid her a warm goodbye, wishing she'd thought of it sooner.

"Take care, Miss Shaw, and God be with you till we meet again."

A barefoot lad fetched Minta. Esmée stepped atop the mounting block and sat sidesaddle. The biting autumn air did her good. She rode out with a last look at the forlorn French encampment before her thoughts ran ahead to Henri.

Nay. The captain is a conundrum I can do without.

'Twas only her aloneness, her loneliness, that sharpened her interest in him. Was it not? Just when she'd adjusted to life without him, made a resigned peace with his absence, he'd reappeared, renewing her girlish hopes and dreams. Alas, she'd soon turn thirty. Henri was older still. Yet when he was near, all the years seemed to slip away and she felt young again. And he was, if possible, even more intriguing than he used to be.

Or had her own spinsterish ways simply deepened her appreciation of him?

Restlessness churned like a current inside her. She felt on the cusp of something new, though she knew not what. Surely it wasn't in the form of a privateer with a questionable reputation.

Lord, what is it You have for me beyond the almshouse and chocolate shop?

CHAPTER *twenty*

Henri's most trusted men, recently returned from shore leave, sat before him in a semicircle at the ordinary's corner table. Despite Hermes's screeching and Mistress Saltonstall's robust chatter with a patron in the open doorway, he wasted no time telling them the latest turn of events.

"I have a recent communication from the frontier, sent by Colonel Washington to Governor Dinwiddie." Henri took out the letter given him, a sad testament to how the frontier fight with the French and Indians was faring, at least at the time the letter was penned. He held the letter aloft as he read, "'Regular troops exposed all those who were inclined to do their duty to almost certain death; and at length, in despite of every effort to the contrary, broke and ran as sheep before hounds, leaving the artillery, ammunition, provision, baggage, and in short everything a prey to the enemy, and when we endeavored to rally them in hopes of regaining the ground and what we had left upon it, it was with as little success as if we had attempted to have stopped the wild beasts of the mountains.'"

"Colonel Washington is referring to British regulars," Southack said with thinly veiled disgust. "Not Virginians."

"Aye, the king's army," Henri said. He read on in confirmation. "'The Virginia companies behaved like men and died like soldiers.'"

"And Braddock, the white-wigged general, was buried overmountain in an unmarked grave, so I heard." Udo shook his dark head. "Is this not Washington's third attempt to rout the French and take Fort Duquesne?"

"Aye." Henri nodded and folded the letter, noting the broken black seal. "And now the French general Montcalm is said to be on his way here."

"Which led to much ado in Williamsburg with the governor's council," Tarbonde surmised, his astute gaze holding Henri's own. "Have you made your decision, sir?"

"Nay."

Henri's reticence had them all studying him keenly. He was not one to dally. He could read their thoughts. And with a new French commander on the way . . .

He leaned back in his chair till it groaned. "If you were in my place, what would your decision be?"

A weighty pause. Rarely did he turn the question round. It seemed to stymie them.

"With Britain hurtling toward war with France and not just fighting Indians on the frontier, our involvement by sea seems critical," Southack finally said. "But just what is our stake in this?"

"We'd be issued a letter of marque and reprisal from the colonial government authorizing us to target French ships, capture them, and plunder them. We'd set sail in a newly commissioned vessel." He paused, noting their surprise. "We'd fly foreign flags, including French flags as decoys, if needs be."

"And the prizes?" they asked in unison.

"Delivered in part to the admiralty court in Philadelphia. Our share would be fifty percent of all prizes." Henri tapped the letter, thinking again of Braddock. "And one hundred percent of the danger."

"A risky endeavor." Ned expelled a breath, always the last to speak. His perspective as sea chaplain usually differed from the others'. "Though no doubt of great benefit to the colonial cause."

Henri nodded, no nearer his decision than he'd been when he'd first heard of the secret foray against the French at the governor's palace. Was that not in itself his answer? Yet when had he shied away from danger or aiding the British colonies?

"And if you say nay?" Ned questioned, folding his hands atop the edge of the table as if he were about to pray.

"If I—*we*—decline, other ships and crews will bear the commission," Henri stated matter-of-factly.

Southack grimaced. "And take both prizes and credit."

"Virginia's governor desires us at the helm," Henri said. Not only Virginia's governor but other colonial authorities as well. He stopped short of revealing anything vainglorious, further tempting them toward a very hazardous cruise.

"You cannot possibly be content to stay on Indigo Island with so dire a threat. Nor sail away on other business." Tarbonde studied him as if seeing him in a new light. "'Twould be a dereliction of duty."

"You could also further establish your reputation as one of privateer and not pirate as the naysayers have painted you," Southack said.

"What would be done with captives?" Udo queried when Henri made no reply. "You are known far and wide for fair treatment, but with the French declared our enemies . . ."

"They'd likely be used in prisoner exchanges or as leverage in treaties. Transported to prison ships." That alone gave Henri pause. There was no worse fate.

And it could be his and his crew's lot as well.

CHAPTER *twenty-one*

Esmée took the tray of chocolate meringues from the kitchen into the shop, each looking like small storm clouds that matched the heavens over the harbor. Airy and sweet, the egg-white-and-sugar confections were among her favorites, pairing nicely with the chocolate tarts on display. With no one to witness her pilfering, she snuck one and let its ethereal goodness melt on her tongue, her stays expanding with every bite.

Sweet indeed. After a morning spent begging bones from the town's butchers, including a promised delivery, she had her reward. Now in the afternoon, business had ebbed, though the coffeehouse never seemed to quiet. Father was there today, distributing newspapers and handbills, conversing about the latest news in Virginia and beyond with any who cared to join him. His unmistakable voice comforted her as she went about her tasks, taking inventory, perusing the long-coveted *Complete Confectioner*, and overseeing orders for social gatherings and whatnot.

When the shop's bell jingled, she looked up from her work to find a stranger shutting the door behind him, his coattails whipped about by a harbor wind. Knowing nearly everyone in York and even Williamsburg, Esmée discreetly took his measure but couldn't place him.

She gave the familiar shopkeeper's greeting, brushing tart crumbs from her apron. "Good afternoon, sir. What do you buy?"

Tucking his cocked hat beneath one arm, he came to a stop at the counter, gaze landing on the meringues and tarts before sliding to the mound of sugared almonds atop a large porcelain dish. Pleasure suffused his tanned features.

"I'm rather overcome," he said, eyes roving the shelves next.

She understood his dilemma, common to first timers. What *wouldn't* he choose?

"I've not had Shaw's chocolate since the last sailing," he told her with a smile. "Now I'm en route to visit kin in the country and I'd rather not arrive empty-handed."

Last sailing? He was no common jack, truly. "Chocolate almonds travel especially well, though chocolate tarts do not," she told him, charmed by his gracious manner. "Care to try an almond?" She held out the dish.

"I'll take them all," he replied after a bite. "Though I can't guarantee they'll last beyond Tobacco Road."

"If some go missing, none will be the wiser." Smiling, she began wrapping them for travel. "You speak of your kin. Might I know them?"

"Ah, no doubt. Forgive me for the frightful lack of introductions. Nathaniel Autrey, lately at sea."

"The Autreys of Mount Autrey?" She did not doubt it. He bore their wide forehead and cleft chin in addition to their telltale fiery locks. "An old Virginia family you have, sir."

"A very feminine one." He was referring to his maiden aunts, no doubt. "You know them, Miss . . . ?"

"Just who's forgetting introductions?" Flushing, Esmée handed him his wrapped chocolates. "I am Miss Shaw, the proprietress of Shaw's Chocolate. My father is—"

"Barnabas Shaw. The famed admiral." His admiration was not lost on her. "No doubt you and your father are acquainted with Captain Henri Lennox."

Nodding, she lowered her gaze. "My father especially."

"I'm sea chaplain of the *Relentless*, or have been these past many years."

A sea chaplain? All frigates and line-of-battle ships allowed them, though not all but the most devout commanders wanted them aboard. And they did far more than keep journals and hold divine service. She busied herself with his purchase. What more could she say? Would mention of Henri always affect her so? Turn a routine, chocolate-laden encounter bittersweet?

"Good day, Miss Shaw." He gave a slight, elegant bow before he went out. "I hope we meet again."

She crossed to the display window, watching him climb into a waiting coach, then drew back as his gaze returned to the shop. Might Henri be with him? As the coach pulled away with a lurch, she rested her eyes on the cloudy harbor, wishing she'd been a bit more forthright.

Are you on shore long, sir? Does Captain Lennox have any plans to set sail again? And are you always so charming at first meeting?

Henri walked the beach, frothy waves murmuring a monotonous lament against the shore with the incoming tide. His crew continued work on the *Relentless* on the island's south side. Cyprian, ill with a mild fever, lay in a hammock beneath oaks fast losing the last of their leaves. Southack hovered, ready to dispense whatever remedy was called for.

Henri stared down at the wave-washed sand, wishing his mind would come clean, but his thoughts were knotted as rigging. He felt akin to a dismasted ship. It had been nearly a fortnight since those gravely serious meetings in the palace. Governor Dinwiddie awaited his reply. All of British America teetered on the brink of war as matters on the frontier grew more explosive.

While he dallied.

For the first time in his entire naval career, he had no wish to return to sea. The *Relentless* could stay beached forever. Somewhere between the last few cruises and setting foot in York, he'd lost something. His moorings. His true north. His mind.

A few months before, a broken spar had knocked him down. Had that something to do with it? He still had headaches but thought himself mostly healed. Lifting a hand, he traced the scar above his left brow. Nay, he could not blame his indecision on an accident. He knew the real reason. But what would he say to Dinwiddie and his officials?

I've decided to forsake all duty to my country and let France gain the upper hand on the high seas, not only on the colonial frontier, while I attend dances and learn to ride and sip chocolate and try to woo the woman I lost a decade ago.

Headache or no, his prayers seemed to reach no farther than the cottage ceiling. The dilemma was even stealing his sleep.

Lord, make Your will plain to me.

"Captain." A familiar masculine voice turned him round.

"You're back," Henri said. Ned had been on the mainland for a sennight. Henri hadn't expected his return so soon.

"I am." Ned wore his town clothes, his buckled shoes digging deep into the sand as he walked toward Henri. A smile lit up his clean-shaven face. "I can wait no longer to share the glad news."

Henri fell into step beside him. "Glad news? Is there to be no war?"

A low laugh. "War is the farthest thing from my mind. I believe I've met the woman I'm going to marry—or begin courting, at least."

Henri's hand shot out instinctively. "Congratulations, then."

Ned shook with vigor, never missing a step. "I suppose you'll not relax your rule about banning married men as crew."

"Never. Especially newly married ones." Curiosity overcame him. "So, tell me about her."

A slow smile transformed Ned's ruddy features. "She rather bowled me over. I forgot my manners. I nearly forgot to remove my hat at first meeting."

Henri chuckled, stunned by his words. But Ned of all people deserved a helpmeet. A pastor, albeit a sea chaplain, shouldn't be alone.

"She's . . . perfect. Small in stature. Comes to about here." He thumped his hand just below his shoulder. "Hair as black as a Brazilian diamond. Eyes a peculiar shade of jade."

"Careful, you're downright poetic."

Ned laughed, a merry sound that further nettled Henri's tempestuous mood. "Isn't that what lovers do?"

"Does this beauty have a name?"

"Her name is as lovely as all the rest of her."

"A Williamsburg belle?"

"Nay. York."

"Where did you meet?"

"Shaw's Chocolate shop."

Henri snapped to attention. "Admiral Shaw's daughter?"

"The same. Miss Esmée Shaw."

Nay. A thousand times nay.

Henri stopped in his tracks. A sound kick in the gut would have made him gladder. For a few seconds he stood speechless. Then at last he asked, "Are you sure you weren't just entranced by a surfeit of chocolate?"

"Not at all. I visited her twice there. Once when I first got to York and then today before my leaving."

"Twice hardly equates to marriage." Henri shot him a chary look and resumed walking in the direction of the Flask and Sword. "Women are far more complex than they first appear."

"Where is your sense of romance, Captain?" Ned expelled a breath, eyes on distant York. "Once or twice is often all that's necessary."

"I would caution you of the lovesick sailor phenomenon. Lovesick chaplain, in your case." Henri assumed his commander's voice. "When one is away months or years at sea, anything remotely feminine appears utterly remarkable."

"In this case there is no such delusion." Ned studied him, a sympathetic light in his eye. "Have you never experienced it?"

Henri kicked at a pebble in his way. *Aye.* Had he not once felt the same? When Esmée had first entered a stuffy Rhode Island parlor, it was as if no other woman existed. Only Ned did not know of his and Esmée's former tie, having been aboard a schooner till joining the *Relentless* crew.

"Lest you think I've completely lost my reason, I questioned my kinfolk at Mount Autrey about the Shaws, especially Esmée," Ned said. "My aunts are a formidable hurdle—two of them, anyway."

"Well . . . go on," Henri muttered over his misery.

"I've made other discreet inquiries." Ned was as earnest as Henri had ever seen him, removing all hope that this was one big lark. "Her character is sterling. Not vain but virtuous. Kind. God-fearing. She stretches out her hand to the poor and visits the almshouse regularly. She is a woman of spirit and industry, managing the chocolate shop like her mother before her. For the life of me I cannot understand why she has never wed."

"A failed love affair, mayhap."

Ned's clenched brow eased. "Perhaps she was simply waiting for me."

Henri would hear no more. "In short, the perfect chaplain's wife."

"Exactly. And since my father and mother are long buried, I ask your blessing."

My blessing. "I suppose you've yet to tell her you're hardly a humble chaplain but kin to the Autreys."

"She did ask, hearing my surname. An insignificant detail."

Henri nodded. This was what he most admired about Ned. His humility. His utter disregard for earthly mammon. In truth, Esmée had all the makings of a genteel chaplain's wife. Together they could launch all sorts of charitable endeavors from Mount Autrey, one of the largest estates in Virginia, a veritable fount of funds.

"Now seems the time to leave the sea and settle down." The note of finality in Ned's voice seemed to seal the matter. "Though we've had many an adventure together of which I'm extremely grateful, Captain, my wanderlust has begun to tire, as we've oft discussed. I'm now intent on resigning my post, and I seek your blessing."

In a few choice words, Ned had stated Henri's own predicament. *My wanderlust has begun to tire. I'm intent on resigning my post.* So succinctly stated yet how infernally complicated. To leave the sea and settle down was Henri's burning desire and had been for some time.

For Ned it was entirely possible, while he himself felt shackled. By his reputation. His resources. His connections.

"I understand." Henri forced a smile, tried to summon some gladness for Ned beyond a half-hearted clap on the back. "But my blessing is hardly needed. I wish you the best in whatever you undertake." He took a breath and added, "There's never been a more worthy man for such a woman."

Ned's brow tightened anew. "You've oft talked of settling down yourself."

"And now a new endeavor has presented itself." Time ticked on. Virginia needed an answer. "I'm beginning to think I will always be at sea. Die at sea."

"No wife. No children." Ned shook his head mournfully. "Granted, able mariners are always needed, but in the end, is it worth it?"

Henri did not answer. Ned had raised the very question that would not let him be.

CHAPTER
twenty-two

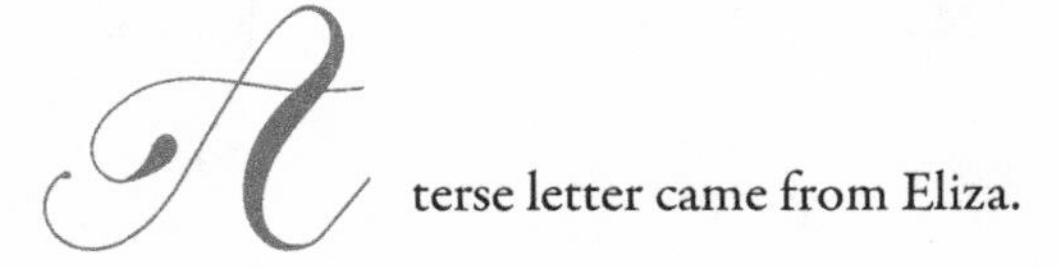

A terse letter came from Eliza.

Dear Sister,

I have been visited by the three aunts from Mount Autrey. Please hasten to Williamsburg where I await you impatiently. Come see the leaves turn color if nothing else.

Your loving Eliza

A visit? Esmée hardly had time, what with begging bones and holding newborns and experimenting with the latest chocolate confections. But what Eliza wanted, Eliza eventually got. And Williamsburg *was* a magnificent panorama of color in autumn.

But what of the spinster aunts from Mount Autrey? Might this have something to do with Nathaniel Autrey?

Esmée pondered it all the way to Eliza's, wishing Father were awake and could distract her. Despite the rumbling coach hitting a bone-rattling bump or two, he dozed, a victim of too many late nights spent working on his marine atlas.

At last he came awake when they rode past Jane Vobe's tavern. "What is that divine smell?"

Esmée leaned nearer the coach's window. "Beef pasty, perhaps."

"I suppose 'tis too late to request the same for our supper from Eliza's kitchen."

"Pasties are a thoroughly English dish, remember."

"I dare not offend the French chef, you mean." He cleared his throat. "What was that marvelous concoction he served us last time when Captain Lennox came to dine?"

Esmée's mind was blank as new paper. Beef ragout? She hardly recalled it, given the company.

With a stifled yawn, her father returned his hat to his head. "I doubt I'll be back in time for supper anyway, as Dinwiddie is fond of conversing so late."

"I hope he serves you something amidst all that secrecy."

"Something Scottish, no doubt, as befits his humble roots." He looked out the window, occasionally raising a hand at passersby who recognized their coach.

She fisted her gloved hands in the folds of her skirts, knowing Henri was somehow at the very heart of these meetings. "Father, if I may be so bold, what have you to do with all this intrigue and conniving?"

To her relief he chuckled. "You make it sound downright villainous. Far more interesting than it is."

"Well? 'Tis how it appears to those of us on the outside."

"On the outside? You have a touch of Eliza's dramatic flair, 'twould seem." He waved again as they passed Bruton Parish Church. "The governor and his officials are merely consulting me about maritime matters in case there's to be a war."

War, war. Would they talk of nothing else? "You don't believe we're in danger of becoming French colonials rather than English ones?"

"Bah! You've been reading one too many broadsides and papers. Coffeehouses aren't called penny universities for naught."

Would he have her believe it was merely gossip? "Perhaps I need to revisit my French lessons of old."

"Which is why Captain Lennox is being considered for the task."

Her gaze narrowed on his shuttered face. "So there's a *task* to consider?" She tried to piece this confounding puzzle together. "Because the captain is part French and speaks French?"

And such mesmerizing French that it sounded like a song. A symphony. *Euphony*, Mama once called it. Years ago, Henri had not simply said goodbye. He'd leaned in, his breath warm against her ear, and whispered *ma belle* and other endearments. Even the memory, long relegated to the trash heap, sent her stomach plummeting to her shoes.

Her father smiled enigmatically, looking like the freebooter he had once been accused of being. "All in good time, my dear."

"No doubt it involves danger," she said grimly. "A prolonged cruise."

The coach lurched to a stop in the courtyard behind Quinn and Eliza's townhouse, sparing him further elaboration. Feeling like a kettle left too long at the fire, Esmée gathered her hat and gloves off the upholstered seat and stepped down once the door opened.

Would she ever have answers?

Dusk gathered about Henri like a gray cloak. Thieves were prevalent along the byways and backroads of rural Virginia. Few traveled at night because of it. He kept a loaded pistol close, careful of shifting shadows. He'd hoped to see Williamsburg by dark, but night was rushing in fast and another stop was required. The lights of the almshouse shone just ahead, and beyond it countless hovels of the French refugees, the smoke from their chimneys trailing crooked gray fingers into the darkening sky. Fragments of French conversation drifted to him as men and women sat outside smoking clay pipes.

Tonight was not the time to ponder their plight, these displaced souls now the bane of cash-strapped Virginia. But the sound of his mother's language never failed to move him, ushering in a dozen different recollections of her, each bittersweet.

He relaxed the reins, slowing Trident to a walk. He'd timed his arrival at the almshouse carefully so as not to attract attention, when most of the residents would be done with their labors and supper and in their rooms, if Jago Wherry had told him right.

The night watch was on patrol, halting him as he approached, lanthorn held high.

"I've business with the trustee, Mr. Boles," Henri told him, dismounting.

"Is he expecting ye, sir?"

"Nay, but he'll be glad of it."

With a nod, the watchman left him, and Henri opened his saddlebags. Soon he was escorted toward a small building that served as both living quarters and office for the supervisor of the entire almshouse. Wherry had spoken well of Boles but less so of the trustee matron. Henri regretted finding them both in one place, having tea by the fire, clearly taken aback by his sudden appearing—or rather irritated by the intrusion, judging from the matron's sour expression.

"And you are, sir?" Boles inquired politely, coming forward.

"Simply a benefactor and champion of the poor," Henri replied, heaving the sacks of specie atop Boles's desk. They jingled as they settled, rousing the matron, who abandoned her tea and came nearer.

"The bequest comes with conditions." Henri fixed a stern eye upon them both. "'Tis to be wisely stewarded for the benefit of all those beneath the almshouse roof—every man, woman, and child as well as the French émigrés in your midst. Not ferreted or spent selfishly by those in positions of authority such as yourselves." Here he held the eye of Mistress Boles. "I have contacts—informants, if you will—who will report to me any suspected double-dealing. Depending on how you conduct yourselves and manage the monies given you, more might be forthcoming in future."

Clearly skittish, Boles began untying the sacks. The knots finally gave way and he stood slack-jawed. Spanish pistoles and pieces of eight were common enough in the colonies, but rarely in such quantities.

"Sir—" Astonishment washed his weary face. "Gold doubloons and silver dollars? 'Tis a fortune."

"Aye. All in need of careful consideration and wise handling."

"May we not ask your name, kind sir?" the matron queried meekly. "Your occupation?"

"Nay." Not even Wherry knew about tonight. Henri wished he could have simply left the specie at the door. "Treat it as you would any endowment or bequest. But say nothing from whence it came."

"You have my word, sir," Boles replied without hesitation.

Their effusive thanks followed him as he went out the door, as glad to get away as he was to lighten Trident's load. Night riding was new to him—dangerously so. In the dark he couldn't see hazards in his path, but Trident seemed to have a sixth sense about him, hastening him to Williamsburg in good time beneath a full moon.

Generosity always left him with a warmth deep inside, an inextinguishable light in a world gone awry. What good were the prizes he'd gotten if not shared? Perhaps such would delight Esmée when she learned of it, even if she'd never know its source.

Truly, the smallest good deed was better than the grandest good intention.

The next afternoon found Esmée hurtling toward Mount Autrey with Eliza to pay a call to the aunts of Captain Lennox's sea chaplain. Though Esmée had never seen the vast estate, she'd heard of it. Her perplexity about their visit was second to her confusion about Nathaniel Autrey's relation to it. She'd thought him a distant relation. A poor sea chaplain and sailor. Eliza was having none of it.

"Really, Esmée." Eliza leaned back on the seat with a sigh. "You look as though you were on your way to a wake!"

"I'm simply pondering what all this means." Esmée smoothed her petticoats, which collided in silky profusion with her sister's. "So the aging aunts paid a visit to you and inquired about me. I don't suppose it was about the abundance of chocolate almonds their nephew brought them."

"Well, they did mention them rather glowingly."

"I don't know why such fuss over a man I conducted business with over the counter a time or two, charming though he was."

"If you would but pull your head out of your receipt books and mind the workings of the outside world . . ." Eliza gave that disarming smile she used when sly. "Your humble chaplain is more a ruse. Rumor has it he might well be the future heir to Mount Autrey and all it entails."

"So?"

Eliza's eyes narrowed in irritation. The baby was making her cross, keeping her up nights with indigestion. "*So*, he has expressed a fondness for you that set these dear ladies all aflutter. And it has nothing to do with Shaw's chocolate."

"Promise me this visit will be brief." But wasn't the reverend's message last Sunday at Grace Church about honoring others with the gift of time? Conscience pricked, Esmée quickly amended, "Though elderly ladies who are oft alone deserve more."

"Indeed." Eliza looked less ruffled. "Most unwed women would leap at the invitation. This bodes well for you and your future."

The coach bumped along the rutted road in dire need of the almshouse men's rocks. Esmée's stomach felt just as gravelly. This was not how she had envisioned her future playing out. Though it might sound unkind, Nathaniel Autrey was little more to her than one of Captain Lennox's crew. That alone made him interesting and of merit. She had no matrimonial aspirations whatsoever.

Still, she could not stem her awe at the beauty of Mount Autrey as they turned off Tobacco Road and moved past elaborate iron gates. The mansion sat on a knoll, lending to its arresting appearance. Of Flemish bond brick, it was a feat of architecture from its multiple porticos to its parterre gardens. Yet she couldn't ignore what kept the Autrey fortune afloat. That alone nullified any romantic prospects.

Eliza's steady gaze was unnerving. "I know what you're thinking, Sister. But you must say nothing of the enslaved here. 'Tis a fact of Virginia life and has ever been."

Even as Eliza spoke, scores of Africans labored in distant fields or scurried to and from the mansion and dependencies. For once the almshouse seemed less wretched. At least the poorest of the poor there were free.

Once the coach deposited them at the entrance amid a storm of dust, Esmée and Eliza climbed wide stone steps and were soon ushered into a wide, deep foyer where a staircase curved upward to three floors. The house was old. Immense. Esmée wasn't surprised when the butler's voice echoed. Into the nearest parlor they went, where three elderly women awaited them. All eyes speared Esmée. There was no other word to describe it. Summoning some of Eliza's charm, she greeted them warmly, again wondering what had led to this unexpected meeting.

"How good of you to visit us," said the aunt who looked to be the eldest, a snowy-haired matron with a diamond-encrusted chatelaine worn at her waist. It glittered as she moved toward several chairs and gestured for them to sit.

Esmée looked from her to the other two aunts. How on earth was it possible to distinguish them if all were the Mistresses Autrey? There was no doubt, however, as to which aunt held the key to the coveted tea chest. The smallest and plumpest wore spectacles and said nary a word while the other began to talk in low tones to the exotic bird kept in a cage by a draped window.

"Allow me to introduce Charis and Dorothy, my younger sisters." The eldest aunt gestured to them with a wrinkled, heavily ringed hand. "I am Margaret."

"Pleased to meet you all," Esmée said. She was at sea with names. Rarely did they make an impression. Eliza, on the other hand, had an astonishing ability to remember names *and* titles.

The five of them sat in low armchairs about the inlaid table. Esmée took in the elegant room redolent of beeswax and something she couldn't name. It smelled ancient . . . unaired. She longed to open a window or two. She craved the salty tang of the sea.

"As soon as I saw you on the drive, I rang for tea," Margaret told them.

Refreshments came, the equipage flawless, and were served in the biggest silver pot Esmée had ever seen. She placed her serviette in her lap, never more mindful of tea etiquette. These antique women looked as if they'd written the rules. Sugar first. Milk at the last, *after* the tea was poured. Eliza performed flawlessly, as usual. But not Esmée. A bit flustered, she added milk first.

"To put milk in your tea before sugar is to cross the path of love, perhaps never to marry," Dorothy said with a slight, reproving smile.

"Such an amusing superstition," Eliza countered between sips. "And may I say how I admire your spiral molded porcelain? Chelsea, I believe? And with handles, all the rage but still so rare."

"Chelsea, yes," Margaret said, holding her cup aloft. "No sense burning one's hands."

"I miss sipping from a dish," Dorothy told them, pouring the steaming tea into her saucer with nary a misplaced drop. "The old ways die hard."

"Have you a chocolate pot?" Esmée asked them.

Margaret made a face. "We are rather chary of cocoa, given what's printed about it in Europe—chocolate being one of many disorders that shorten lives."

"Oh? Our York physic espouses its health benefits—" Esmée startled as the bird squawked, her cup rattling in her saucer. "Of which there are many."

"Chocolate is but a lure for any who happen down Water Street," Dorothy said in whispered tones. "Heavens! A woman such as yourself doesn't plan to keep tending shop forever, do you? And at so disagreeable a place under the hill as Water Street!"

Did they disapprove of her trade or mainly her location? Though there were many women who kept shop, it was mostly left to the middling sort, of which these women were most decidedly not.

"I'm continuing in my mother's stead," Esmée told them quietly. "Proudly so. As for Water Street, little else could be had as far as buildings go when my father bought it. We're making the waterfront more respectable, I hope."

Charis held up her empty cup, eyes plaintive.

Dorothy clucked sympathetically. "Sister is in danger of rivaling Dr. Johnson's tea consumption at five and twenty cups in one sitting."

Truly, Charis's cups exceeded them all and she'd yet to speak a word. Was she mute?

A lengthy silence followed, with no explanation given about Charis's silent state.

"Tea amuses the evening, solaces the midnight, and welcomes the morning, I believe Dr. Johnson said." Unable to endure the tense silence, Esmée finished her own cup and placed an upturned spoon atop it. Would Eliza take the hint?

Her sister merely smiled serenely and stirred more milk into her cup. No doubt she was missing her pot of cream. Despite their means, these sisters appeared quite frugal.

"I've always thought hyson smells of roasted chestnuts," Dorothy told them.

Margaret focused on her sister. "Oh? I prefer souchong's delicate, floral flavor."

"And you, Miss Shaw? Which is your favorite?" Dorothy inquired.

"Gunpowder tea. Such a honeyed taste," Esmée replied as the mantel clock struck three. "'Tis the freshest on long trade routes, my father said."

"Ah, your father." Margaret's eyes narrowed. "The esteemed admiral from Rhode Island."

The sisters exchanged a furtive look.

"Which puts me in mind of Captain Lennox, cut of the same cloth," Charis told them. "Our nephew's daring sea captain."

Esmée nearly sighed aloud. Clearly Charis wasn't mute. And what a topic she'd chosen to expound upon! Would everything always circle back to Henri?

CHAPTER
twenty-three

Henri was on the verge of saying nay to the proposed mission, and he sensed that the governor's council, a body of astute, shrewd men, knew it. The temperature in the paneled room was cool, but tempers were a-simmer. And it had little to do with the French threat.

"Provisions for several months at sea are needed and as follows . . ."

Henri listened as quartermaster Udo detailed the provisions required for such a mission before the chamber of officials, who sat rapt if stony-faced and silent. That they were listening to an African, an able commander in his own right, was an extraordinary occurrence. That Udo was free was an affront to these slave-owning Virginians. But Henri would not pander to their preference to exclude his black crew. Nor would he set sail without them.

Udo's smooth, robust voice filled the chamber's farthest corners. "Thirteen tierces and forty-five barrels salt beef and pork. A cask of oats. Five hundred gallons rum. Three tons beer. Five hundred pounds cheeses and butter. Fruit to stave off scurvy. Vinegar. Four hundred pounds brown sugar . . ."

Minutes before, Henri himself had finished telling the council of the weapons and artillery required to take on any enemy ships encountered, a presentation that smacked of an unwanted war, dug deep into Virginia's depleted coffers, and raised many a testy question. On either side of him sat Tarbonde and Southack, as well as his first mate and master gunner, all experienced men who knew the sea and its many moods and dangers as well as himself.

His foremost ally among Virginia's officials was missing. Lord Drysdale—Quinn—had been called away on other business. Henri hoped he'd return by next meeting. Across from Quinn's empty seat sat Admiral Shaw, ever attentive, occasionally asking a well-placed question and keeping the conversation on course. For all his years—and Henri guessed him to be nearing seventy—his mind was rapier sharp, and he'd not lost his passion for maritime affairs. Which led to a question that had nothing to do with the present company . . .

Was Esmée also in Williamsburg?

He looked toward a window that bespoke an easterly breeze. The airtight chamber left one pining for the outdoors and a walk about town. The Raleigh flashed to mind, Carter's brick store beside it. He needed a shaving razor. A woolen frock coat against the chill. Some minor items to tide him over while he lodged at the Raleigh and the governor's business was being done.

"Captain Lennox, we are prepared to reward your crew with payment of three months' wages in advance of their service, in addition to all of the provisions outlined by your quartermaster."

Henri returned his attention to the governor as Udo sat down.

Dinwiddie said with some pride, "A new seventy-four-gun man-of-war is at your behest, en route from the Wharton shipyard in Philadelphia to York."

Henri sensed his crew's surprise. They were not easily impressed, but this was a major coup for all. Only the newest and most capable ships were thus equipped. Wharton was the premier shipbuilder in all thirteen colonies.

Did they ken their captain wanted nothing to do with it?

All attention was on Henri again. He simply listened as Dinwiddie called for yet another meeting the next morning, at which time they would discuss the French navy and its ships of the line en route to British North America, as well as the latest intelligence coming from the harbor of Brest.

"I regret we must adjourn early today, gentlemen. I've death warrants to sign for deserters, a decision to be made on the issuance of paper money, appointments to be confirmed, and visiting Indian dignitaries to entertain." Dinwiddie put a hand to his high forehead, his normally florid face the hue of his powdered wig. "Till tomorrow, then. Ours is a most pressing matter that begs resolution by sennight's end."

Henri stood, his attention on the beleaguered official's back as he exited the chamber. The responsibilities of office dogged the governor, a true servant of the crown. Fatigue of body and vexation of mind were what plagued him, he'd told Henri earlier. As he was charged with taking back Fort Duquesne from the French on the frontier and trying to raise Virginia's fighting forces, a war by sea seemed another extraordinary complication.

"Won't you join us, Captain?" Southack asked him, moving toward the door. "A pint or two at the Raleigh seems in order, for some of us, at least."

"Later, mayhap," Henri said, putting on his hat. His black jacks would return to York and their lodgings at the Colored Seamen's Home on the outskirts. "For now I've other business to attend to."

He left the crowded room, slipping out the front door and the palace's forecourt onto the street, and noticed the Indian delegation recently come to town. The gathered Cherokee were beaded and befeathered, a tall chief having his portrait painted beneath a brilliant red maple. With Publick Times in October over, the town had a quieter feel, a thoughtful and more peaceful cadence.

He took a backstreet toward the Raleigh, trying to recall what it was he needed from Carter's store. He tipped his hat to a trio of straw-hatted young ladies who tittered and gawked at him as he passed. Comely as they were, they didn't hold a candle to Esmée.

Why was his every thought ensnared by her?

He pressed on, his coattails whipped about by the strengthening wind. Nigh on three o'clock. His stomach rumbled, making him consider supper options. After a day crowded with people and war talk, he wanted nothing more than the sanctuary of his lodgings and a fire to ward off the evening's chill. Quinn had lent him a book from his growing personal library. Fielding's *The Journal of a Voyage to Lisbon*.

But first, Carter's store.

How good it felt to be out in the open air. Even without a harbor view, Williamsburg had a charm all its own. Eliza had wanted to send a maid in her stead, but Esmée felt the need to walk about alone while her sister napped. She hastened from Nassau Street toward the town's wide-set thoroughfare with a decisive step, as if anxious to outpace any memories of yesterday's tea. Mount Autrey cast quite a shadow in her thoughts. But for the moment she didn't care to contemplate being courted by the sea chaplain, despite Eliza's glee as they returned to the townhouse in the coach.

"Just think, Sister, we could be nearer neighbors. Mount Autrey lies just beyond Williamsburg. Not only that, you'd be ensconced at one of the oldest plantations in all Virginia, though the old aunties might take some getting used to."

"You can put all that out of your head once and for all." Esmée fingered her chatelaine, lingering on the tiny silver lighthouse. "I'm in no more danger of becoming an Autrey than you are being crowned queen of England."

For once Eliza had made no reply.

Pulling her cape closer about her, Esmée slowed by Williamsburg's jeweler. A woman jostled her as she went past, causing her to hold tighter to her pocketbook. Pickpockets were commonplace, be it here or York. She looked through the store's large front window, assessing pinchbeck broaches and necklaces displayed next to sobering mourning jewelry and the pointe naive diamond rings capable of writing on glass. She'd always been most drawn to simple posy rings with their poignant inscriptions exchanged by lovers.

Far off yet not forgot.

God above increase our love.
In Christ and thee my comfort be.
Meet me at midnight.
Yours in heart till death depart.

Charmed, she nearly pressed her nose to the glass but for her wide hat. The longing building inside her became a full-fledged ache.

Early in their courtship, Henri had hinted at giving her a posy ring. Why had he not? Rather, why did it matter? She turned on her heel with renewed purpose and walked on to Carter's store. Up the bricked steps and through the jingling door she went, always at home among her fellow merchants.

"What d'ye buy, Miss Shaw?" the shopkeeper asked, despite being busy with other customers.

"Pounce and wax." Esmée took in the many shelves and displays crowded with all manner of tempting goods in a dizzying array. She missed the familiar York shops, but truly Williamsburg dazzled.

The shopkeeper's voice carried pleasantly. "What you seek is at the back, in the south corner opposite the men's coats."

Thanking him, she slowly made her way in that direction, perusing cheesecake pans and ambergris wash balls, buttons and hand fans and handkerchiefs, China toy tea ware and imported garden seed. An embroidered bergère hat with velvet ribbons begged closer perusal, yellow silk roses adorning it. As she took the hat from its stand, she glanced past the display to the man in the near corner before a gilt-edged looking glass. And froze.

Henri?

What an arresting picture he made, even with his back to her. The coat he tried on was of fulled wool, suitable for winter, with a collar and deep cuffs. It fit his wide-set shoulders snugly before falling to the tops of his black boots. This one was a smoky gray, while the shop clerk held another in Prussian blue.

"Do you have a preference, sir?" the clerk asked.

A pause. Henri had a knack for weighing his words before speaking.

"The blue one," Esmée whispered behind their backs.

Brow arched, the clerk turned toward her, as did the captain. Surprise crossed both their faces, and then Henri shrugged off the gray coat and exchanged it for the blue one. With a bob of his head, the clerk bowed and excused himself, leaving them alone.

"Blue it is," Henri said with aplomb, turning back to the mirror.

Taking a deep breath, Esmée stepped clear of the hat display, forgetting she still clutched the bergère. Her head swam traitorously. She'd not eaten since breakfast, and then only sweet cake.

He looked at her reflection in the mirror, meeting her eyes. "So you are not only a chocolatier but a purveyor of men's garments."

"We are old friends, are we not?" She came to stand beside him, her wide petticoats brushing the leg of his breeches. "And as your friend I can make recommendations about your coat. Though the gray is handsome enough, you are altogether elevated in blue."

"Your turn." He faced her, gaze falling from her face to the hat she held. "Try it on."

He reached out a hand to hold the bergère as she pulled the hatpins from her hair and removed the plain bonnet she wore. As she set the hat in place, the admiration in his eyes warmed her all over. She scarcely consulted the looking glass. Yet she must have the hat.

"I know nothing of women's fashion, Miss Shaw, but it does become you . . . more than a little."

So they were back to formal names, were they? The sting of it poked a hole in her swelling pleasure. Still, she smiled at him, caught up in this cozy corner while the world spun around them.

"Thank you, Captain. I believe I shall buy it."

He took off the greatcoat and folded it over one arm while she removed her new hat. Stepping to the mirror, she pinned her old hat back into place.

"What brings you to Williamsburg?" The intensity of his gaze nearly made her forget his question.

"My father had meetings of which I'm sure you were a part. And I'm always happy to see my sister."

"Lord Drysdale was absent today. Please give him and Lady Drysdale my regards."

"I shall. We expect him home late this evening." She paused, awkwardness building. But she was unwilling to end their chance encounter. "Are you lodging in town?"

"At the Raleigh, as palace quarters are full. But alas, Williamsburg has no harbor. And no Shaw's Chocolate."

That cheered her, though he'd yet to darken their door. "You miss the sea."

"Aye, among other things."

Other things?

She would not let herself think she was one of them. Her eyes met his again, and she found his gaze warm and lively, as if holding some invitation.

He gestured for her to go ahead of him. She did so reluctantly, having forgotten the time. The clock on a far wall told five o'clock. Esmée wanted to still the mechanical hands stealing the moment away from her. She could easily have stood there all night. But the store was closing soon, and a queue of people waited to purchase their goods. Somehow a gentleman got between them, ending any further conversation.

And Esmée realized she had completely forgotten Eliza's pounce and wax.

CHAPTER twenty-four

The November morning glowered, threatening rain, but nothing prevented Esmée from heading toward Matthews Street to see Kitty Hart. She'd begun to walk about York more often of late since returning from Williamsburg. Doing so helped clear her head. With those tall-masted ships in the harbor at her back, she wasn't reminded at every turn of Henri Lennox like she was when at the chocolate shop. On the other hand, she didn't need reminding, as he'd taken up permanent residence in her head *and* her heart.

"Good morning, Miss Shaw." A mob-capped servant bobbed a curtsy as Esmée drew near.

"Is Miss Hart at home?" Esmée asked, and the servant pointed the way.

The tea garden had been readied for winter, a somber sight after the recent black frost. Each flower bed seemed asleep, some covered with thatch, others with earth. At the heart of it all was the brick tearoom with its many windows, a wisp of smoke floating above it like a white flag. Esmée missed the music of the fountain and vendors strolling about selling refreshments. Many a romantic assignation had occurred here and still did.

Through the glass of the tearoom, Esmée saw Kitty bustling about in an apple-green gown. She approached, a gift of chocolate in hand. Nothing sounded so good as a steaming cup of tea or cocoa with her closest friend and confidante. If not for Kitty, who would she spill her secrets to?

"Esmée! Your timing is perfect. We just bid goodbye to our last guests." Smiling, Kitty embraced her and welcomed her in. "As soon as I saw you at the gate, I sent for tea. I've a fresh loaf of bread with newly churned butter and a jar of cherry preserves for just such an occasion."

That was Kitty's appeal, making much of an ordinary occurrence. Esmée took a seat nearest the coal stove, an ornate contraption that warmed every corner of the tearoom.

"'Tis delightful—warmer than wood!" Esmée stretched out cold fingers, her gloves in her lap. "Does it smoke?"

"More than I like. And coal dust is quite unattractive. I miss wood ash for fertilizing the garden to boot." Taking a seat opposite her, Kitty eyed a near coal bucket with fire tongs. "But Father is rather pleased with it. Soon all the lumber in the colonies will be gone and coal must suffice, he says."

Esmée passed her the chocolate. "A little something for when winter truly sets in."

"Winter, indeed. Have you heard? The almanac predicts early snows." With a shiver, Kitty opened the sack of shaved chocolate. "I shall weather the season in the tearoom, sipping hot chocolate and reading books."

"Shall you traipse through the snow?"

"Father is contemplating building a covered passage so we shan't get our feet wet. But enough of that." Kitty's expression turned imploring. "I'd much rather hear about you. I've not seen you riding by of late, not even in your coach."

"I've been in Williamsburg. Eliza is wanting company as she nears her confinement, and Father has meetings at the palace."

"I trust your sister is well. She's frequently mentioned in the *Gazette*. The baby has hardly slowed her in society."

"Irrepressible Eliza." Overwarm, Esmée worked the clasp of her cape free and let it slip from her shoulders. "She's already searching for a wet nurse and nursemaid."

"I didn't expect otherwise. As Lady Drysdale she would have help."

"I do wonder though . . ." Esmée paused, voicing her ongoing prayer. "I hope Eliza doesn't exchange family life for society."

"Many genteel women do." Kitty quieted as the maid came in with a tray. "A little gunpowder tea today, shall we?"

"Oh?" Esmée breathed in the welcome aroma. "I was just telling the ladies at Mount Autrey that gunpowder is my favorite."

"Mount Autrey?" Kitty studied her, then took up the sugar nippers to indulge her habit. "We have much to discuss, then."

With a slight lift of her shoulders, Esmé replied, "Their nephew, Nathaniel Autrey, is Captain Lennox's sea chaplain."

"The captain?" Kitty looked up from the sugar, wide-eyed. "My, how the plot does thicken . . ."

"A minor detail." Esmée busied herself with reaching for the cream pot. "You see, Chaplain Autrey visited me in the chocolate shop on two occasions and seems to have told his aunts he found me . . . agreeable."

"He's smitten, you mean." Kitty laughed. "Well, I wonder what Captain Lennox thinks of that!"

"Very little, I'm sure. 'Twould seem Chaplain Autrey will no longer be sailing but, according to his aunts, returning home to assume his rightful place, whatever that might be."

"With you by his side, no doubt. Is that where this fairy tale is leading? His aunts are rather ancient, and the sea chaplain could well be the heir, making you mistress of Mount Autrey."

Esmée looked askance at her. "How easy you make it sound when it is in fact quite complicated."

"How so?"

"Nathaniel Autrey seems gentlemanly enough, but . . ."

Kitty began pouring tea. "I suppose the question remains—do you want to see him?"

"Nay."

"Because your heart is already taken."

There was no fooling Kitty. Taking a steadying breath, Esmée confronted the matter head-on. "I regret that I still have . . . feelings for the captain." There, she had confessed it. Now perhaps she could amend the matter.

"Ten-year-*old* feelings. And have you seen the captain recently?"

"I have." Their recent encounter was all too fresh. She pondered it and took a sip of tea. "Quite by accident at Carter's store in Williamsburg Thursday last."

"I don't believe in accidents, nor coincidences, but rather divine instances," Kitty said, passing both butter and bread. "Especially in matters of the heart."

Esmée took cherry jam next, hardly knowing what she did, so sunk was she in the memory. "I helped him choose a greatcoat." Had his pleasure in the moment only been imagined? "He seemed to welcome my advice. We parted as friends."

"Friends." The disappointment in Kitty's tone rivaled Esmée's own.

If she could take the word back, she would. She'd only meant to smooth an awkward moment. *Friends* had seemed the perfect word to gloss over her imperfect feelings.

"How long has the captain been in Virginia since his return?" Kitty asked.

"Two months is my guess."

"And you've been thrust together how many times since?"

"Once at Lady Lightfoot's ball, then when Quinn invited him for supper and to see the illuminations on Palace Green, at church, and lastly at Carter's store. Though I did spy him going into Father's coffeehouse on one occasion."

"Has he not come by the chocolate shop?" At Esmée's nay, Kitty said, "Then that is your answer."

"Meaning he would have stopped by had he any feelings for me."

"Perhaps he's lost his fondness for cocoa," Kitty said gently, adding more sugar to her tea. "Or he's still somewhat burnt from your prior association and doesn't know how to proceed."

Esmée swallowed a bite, the dismay welling inside her rendering the refreshments tasteless. "Then what would you suggest? Your plan of . . . attack?"

Kitty laughed again. "How like your father you sound! Plan of attack, indeed." Her eyes glittered. Kitty liked nothing better than a little intrigue. "Well, I do have one daring idea . . ."

CHAPTER *twenty-five*

Esmée clutched her cape tighter about her as she left the tearoom and walked home, noticing York's streets emptying fast in the face of a rising wind. Ships in the harbor pulled restively at their anchors, and Water Street seemed oddly quiet, as it always did in the face of great gusts. Such brought to mind the autumn squall of 1749, when a great many dismasted ships left their moorings and tobacco houses were overturned, all followed by a violent snowstorm. Kitty's prediction of an early winter might not be far off.

She began to hurry, head down, as great drops of rain spattered her cape, turning it from purple to black. Passing through the iron gate of their residence on fleet feet, she thought again of Kitty's bold proposition. *Daring idea* did not do it justice.

Up the steps she went. Their housekeeper, always having a sixth sense about such things, was at the door to greet her. "Come in, dear, and let me take your cape to dry by the fire. I can ready hot tea if you'd like."

"No need, thank you, as I've just been to the tearoom." Esmée removed her cape and smoothed her hair, looking toward Father's study at the end of the hall, where the door was shut. Father often had visitors.

"The admiral has asked not to be disturbed." Mrs. Mabrey whisked the cape away to the front parlor, where a fire roared in the grate. "Supper may be late. Cook has prepared your favorite, chicken fricassee."

"Ah, I must thank her. And I'll wait to eat with Father."

"Very well." She left for the kitchen belowstairs while Esmée started up the steps to the second floor.

At the sound of masculine laughter, she stopped. Company never much concerned her. Any number of merchants and townspeople came and went from Father's study on any given day. The fragrance of tobacco smoke, pungent and heady, snuck beneath the door. Many women abhorred it, but Esmée found it indescribably masculine and far better than snuff. The captain once smoked a handsome pipe with premium Tidewater tobacco. Did he still?

Her father's voice crested as if he were enjoying himself immensely. More laughter rumbled, followed by a voice she knew all too well, deep and heart-tuggingly distinct. Henri, without a doubt. A third man was present, his voice begging recognition, that failed to take root.

She hastened her steps. But before she was halfway up, the study door opened and a blue-coated figure stepped into the hall, closing the door behind him. Though she tried to tiptoe and avoid every creak in the stair, the whisper of her petticoats gave a warning.

The captain looked up and slowed his step. Was he on his way out? He stopped at the banister, resting one hand on the elaborately carved newel post at the stair's bottom. Their eyes locked. A moment of indecision racked her. Should she simply acknowledge him and continue her climb? Or return downstairs for conversation? Her feet, having a mind of their own, began their descent.

"Miss Shaw."

"Captain Lennox." She looked to the closed study door in question.

"I was on my way to my lodgings. Chaplain Autrey has asked to speak with your father alone."

Her stomach turned to jelly. She nodded, trying not to frown, remembering too late how disheveled she looked. Some of her upswept hair had escaped its pins and dangled about her shoulder. And Henri . . . he looked for all the world like he wanted to right it. She hovered on the bottom step, eye level with him now. Above his creamy neckcloth a faint line of color began to show.

"I don't mean to prevent you going upstairs," he told her.

"You didn't." She mulled her next words as the hall turned deathly quiet. "Another chance encounter, 'twould seem."

"We have a knack for those." He glanced toward the closed study door. "I came by to speak with the admiral about the light on Indigo Island."

"Of course," she replied, fingering her chatelaine. "How did that go?"

"He's in full agreement a keeper be found as soon as possible. Virginia's coastline, including the Chesapeake, has never been so vulnerable, despite guard ships."

Even now the names of foundering ships played in her head like a song. *La Galga. Invincible. Severn. Royal Fortune. Rebecca. Pembroke. Blackwall.* So many lives lost, not to mention treasure, including the herd of Spanish mustangs that swam to safety on one barrier island and were there still.

"So 'tis finished?" she asked quietly, almost sadly, as if she were outside the glass looking in.

"Finally, aye."

"Will you be its keeper?"

His face clouded, adding years. Was that a drift of silver through his dark hair or only a trick of the light? "'Twas the original plan . . . our plan, remember? But it seems I'm most needed at sea."

Nay, you are not.

His words weighted her, underscoring the chasm betwixt them. Separate paths. Separate ambitions. Separate lives.

"I'm considering several men who've applied for the position." With that he seemed to nail shut the coffin on their once shared dream.

Despite it, she gave way to a wistful longing. "I've always wanted to set foot on Indigo Island."

His eyes flashed surprise. "I nearly forgot you've not been there."

"'Tis beautiful, I hear. Serene. Is it true your cottage was built from Montserrat stone?" The question bordered on the intimate, but she forged ahead, uncaring. "And the lightkeeper's cottage is the same?"

"The both of them. Hurricane proof if not earthquake proof."

Hearing about him and his island life secondhand always chafed, but 'twas better than no news at all. "Mistress Saltonstall is a customer of ours," she said. "I suppose she's left the island for the winter."

"She has. Hermes remains behind."

Mistress Saltonstall's marmoset? She'd nearly forgotten Hermes. His antics were said to entertain tavern patrons far and wide. "I hope you've not been put in charge of him."

"Nay. The contrary creature is in the keeping of my steward."

"Poor thing. Might I send him some chocolate?"

"Oh, aye. Hermes is fond of your chocolate almonds especially."

"I meant your steward—"

"I ken what you meant, Esmée." He winked, the light remaining in his eyes. "Is there no laughter left in your soul?"

The gentle question was still more a dousing of cold water, though his return to her first name assuaged her somewhat. Tears hovered that had nothing to do with sweets but with his belonging to the sea. Of their shared lighthouse dream gone awry. She set her jaw lest she dig for a handkerchief.

Once they had laughed. His winking at her was commonplace. Once she'd felt she hadn't a care in the world with him near. Somehow time had turned her somber. Older, if not wiser. "I am not the woman—the girl—you remember. Ten years has wrought many changes."

He nodded, never taking his eyes off her. "Changes . . . not all of them welcome."

She looked to her slippers. She had no clue what raced through his thoughts, but half a dozen thorns were uppermost in hers. So many changes. Did he notice what a shell their townhouse had become without her mother and then Eliza? How she'd become unmoored, trying to salve her sorrow in her mother's endeavors, from chocolate shop to almshouse? How she was half-angry with him for forging ahead with the lighthouse and leaving her behind in his wake?

The study door opened. Esmée gave the captain a last, fleeting look before turning and hurrying upstairs lest Father and the sea chaplain see her.

CHAPTER *twenty-six*

Supper that night was a quiet affair. Father seemed preoccupied, at least until dessert was served—his favorite flummery with brandied cherries.

"Cook has outdone herself," he said as a servant removed his supper plate and served dessert in small crystal dishes.

Fighting a headache, Esmée drank a cup of coffee, adding so much cream and sugar it reminded her of Kitty. Her mind was not on the meal, and it seemed her father knew it, for he regarded her thoughtfully.

"Cat got your tongue, Daughter?"

She moistened her lips, which had suddenly gone dry. "We have no cat, Father."

He chuckled as coffee was poured on his side of the too large table. Mama's and Eliza's places remained empty, gaping holes where laughter and talk had once been effortless. Esmée sipped from her cup without savoring the coffee.

"You're not going to ask me about our gentleman callers?" her father asked.

Surprised, she held her cup aloft and peered at him over the rim. "Since they met with you and not me, do you care to divulge it?"

His smile seemed rueful. "Chaplain Autrey—Ned, I believe the captain calls him—came specifically to ask about you."

"I'm flattered, but . . ." The thought of him romantically was no more palatable than before. "He has since left for Indigo Island, has he not?"

"Aye, but his plan is to quit the captain's crew and settle at Mount Autrey within a fortnight."

"With his maiden aunts."

"Whom you've met, thanks to Eliza's roistering."

"So far I've been catechized by his aunts, not courted by Chaplain Autrey."

Her father chuckled as he plied his spoon. "The man, however latent, may well be heir to a prosperous plantation in need of a mistress."

So Father approved, did he? Their terse talk felt more like verbal sparring. She sipped her coffee, waiting for the next volley.

"I was rather taken aback." He brought a serviette to his lips. "I thought the captain had come not to talk about the island's light but something else entirely."

His resumed courtship of her, perhaps?

"I find the light altogether fascinating," she replied, certain of where he was headed and desperate to turn the tide of conversation. "Such a beacon is overdue."

"Long overdue. The captain even made mention of it being your idea to begin with."

Had he? The words rang hollow.

"But I digress." Her father's face beneath his unpowdered wig looked grave. "With Chaplain Autrey's pursuit, you have an opportunity for change."

Her spoon hovered over her untouched flummery. "You would have me be the mistress of a plantation of over a hundred Africans, in direct opposition to our faith and even the Freedom Society you are a part of?"

"Nay. That is not my decision but yours. Yet it begs considering. As mistress, you might implement change."

But not the one she wanted. Not the change that would come from loving a man so much she'd face those challenges gladly.

Her headache thundered between her temples. She set down her spoon, half sick.

"I thought perhaps that after visiting the Autrey aunts, you had some regard for him," her father said.

"'Twas Eliza's doing. Repaying a social call."

"Will you receive him, then, once he is settled at Mount Autrey?"

Would she? The prospect was as appealing as yesterday's porridge. "I shan't play him false and encourage him. So, nay."

"Keep an open mind, Daughter." He motioned for more coffee as a servant reappeared. "When your mother and I were courting, she herself was unsure at first. Her family had higher hopes for her than a mere sailor. But I finally won them—and more importantly, her—over. I practiced patience until she came to know me better. With her by my side, I soon rose in the ranks of the Royal Navy. I'm a better man because of your mother, and there's not a day goes by that I don't wish she were still by my side. I simply want to see you settled, a family about you, like your sister."

Rarely did he speak of the past. Eliza's fortuitous match had been a joy to him. He was very fond of Quinn and anticipated his first grandchild. Esmée, on the other hand, had been at home with him all her life, nursed Mama till the end, and fully expected to do the same with him when his time came.

A niggling suspicion bloomed. Might he have another reason for seeing her settled? If she wed, would he return to sea as she suspected?

His gaze grew shrewd. "I sense you are still torn over Captain Lennox."

Could he see straight to her heart? *Torn* was an understatement. "Captain Lennox and I are now . . . friends." The word pained her no matter how much she used it. To be just friends made her especially heartsore.

"Friends? Glad I am to hear it." He nodded as if it confirmed something that had passed between him and the captain about the matter. "There are men made more for their professions than marriage.

Captain Lennox is one of them. He is too great an asset to the colonial cause—to England's cause—to remain ashore at such a critical juncture. The sooner you reconcile yourself to that fact, the better."

His firm words snuffed the last of her hopes. Why had she let hope take hold? Hope that Henri had had a change of heart. That he'd had enough of the sea. That they'd have a future together after long years apart.

"Sir . . ." The messenger at the door brought her father to his feet. "There's been a disturbance at the coffeehouse. Thievery, one of your indentures is saying."

With a last word to Esmée, her father excused himself to return to Water Street and the trouble there.

Esmée watched the candelabra cast shadows on the portraits of prior Shaws hanging upon the paneled walls, the beeswax candles melting lower and lower, her spirits with them. What did the Lord have in store for her? Was it in the form of Nathaniel Autrey and not Henri Lennox? Was she blinded by the one and not able to clearly see the other? She knew little of Nathaniel, but in truth, her would-be suitor was not of the same caliber. He was shorter, slender, and more softly spoken, with eyes so nondescript they almost held no color at all. But for his blaze of hair . . .

For the Lord seeth not as man seeth; for man looketh on the outward appearance, but the Lord looketh on the heart.

Duly chastised, Esmée closed her eyes and confessed all dissatisfaction. Who was she to discount the man if he was the Lord's choice for her? Many married for reasons other than love. Was it not better than life alone? Yet was that reasoning not flawed? Didn't Nathaniel Autrey deserve more than a half-hearted bride?

As for remaining a spinster, she'd grown used to her solitary state. But she did not sit idly by and lament she had no mate. Her hours were filled with family. The almshouse. Business. Friends. And she was about to become an aunt, if not a wife and mother.

Life was all about how you looked at it, was it not?

CHAPTER

twenty-seven

The next morn, Henri and his crew sailed from York with the tide. Theirs was a quiet passage, the blustery weather of the previous day and night a memory. The shallop soon had them across the Chesapeake, the island before them a shimmering mirage. High above the pines and dunes and beach heather rose the finished stone tower, soon to shine a piercing light to mariners. No more kindling sporadic bonfires on cliff tops to aid navigation, nor witnessing ships dashed to pieces on reefs or other perils of the deep.

"If there's to be a war, the light shall go dark lest the French be guided by it," the admiral had told Henri. "But in times of peace 'twill be a sure boon for ships coming and going, whether in stormy seas or no. Virginia should have risen to the occasion long ago."

"The Norfolk architect who designed it will soon make a final inspection," Henri replied, though the satisfaction he expected to feel was denied him. Why, he didn't know.

"You've seen it through to fruition and have shouldered considerable expense."

"'Tis a beauty at such a great height and crafted of local granite." Henri carefully enumerated the details that had occupied him since he'd first taken to the sea and seen countless lights around the globe. "Hanging oil lamps, at least twelve of them, though candles will suffice if oil is scarce. A platform around the light's lantern room will keep the glass free of snow and ice in bad weather. And a small cannon has been cast to answer ships in the fog."

"Much like the Boston harbor light." The admiral had looked pleased, even proud. "Lord willing, it shan't be so cursed."

Henri contemplated it now. Lord willing, it would only be a blessing, not just to the coming lightkeeper but to all those who encountered it. His vision was but one step from being realized. Nay, his and Esmée's vision. Though he'd seen the project to a finish, he'd not forgotten it was her idea from the first.

"There's but one matter that confounds me about Admiral Shaw."

Henri had nearly forgotten Ned was close. The chaplain moved nearer him in the bow.

"He seems somewhat reserved about my pursuit of his daughter," Ned confided, his tone perplexed. "And more than a little surprised."

"As I wasn't privy to what passed between you, I can offer little insight," Henri replied, trying to dismiss his meeting with Esmée on the stair. But every detail badgered him like sand fleas. Her fragile expression. Her wind-tossed hair tumbling to her shoulder. The beguiling way she held his gaze.

"I presumed my ties to Mount Autrey would be of more merit than being a simple sea chaplain."

"Admiral Shaw is an opponent of slavery. He may well wonder why a chaplain would espouse such by living there, even if you don't inherit the plantation."

"A predicament I've no peace with myself." Ned shook his head.

"You should know he and Mrs. Shaw were among the founders of a Rhode Island society for freeing those in bondage. His daughter is assuredly of the same mind."

"Then I am in a maddening quandary, am I not? A mere nephew, yet tainted by my relation. It does not help that the overseers are said to be cruel to Mount Autrey's slaves."

"Consider manumitting the enslaved Africans if it's in your power to do so. Employ tenant farmers instead."

"Like the mother country."

"Cease growing tobacco and turn to more profitable endeavors like grain and white wheat."

"You are ahead of your time, Captain. And you sound a farmer at heart, not a sailor."

"Truth be told, I've grown weary of the sea."

"Yet the governor and his minions are so desperate to foil the French they've agreed to all your terms, even your African crew."

Henri said no more as two jacks reached for the mooring lines with which to dock. With a lightness he didn't feel, Henri leapt to the pier.

Ned followed, expression still grim. "You've not yet said what you think of her."

Henri walked on, caught off guard by the question. Had the admiral told Ned of his and Esmée's former tie?

Finally he faced Ned, well out of earshot of the rest of the crew. "What do I think of her . . ." Heat sidled up his face, much as it had done when he was in the stairwell alone with her. Dare he say it? *Speak truthfully.* "I was in love with her once."

Ned's soberness turned to astonishment, and he parroted the words back to Henri. "In love with her?"

"*Once*," Henri stated firmly. "I hardly know her now."

Ned stared at him. "You've never spoken of it."

"'Twas long ago. Before you came aboard. It seemed of little consequence."

"May I ask what happened to end your misalliance?"

"I scarce ken how to frame it." Henri shrugged. "She wanted me to stay on land. I craved the sea."

Ned looked aggrieved. "You spurned her."

"Nay." The mere thought raked Henri's composure. "'Twas mutual. And I do not care to remember."

"If 'tis still sore, then some feeling must remain."

Henri turned away, done with the conversation. "Tell the men I want a meeting at six bells in the forenoon."

They parted, Henri going to look at the light tower but mostly at the finished keeper's cottage a stone's throw from it. A short, covered passage connected the two for protection in times of inclement weather. Pushing open the cottage door, he paused before entering, trying to see it with new eyes. He'd taken care to furnish it comfortably, culling items from his travels and carefully storing them in the ship's hold with the future lightkeeper in mind.

Twin Venetian wingback chairs upholstered in blue tapestry with a nautical theme rested by the fireplace. On a game table was a Russian scrimshaw cribbage set. Tole lanterns hung from the beamed ceiling, each unique. A teak shipwright's trunk adorned one plaster wall beneath a shelf that held a spyglass and tide tables. He was partial to the humble ship's barrel for storage in a kitchen corner and the handsome chest of drawers in the bedchamber, its painted surface of a ship at full sail. The generous bed was hung with soft if plain linens. Sparse, well intentioned, and well crafted, the cottage simply lacked a keeper.

His next order of business was to supply just that, one he could oversee till he sailed under a letter of marque for Virginia. Decision made, he still craved a different sort of future.

CHAPTER twenty-eight

Surely babies were made to inspire hope, especially in the dreary days of November. As soon as Esmée sat down by the hearth's fire in Miss Grove's cramped almshouse quarters, Alice's baby boy in her arms, a sweet peace settled over her. Asleep, bundled in one of the blankets she'd made, a wee fist tucked under his dimpled chin, Alden was the picture of contentment.

"Such foul weather of late, though you seem to have brought the sunshine with you today, at least," Miss Grove told her as she cleared away the tea tray they'd partaken of. "'Tis good to have you back. We seldom have company, especially when the roads turn to mud and ice."

"I had to see how you all were faring, including this wee cherub." Esmée smoothed a wisp of the baby's russet hair showing beneath his bonnet. "And replenish your cocoa stores before winter sets in."

Miss Grove settled opposite her in the wing chair, a worn affair of scuffed walnut. "Of all the things you bring us, Shaw's hot chocolate is the unrivaled favorite of all the residents."

"I confess to an overfondness for it." Esmée looked out a near window, where the sun had the shine of May, not November. "When the snow flies and York comes to a standstill, there's little better."

"We've no one to bring us such fancies but you." Leaning forward, Miss Grove darted a glance at the door before saying conspiratorially, "Though I must tell you in secret, we are of late well supplied. Even with the French refugees on our doorstep."

"Well supplied? You don't mean all those bones I begged?"

Miss Grove chuckled, revealing a missing tooth. "Those bones are much appreciated. But nay, I'm referring to another benefactor. A furtive one. Not long ago a gentleman stopped by here under cover of darkness and met with Mr. Boles and his wife."

"Is this gentleman known to you?"

"Nay, and he insisted on remaining anonymous. The night watch did say he wasn't a great age but younger. Hatted and somewhat disguised." Her eyes shone. "He left an enormous sum with the express wish of seeing it well used. He spoke of having contacts who would apprise him of anything misspent."

Esmée warmed to the mystery. "Meaning the bulk of the money is to go to the poor for their well-being and comfort, not the trustees' pockets."

"Precisely. It seems to have struck some fear into the heart of the Boleses and even the lesser staff. Depending on how the behest is managed, more might be forthcoming. Or not."

Esmée felt stark relief. "'Tis hard to persuade people to be openhanded, yet this man did it unbidden."

"Perhaps the gentleman is known to you?"

"I know of no such gentleman. But I like that he did his giving in secret, as Scripture praises. No naming the almshouse after him."

"Indeed." Miss Grove's wide smile made her appear less careworn. "'That thine alms may be in secret: and thy Father which seeth in secret himself shall reward thee openly.'"

"Still, I am curious . . . and intrigued." Esmée looked down at the sleeping baby, her thoughts far afield. "'Tis good only God knows."

Miss Grove reached up a hand to touch the new mobcap Esmée had brought her. "Mr. Boles has even promised a chapel and a walled garden in spring now that we're not so dependent on parish levies."

"A chapel *and* garden? How delightful! Then I shall be doubly relieved all winter, knowing none here are in need." Esmée felt one burden lighter. How quickly life could take a turn. Only recently she'd been sitting at her father's table feeling as spent as the guttering candles, and now this.

Might the captain have done the benevolent deed? Or . . . had the sea chaplain decided to somehow curry her favor by giving to a cause dear to her heart?

"I've need of guidance." Ned paced before the hearth as rain drummed a steady rhythm on the cottage's shingled roof. Since their return to the island, the weather had been fitful. "You're the best one suited to offer advice, given you were once fond of the woman I now favor."

Henri leaned back in his wing chair, feet extended to the roaring fire. He could feel the heat through the worn soles of his boots. "Since I failed in that respect, mayhap you'd best consult Southack or Robbins."

"Southack, who cavorts with every native woman he sees? Or Robbins, so prudish a first mate he can't speak of a woman without a feverish blush?"

"What are you in need of knowing?" Henri asked grudgingly.

"How to proceed." Ned raked a hand through lank hair and came to a sudden stop. Leaning into the mantel, he seemed so perplexed that Henri bit his tongue lest he laugh. "I've gained her father's approval. Now hers is needed. But how do I call upon her? What should I bring?"

"Bring yourself." Henri moved to add another stick of wood to the fire. "State your intentions and see what she says."

"But—"

"Take care to not overthink it lest you appear a straw man. Speak from the heart."

"How easy you make it sound."

"You'll know soon enough if she favors you."

Ned looked to the Bible open on the table as if contemplating his most biblical option. "Perhaps I should ponder the Song of Songs first."

Henri uttered a warning. "Careful lest it inflame you before your time."

"What?"

"'Tis a biblical celebration of marriage, not courtship. An unabashedly sensuous book."

Ned assumed an injured look. "I am a chaplain, remember. I well know what it says, though in all truthfulness, I've not visited its passages in some time."

"Here's another caution." Henri cleared his throat, bracing himself against the onrush of carefully stowed memories. "Speak no French."

"French? Miss Shaw does not care for it?"

"It may remind her of my doing so and slow your pursuit."

"Touché, Captain." Understanding lit Ned's features. Then a shadow darkened his brow. "I confess she bears a striking resemblance to Verity."

Verity. Ned's betrothed who'd died of fever. As he'd never met her, Henri was in the dark.

"Same hair and eye color," Ned murmured mournfully. "Same penchant for confections."

"If your attraction is based on a dead woman," Henri told him curtly if kindly, "'tis rocky ground upon which to proceed."

"Well taken." Ned began pacing again, no small feat given the close quarters, and looked so troubled Henri sensed something more was on his mind than courtship.

"What weighs on you, Ned? Surely not the lovely Miss Shaw."

Ned shook his head. "The thought of living with my maiden aunts on a sprawling plantation is . . . daunting."

"'Tis nothing like the sea." Henri stared at the dog irons, pondering Ned's predicament. "Though if you can handle shipboard conditions as well as you did, several women and a great deal of acreage seem less burdensome."

"I'm considering a pastorate. A parish. There are many in need of shepherding in various places in Virginia and elsewhere."

"Why not preach and minister to the Africans within your sphere at Mount Autrey?"

"And be cast out of Virginia? Labeled a heretic?"

"Pray about it foremost."

"Aye, pray." Ned looked at Henri, his bloodshot eyes indicating a sleepless night or two. "I will miss your company and our wooden world."

Henri took hold of a black glass bottle, removed the seal, and poured them both a drink.

Ned took a bracing sip. "Vinho da roda."

"Aye. Madeira Terrantez. Aged by our last trip around the world."

"You brought that pipe of Madeira aboard when we were in the West Indies, if memory serves. Some five hundred bottles. This must be one of them."

They lapsed into silence, the drone of rain and snap of the fire a drowsy melody. Soon Ned departed in better spirits, leaving Henri alone. But his own thoughts were poor company, his feelings in chaos. Ned had stirred them up like storm petrels, those ominous birds that flew alongside ships, foretelling a gale. Here he sat, attempting to support his longtime sea chaplain, needing to pray for him at so critical a juncture . . .

When what he wanted was to throw him overboard.

He shut his eyes and took a deep, measured breath. *God, forgive me.*

CHAPTER *twenty-nine*

Esmée smoothed the lace sleeve of her gown, a lush rose brocade never before worn. She hovered on the stair landing of the Williamsburg townhouse, trying to warm to the idea of the party below. Voices floated up to her, scraps of spirit-sated conversation and laughter, inviting her to join in when what she craved was a quiet corner. A book. A window seat from which to watch the stormy weather.

'Twas Eliza's last soiree before her confinement. And what a soiree it was, with an ice sculpture adorning an enormous punch bowl and no end of savory items from the kitchen, even a table reserved for Shaw's chocolate in all its forms. A liveried servant was at hand to concoct hot cocoa, rich with cream and beaten to a froth and topped with West Indies spices.

Since Eliza had only hinted at the guest list, Esmée tried to prepare herself for elation or deep disappointment. The one voice she hoped to hear was lost to her, either missing or muffled by upwards of two dozen people.

She began her descent, glad the foyer was empty. A fan dangled from her wrist by a golden cord. With so many people in the parlor, she'd certainly need it. As she was missing her chatelaine, it gave her something to do with her hands.

"Esmée, there you are!" Eliza's voice rang out and turned every eye to her, if only momentarily.

Smiling rather stiffly, Esmée entered the melee, candlelight glittering off a great many gowns and jewels and faces. The governor was there with his wife and daughters. Rebecca Dinwiddie smiled at her, no doubt recalling their rather controversial tea of weeks before. Her own father held court by the marble fireplace, surrounded by old friends. Several officials, burgesses among them, gathered round the punch bowl, their conversation rousing and reminding her of the coffeehouse. No merchants here or any middling folk, just Williamsburg's leading lights as befitting Lord and Lady Drysdale.

"Miss Shaw, just the lady I was hoping to encounter."

She turned. Nathaniel Autrey gave a gallant bow to one side of the parlor door, as if awaiting her entrance. She tried not to stare, but she'd not seen him so well dressed nor smelling like a perfumery—eau de cologne? He wore a powderless wig tailed down his back with black silk ribbon. She nearly didn't recognize him.

Tongue-tied, she inclined her head, wishing for a little music. As there was to be no dancing, she braced herself for a long night of conversation.

"Are your aunts here?" she asked, gaze sweeping the crowded room.

"They rarely venture out in foul weather, given their advanced age."

"Of course." Relief flooded her. "You're brave to come. The wind is wilder by the hour."

"I can only imagine Indigo Island about now." Ignorant of her thoughts mired there, he looked briefly toward a window. "Hurricane season is still upon us." His eyes sought hers long enough to fill her face with fire. "Would you care for punch, Miss Shaw?"

At her smile and nod, he threaded his way through the parlor to the punch bowl being refilled while she seated herself on a vacant chair. Eliza's laughter rang out, reminding Esmée anew her sister had gotten a double portion of hostessing while she herself had not.

Though Eliza's entertaining was faultless, Esmée worked to stifle a yawn. It didn't help she'd visited the Williamsburg bookseller and had a novel waiting upstairs. The bestselling *Love in Excess* raised her father's brows and left Eliza laughing, but Esmée was drawn to the daring premise, challenging the custom that forbade women from declaring their romantic thoughts. Since when were men the only arbiters of affection?

Chaplain Autrey returned, two glasses in hand. She took the cold punch with gratitude, as the room was overwarm.

"So have you come to the mainland permanently? Left Indigo Island and the service of Captain Lennox?" she asked.

"I'm now at Mount Autrey, aye, trying to come to terms with my land legs." He looked down at her, studying her more closely than she wished. Or was she being too sensitive?

"What made you seek the sea to begin with?" She was sincerely curious, but the pained look on his face told her she'd misspoken. "I'm sorry, I—"

"Nay, Miss Shaw. 'Tis an honest question that deserves an honest answer." He stared down into his glass. "My betrothed died on the eve of our wedding. Verity was everything to me. Perhaps too much so. Idolatry, if you will. When she died I took to the sea, thinking to outrun her memory."

"And did you?"

"Nay. But I found instead the only One worthy of worship. And Verity's loss, while still painful, assumed its rightful place."

Esmée stared at him, forgetting herself. Could idols be of flesh and blood like Verity, not just carved stone or wood? She pondered this, unprepared for his next words.

"You undoubtedly know where my future interests lie where you're concerned, Miss Shaw."

"My father told me." Though she was well versed in resisting suitors, she still found it awkward, her palms damp. She gave an apologetic smile. "And being a forthright woman, some say a spinster, I thank you but must say I am not the wife you are desiring."

"I appreciate your honesty." Was it her imagination, or did his eyes twinkle? For so plain a rebuff, he weathered it well. "My fondness for chocolate may well have blinded me to the Lord's leading. And your agreement."

As if they'd orchestrated it, her sister drew near, a belle on each side of her. "Allow me to introduce Miss Carter and Miss Marriot." Eliza was all smiles, the Drysdale tiara she wore flashing in the candlelight. "They've yet to meet the new resident of Mount Autrey."

Turning her back on them, Eliza gave Esmée a piercing look. Knowing that look, Esmée followed her around the parlor's perimeter and into an alcove half-hidden by exotic potted plants.

"The governor's tongue has been loosed by too much punch," Eliza whispered with vehemence, her back against the wall. "He's been spilling details about all those closed-door meetings at the palace."

Esmée sensed it all had to do with Henri. Would Dinwiddie's revelations endanger his mission? She took another bracing sip of punch.

With a flutter of her fan, Eliza continued. "A declaration of war is imminent, and the battle will soon be fought by sea, not only by land. Stalwart captain that he is, Lennox will carry a letter of marque from the colonial government, acting as an ancillary of the Royal Navy."

The sweet punch soured on Esmée's tongue. She wanted to raise a hand to stay the words, understanding why Father had spared her the details. A grim mission indeed. "So Captain Lennox will command a vessel of war."

Dinwiddie was rabid for war, the newspapers printed, eager to defeat France with whatever manpower was available to him. Hadn't the irascible Scot ignited the frontier conflict by sending Colonel Washington west to begin with? She looked across the room at the governor speaking with Quinn and fellow burgesses so intently.

"But that is not all of it." Eliza's color was high, her voice a bit breathless. "Quinn is behaving quite strangely."

"What means you?"

Eliza darted a look in his direction. "At the last minute he cut half the guests from the guest list. Something about vain persons and dissemblers and evildoers, all of whom are the foremost critics of Captain Lennox."

Esmée felt a flicker of triumph. "Oh?"

"Brace yourself further." Eliza's fan fluttered harder. "He insists our party conclude before midnight."

With a look at the mantel clock, Esmée said, "Your parties oft last till dawn. Perhaps he is merely concerned for you and the baby—"

"Ha! He doesn't want to be late to Sabbath service. We haven't missed church for weeks now. He listens raptly to every word Reverend Dawson utters. He even wants to discuss his sermons once we are home."

"Fancy that," Esmée said dryly.

"Of late he's become an ardent admirer of Mr. Whitefield, the evangelist, and his writings and stance on slavery. I tell you, I have great cause for alarm."

"Sister, if you'd told me Quinn is in his cups, had insulted Reverend Dawson, and committed adultery, that would concern me. As it stands, I can only offer you my congratulations."

With a huff, Eliza moved on, her gown cleverly disguising the baby's bulk, leaving Esmée alone in the alcove. She finished her punch, and a servant came to replenish it. The hour was early, only nine o'clock. Esmée looked toward the window again as a gust of wind shook the pane.

What was the captain doing on such a night?

Hunkering down by the fire, likely. Once he'd been fond of books. They'd talked of poems and plays and novels. They played cribbage. She made them both flip, which frothed into foamy waves atop blue Meissen mugs. Feet to the hearth in her father's study, they heard the clock chime midnight many a time, but her parents said nary a word. It had been, in hindsight, the richest, most exhilarating time of her life.

If not his.

CHAPTER *thirty*

"Good day to you, Widow Radcliffe." Esmée smiled and helped the bent-backed woman to the chocolate shop door with her purchases, glad for so busy a morning, as it kept her mind off the heart-pounding present. But now, with no more customers at hand, a dreadful lull ensued, though one of the indentures was singing a slightly off-key tune in the kitchen.

Esmée moved to the front window, her vista mostly gray as winter approached. The days were growing shorter, the weather crisp as a Hewes crab apple. Next door, the coffeehouse hummed, patrons enjoying fresh-pressed cider. She could smell its spiced tang through the open Dutch door. Occasionally a gentleman would cross the threshold and buy a sweet to partake of with his beverage or carry home to a wife or sweetheart.

But not Henri Lennox.

She'd not seen him since their week-old encounter in the townhouse foyer when he'd been wearing the handsome coat she'd helped pick out at Carter's store. Though she looked for him—and his horse—about town or on the road between York and Williamsburg, he stayed hidden. The papers had ceased printing his whereabouts and business, giving rise to her belief he remained on Indigo Island.

Esmée rearranged the display window, moving chocolate pots and porcelain cups nearer the glass. Taking up a cluster of turkey feathers, she dusted, an unnecessary task, as Simon had done it just that morning. What once brought her a sense of satisfaction now turned to ashes no matter what she set her hand to. Blame it on the news heard at Eliza's soiree. She'd hardly slept since. It wasn't only Henri's future she was concerned with but her own. And enacting her plan required all the courage she could muster. It might all come to naught and haunt her the rest of her life, but still she must try.

Crossing the shop to the kitchen door, she bade Molly take her place. "I must go out and shan't return to the shop today. But Father is near should you need him."

Molly simply smiled, used to her midday jaunts, and exchanged her soiled apron for a clean one. "I'll gladly swap, Miss Shaw. I'm weary o' Josiah's singing."

Esmée removed her own apron and reached for her cloak. Hurriedly she passed by the chocolate stones heating at the hearth and was reminded of the cocoa grinder Father spoke of getting from Boston, capable of producing one hundred pounds of chocolate in six hours. No doubt the indentures would prefer that, freeing them from kitchen labor better spent elsewhere.

Down Water Street she went on foot, then took a sharp right up the rutted road that climbed to Main Street and their residence. She stopped at the stable, telling a hand to ready her mare. Minta nickered at her voice, anticipating a ride. It gave Esmée time to go to her bedchamber and change into her riding habit.

And reconsider her foolhardy plan.

She pressed on nonetheless, boots on and plumed hat pinned tightly, glad Mrs. Mabrey hadn't questioned her and Father was busy at the coffeehouse. He'd put a stop to her rashness at once if he found out. Yet as she turned down the lonely road that led to the almshouse, she felt an odd peace settle over her. From the top of her head to her leather soles, it seemed a cool draft of water passed through her, settling her, encouraging her, leading her. So stark was the absence of her recent turmoil that tears stung her eyes.

Was this what the Lord had for her then? This rash mission she'd undertaken in her own secret thoughts, only to be confirmed by Kitty? How was it possible to feel any peace? Yet peace was what she had. At least for the fleeting moment.

Lord, I am a foolish, lovestruck woman. Please guide me and keep me from harm.

She prodded Minta into a gallop, wanting her mission over with as soon as possible. 'Twas fortuitous Jago Wherry was getting wood in the saw lot away from the almshouse. The few men with him tipped their hats and moved away as she neared. He dropped his armload of wood as if sensing her business was with him as she reined in a few feet away. She rarely spoke with him, not since her mother was alive and they'd visited weekly. Wherry came and went as his fortunes rose and fell at the track and elsewhere.

"Good afternoon to you," Esmée said, staying atop her horse.

"G'day, Miss Shaw." He removed his hat, clutching its battered edges in workworn hands. "We don't oft see you unless you're pulling a cart full of relief."

"No need for that of late, thankfully." Did he know who had given the fortune to the almshouse? She took a breath, a bit winded from her ride. "I've come to ask something of you. A private matter."

He took a step nearer, his features sharpening. "At your service, ma'am."

"I want you to row me to Indigo Island." Her gaze held his. "Stone-cold sober."

A smile curled his thin lips. "But I've no boat, Miss Shaw."

"Well, you're clever enough to get one. And I'll reward you handsomely for it."

He pondered this, amusement and concern playing across his craggy face. "Ye've not set foot on the island before?"

"Never. 'Tis time." Even as she spoke the confident words, she had second thoughts. She felt a bit like Eliza with such scheming.

"Does the captain know of yer coming?"

"I'd rather he not."

"Um . . ." He seemed to reconsider.

"For all you know, I might be visiting Mistress Saltonstall," she said.

"I doubt it, given she's now on the mainland." He returned his hat to his head and peered at the glowering sky. "A bit chancy with November well upon us. When are ye thinking of going?"

"The next fair day."

He studied the sky. "Could be tomorrow . . . could be sennight's end." A nod. "I'll be ready."

"We'll meet at eight bells in that little cove where you saw the captain off."

"Yer the admiral's daughter, for sure." His chest shook with suppressed laughter. "I must warn ye yer taking a frightful risk. A northeaster could blow in, keeping ye on the island for days and days if ye do get there."

Esmée nearly sighed aloud. The sweet relief she'd felt—the elusive peace that flew in the face of this mad plan—began to crack beneath his caution.

Lord, help.

CHAPTER *thirty-one*

The weather continued to defy Esmée and beg her to reconsider. There was plenty of time for Wherry to change his mind . . . or borrow a boat. Plenty of time for her to revisit her trust in this man, a stranger nearly, with a questionable reputation. But who else would she involve in her plan? Henri had entrusted Wherry to give him riding lessons. Was she wrong to rely on him as well?

Midweek, she stood at her rain-smeared bedchamber window, gazing past York to the Atlantic that beckoned. She fingered her chatelaine, intent on the little lighthouse. If all this went awry, she would hurl the tiny token into the sea. But . . .

Her Bible lay open on the table near her empty teacup. She'd been too preoccupied to partake of much breakfast. Only Kitty knew of her plan. Kitty was praying for her and watching the weather.

Father was absent while she waited, busy with matters in town. He even went to Williamsburg all of a sudden, as secretive as ever as to why, but Esmée was certain it had to do with Henri. Instead of it weakening her purpose, sensing Henri might set sail at any moment only hardened her resolve. She would act with grace and dignity despite her boldness, lest she spend the rest of her life ruing her cowardice and failure to move forward.

Lord, let me not make myself a fool by either rashness or overthinking the matter.

One verse in particular kept her grounded.

For God hath not given us the spirit of fear; but of power, and of love, and of a sound mind.

Even the timing was the Almighty's own. And the weather.

At last, sennight's end found Esmée in the agreed-upon cove. She stood on the sand, clutching her purse of coin, wondering if she'd dreamed the plan up. She was alone on the launching site. No vessel. No Wherry at hand. Had he succumbed to spirits and forgotten their agreement? Suddenly weary, she sat down upon a log and faced the wind.

The water was calm. Dead calm. And it might not be again for some time.

But the wily Cornishman did not disappoint. A sudden shout carried over the water. She turned in its direction. A handsome jolly raised her brows in admiration. Jago Wherry and a lad from the almshouse plied the oars. She wouldn't ask where Wherry had gotten the vessel. She prayed he'd not stolen it. Such boats usually hung from davits at a ship's stern when not in use.

He docked and helped her in, and she took a discerning if discreet breath. He didn't waft of spirits, though she spied a bottle half-hidden in rain gear stashed in the boat's bottom. With a practiced air he took up the oars again, reminding her of his history. Word was he'd once served under an Admiral of the Fleet in the Royal Navy. Surely she was in good hands.

From her stern seat she was rendered speechless, aware of a great many things at once. The still blue of the water on a nearly windless day, its fathomless depths a mirror of the heavens above. Was this what enticed the captain time and again?

While the men rowed, she took in York in a way denied her before. How small it looked. How insignificant. It faded from her line of sight as if melting like a confection on the horizon, all the ships at anchor like a child's toys. Down the relative safety of the York River and into the treacherous bay they went, all manner of vessels around them.

Breathless she was. Not from any exertion but from the risk she took. What if the jolly capsized? Whales did much mischief, upending boats without warning. What if—nay, she could not bear it—the island was less than she'd hoped and dreamed? She kept her eye on it beneath the shade of her cloak's hood as the flutter inside her intensified.

What if the captain was not there? Or—the latent realization turned her leaden—he'd already set sail or hired a lighthouse keeper?

She took in the mound of land resembling a sea turtle's back. There were more trees than she'd imagined. Wind-stunted pines. An abundance of seagrass. Gulls careening overhead. By the time they neared the island, the wind had strengthened, stirring her cloak and nearly pushing her hood back.

The light could not be seen yet, situated as it was on the backside of the island, facing the Atlantic. The captain's cottage was not far from it, or so Father once told her. The keeper's cottage too.

Where would she find Henri? And would Indigo Island become a beloved memory or another sore reminder?

CHAPTER *thirty-two*

It was late November. Painfully aware of the time, Henri stood with arms folded, legs apart, and boots firmly planted on shifting sand as he watched his men coat the bottom of the *Relentless* with tar, tallow, and sulfur. Its potency carried in the rising wind, but it was a pleasant smell, at least to him, evidence of enormous effort. Behind him were the ship's guns and top masts that needed to be returned to the careened vessel before severe weather set in. His crew had finished with little time to spare. Even old Jacques's bones ached, a sworn precursor to a gale.

"Well done!" His voice rang out, meeting with huzzahs from all sides. "An extra half gill of rum at day's end for every man."

The beach where they'd chosen to work was ideal, shallow and secluded. Of all the coves and inlets on this seven-mile island, this was his favorite. It held the lush richness of the Caribbean, with warm azure waters and glittering sand but none of its venomous snakes.

"Blasted teredo worms!" he overheard Cyprian say from down the beach as he spat into the sand.

Tarbonde smiled patiently. "'Tis only the third careening we've endured this year."

"Next time we'll not stay so long in the Caribbean," Henri replied, thinking shipworms one of the few hazards of the tropics.

Southack scratched his chin. "Still no word from the governor about our departure?"

"Any day now," Henri replied quietly.

"The men are enjoying their freedom meanwhile," Southack said. "They've struck their tents and moved to the Flask and Sword since it's been shuttered for the winter. Generous of Mistress Saltonstall to offer up quarters while we wait. But I suppose you paid her handsomely to do it."

With a nod, Henri privately recounted her glee as they'd dickered about a price. She'd come away with a sack of silver ingots and a Burmese ruby she fancied besides.

"Captain." Udo approached, a list in hand. "I've sent to the mainland for another fortnight's victuals and drink. Jacques is quite at home in the tavern's kitchen . . ." His voice died away as he looked toward the water.

Henri, intent on the careening, widened his focus. Half a league out was a trim little jolly, three figures within. Two were at the oars, one of which was Jago Wherry. Another was in the stern, her purple cape fluttering against her full figure like a flag. He'd seen that comely garment before . . .

Esmée?

The bottom dropped out of his belly. Some of his crew were now gaping, forgetting their work. As the vessel floated by, Esmée turned her head toward him as if captured by the activity on shore and the hulking vessel that lay on its side like a beached behemoth. Were they on their way toward the end of the island? His cottage? Or the light?

Run, man.

Without a word to anyone, he bolted, kicking up sand as he sprinted toward the trees and trail that led to his end of the island. His boots clattered on the boardwalk. Winded, even dazed, he thrust open the door to his dwelling and made for the washstand in his bedchamber. He poured water into a basin and all but dunked his head in, ruing the bristles scrabbling his jaw, his uncombed hair. If ever he'd had the look of a pirate . . .

Rearing back, he toweled himself dry. Too late for a razor. Missing a comb, he ran both hands through his black mane, then tied the mass back with black ribbon. His garments would suffice. One unsatisfactory look in the mirror sent him from the bedchamber outside again.

To he knew not what.

While he awaited the next sighting of the vessel, he battled for composure. Why had Esmée come? Had Admiral Shaw fallen ill? Was she somehow bringing word from Lord Drysdale and Williamsburg?

His impatience was soon rewarded when the jolly sidled up to the pier. Despite the sea jaunt, Esmée looked as comely as he'd ever seen her. A queenly posture. Cape hood pushed back to reveal upswept hair with nary a pin awry. And a triumphant smile—was it slightly tremulous?—on her upturned face as he put out a hand to lift her to land. At least some of his fears were allayed.

"Good morning, Captain."

His heart beat hard against his rib cage. "To what do I owe the pleasure, Miss Shaw?"

"I've always wanted to see your island," she answered as lightly as if they were exchanging pleasantries about the weather. "And have a private word with you, if I may."

He darted a glance at Jago, who was busy with the mooring lines. "I'll escort you to my study, then."

"Thank you."

Hand cupping her elbow, he led her up the steps to his cottage, second-guessing himself all the way. Should he have taken her to the light instead? His study—did it look hurricane struck? Of late the chaos in his spirit was reflected in his normally tidy surroundings. Too late to right them. He opened the door for her reluctantly, and she entered in ahead of him, her face alive with interest.

"Your first visit to the island," he said, overcome by a guilty negligence.

She simply smiled again as he led her to his study. It wasn't as disheveled as he remembered, just dusty, and they both sat, the desk between them. Her attention drifted from him to the cowrie shell atop his desk. Removing her gloves, she reached out a hand to touch it.

"I've never seen the like," she said, looking a bit awed. "It has the shine of porcelain."

"They're most abundant in the Indian Ocean. A gift to me from the African chief liberated from the *Swallow*."

Her expression brightened. "Ah, the heroic deed that will not die."

He nearly flushed at her open admiration. Fisting his hands atop his desk, he wondered if his pleasure in her company showed on his face. "I'll be honest and say I'm rather thunderstruck by your coming. 'Tis not every day a lady of quality hazards a crossing to a barrier island in the chill of November."

"Expect the unexpected, 'tis said." Her quiet words rolled over him as her green gaze held his. "I've mainly come because I'm seeking the position of lightkeeper."

He swallowed, not entirely astounded, but still . . . "The position."

"After much thought . . ." Her lovely face turned pensive. "If you've not already decided on a keeper, that is."

He looked down at the papers before him, half a dozen men's names scrawled as possible appointees. None but two seemed fit for the task. Both were capable. Middle-aged and able-bodied. Proven Virginians who had seen military service.

"Why do you wish to turn lightkeeper instead of being the successful chocolatier and almshouse benefactress you are?" He felt beyond his ken questioning her, this woman who had his heart so entangled, but there must be some semblance of an interview even if he refused her the position.

"Shaw's Chocolate was my mother's business and the almshouse her heart's cause, though I've been glad to stand in her stead." She folded her hands atop her lap, her lush cape settling in lavender folds about her. "But in truth, I'm unnecessary to its continuance now that it's well established and worked by indentures. As for the almshouse, the poor will always be with us, sadly."

No refuting that. Scripture said the same. But another matter still tore at him. Ned's presence seemed to come between them, a question that begged settling once and for all. Did this mean she'd refused him? Even after he'd sought her father's permission to court her? The silence needed filling, but how to frame such a delicate question?

"Have you no other . . . opportunities, Es—Miss Shaw? Choices?"

She lowered her gaze, a pink cast to her features. "If you imply any suitors, nay. I am not meant to reside at Mount Autrey. And I have said as much to your sea chaplain."

Relief nearly made him light-headed. Still, there were other hurdles to overcome. "You realize island life is very different than living on the mainland."

"Understandably. But I would do my part for Virginia and the Chesapeake."

"You'd be the first lady lightkeeper in the colonies. Other than the woman in Rhode Island who took up the task when her keeper husband died."

"First of many, is my guess."

"What does your father say?"

A pause. "He knows nothing of my coming here." She looked past him to the map pinned to the wall behind him. "I am, I remind you, of an age to do what I will."

He'd not forgotten her age, nor his. Even now the pinch in his knees reminded him of the rheumatism that plagued aging seamen. "'Tis often lonesome and dangerous. As keeper you'd do far more than clean and polish glass."

"Do you doubt my abilities, Captain?"

"Nay, I admire you for rising to the challenge." He leaned forward, resting his forearms on the desk. "You make me think twice about the men who seek the appointment. None of them rowed out in a jolly to win the position."

She smiled, then grew serious again. "I can swim, surely a requirement. I keep a cool head under trying conditions. I prefer solitude to society." She took a breath. "I'm stronger than I look."

The sun slanted through a window, casting her in angelic light. It made her look . . . vulnerable. Too fragile for the rigors of lighthouse keeper.

"You must be thirsty." He gestured toward the bottle on a tray at the edge of his desk. "Madeira?"

With a nod, she reached into her pocket and produced a small brown package tied with twine. "Madeira pairs nicely with chocolate."

Her smile warmed him all over. He reached for the wine and poured it into two glasses engraved with fruiting vines while she unwrapped her offering.

"Chocolate meringues," she told him, passing him a confection. "Though I've also brought some almonds, as I recall your fondness for those long ago."

He'd had no Shaw's chocolate since his return to the island, and these were like a siren's song. Only there was no ship's mast to tie himself to so he could stay on course. He was now in dire straits, his good intentions sinking as he came under her spell again.

He passed her a glass, the wine a rich brown not unlike the chocolate. "Are you attempting to bribe me, Miss Shaw?"

Laughter lit her eyes. So she did have some merriment left in her soul. "Guilty, Captain Lennox—unashamedly so."

He raised his glass in a toast. "To the newly appointed lightkeeper of Indigo Island."

Lips parted, she stared back at him, her glass suspended in midair. "Surely you do not jest."

"On my honor."

Their rims clinked, and then they each took a celebratory sip. Next he sampled the meringue, the sugary goodness melting on his tongue.

"With conditions," he amended, hating the harsh sound of it.

"Conditions?"

"The first is that you'll not be here alone. A maidservant must accompany you."

"I know just the one from the almshouse."

"You'll be relieved every six weeks by an assistant, giving you leave to return to the mainland for a few days."

"Fair enough." Her posture seemed to relax, and she sat back in her chair, wine glass in hand, meringue in her lap.

"You'll keep a detailed log to be given to me or to colonial authorities upon request."

She listened, looking thoughtful.

"Your wages will be a hundred fifty pounds a year, payable in silver ingots or pieces of eight. Your preference."

She merely nodded pleasantly.

"And you'll prepare yourself for the onslaught of gossip that will ensue once the mainland gets word you're ensconced as lightkeeper here by the man who was once your would-be husband."

Her eyes flared, not at the mention of gossip, he guessed, but his calling out their former intimacy.

"Not only that, but a man who is even now awaiting orders of a letter of marque and who will be your nearest neighbor till that happens."

She took a bite of meringue, which slowed her reply. "Let them say what they will. I care not."

"Spoken like an admiral's daughter." He savored his Madeira and this rare moment. The look on her face bespoke a sudden hesitation. Had he alarmed her with such plain speaking?

"You're not appointing me to the position because my father is admiral or—" She wavered, groping for the words he already knew hovered on her tongue.

"Because I feel guilt or some sort of indebtedness to you because of our former impasse?" At her pained nod, he removed all doubt. "Nay. Your father as admiral doesn't hurt your cause, but you are entirely capable of keeping the light, come what may. I have no qualms on that account."

"Nor do I," she replied, a new gleam in her eye, lifting her glass in another toast.

CHAPTER
thirty-three

Henri's firm nay removed any doubt Esmée had about why he was appointing her lightkeeper. Still, her suddenly shifting world made her a little light-headed, which had nothing to do with the wine and everything to do with his proximity and her new position.

She, the lady lightkeeper of Indigo Island.

She'd expected some naysaying. An outright refusal. As if to ground herself, she touched the tiny silver lighthouse on her chatelaine beneath the folds of her cloak.

"May I see my future quarters?" she asked when they'd finished their refreshments.

"Of course. Right this way."

Out they went, her spirit and step more buoyant than when she'd arrived. The path connecting his cottage to the light and her quarters had recently been scattered with shells. Their footsteps crunched as they walked it, a distance mercifully short.

Or brow-raisingly brief.

If the wags got wind of it . . . She shuttered the thought and followed him, eyes on his broad back until she laid eyes on her new home. *Home.* 'Twas not as she imagined it. 'Twas even better. Made of rubblestone and brick, the lighthouse shot into the sky some one hundred sixty feet high, its foundation staked into the ground with iron spikes. But 'twas the cottage that called to her. Quaint. Well-built. Its door and windows seemed almost in miniature, especially when the captain ducked beneath the lintel, his shoulders nearly touching the doorframe.

Once they were in the main room—the parlor—her gaze was everywhere at once. The cold hearth that begged for a warm fire vied for her attention, along with the simple furnishings that bespoke exotic ports. All was masculine and spare, something she would enjoy making her own. She'd put curtains at the windows and bring over a few of her treasured belongings to start.

"So, how does it strike you?" Henri stood back as she began to roam.

Withholding her answer, she passed into a bedchamber, its windows facing the sea. Would she hear its music night and day?

The kitchen was trim but adequate, with room enough for a small table and two chairs. Cooking vessels rested on the hearthstones. The room simply lacked a teapot and pretty porcelain cups. The larder was large, as befitting a home so far from a market. Supplies would need to be gotten, especially for the coming winter.

"At the risk of sounding too forward, I'm rather smitten," she finally said, garnering his smile.

They went outside, where the back of the cottage was level enough for a small garden. Next he took her into the light, up the twisting stair to the very top. The dizzying height and view stole her breath.

All around them rested lanterns waiting to be lit and a great many candles. Unkindled, the tower seemed a hollow place, a body without a soul. Echoing and awaiting its purpose. Henri was standing near her, one protective hand on her back as if the glass was not there at all and she was in danger of falling. She felt his hand through the thick folds of her cape. Warmth flooded her.

"Look, there's a sloop approaching." Her words were awed. She felt she looked down upon the open sea with the view of a gull.

The Atlantic seemed merry today, a brilliant blue, the wind making a lacy ruffle around the island's shores. She'd pray for days more fair than ill.

"Will the light withstand a hurricane?"

His reply was slow in coming. He placed a hand upon a beam. "Only the Almighty knows. But I had a Norfolk architect construct it like a ship for that very reason. The internal structure is of stalwart oak like a mast, the wood coated in oakum and pitch, much like a hull. The iron spikes you saw anchor the whole to the foundation."

"Since you've overseen it, I'll trust it in a storm."

The accolade hung in the tower's windless air. He looked down at her, making her feel small and awed and wonder if she was up to the task. If she'd ever wished she were a taller, stronger woman, 'twas now. His hand fell away, and he turned toward her, filling her view, his back against the glass.

"Esmée, tell me. Is this what you genuinely want?"

She looked up at him, missing the touch of his hand, wishing it at the small of her back again. Something burned in his eyes. A banked fire from of old? A familiar heat radiated between them. She felt it to her bones. He looked at her like he had before he'd kissed her that first time. Her own need sparked, making her place a hand on the front of his coat, not to push him away but to enfold the fine fabric in her fingers and draw him closer.

He leaned in, so intoxicatingly near she sighed. Her eyes closed as she awaited the brush of his lips.

"Captain Lennox, sir?" an unfamiliar voice said respectfully. "Surgeon Southack has need of ye at yer convenience."

Her hand fell away as Henri answered in a voice that echoed down the stairwell. "A half hour, then."

Intimacy gone, she started toward the steps, which seemed impossibly narrow and steep, more a hazard going down than up.

"Take my hand and let me go ahead of you," Henri told her.

She reached for him again, a rush of memories filling her. Once they'd held hands so often, it felt odd when they didn't. If his gloves had been off, she could have felt the strength of his fingers again, skin to skin, and the jagged scar along the thumb where a sword had once slashed him. She'd not asked him about the scar on his brow. Would she ever know its cause?

They took their time coming down lest she misstep and returned to the sunlit air. Jago and his oarsman were nowhere to be seen. Had they sought out the Flask and Sword to slake their thirst? The sun bespoke the afternoon, just ahead of her usual two o'clock dinner hour. The bit of wine and chocolate they'd shared still lingered on her tongue.

Henri gestured to a plot of leveled ground. "A fog cannon will be installed within a fortnight. But you won't have to fire it. One of my crew has been assigned that task."

They stood near the pier, the jolly bobbing in the water, the lighthouse at their backs. A comfortable silence ensued, rife with emotion.

She stifled the thornlike worry that reared its ugly head. *I know you are soon to sail under a letter of marque for the colonial government.* She wanted nothing to intrude on this day, this moment. This *peace.* Did he feel it too?

Curiosity got the better of her. "How do you come by your meals? I see no cook or housekeeper."

"Most of the time I take a long walk west to the Flask and Sword, where the *Relentless*'s cook has command of Mistress Saltonstall's kitchen."

"So you eat with your crew."

"Aye. And then I walk the beach home again. The sunsets are spectacular."

She looked west toward York, a thin line of green on the horizon. "I shall look forward to the sunrises too."

He studied her with an openness that told her they'd overcome some barrier, moved past the unease that had held them captive since his return. "I'll collect you by pinnace Saturday next in York's harbor. Bring anything you wish to make yourself at home here. And if you should change your mind—"

"I shan't."

Jago and the oarsman appeared as if materializing in thin air. "Ready to depart, Miss Shaw?"

She wasn't at all ready, but what choice did she have? If she had her druthers, the wind and the waves would keep her here. But the water was only slightly more ruffled now than when they'd left, a reminder of the hurdles to come. Telling friends and family. Fending off gossips.

She took a last look at the light and cottage with a keen yearning as Henri handed her into the boat. Raising the hood of her cape, she cast a look at him.

He stood unsmiling, looking thoughtful, making her wonder what he was pondering.

Lord willing, he'd still be here by Saturday next. She couldn't imagine the island without him.

CHAPTER *thirty-four*

"You're *what*?" Eliza stared at Esmée as if she'd sprouted horns in their very parlor.

"I'm to be the new lightkeeper for Indigo Island," Esmée repeated, marveling at the calm that accompanied the decision, only slightly bestirred by her sister's disquiet.

"A female lightkeeper? All your novel reading is giving you fancies! I can't imagine it!"

"'Tis no different than any female tradeswoman," Esmée replied, taking a seat on the sofa. "We've female printers, bookbinders, blacksmiths. Even an apothecary."

"But my confinement—I—you won't be here for the baby's birth!"

"I'm hardly a midwife or nursemaid," Esmée said in soothing tones. "And every six weeks or so I'm to have shore leave."

"You know your sister is not one for society." Quinn took a seat beside his wife, stroking her hand as it rested on the sofa. "Nor is she at your beck and call."

A tear slid down Eliza's plump cheek. "But . . ."

"I'm rather proud." Father stood by the crackling hearth, arms crossed. "The admiral's daughter has achieved something I never thought or expected."

"'Tis partly Captain Lennox's doing," Esmée told them, passing Eliza a handkerchief. "He has had several interested parties, all men. I wasn't sure he'd take me seriously."

"He considers you because he's still in love with you," Eliza said with conviction. "I witnessed it in my own parlor but a month ago."

The men chuckled as Esmée shook her head. "'Tis not what it seems—"

"Oh? 'Tis what all Virginia will think!"

"Let the naysayers spew what they will," their father put in. "My daughter and Captain Lennox are above reproach."

Eliza managed a short, tearstained laugh. "You do have a bold bone after all, Sister, if a tad belated, running off with the captain this way."

Esmée sighed. "We are not—"

"What of the almshouse and your charitable endeavors?" Quinn interrupted gently, still smiling. "You will be missed."

"The almshouse has had a windfall of late." Esmée still longed to unravel that mystery. "An anonymous benefactor has given so generously, 'twill carry them through the winter and far beyond."

"And the chocolate shop?" Quinn queried.

Father cleared his throat. "I've just purchased a hand-operated machine from Boston. 'Tis time Esmée was relieved of her duties there."

Esmée warmed at her father's words, for she'd been unsure of his reaction. Eliza still looked sullen, her usual high spirits dampened by sleepless nights and indigestion. Even now she winced, moving a hand as if to counter an uncomfortable kick.

She continued to pout. "When does your island sojourn begin?"

Four more days. Each stroke of the clock brought Henri nearer. "Captain Lennox is coming this Saturday to collect me and my things."

Eliza persisted. "Why don't you two just elope? 'Tis what it amounts to, does it not?"

"Employment is not the same as elopement." Father sent a stern look Eliza's way. "Some felicitations are due your sister, are they not?

She has served all of us well, even caring for your mother till she passed, and is late to living a life of her own."

"I gather this is a resounding nay to Nathaniel Autrey's pursuit." Quinn's voice was absent of any censure. "I've just learned that lately he has been in the company of my cousin Elinor from Norfolk."

"Elinor?" Eliza's vexation vanished as surprise rushed in. "Why, she's homely enough to stop a clock. What on earth does he see in her?"

"Pretty is as pretty does, as Mama oft said," Esmée reminded her. "I've met Elinor, and she's lovely."

"Pish! Nor does she have any dowry I know of."

"Chaplain Autrey has little need of it, given he might inherit Mount Autrey one day." Quinn gave a small, knowing smile, which left Eliza eyeing him curiously.

"I wish Chaplain Autrey all my best." Esmée felt relief just saying it. "And his bride-to-be, whomever she is."

Quinn took a cup of punch the maid brought round while Eliza turned up her nose at a cup of chamomile tea before accepting it. "Will Captain Lennox replace him, do you think?" she asked.

"Likely, if he can find a man willing to serve on a ship of the line in dangerous waters." Father downed the last of his punch. "Not many would."

Weary of any ominous talk, Esmée steered the conversation in a safer direction. "You should see the cottage I'm to occupy. 'Tis like something from a fairy tale. There's even room for a small garden come spring."

Father held out his cup as the punch was replenished. "I'll visit you as often as I can. I've seen the lighthouse plans but not the finished structure."

"What of a maidservant?" Eliza asked between sips of tea.

"'Tis one of the captain's conditions." Esmée pondered the miss she had in mind. "I've already sought permission from the almshouse and the girl in question. Lucy Barlow is willing to accompany me. She's skilled in needlework and housework, including cookery. There's even a cozy room for her off the kitchen."

"I'm relieved," Eliza exclaimed. "'Twould not do to be the only woman on an island of men, even if they are under Captain Lennox's command."

"The island will soon be absent of all but a trusted guard." Father moved closer to the fire since the room's corners were cold, chilling Esmée with his words as well. "And Mistress Saltonstall shall return in spring."

"I do wonder," Quinn remarked, looking to Esmée, "if you won't tire of the isolation in time, having become used to town, with an ability to roam at will. The island is not unlike being shipbound, one would think."

"I hadn't thought of that," Esmée told him. "But time will tell."

"Promise you'll visit me once you return to shore." Eliza set her unfinished tea aside. "I simply must be the first to hear all about it."

"Of course I shall," Esmée reassured her. Eliza was not usually so cross. "Perhaps you'll even set foot on the island one day."

Eliza rolled her eyes, though a wry smile played at the corners of her mouth. "Another one of your fancies, Sister. I give you a fortnight before you're missing us and wanting to forsake your island duties."

CHAPTER thirty-five

Esmée turned the spyglass on York's harbor from the anonymity of her father's study, where she'd been waiting for the last quarter of an hour. A small crowd gathered at the landing just below Shaw's Chocolate. The *Relentless*'s pinnace had just docked amid the many frigates and merchantmen and sloops already at anchor—a cardinal among crows, from the attention it garnered. With its ornately decorated sterncastle and three masts, not to mention half a dozen crew, it looked dashing and fit for anything, if only to carry a chocolatier turned lightkeeper to a near island.

Her heart skipped as she watched Henri step onto the pier, his cape furling and unfurling like a sail in the November wind. A few jacks remained on the boat save two lads who accompanied him onto Water Street and up the hill to the Shaw residence. Breathless, she rushed to her bedchamber—her soon-to-be-former bedchamber—and readied to leave as Mrs. Mabrey greeted the captain in the hall below.

Soon three trunks, a chair and tea table, and several other items were loaded onto a waiting wagon. Esmée walked behind as the conveyance rumbled back down to the waterfront, glad to stretch her legs after two days of packing. Kitty was on hand, the two of them giddy as schoolgirls, for the day was clement and spirits were high. As the captain bowed from the waist when he greeted her again, Kitty blushed to the roots of her fair hair.

"So gallant," Kitty whispered to Esmée when his back was turned. "For a widow of one and thirty, even I feel a bit smitten."

Smiling, Esmée linked arms with her. "I shall miss you and your tea garden. But when I come ashore, we shall celebrate."

"And I shall come to the island in turn, spend the night at your cozy cottage, climb to the top of the light, and take in the princely view."

They chattered so exuberantly Henri turned around and smiled at them as they neared the water. Father was on hand, coming out of the coffeehouse to bid them farewell. His appearance caught the attention of one too many wags about town. Soon the papers would buzz with the news of Esmée Shaw leaving York.

Lucy arrived, brought from the almshouse by Jago Wherry in a pony cart. Her few belongings were in a small bag, a kitten included. For every new home needed a cat, did it not?

Esmée greeted Lucy, praying the both of them wouldn't be seasick, as the wind was brisk. Dressed in a plain striped cotton gown with a darker petticoat, a clean apron about her waist, and a bonnet framing her face, Lucy looked expectant and a tad fearful. Scuffed shoes and white-thread stockings were on her small feet. The humiliating mark of the almshouse was missing from her garments. But had she no cloak? Before Esmée could reach for the clasp of her own cape to give her, the captain removed his and draped it about the maid's shivering shoulders. Esmée smiled her thanks, touched by the small courtesy.

"'Tis colder on the open water than here in the harbor," he said, returning her gaze as he helped her into the pinnace.

Warmed by his touch, Esmée watched as Lucy smiled up at him, a bit wide-eyed at the gathering crowd. Seated in the vessel, Esmée steeled herself against the late autumn wind, her excitement building with every second.

"How long will it take, Miss Shaw?" Lucy asked beside her, her kitten in her lap.

"With those sails unfurled and the captain at the helm, no time at all."

Esmée let out a breath as the mooring lines were loosed. Jacks she'd never seen worked around her, the captain standing tall. The boat took to the open water, leaving her a bit winded as they gained speed. Every ripple seemed to roll through her in turn, not sickening but exhilarating. A far different ride than the slow-as-molasses row in the jolly. She looked out on the York River as they sailed into Chesapeake Bay, which winked sapphire blue in the sun. Beyond it lay a mound of land bitten by autumn's first frosts.

His island and now hers.

CHAPTER
thirty-six

The cottage was better than she'd left it. Pushing open the door, Lucy on her heels, Esmée could hardly contain her delight. A second Windsor chair had been placed near the hearth in the front parlor, the fire crackling merrily in welcome. Striped curtains were at the windows, making the cloth she'd brought unnecessary.

"My sailmakers have had a heyday outfitting your windows and your maid's bedding," Henri told her.

"You have a very able crew." Esmée went to a window, marveling at how well-stitched the curtains were. "Please thank them for me."

He supervised the men moving their belongings while she and Lucy wended their way through the cottage, exclaiming over this or that. A vase of dried flowers adorned the kitchen table. And not only flowers but a crusty loaf of bread and a small pot of salted butter. Thyme and roast chicken teased their senses, enticing Lucy to lift the lid off a pot in the embers.

"Jacques—the *Relentless*'s cook—prepared your supper." Henri stood in the kitchen doorway, answering the question Esmée wanted to ask.

Smiling, she turned toward him. "A warm welcome indeed. Won't you join us?"

He hesitated, his lips parting as if he was considering, then curving in an apologetic half-smile. "Another eve, mayhap. Tonight I'll leave you to get your bearings."

She nodded, pulled in a dozen different directions at once. Lucy was already in her room off the kitchen while the crew brought in the last of Esmée's trunks and furnishings, inquiring as to where she'd like them. When she looked up again, Henri had disappeared. But how far could he go with his quarters a stone's throw from her own?

By nightfall, they'd settled in and stripped Jacques's delicious chicken to the bone. Saving half a loaf of the bread for their morning tea, Esmée invited Lucy to sit by the fire in the small parlor. Taking out her sewing, Lucy stitched a handkerchief while Esmée read aloud from *Robinson Crusoe*, the kitten, Tibby, curled up at their feet.

> "By this time it blew a terrible storm; indeed, and now I began to see terror and amazement in the faces of the seamen themselves. The master, though vigilant in the business of preserving the ship, yet as he went in and out of his cabin by me, I could hear him softly to himself say, several times, 'Lord be merciful to us! We shall all be lost! We shall all be undone!'"

Lucy's hands stilled, her needle midair. A moody wind began to blow about the cottage, adding to the moment's intensity. "D'ye think, mistress, that Captain Lennox would be so afraid of a storm?" she asked.

"Afraid of the storm, perhaps, but hopefully confident in the storm's Maker who can still the waves and even walk on them."

Lucy's capped head bobbed in vigor. "When ye asked me if I wanted to come to the island, I was a bit afraid, though it be a good deal better than the almshouse. But what if a rogue wave comes over us and sweeps us out to sea?"

"You must take care not to go out in foul weather. You and Tibby shall stay secure right here by the fire, at least for this winter, while I tend to the light and pray for safety."

"Yer as brave as the captain, mistress. To think ye must climb all those tower stairs no matter the weather!"

Esmée smiled, setting the book aside. "'Tis for the good of many, all those brave sailors who seek a safe harbor."

"Including the captain, aye." Tibby pressed against Lucy's skirts, and Lucy reached down a hand to stroke its caramel-streaked back. "Ye'll light his way back when he goes to sea again?"

The bittersweet thought intruded on Esmée's quiet joy. "I should hope so. And pray for his return."

"I'd best hie to bed and say my prayers so I can wake early and make our tea and toast." Yawning, Lucy scooped Tibby up and excused herself. "I shan't forget Mrs. Mabrey's peach preserves."

"A delightful breakfast awaits us."

At the close of her door, Esmée went to the window. With the tower unlit till tomorrow, the darkness was profound save the square of yellow gleaming from the captain's own cottage. Though she couldn't see it, she could hear the surf beating against the beach and the moan of the wind that drove it there. Yet she'd never felt so secure. So . . . serene.

Was God's leading not the way of peace? She sought the hearth again, already at home in her chair, thankful for all the little things Henri had superintended for her comfort. Or was she making it more significant than it actually was? He would, in truth, have done the same for any keeper, would he not? She settled back in her chair and tried not to think of his leaving. She mustn't let her present happiness and the blessing God had given her depend on the captain and his future.

CHAPTER *thirty-seven*

The following day Henri pulled on his boots, the gray day beyond his cottage like a woolen blanket, in direct contrast to his sunny mood. The island smelled clean, as it always did after a windy lashing—of wet rocks and sodden sand and foamy treasures pushed ashore from the deep.

His first thought on awakening had been Esmée. Mayhap her last thought had been of him. He'd seen her at her parlor window around nine o'clock when he'd returned from his usual rounds before retiring. He nearly couldn't sleep. Thank heaven she wasn't on the other end of the island, miles distant. He chuckled. Thank heaven Hermes and crew were.

He stood and exchanged last night's rain gear for a woolen coat, his red Monmouth cap for a tan cocked hat. Used to being alone on his own stretch of beach, especially in the morning, he left the cottage to a pleasant surprise. Esmée was walking away from him as the tide went out, her purple cape aflutter. Every now and then she bent over to pick something up and examine it. Just like her shelling that day they'd first met.

He headed toward her, coming up from behind slowly so as not to startle her. "Good morning, Miss Shaw."

"A fine day to you, Captain."

He wanted to say *Esmée*, but a new formality had crept in with her position. It weighed on him, but he let it pass. "What have you there?"

She held out something blue and jagged. She'd said on her arrival she was hoping for a pearl.

"Sea glass." He took the piece and held it up to the light, its green tint visible. "Likely from a bottle of spirits. Pearls suit you better."

She smiled at him, her upswept hair pillowing a bit loosely about her face, two long curls over her shoulder. "I'll keep looking."

Farther down the beach he heard laughter. Cyprian was on hand, entertaining the maidservant, who had an egg basket on one arm. No doubt he'd visited the hens roosting at the Flask and Sword as a way of introduction. Clever, that.

"Tell me your maidservant's story," he said, falling into step beside her.

Esmée kept her eyes on the sand. "Lucy is but eighteen, orphaned after her parents died of fever. She was at the almshouse long enough to take a dislike to it. Being skilled with a needle, she was on her way to being bound out to a mantuamaker. When I gave her the choice to come with me, she readily assented. But I do wonder about keeping her isolated here long."

"At the moment she seems happy enough."

Laughter erupted again, Lucy's mingled with Cyprian's.

"Is that a monkey I spy on the shoulder of your cabin boy?" Esmée asked. "The renowned Hermes, I take it."

He chuckled. "You've yet to be formally introduced. Cyprian is my steward and has charge of Hermes for the time being."

"I've never seen a better dressed youth."

"Once he laid eyes on fair Lucy, he must have decided to bedeck himself in the finest garments to be had from the common chest."

"Ah, the slops chest, Father called it. Plunder."

"Aye, from seized enemy vessels."

The lad did look a tad ludicrous, having traded his humble working trousers and shirt of yesterday for ruffles and silk. But Lucy seemed to be enjoying the attention, and Henri would rather they be here than in the alleys and gin shops ashore.

"Tell me his story." Esmée looked at him, another wisp of hair tumbling down. With a gloved hand she looped it behind her ear, jarring the bonnet that matched her gown.

He was having a devil of a time trying to stay his hand and not right it for her, staunching his urge to throw her hat to the wind, take out all the pins, and tumble her hair further. "Cyprian is Portuguese. I found him begging at the port of Lisbon. He's served aboard the *Relentless* for several years and is well into manhood, though he looks younger."

"They've known such hardship already." Esmée's expression turned pensive. "Their laughter does me good. Let them have their amusement while they may."

They walked on in silence for a time, pausing now and again to examine something interesting on the beach. When he gave a little bow and held out another piece of sea glass, she curtsied prettily in return, making them both laugh.

"'Tis the blue of your gown," he remarked. "The one you wore when we first met."

She looked at him, near disbelief in her eyes. "I still have it but haven't worn it since—"

Since you left.

He'd tried to pin that blue down a thousand times in the last decade. Caribbean blue. Delft blue. Egyptian blue. Marine blue, the official color of British naval uniforms. Cobalt blue.

Lapis lazuli. Aye, that was it.

She squinted into the sunlight, and he looked to the sea and then the lighthouse when she said, "So shall we kindle the light tonight, you and I?"

How romantic she made it sound. A joint effort. The first of many, he hoped. "Aye, I want you to shadow me for a sennight or so, till we know the ins and outs of the tower and its workings and you're comfortable enough to handle it on your own."

"Will you be here a sennight more?" The shadow he'd found in her face when he'd seen her at Lady Lightfoot's ball returned, eclipsing her loveliness.

"I know not." How he wanted to throw any future cruise to the wind and remain right here. Even now he sensed there was more to her arrival than keeping the light. His appointing her as lightkeeper had been far from objective.

Would it all play out like it had years before when they'd first parted?

He sent his concerns heavenward, the sunlit moment weighed down by dark thoughts.

"Then we shall make the most of the time given us." Her smile was soft, a bit sad. It tore at him in a way little else did.

Gone was the spirited girl who had objected so strenuously to his going to sea. He hardly knew what to do with the composed woman in her place.

She took his extended hand, and he helped her over a rocky outcropping. "Is it true you forbid married men from joining your crew?"

He gave a nod. "Mostly out of respect to you."

Her green gaze came back to him. Tears stood in her eyes. His own throat closed and threatened to choke him.

At last he said, "I took to heart all you said back then—the toll on your family with your father away, your mother especially."

She leaned down and picked up a cracked shell. "I wish I'd known. It might have softened my regard of you."

He took a breath and revealed the rest. "I had a small chest of letters I wrote you but never sent."

The shell was discarded. "Do you have them still?"

His aye earned such a bittersweet look it sank his stomach to his boots.

"Might you give them to me after all?"

Would he? "The heartsick ponderings of a sailor?" He'd nearly thrown the chest overboard on more than one melancholy occasion. "Mayhap when I sail again."

"Please." The entreaty in her voice decided the matter.

"Do you forgive me for leaving?" He looked toward the line of smoke that marked the Flask and Sword's chimney. "For forsaking what we had?"

A gull swooped in, shattering the air with its cry.

"Only if you'll forgive me for making it an all-or-nothing arrangement." The mist in her eyes returned. "That was unconscionable."

"We were young. Foolish."

"And now?" Pensiveness limned her words. "We are . . ."

"Older. Wiser." He said the last word with a shake of his head. "Friends."

"Friends." Her echo came soft, a bit disappointed, he thought.

Hope took hold. "Unless you want to be otherwise."

She halted then and looked up at him, her sandy fingers full of beach treasures. "I scarcely know how to start over, if that's what you mean."

His heart began to pound. A deluge of emotion akin to a tropical monsoon swirled inside him. Never did he imagine this turn of events—having her here beside him, removing the distance between them in one stunning move. And now looking as if they might reconcile, fall in love again.

If they'd ever stopped loving each other to begin with.

"I want what you want, Henri." She began walking again, her full skirts dragging on the wet sand. "Maybe 'tis a bit like dancing," she said, a beguiling light in her eye. "I shall simply follow your lead."

He caught up to her, wanting to take her hand again yet wanting to be careful with her. Not wreck the both of them like before. How did one let go of the past and risk love again?

CHAPTER *thirty-eight*

The next day Henri sat with his officers at a tavern table, the rest of the crew spread out across the taproom. The Flask and Sword had never looked better, the floors mopped, every stick of furniture shiny as a newly minted shilling. Even Hermes looked content perched on a window ledge, eating pecans and occasionally emitting a shrill screech. Henri smiled his amusement, wishing Mistress Saltonstall back, if only to have another woman on the island. In the meantime, if there was a cruise, half a dozen of his men who were injured and ailing would remain behind, the penalty being caretakers of a cantankerous marmoset.

He finished his ale and set down his tankard, careful to avoid the letter of marque and reprisal lying atop the table. It had been delivered that afternoon by a courier of Virginia's governor in the name of the king, and Henri had just read it aloud. Their future mission sounded simple but was infinitely complex.

George the Second, by the grace of God, King of England, Scotland, and Ireland, defender of the faith, &c. To Captain Henri Lennox, commander of eighty men and mounting thirty carriage guns. You may, by force of arms, attack, subdue, and take all ships and other vessels belonging to the inhabitants of France, on the high seas, or between high-water and low-water marks . . .

His crew's conversation had risen around him like a headwind ever since.

"We're fully outfitted and ready to sail at a moment's notice."

"Lest fortune frown upon us, I shall place a silver coin beneath the main mast when we weigh anchor."

"Superstitions don't become you. Coin be hanged. I saw you on your knees petitioning Providence at the last violent squall."

"A misfortune the French often fly false flags, hoping to avoid capture."

Hermes screeched at Cyprian's late entry, then ran to the lad, who hoisted him on his shoulder. Laughter rumbled through the watching men while Henri looked out a near window at the sunset.

"How many other privateers are operating under letters of marque, Captain?" Tarbonde asked from across the table.

Henri came to attention. "New York leads the colonies in sending twenty-six privateers bearing three hundred fifty guns and nearly three thousand men. Virginia is second in force."

A pronounced hush ensued as the gravity of their mission took hold.

Henri stood, bringing the din across the room to a slow halt. "I need to tend the light."

Chuckling and elbowing greeted his announcement. "Don't you have a lady lightkeeper for that, Captain?" Southack dared to ask.

With a wink, Henri settled his cocked hat on his head. "A lady lightkeeper in training."

"No matter who tends it, 'tis most welcome," Cyprian said as Hermes scrambled to his opposite shoulder. "Far better than the hilltop fires of old."

Henri went out, glad for fresh air and quiet. His walk was an enviable one, energizing him after the tobacco smoke and chatter of the tavern. The beach lay in winsome white curves all the way to his end of the island, easily navigated by moonlight. He was beginning to look forward to the hour when darkness descended. Once a trial to him, lonesome and full of memories, it now marked the time he could see Esmée.

By now she'd have finished her supper and was likely seated by the fire with Lucy. Esmée had mentioned knitting him stockings, even a hat and gloves—simple, practical things that a man had need of. He considered getting sheep so she'd have a supply of wool at hand, but that was in the distant future.

He rapped at the door, and it opened. Lucy gave him an unnecessary curtsy and excused herself, retreating to the kitchen. Esmée's eyes shone with quiet delight, another step away from the guarded woman she'd become.

"Good evening." He removed his hat as she rose from her seat.

"A good evening indeed." She gestured to the chair Lucy had vacated. "Won't you sit for a moment and warm up? 'Tis not quite dusk."

He did so, noticing all the little things she'd done to make the cottage hers. Over the hearth hung a landscape painting of a garden in bloom, while a smaller painting of her father's last ship rested on the mantel.

He leaned in to get a closer look. "A remarkable likeness of the *Indefatigable*."

"Mama painted it for him shortly before she died. 'Twas the great love of his life after her."

He added another log to the fire, thinking how cozy the cottage was compared to his own quarters. "Your mother was very gifted. And I'm sure very missed."

"Always." She returned to her knitting, her movements smooth and sure. "The oil landscape was in my York bedchamber. I've a fondness for gardens. Cook has a kitchen garden at our townhouse, but I've always dreamed of flowers. This painting gave me a little of what I lacked."

"In summer you'll find rose mallow, goldenrod, and wildflowers on the island."

"I've in mind roses, lavender, and larkspur. Even my favorite, sweet peas—the new variety of painted lady in particular. They symbolize goodbye, adieu, bon voyage."

"Don't remind me," he replied.

She eyed him in surprise, needles stilling.

"I'd rather remain and build you a wall to enclose your garden. Protect it from the wind."

"I can't imagine you doing something so small. Not when you've seen the gardens of Versailles and the Alhambra."

"Mayhap it's because I've seen them that my true north is now home."

"And is Indigo Island your home? Can you be content to live on an island so small?"

"My life has already been enlarged by your coming here, Esmée."

"You flatter me." Her needles picked up again, faster than before. "'Tis been but two days."

"The best days I've spent." Reaching out, he took her nearest hand, the yarn falling to her aproned lap. "I have no desire to sail."

"But has it not been decided?" She clutched his hand, her eyes sharp with intensity.

"I've a letter of marque and reprisal, aye." He continued to hold her hand and her gaze. "We could sail at any time now. We merely await word from Williamsburg."

And what a cruise it would be. An all-out battle. The potential loss of his ship, his crew, his life. He couldn't recount the close calls he'd had previously, both aboard ship and in foreign ports. Then, he hadn't half reckoned with the danger, but now . . .

"Imminent, then." She looked to the fire as it sputtered and hissed. "When once I had you not at all, even a little of you now is heaven-sent. Every second."

"Now you flatter me." His smile summoned her own. "But in truth, I feel the same."

They sat in sweet silence save for her knitting till a clock with a musical chime struck six. She was the first out of her chair, gathering her cloak and gloves. He held the door open, and they went out into moonlight and silence.

What he wanted was to gather her in his arms.

CHAPTER
thirty-nine

Esmée was far more aware of Henri than the task at hand. Up the steep stairs they went, his lantern throwing low light in the tower. The first time she'd climbed she'd been slightly winded, but now she hardly noticed. At the top she watched as he hung the lantern from a hook near the giant compass lamp, which held twenty-four lights.

"I've received confirmation our light can be seen by telescope from three leagues away."

Our light. How sweet the sound. They began to kindle each candle, and the tower was soon ablaze. When Henri was away, she'd have charge of them all. Red leather fire buckets filled with sand and water were at floor level. A tinderbox and brass candlesnuffer lay in a tray near at hand, a second lantern alongside it. Plenty of light to read by if the tower wasn't so cold. In summer she might bring a book.

Once the candles were illuminated, they stood by the glass facing the Atlantic. This was their ambition realized, a lighthouse for treacherous shoals and shifting sandbars, a warning of the infamous middle ground that marked Chesapeake Bay. No telling how many ships and lives had been lost there, casting crew and cargo into the deep.

And now she had a small part in it all.

Down the steps they went. She fully expected him to open the door at the tower's bottom as he usually did, lantern held high in the other hand. But instead he set the light on the floor, illuminating her yellow quilted petticoat and his dark breeches and boots, casting the rest of them in shadows.

"Esmée."

Her name, so tenderly spoken, sent a tremor through her, as did his sudden nearness a handbreadth away. She leaned into him, her knees a bit weak, her breath short.

He placed his hand on hers, holding it against his cheek. "I never stopped loving you, Esmée. No matter how far I sailed nor how many years passed, there's been none but you."

His words came slow and earnest, further mending the hurt the past had wrought. Her throat tightened, tears close. What could she say to this? She had no words. Only a tempest of fine feeling, joy foremost. Standing on tiptoe, she shut her eyes and pressed her lips to his. Their kiss was known yet different. Richer and sweeter than ever before. His arms went around her immediately, stronger than she remembered yet just as tender.

"*Ma belle.*" The old endearment hadn't lost its luster. His lips brushed her cheek and then her hair, his breath a tickle against her ear. "Was it you who gave me the riding crop?"

"I confess." Another kiss, long and lingering. Breathless, she rested her head against his chest. "And was it you who gave me the confectionary book?"

"Guilty."

"And 'twas you who blessed the almshouse so abundantly."

"I knew there was a need." He stroked her hair. "I knew it was important to you. And so it became important to me."

She looked up at him again. "Your doing so made it easier for me to come here, not worrying about their lack in another lean winter season."

"If you are as good a lightkeeper as an almshouse patron, of which I have no doubt, then Virginia is blessed indeed."

"Alas, you, Captain Lennox, are a terrible distraction."

His low laugh held a hint of mischief. "Who knew lighthouses were made for liaisons like this, Miss Shaw?"

He kissed her again, stealing her breath once more, his arms about her so warm and enveloping she forgot the cold stone and plummeting temperatures around them.

"I want this night to never end." His bristled cheek rested against her smooth one. His heartfelt words echoed her own unspoken thoughts. "Marry me, Esmée."

The words she'd heard years before now seemed doubly knee-bending as she grasped the enormity of the question. "When, Henri?"

"Upon my return. A few months, Lord willing."

"Then I shall, without question."

"All that matters to me is you will soon be mine at last. Esmée Shaw Lennox."

The wonderment of it stilled her tongue. Could it be? She'd come to the island with small hopes of being the lightkeeper or residing on the island at all. And now this . . .

"We'll redeem those lost years, you and I." His voice held a promise and the solemnity of a spoken vow. "Our future is finally at hand."

CHAPTER *forty*

Esmée slowly awoke, her new bed not quite familiar with the sun slanting down through an equally unfamiliar window. She'd slept late, Henri having kept the last watch of the light. Tonight she would spell him in turn, but for now she lay beneath the counterpane and closed her eyes again, reliving those minutes in the tower when their shared passion spurred such sudden, unexpected declarations. It seemed naught but a vivid dream.

His lips against hers, trailing the curve of her neck . . . Burying his face in her hair. *Marry me, Esmée.* They'd stayed in the tower a long time, neither of them wanting to part. And even after that she'd lain awake, the feel and scent of him lingering.

Nay, she'd not dreamed it.

Pushing the covers back, she swung bare feet to the floor. Beneath the closed door came the beckoning scents of coffee and breakfast as Lucy clattered about the kitchen. From the parlor chimed the mantel clock. The fire in her bedchamber hearth gleamed red with a few sooty ashes that needed replenishing. All in good time.

Positioning her stays over her shift, she tied the front laces and dressed in layers as befitted the cold, then donned a woolen petticoat.

She unraveled the braid from her hair and began to pin it up, the small mirror over the dresser capturing her joyous expression instead of her usual pensive one.

Lucy's voice pushed past the door after a timid knock. "Mistress, will ye breakfast soon?"

"Coming," Esmée replied, pulling a shawl about her shoulders and pinning it in place with a crystal brooch.

The warmth of the kitchen was like an embrace, the hearth's robust fire making the teakettle sing. At the table were bowls of steaming porridge and a small pot of cream, bread and butter, and peach preserves.

"Good morning, Lucy." Esmée sat down, glad she'd brought over some of Mama's beloved porcelain china.

"And a beautiful morn it is." The maid sat down across from Esmée and poured them tea.

Stifling a yawn, Esmée took in the red-checkered gingham tablecloth spread with care and the shell centerpiece, her stomach rumbling. "I overslept without meaning to."

"Ye look refreshed. Sweet dreams, mayhap?"

"Aye, very sweet." She took a breath. "You shall be the first to know . . . Captain Lennox and I are to wed."

Lucy's mouth popped open, her eyes round as saucers. "When, mistress?"

"As soon as he returns from his next cruise."

"Oh, glad news indeed! Shall ye marry here on the island? The beach perhaps, or the deck of his ship?"

Esmée reached for the preserves, delighted by all the possibilities. "I haven't given it much thought."

Joy seemed to sit at the table with them, the sunshine a benevolent guest as it streamed across the table, illuminating gilt-edged cups and saucers. Unhindered by clouds, the sky beyond the kitchen window was as blue as the ocean below it.

"And yer gown, Miss Shaw?"

Esmée pondered it. She'd brought mostly serviceable garments, leaving all but two of her most costly gowns behind. "Perhaps the Spitalfields silk with the matching shoes I brought. And pearls."

"And yer bouquet?" Lucy, obviously schooled to weddings despite her humble station, looked perplexed.

"Seagrass and shells, perhaps?"

They laughed, trying to take the unexpected in.

"Ye'll need a bride's cake and a groom's cake. I'm guessing that French chef of the captain's could concoct something special."

"I should hope." Esmée sipped her tea, sure it was more likely Cyprian who drew Lucy than cake. "For now we'll keep the news between us two. Anticipate a special occasion."

Lucy's eyes shone with delight in a way they'd never done at the almshouse. "A frolic is most welcome, especially on the heels of a wedding."

An island wedding as opposed to one at Grace Church or the Shaws' formal parlor. Eliza might never forgive her, but Father would understand. A memorable wedding it would be with a crew of sailors as guests, perhaps even Hermes.

"We've much to look forward to. Glad I am to have such a capable young woman by my side to help me," Esmée said with gratitude, and Lucy flushed.

Breakfast done, Lucy set off to get milk from the Flask and Sword's lone cow while Esmée betook herself to the captain's cottage, comfortably close to her own. The shutters weren't closed, nor was the door locked.

Was Henri asleep?

She pushed open the cottage door, and there she found her beloved in a chair by the hearth. Even at rest he emanated an immense vitality she found irresistible. His hair was unkempt as if he'd run his hands through it, his still form draped by a woolen blanket.

She shut the door soundlessly and tiptoed to him, her heart on tiptoe as well.

CHAPTER *forty-one*

A trace of perfumed soap brought Henri to his senses. Lavender? Nay, rose. *Esmée.* Her very essence. His limbs were heavy, his eyes closed. Fragments of their time in the tower washed over him like storm-tossed flotsam.

Was he dreaming again?

When warm lips met his own, he came fully awake. His bride-to-be knelt in front of him, blue skirts swirling around her in a frothy mass not unlike a wave.

Her voice held a teasing lilt he'd not heard in . . . years. "I wanted to ask if you'd repented of your bold question last night in the tower."

He chuckled. This was the Esmée of old shining through, the one he'd missed so desperately. "I have not nor will I ever, especially with a greeting such as that."

He leaned forward, holding her face between his hands. She looked as lovely as he was disheveled. But her gaze told him she liked his roguish, rumpled appearance. Drawing back, he reached into his pocket. Taking her left hand in his, he slowly slipped the jewelry on her finger. "I meant to give you this last night. But now seems a better time."

His mind flashed to Williamsburg as she said, "Did you see me gazing at posy rings on the street that day we met in Carter's store?"

"Nay." He brought her hand to his lips and kissed it.

Noticeably moved, she removed the ring, peering at the inscription within. "'In Christ and thee my comfort be.'" She stared down at it, a glitter of gold flowers and vines encircling her finger once she put it on again. "I've never seen one so beautiful, the words so fitting."

"Not too small nor too large?"

"'Tis perfect."

"Even after ten years," he murmured, relieved.

Her lashes lifted, her gaze beseeching. "You've had it all this time?"

He nodded. "It seems Providence was intent on being my comfort before I could have you as my bride."

"Oh, Henri . . ." Emotion made her voice tremble. "Had you brought it with you that terrible day? When we quarreled in the townhouse parlor and then parted?"

The memory had finally lost its barb if not its regret. "I returned to the ship and put it away in the trunk that would hold the letters I wrote you."

A single tear wet her cheek. She dashed it away with the back of her hand before he could reach for a handkerchief. "Which you'll give me on your leaving."

"If you still want them."

"Want them?" She took his hands in hers and squeezed. "They'll be my stay till you return. That and this." She looked to the ring again, more touched than he'd anticipated.

Despite her brave words, he saw sadness in her eyes—the dread of their future parting. He took her in his arms where she knelt, her head resting in the hollow of his shoulder. "If God has brought us this far, we've no fear of the future, Esmée."

They grew quiet, the companionable silence dear if emotionally laden. How would their lives have been different had they wed long ago?

"I cannot wait." She pulled away from him and stood, smoothing her skirts and the comely apron that cinched her waist. "For now I'll practice being your wife."

He looked on, amused, as she added wood to the fire and stoked it into a snapping, popping crimson. Next she took the blanket that he'd set aside, folding it neatly before going into the kitchen. He heard—rather guessed at—her movements as the crane creaked and water splashed in a teakettle.

So this was what wedded life would be like. Not going it alone. Not being surrounded by unending sea and crew. Not hearing the cottage echo. Her presence already infused it with her rose scent and warmth and liveliness. She was nearly his. Forever.

Yawning, he pushed up from his chair and sought his bedchamber, on the opposite end of the cottage where Esmée commandeered the kitchen. There he peered into the looking glass of his washstand, his bristled jaw begging a razor. He'd bathe and change clothes once she left. But for now he'd just ready for breakfast.

She began humming a low tune, and it buoyed him as he made his way back to the kitchen. She looked at home there, her expression serene, the table set for him. Despite his not having told her where anything was in the larder, she'd set bacon to frying and eggs awaited their turn. Toast too. But for now, tea.

"Mightn't you like coffee better?" She looked at him as he sat down and fisted his hands atop the table. "I see you have no chocolate."

"I'll like whatever it is you serve me."

She smiled, a pink tint to her cheeks. His own were ruddy from more than the razor. Despite their longstanding tie, there were a great many things to be discovered between them, both mundane and otherwise. As she poured his tea, Henri bowed his head in a silent prayer, thankful for far more than breakfast.

He'd barely finished setting down his fork when a voice boomed. "Captain Lennox, sir!"

The bellow came from beyond the cottage but brought him to his feet. Esmée looked at him, then passed to the nearest window. Together they looked out on not just the rise and fall of low waves hurrying to shore but a ship's bow cutting through the water like scissors through blue silk, its masts as tall as the oaks felled to make them, heavy guns on two decks. The *Intrepid*'s topsides were painted black, the figurehead of a woman striking.

Their intimacy of the hour before abruptly ended. A full crew of men scurried over the deck in all directions as the ship rounded the island and prepared to drop anchor. The hour had come.

CHAPTER *forty-two*

Though Esmée had long grown used to vessels of every size and description, nothing could have prepared her for the sight of the ship that would take Henri away from her. Her heart quailed at the coming separation. The *Intrepid* was one of the handsomest ships of the line she'd ever seen, built to inspire awe among its allies and fear among its enemies. 'Twas a two-masted brigantine, outfitted superbly, guns and cannons on full display.

Henri turned back to her. "I fancy the figurehead resembles you."

"Should I be flattered?" Esmée thought it an odd likeness, dark hair and all. "I even have a yellow dress of that same color."

"Though expertly carved, she's very wooden. You're far lovelier." He winked at her. "You well know female figureheads are said to calm angry seas with their beauty."

"Not only that, when I was small Father told me fairies lived in the figurehead and watched over the crew." Her attention returned to the window. "He was telling me about the ship as it was being built. A maritime feat, he called it. And now yours to command."

"Pray I keep my wits about me."

"Why? You've never been otherwise."

"I've never been betrothed."

"Does this mean you must alter your rule about unmarried crew, Captain?"

"What is your recommendation, Miss Shaw?"

She smiled. She always seemed to be smiling of late. "Why not query your men?"

"Fair enough. This shall, God willing, be my final cruise."

Lucy's words echoed in her mind. Mightn't they marry on the ship's smoothly planed deck? A sort of declaration of her love for him, a way to redeem the past. A rebuke to the foolish girl she'd once been. But for now Henri had hold of her hand, leading her out the door.

Even anchored at a distance, the *Intrepid* loomed as large as the island itself, dwarfing everything except the light. In time, the jolly was lowered and several crew disembarked, intent on the landing.

When ashore, one man gave a little bow, cocked hat beneath one arm. "Richard Farr, sea chaplain, at your service." He lowered his bald head once again. "Miss Shaw, daughter of the renowned Admiral Shaw, I presume. I am an admirer of your father and his coffeehouse."

Charmed, Esmée greeted him just as warmly, thinking how different he was from Nathaniel Autrey. Behind him came several other new crew, lured more by the captain's reputation than the colonial government's lucrative sign-on bonus, Father had said. They regarded her with deference and downcast eyes, obeying Henri's command to repair to the Flask and Sword.

"This is Dr. Gerard, ship's surgeon." Henri made introductions to a tall, bespectacled man of middle age.

He bowed. "Good morning, Captain. At your service."

Two ship's surgeons? She'd thought only Southack would sail. The significance was not lost on her. Henri exchanged a few pleasantries with the newest medical officer before he walked on, joining those en route to the tavern.

"A full complement of hand-selected men," she mused, "including your Africans who form the foundation of your crew. Fiercely loyal, all of them, or so I've heard."

"'Tis what keeps ships afloat and mutiny at bay," he replied, attention still on the ship.

Esmée shaded her eyes, having forgotten her hat, as another figure in the full uniform of a naval officer walked toward them. "Father? What are you doing here?"

Her father embraced her, holding her tight as if she'd been gone months instead of days. His gray eyes sparkled, his navy felted cape expertly tailored. "And do you think I'd be absent from this launch? And the frolic beforehand?"

"Frolic?" She drew back as Henri explained there would be a bit of revelry before sailing. "Of course you must be in attendance, Father. 'Tis your lifeblood, this."

"Eliza nearly accompanied me. She misses her older sister dearly." He smiled enigmatically. "Of course she sent a little something to you. Her gift is in the captain's cabin."

"Does it require tending or feeding?" Esmée asked, knowing Eliza's preference for the outlandish.

"Neither, thankfully." Her father faced into the wind, pulling his cocked hat lower. "Now if you lightkeepers will excuse me, I'll be on my way."

"When you return, we'll show you the tower," Esmée told him with a squeeze of his arm.

"All in good time, my dear. For now I must quench my thirst and be among my maritime fellows." With a smile, he bid them farewell, following the well-trod path that wended through sheltering pines, the new chaplain accompanying him.

Alone with Henri, Esmée watched them go, then returned her attention to the ship.

"You look befuddled, *mon amour*," Henri said.

The endearment brought heat to her cheeks. "After years of sameness, I'm reeling from the unpredictable, however welcome."

He smiled and adjusted his own hat, the cockade a flourish of red and blue, the king's colors.

"Never mind me." She looked to the water. "Your ship awaits."

"How about a tour?"

Her plans for the morning were set aside. "Of course."

Into the waiting jolly they went, his gaze attentive lest she misstep. She'd not been on one of her father's ships for years. He'd had but one that rivaled the *Intrepid*. He still spoke of it fondly.

As they bridged the short distance, they were welcomed by the remaining crew on deck. Esmée stood to one side while Henri greeted the men, who then went about their duties.

She ran a hand along the taffrail. "Father said they launched from a secret location. Why not York's harbor?"

"Our mission is unknown to most. No need to garner undue attention or alert French spies."

He led her over the gleaming deck, walking forward and aft, his expression so schooled she couldn't guess what he was thinking. He opened the door to his quarters, the paneled chamber appointed in blue and gold and spanning the width of the stern. Its large windows faced away from the lighthouse and cottages and took in the sea instead.

He surveyed the bower before them with an amused appreciation, while she was nearly speechless. "The great cabin is fitted up rather like Eliza's parlor."

He showed her several interesting features, including his mahogany desk with brass loops that lashed it down during heavy weather and a china cupboard adorned with pewter and silver. A pleasing arrangement of sofa and chairs were atop a large turkey-red rug.

"Forward of the great cabin is my night cabin for sleeping. Small but adequate."

Her gaze landed on the richly appointed bed through the open doorway. "Hardly a hammock or cot."

Everything smelled of wood shavings within these timbered walls. Sunlight streamed through the stern's span of windows and gilded the dark paneling like gold dust. Despite her cape, she shivered. She'd always found it harsh that ships had no heat other than the galley's cookstove. Not even the captain's quarters.

Henri picked up a box wrapped in decorated paper and silk ribbon from atop his desk. Eliza's gift? She read the attached card.

Dearest Esmée,

A silhouettist came to town recently and amused us. He captured my profile perfectly, so I am giving it to you lest you forget your younger sister while stranded on that desolate island of yours.

Your loving Eliza

Delighted, Esmée held the paper up to the light, astonished a simple paper silhouette could capture so much of her comely sister.

"Shadow portraits." Henri smiled. "Or *à la Pompadour*, as the French call them."

How like Eliza to send something unusual. Esmée returned the gift to its velvet-lined box, wishing she missed Eliza—and the mainland—more than she did.

Henri came to stand behind her at the windows, enclosing her in his arms. "When I sail, I want to remember this." He rested his cheek against her upswept hair. "Your being here with me in this place, if only for a brief time."

Already she felt the emptiness of his going. The slight creaking of the ship and cradle-like motion of its gentle rocking gave her only an inkling of what shipboard life was like.

"How is it on the open sea?" Though Father had told her, she wanted to hear it from Henri himself.

"Noisy. Crowded. A great many sights and smells and sounds on board."

Was solitude as dear to him as it was to her? "Can you retire to your cabin and just be alone?"

"Rarely." His voice held a hint of pathos. "But mark my word, when I do I'll be thinking of you."

CHAPTER *forty-three*

Back in the lightkeeper's cottage, Esmée and Lucy began preparing refreshments. Father and Henri were in the front parlor talking by the hearth. Scraps of conversation drifted to her as she placed cups in saucers and fetched spoons and sugar. Her father preferred gunpowder tea. Henri's choice was chocolate.

Her father had brought them several high-quality bricks. His silver pocket grater rested on the table, and she used it to shave some of the cocoa into warm milk, added sugar, and whisked it into a froth with a molinillo. Tasting it, she made a face. Had they vanilla? A few steps to the larder made all the difference. Not only vanilla but cinnamon, nutmeg, and star anise too.

Father's voice held the authority of his admiralty of old. "Here are more details concerning your mission from the governor . . ."

A rustle of papers. Henri made some remark she couldn't decipher. She carried in the tray, set it down, and served them. Henri's appreciation was not lost on her as he set the papers aside and took his cup. Her father poured tea into his saucer as was his custom, while she took a third chair nearest the fire and sipped her own.

Henri winked. "You do realize I'm marrying you for your cocoa making."

"I did wonder," she replied with a smile. "Shaw's Chocolate makes a delicious dowry."

Her father's pleasure was palpable. "Now that I'm aware your courtship has commenced, I shall be unstinting with our cocoa. As it stands, I made sure the galley holds a hefty supply since there'll be no visiting the premier cocoa growers in the Caribbean on this voyage."

"Nay." Henri stared into the fire, dark brows knit together like thread stitched too tight. "We'll bear away to the north, off the Virginia capes."

The pause that ensued was onerous, and Esmée felt a sudden, swift terror. She looked to a sleet-streaked windowpane that reminded her of their slippery walk to the light but an hour before, wishing someone—something—would intervene and prevent Henri's going.

Henri's gaze shifted to Esmée. Firelight played across her serene features, but he detected a shadow beneath. The looming cruise made a dismal backdrop to the evening.

"When shall you put to sea?" she asked, pulling her gaze from the window to meet his.

He gestured to the papers. "'Tis likely in Dinwiddie's correspondence . . . which I am in no hurry to read."

Her slight smile assured him not a whit. They'd not discussed the future in depth except in the vaguest terms. The sea had driven a wedge between them years before. Would it again?

The admiral finished his tea, and Esmée poured him more, trailing that telltale rose scent that had been his delight and undoing in the night. Though the *Intrepid* sat at anchor just offshore, its wintry decks fit for skating, this was not the time to broach the onerous task before him. He'd rather talk Christmas and weddings. But for the admiral—

"You do understand, Daughter, the critical nature of your betrothed's mission."

Esmée surprised Henri with her swift answer. "Intercept French supply ships en route to Scotia and their militias fighting on the western frontier."

Henri nodded, unwillingly drawn into the conversation. "Specifically, intercept and capture the fleet that bears three thousand French regulars en route to North American posts, along with a number of officers."

The admiral took another sip from his saucer. "Beware the newly launched *Raisonable*, a sixty-four-gun ship of the line and the pride of the French navy. Rather, be wary of Admiral Comte du Bois de la Motte and Pierre de Salvert." He rattled off the French names with admirable flair.

Esmée looked from her father to Henri again, her chin raised in a bid to be resolute. But he knew better. The admiral, however, enjoyed nothing more than discussing ships, strategy, and the coming conflict.

Henri shrugged. "One maneuvers. One encounters. One fires cannon. Then each of the two fleets retires and the ocean is as salt as ever, so the French navy says."

Though a low rumbling laugh built in the admiral's chest, Esmée's eyes glittered. "I shall fetch you more chocolate."

The sudden clutch in his belly was more ache. Admiral Shaw continued his tea drinking. The mantel clock struck seven, and at last Esmée returned to the parlor, looking more composed than when she'd left and bearing an entire chocolate pot.

To Henri's surprise—and relief—the admiral set down his empty cup with a yawn. "I shall leave you two lovebirds alone and retire to bed and dream of my seafaring days."

"Good night, Father." Esmée kissed him on the cheek. "'Tis a bit slippery tonight. Mind your step."

He went out, carrying a lantern, while she resumed her place by the fire.

"To our future," Henri said, lifting his cup and wanting to take the worry from her face. "'And if one prevail against him, two shall withstand him; and a threefold cord is not quickly broken.'"

"A beloved Scripture." She raised her cup to his. "Still, I would be aware of the realities of this cruise and pray accordingly."

"I'd rather tell you about the Patagonia coast, where countless butterflies swarm the decks and rigging." He took a long, sweet drink. "Or the colorful coral beds off of the Turks and Caicos Islands."

"Nay, Henri."

"All right. The realities . . ." He lingered on the pale oval of her face and her remarkable eyes, arguably her best feature. "We could founder in heavy weather."

"You haven't yet."

"French buccaneers could trouble us. Or the Spanish."

"Not to mention their navies."

He took a deep breath. "We could be ambushed. Torched. Stranded. Imprisoned."

"Confined to a prison ship." She shuddered when she said it.

"The crew might mutiny."

"Nary a chance."

He studied the cocoa grounds at the bottom of his cup. "There ends all the hazards I can think of."

"'Tis enough." She poured herself a second cup. "I'd worry except for this. Surely the Lord didn't bring us together to tear us apart."

"Agreed. And your prayers go with me."

Her eyes held that glitter again. "There was a time I nearly gave up on prayer. I prayed and we parted. I prayed and my mother died. But I also prayed and good came to the almshouse, Eliza made a wonderful match, and you came back to me."

"It helps to remove yourself from the equation." All the times he'd wrestled in prayer returned to him like a rogue wave. "I've learned to pray 'Thy kingdom come, Thy will be done on earth as it is in heaven.'"

"'Tis a brave prayer."

"'Tis the best, most honest prayer."

They fell into a companionable silence, solaced by the snap of the fire and cups warm against their palms.

She looked at him pensively. "Tell me about the home you have in mind here."

Setting his cup aside, he added two chunks of pine to the leaping flames. "Before I sail I'll show you the place. If you agree, we can break ground in spring for a three-storied house with southern porches, a great many windows, and a walled garden."

Her eyes lit like the candle between them. Did talk of the future lessen the anxiety of the present? He felt it too, a subtle but tangible anticipation, the future no longer hazy. No longer consumed with missing the other.

"Might you draw me a sketch?" she asked.

At his aye, she assembled paper, a stylus, and a lap desk.

"Alas, I am no artist," he lamented, wanting to please her. Still, he began a fair etching of a handsome house and floor plan, her enthusiasm spurring him on. Half an hour later he had the details on paper, the walled garden with them.

"I'm enchanted," she said with a smile.

His hand stole across the table to hold hers, his signet ring glinting just as her posy ring caught the candlelight. "There's another matter not nearly as lighthearted."

"Such as?"

"If there's to be a war, the light will stay unlit. I want you to return to York. Better yet, Williamsburg, safe from enemy incursion and especially corsairs." He knew all too well the French and Spanish buccaneers, sea rogues who inspired fear and did far worse. "Take your maid with you."

"I shall. Lucy has left the almshouse for good. She wants to remain in our employ." Her face clouded. "So my time here as lightkeeper may be brief."

"Mayhap. For now there's enough crew remaining behind for a guard as well as an ample supply of powder and munitions. Your safety is essential and as assured as I can make it."

She squeezed his callused fingers. "If only I could ensure your own success, your well-being. If anything happens to you—"

"Nay, Esmée." He had hold of her hand more firmly now, and she seemed to lean into his strength. "God alone is our refuge. Our guide."

CHAPTER *forty-four*

Frost hardened the ground during the night, widening winter's icy grip. By the time Esmée ate her tea and toast, the sun had made a tentative appearance, a boon for the planned frolic at hand. Her heart gave an expectant leap only to fall like a stone at her next thought.

Henri's sailing was imminent.

Lucy began clearing the table, her usual query less cheery. "Did ye sleep well, mistress?"

Esmée set her cup down and stifled a yawn. "Excitement is a poor bedfellow, I'm afraid."

"I slept nary a wink myself, so I up and pressed yer gown and brushed yer cape, but unless it rains ye mayn't have need of it. Yer gown is too fetching to cover up."

"And your gown, Lucy?" In the rush, Esmée hadn't considered Lucy's attire. Did she even have a best dress?

The gentle query still left Lucy shamefaced. "I sold all I had to keep out of the almshouse but still ended up there."

"Well, we must send the *Intrepid* off royally, and I have just the gown for you." Esmée got up from the table and went to her bedchamber. "With your pale hair and skin, you'll look especially fetching in rose."

A trunk had her best gowns folded within. She'd not even thought to air them properly. The desired dress was at the bottom, lustrous and full, a gift from Eliza. Lucy was slender, and it likely needed alteration, something they could manage hurriedly with a few discreet pins. When she brought the garment to the kitchen, Lucy gasped.

"Fit for royalty, Miss Shaw, not for a girl from the almshouse!" Flushing, Lucy looked to her soiled apron. "Reminds me of the tale my mother told when I was small, complete with a fairy godmother, a pumpkin, and a glass slipper."

"Ah, the French fairy tale *Cendrillon*. In truth, you are the King's daughter, and 'tis all that matters." Smiling, Esmée smoothed a bold wrinkle that cried for ironing. "I want it to be yours."

Tears came to Lucy's eyes. For a girl so young, she'd endured much and hadn't yet lost the shadow of the almshouse.

"Best heat the iron to press it," Esmée encouraged. "I cannot wait to see you in it."

Lucy set the iron in the hearth near the flame. "Now, Miss Shaw, we must see to yer hair. No powder, to be sure. Spirals and a bit o' silk ribbon instead."

"Papillote curls?" They were Eliza's favorite. "I've some tissue paper and a pinching iron."

Lucy came alive in a way she never did when porridge making and pot scrubbing. "Captain Lennox will call ye his beautiful bride-to-be . . . *ma belle*."

So, she'd overheard the endearment.

Lord, let me hear it for always.

Henri had prayed for clement weather. Taken a frigid bath in a discreet cove. Donned his best suit of clothes. Forgotten breakfast. The empty jab to his ribs followed by a fierce rumbling reminded him of the celebratory feast to come.

"Have you any qualms, Captain, about your mission?" his new

sea chaplain asked him as they stood on the Flask and Sword's porch moments before the frolic was underway.

"Qualms?" Henri looked to the *Intrepid*, now at anchor offshore. "At five and twenty I would have been at sixes and sevens. At five and thirty I'm simply wanting it done."

"Splendid. Life's tragedy is that we get old too soon and wise too late, as Mr. Franklin said." Richard adjusted his cocked hat. "As for myself, I am in the prime of senility."

Henri smiled, appreciating his wit. It boded well for the coming voyage. His crew, old and new, was assembling. The festive air was undeniable. Cyprian had raided the slops chest again from all appearances, earning more than a few back slaps and guffaws. Henri and Richard entered the tavern and stood by the hearth, which glowed red-hot with burls of pine.

His sea chaplain removed his hat. "'Tis your lady, sir."

The hush that descended was akin to when a ship was sighted, that breathless, defining moment that determined friend or foe, all hands held captive. Henri stood taller, hands fisted behind his back as Esmée crossed the tavern's threshold with her father. He took her in, from her curled head to her buttery silk dress to her slippered feet. Her hair was woven with ribbon, curls cascading to the shoulders of her gown. A short, fur-lined cape covered her bodice. He spied pearls and shoes with gilt buckles.

When her gaze met his, he was overcome with love for her. And second chances. The emotion shining in her eyes raised such a knot in his throat, he wondered how he'd be able to voice the order to weigh anchor once it came.

The door shut on the wind and cry of gulls, and then the ensuing hours became a blur of delight. Punch. Sweet cake. Unending jigs and reels and country dances. Lucy in her gown had a ready supply of partners, Cyprian foremost.

When the first shades of evening began to gather, the merriment slowly faded. Though she'd danced with a great many men, Henri included, Esmée looked as lovely as when she'd first set foot in the Flask and Sword. Suddenly he wanted to be alone with her, if only to tell her what he couldn't withhold any longer. The governor's paperwork had been crystal clear.

He and Esmée exited the tavern, taking the path that would return them to the cottages. Tonight the heavens were spangled with stars, diamond bright, reminding him of their going up-scuttle atop the York townhouse long ago.

"Day after tomorrow we sail," he said.

Was she as loath to hear the words as he was to say them?

Without so much as a pause, she held up her hand and admired the posy ring. "When you are gone and all this seems like a dream, your gift shall remind me I am indeed to be married."

He came to a stop on the path. Moonlight cast her in silvery light. Tenderly he kissed her. "*Adieu, mon ciel étoilé.*"

Goodbye, my starry sky.

CHAPTER *forty-five*

Early the next morn Esmée arose and did as she'd begun to do every morning, crossing to the window to look out at Henri's cottage and the lighthouse before dressing and breakfasting. She'd just finished eating when Lucy answered the knock at the cottage door. Henri stepped inside with a greeting, gaze slanted toward the kitchen, where Esmée was rising from the table.

"Good morn to ye, Captain Lennox." Flushing furiously, Lucy bobbed a quick curtsy before snatching up her cloak to fetch firewood and hastening out the door.

"I do think she's afraid of me," Henri said with a slightly puzzled look. "Or my exaggerated reputation."

"She's in awe of you, rather," Esmée told him with a smile, gesturing to the refilled teapot. "Won't you join me?"

"How about a walk?"

In moments she was bundled up in her sturdiest shoes and cloak, hood covering the remaining curls from the frolic. A walk would do her good. She must do something to offset her moody thoughts.

A blast of wintry air buffeted them as they stepped outside, arm in arm.

"A cold courtship," Henri said wryly, pulling his coat collar tighter.

She held on to her hood. "Good thing my heart is far warmer than the weather."

"We'll take the pine path instead of the beach."

There amid the evergreens they were somewhat sheltered from the wind.

"Feels like snow," he said, his breath a milky cloud.

"Am I wrong to wish we'd be snowbound?"

"Ships are rarely snowbound. But ice is another matter."

Would they have snow for Christmas? She wouldn't voice her melancholy that he'd be away for the holiday. Nor would she ask what they did to observe it aboard ship. Precious little, she wagered.

Now that they were away from the fire, the day felt bone-bitter. They walked on, the path winding in places and often picturesque, a cove here or there, the sky and ocean a shining pewter. Finally they came to a sandy rise where the trees gave way. She'd not been to the leeward side of the island. The view was breathtaking.

"'Tis the driest part of the island, protected from prevailing winds. A fine place for a foundation." Henri gestured to a rock border. "I had my midshipmen lay out stones to mark the boundaries."

"Our home," she breathed, a bit awed.

Arranged so plainly and paired with his sketches, the vision assumed a reality previously denied her. A blessed start.

"We'll bring over sheep and other livestock from Hog Island." He walked to what he called the garden spot, but she shook her head.

"*Two* gardens." The vision was clear as a painting in her head and heart. "A vegetable patch on one side and the formal walled garden on the other."

He smiled. "So be it, then. How do you want the dependencies?"

Smokehouse. Milk house. Laundry. A summer kitchen. They debated, rearranged, and amused themselves by laying out more stones. For a time they forgot the wind and weather and imminent departures. Paramount in Esmée's mind was making their last hours memorable. She'd not leave Henri with a sore memory like last time.

Ruddy-cheeked, eyes flashing, he was exhilarated in a way she'd seldom seen him. "We'll hire stonemasons rather than bricklayers. Put in gardens as soon as possible in spring. I'll leave it to you to order seed and plants from Bartram's in Philadelphia."

"I'll do all I can while you're away. Father has a great many connections and can arrange for shipping of building materials to the island."

Their shared excitement was palpable, adding an element of God-ordained joy to the winter's day. Pale sunlight broke through the clouds, brightening their vision. Their future.

"I've always wanted a stone house," she told him. "Brick is so common in Virginia. This island is better suited to stone."

"Potomac River stone and sand." He wrapped hard arms around her. "And we have the Norfolk house if you develop a taste for the city."

"I shan't." Standing on tiptoe, she kissed him. "Now that I'm here on the island, I never want to leave it."

"I once felt the same standing on the quarterdeck. But not any longer."

"If a ship has a name, then a house should." She thought of all the grand residences she knew across Virginia, including Mount Autrey. None held the slightest appeal.

"Ours will be a humble house. No enslaved, just indentures or those willing to work from the almshouse. Mayhap even a few of my crew." Henri stepped toward the pine path, holding her hand. "There's something else I need to show you not far from here."

He led her to a secluded grove, the pines so thick they nearly touched. Her attention shifted to the ground, where loose pine branches lay as if downed in a windstorm.

"Beneath those branches is a buried cache of prizes, including treasure from a sunken Spanish galleon." He looked over his shoulder toward the lighthouse. "And beneath a floorboard in my cottage there lies a map marking more."

His tone told her what his words did not. 'Twas vast. A king's ransom.

"Of which you gave the almshouse part," she said quietly, the pieces falling into place.

His eyes weren't on her but on their surroundings. Did he think someone might be watching? Listening? "If something should happen—if I don't return—"

Her fingers touched his lips in warning. "Say nothing of the sort."

"You'll have enough for two lifetimes." With a tug of her hand, he led her back toward their house's boundary stones and the open, windswept beach.

Upon hearing the *Intrepid* would sail with the tide, Lucy took the stockings and shirt she'd made for Cyprian and walked to the Flask and Sword to bid him goodbye. Esmée's father accompanied her, leaving Esmée and Henri alone. Likely this was his intent, as he knew how precious their remaining time together was. Supper awaited on the table in Esmée's cottage. A loaf of wheaten bread and Gloucester cheese. Potato soup as well as roast chicken and apple tansy.

"Lucy has outdone herself," Esmée exclaimed in gratitude as she and Henri sat down.

"It has the feel of the Last Supper," he replied, surveying the bounty. "A veritable farewell feast."

"I'd rather talk about our nuptials," she said, putting her serviette in her lap. "Shall we wed without ado upon your return?"

"Without ado, aye." Henri cut his meat as she sampled her soup. "Something small and private. Or do you wish otherwise?"

"I'm relieved, truly. Eliza's wedding was nothing short of a carnival."

Too many guests had crowded into their York parlor, and one man had suffered an apoplectic fit. The cake had collapsed in the heat, and a wharf rat had crossed the carpet, leading to a woman's fainting. Still, Eliza had shone, undaunted.

Henri winked before taking another bite. "You are as bold as your sister in your own right, rowing here and proclaiming your passion for me."

Amused, Esmée spooned her soup. "So you saw through my little ruse and appointed me lightkeeper anyway."

"I know an answered prayer when it comes, however cleverly disguised."

Their eyes met, the flickering candle between them.

"There's a saying you may well know," he said. "'Let those that would learn to pray go to sea.'"

Her throat tightened. "Perhaps we should pray now that we are not long parted. Or . . ." A new idea bloomed, however impossible. "You could take me with you."

"You would sail with me?"

"Rather that than be away from you, though I know women aboard are considered ill luck."

His face took on a studied solemnity. "I'd rather you mind the light. Guide me home. Your father wants you to spend Christmas with him in Williamsburg."

"Of course." Eliza wouldn't travel to York so near her confinement. Esmée and her father must go to her. The twelve days of Christmas leading to Epiphany in January were treasured by them all.

"There's an assistant keeper—a widower and former mariner from Norfolk—who'll stay in my cottage and spell you for your time on the mainland. George Haller."

"I'd rather think about next Christmas."

"Our first married Christmas, aye." His expression brightened. "In our new home right here, Lord willing. At least what's standing by then."

The tick of the clock chafed, tugging at Esmée's heart. She tried to grasp the present and savor its sweetness but already felt it slipping away like sand.

The only certainty about life was its uncertainty. Only God stayed steadfast. Only the Almighty could walk her through life's many changes. And when she felt overwhelmed, like now, she simply had to look back to see how faithful God had been, did she not? The heartaches and closed doors of the past had made the present more beloved.

She set down her fork. "Suddenly on the eve of your departure I want a great many answers."

"Such as?"

She pondered all she didn't know about him or had forgotten. "Your favorite color?"

His slow smile gave her butterflies. "The green of your eyes."

Was he ever at a loss for words? "Favorite place?"

"Other than right here, right now? Corfu off the coast of Greece."

Father had said the same. She could only imagine the beauty. "Best memory?"

"The spring we first met."

"Mine too." She looked to her posy ring, her fingers wrapped around the stem of her glass. "Best dish?"

"My mother's cassoulet."

"Best holiday?"

"Christmastide."

"Best book?"

"The Bible." He leaned back in his chair until it groaned. "Your turn, Esmée."

She smiled, trying not to dwell on the hands of the clock or the candles sinking lower in their holders.

"Best friend?" he asked, taking a drink.

"Kitty Hart. Other than you, that is."

"Foremost wish?"

"To marry you." Her voice held a touch of wistfulness. "To live here on the island with our children and savor every sunrise and sunset."

Their eyes locked.

We've not talked about children.

Heat filled her face as a smile came to his. Children. His thoughts ran ahead like hers, she knew it.

"A good half dozen of them is my hope," he said. "I've always wanted a son to call my own. And daughters."

He took the words right out of her mouth. 'Twas almost too much happiness to hold. Her soul overflowed with it. His gaze intensified. Was she making it harder, their parting? 'Twas not her intent.

His gaze canted toward a window. "'Tis time to mind the light."

One last time. Together.

CHAPTER

forty-six

The cry of gulls woke her. For a moment Esmée drifted, eyes closed, before a heady reality rushed in. Today was the day of Henri's departure.

Snowflakes crystallized against the wind-beaten pane in icy elegance. All night the tower had illuminated a white world beyond the cottage, but she felt as unprepared for the cold as the events of the day. The next hour was spent in the usual routines of dressing and breakfasting that were now anything but normal. One look out the window at Henri's cottage, the chimney furiously puffing smoke, reminded her how cold he'd be aboard ship.

Lucy accompanied her to where the *Intrepid* lay at anchor. Men crawled over it like ants, readying for departure. Snow festooned the vessel like it was Christmas morn.

She would be strong. Brave. She would not let him see her sorrowful.

Snow turned the *Intrepid* into a ghost ship. Henri stood by the quarterdeck rail, turned away from Esmée rather than toward her.

No need to make their leave-taking more difficult than it already was. There was little time for it anyway, the holystoned decks a frenzy of activity. The crew was busy obeying Henri's order to put to sea, catting the anchor and securing it to the side of the ship.

Goodbye, ma belle.

The sentiment was cut short by the exhilarating rush he always felt upon facing the open ocean, the wind a roar in his ears, snowflakes stinging his skin. The cold drove all warm thoughts of Esmée away, at least temporarily. The *Intrepid* bore northeast in a squalling snowstorm, the waves hitting the ship's black sides and lifting the bowsprit skyward, sending a shudder through the vessel as it rolled then resettled into an even keel. His balance, finely honed over the years, took every pitch, roll, and heave in stride. Even the groans of the woodwork failed to unsettle him.

How many journeys had he made? He'd lost count of them all. He stood frozen in place by the capstan, a prayer for safety and wisdom on his lips, and looked up through white, stinging sleet, barely able to discern the lookout high above. A frostbitten business on such a day. Once upon a time he'd climbed the mizzen rigging and ratlines like Hermes, clutching his spyglass all the way. But now all he wanted was the leaping hearth's fire of the cottage and Esmée's company.

That night in his cold cabin, he sharpened a quill and opened his leather journal.

We got under sail with a snow. Heavy seas.

He would not pen his own feelings about the matter. *If I could have jumped overboard and swum back to the island, I would have.*

Their goodbyes had been whispered in the lighthouse shadows, a dozen lingering kisses in between. He'd pressed his lips to her hair. Her fragrant throat. The little hollow of her shoulder.

And then the next morn, once the *Intrepid* was far enough out that the island was reduced to a mere speck, he'd turned his back toward Esmée, not trusting his reaction. But her memory held, as real and intoxicating as if she'd been standing on the quarterdeck beside him.

All day Esmée had been restless. Had Henri really been away but a sennight? It seemed far longer. Sewing could not hold her. She had no taste for tea. A discarded novel lay at hand. By nightfall, a chill had trailed down her spine that had little to do with the change of weather. It sent her to her knees at sunset, a peculiarly scarlet sunset bright as holly berries. Or blood. Kneeling beside the trunk of letters Henri had left her, she bent her head, hardly knowing what needed praying for.

Lord, You are with him wherever he is. I know not. Please hedge him and his crew from harm and bring him back to me.

Henri missed the sound of birds singing. The drowsy warmth of a hearth's fire. The scent of baked bread. The sigh of the wind in the trees and firm ground beneath his feet. Not screeching gulls or the knifelike wind. Nor tasteless ship's biscuits and endless water—one moment blue and the next silver, always uncertain, at the whim of wind and weather.

But mostly he missed *her*.

Taking up his spyglass, he studied the handsome French frigate at a distance. Till now they'd not come to close quarters with the enemy. Just two false alarms from English merchantmen before this. But now . . .

His soul went still. "All hands clear the ship for action."

At his command, organized chaos ensued, everything scuttled on behalf of the guns. The galley's fire was put out. His own quarters became almost unrecognizable as furnishings were shoved aside and all munitions were prepared to the last detail.

Chasing the French had never been so straightforward. They'd been at sea only a sennight. Now with the enemy bearing toward them, he could nearly smell the powder and smoke. Already his body seemed to brace for the coming confrontation, the roar of cannon and oft fatal splintering of wood. His aim was not to sink the vessel but put the enemy cannons out of action and capture the crew and ship.

Before his steady eye, the frigate changed course. Seconds later the *Intrepid* gave chase. While they bounded after the *Sauvage* on a favorable wind, netting was fitted over the decks to shield the crew from debris, and numerous casks of water were prepared for fire. Cyprian and two other lads sprinted past, strewing sand everywhere. The lookout shouted what Henri had been prepared to hear. The enemy frigate was part of a fleet of five merchantmen, perhaps the very ones he'd been advised were carrying troops and provisions, important personages, and critical documents.

"Ship cleared for action, sir," came the call from the quarterdeck.

He steeled himself for what was to come. A battle fleet such as theirs might prevent an outright declaration of war and save the colonies the cost in untold lives and materials.

Still, despite the mounting melee, Esmée danced at the corners of his conscience, making what transpired more critical than it had ever been.

He swung his spyglass in another direction. More enemy ships amassed over the horizon now, the topsails in plain view. He trained his glass on them, his heart shifting from a dull thud to a roar between his temples. Five ships of war to dismantle. Could there be more? His crew worked feverishly as the *Intrepid* rolled, preparing to discharge shot fit to cut rope and tear sails in an instant.

In the chaos he'd forgotten the weather. The scent of rain filled his senses. The start of a squall? A rainstorm would shroud these ships and hinder the action. But better rain than snow. He shivered, more from foreboding than the cold.

Lord God Almighty, help.

Behind the *Intrepid* sailed a force of Royal Navy ships. Henri held the lead, gaining on his prey until the *Intrepid* was close enough to fire two shots across the French frigate's proud bow. The *Sauvage* heaved to with a great shudder and splintering of wood, its crew frantic and furious. His men gave a loud cheer, which was followed by a shuddering thud as one ball raced past him, making him reel. Another struck the *Intrepid*'s hull.

Through the smoke he could see the *Sauvage*'s main topmast

fall. In that moment, his own helmsman plummeted to the deck. Cyprian stumbled and stared down at the lifeless body, his own face masked in blood. At once Lucy's entreating face flashed to Henri's mind.

"Go below and tend to your wound," Henri yelled to Cyprian as shot poured forth all around them.

Nearly deafened, he barked orders as he sought to stay ahead of the storm and scatter the convoy, leaving the farthest-lying French ships to the Royal Navy. His prize was before him, the frigate that he sensed held the most important cargo, human and otherwise. His gaze swung to the frigate's deck, where a great many Frenchmen had fallen as the *Intrepid* ran alongside her, both pointed north.

"Lie down between the guns!" he shouted to his men on the main deck, mere seconds ahead of enemy shot ravaging them like a hailstorm.

He himself stayed standing while the *Sauvage* became incapable of the fight and its captain surrendered just as the sun sank lower on a now fiery horizon. With a few words, Henri sent an armed party aboard her. He stood by the taffrail, hands fisted behind his back, taking in every detail of the ship he'd just maimed. It was a masterpiece of French shipbuilding for the Marine Royale, launched from Brest most likely, a prize of extraordinary proportions for the British. Forty guns from the upper deck to the gaillards.

In minutes, the French captain faced him—grim, eyes flashing—and burst forth in a volley of fury that even Henri was hard-pressed to follow. Chest heaving, Henri continued to give orders as the British flag was hoisted and announced the frigate's capture. Rain began spattering, blessedly cool amid the heat of the fracas but making the decks a shocking stream of scarlet. Few of his men had been killed, but many were wounded, dulling the victory.

No more, Lord, no more.

A cluster of women appeared, huddled by the companionway. French officers' wives? They stared at him in mute misery, their stricken faces white as sailcloth. Choosing his words with care, he instructed them to board the *Intrepid*, but they hung back timorously as if going to the guillotine instead. Finally they made their way onto the deck, their rich silks and fur-lined capes held up above the mess as the captured officers and crew followed.

Even as the thunderous battle of other ships played out all around them.

CHAPTER *forty-seven*

Shortly before Christmas, Esmée left the island in the company of her father and Lucy. They exchanged a cold, choppy journey in the wherry for a somewhat warmer ride in the coach, brass foot warmers filled with hot coals at their feet. For Williamsburg, the holiday season meant greenery adorning mantels and candles on windowsills. The snow that had sent the *Intrepid* sailing still lay upon the ground, half a foot deep now, freezing all but the holiday merriment.

Esmée hid her shock upon arriving at the townhouse and seeing Eliza again. Clad in a sultana, her hair undressed, feet swollen and face flushed, her sister lay upon a parlor sofa, her Angora cat, Dulcet, in her lap.

Truly, Eliza had lost her joie de vivre.

Taking Quinn aside, Esmée asked, "Have you consulted the physic of late?"

He nodded, then confessed as he readied to leave on business, "Dr. Anson is here nearly every day but says till the birth there's little to be done. By the ninth month, women tend to be overtaxed in every way."

In the days following, Eliza fussed continuously over a stray kitten.

Cried at underdone mutton. Rearranged the nursery thrice. Sent the servants to market for this or that at every whim. Pelted Esmée with fractious questions. Lambasted Quinn.

"A friend loveth at all times," Father muttered. "Rather, a husband and sister."

Then and there Esmée vowed to never try Henri so, not if she could help it.

"Did you read my advertisement in the *Gazette*?" Eliza asked her when they were alone. At Esmée's nay, her sister took up a paper. "'Wet nurse wanted immediately, a young healthful person of good character, with a plentiful show of wholesome milk, if from the country the more desirable. Good wages and advantageous terms.'"

"That would be Alice Reed from the almshouse," Esmée told her, taking out her embroidery. "She was brought to bed but two months ago with a son. She's fallen on hard times as her husband is away with Washington's army. Shall I seek her out on your behalf?"

"Is she gentle, quiet, and well-tempered?"

"She seems so."

"And her hair? Is it red? Redheads have a milk-curdling effect with their temper, according to Dr. Guillemeau of France."

Esmée hid her exasperation. "Dr. Guillemeau is dead, and his nonsense with him. Alice's hair is flaxen, anyway."

"What of her child-rearing principles? I cannot conscience the use of Godfrey's Cordial to quiet a baby."

"Rest your mind. Alice cannot afford such." Esmée worked a flower with silver thread. "Would you like me to send word to the almshouse and see if she's agreeable to your plan?"

Eliza affected her most pronounced pout. "I suppose so, though I do wonder what the wags will say when they learn an almshouse castoff is beneath my roof."

"They shall say 'tis your sister's doing."

"I suppose. But what else can I manage? I've had no success with a wet nurse as advertised."

"You'd do well to disregard the wags and dwell on Alice and how you both might benefit the other."

Eliza began a whipstitch on a handkerchief. "Sister, you seem to have an answer for everything and no trouble expressing it."

"Have you given serious thought to nursing your own child instead?"

"I have not." Eliza made a face and rang for tea. "Your bluestocking notions are most unwelcome. I shan't be tethered to an infant night and day."

"Then if you're sure, I'll seek out Alice on the morrow. She's friend to my maid, Lucy."

"Very well, then. I lack the time and temper to take care of it. My confinement is nearly at hand." She rang for the fire to be tended next, as she was cold, despite the shawl Esmée had settled round her shoulders. "Enough talk about mundane matters. I'd rather hear about Captain Lennox."

Esmée took her time answering. "Henri has been gone more than a fortnight in what is thought to be a two-month sailing." She bit back a sigh as she stitched. "Sealed orders."

"Sealed orders indeed. Quinn is quite tight-lipped about the matter. No doubt your stalwart captain is in pursuit of French ships, fooling them with false colors and all the rest."

"He's left me a sea chest of letters." Esmée felt aflutter even voicing it, the chest's tiny key on her chatelaine.

"Letters? From the past?"

"He began writing them years ago when we parted. I find it quite romantic. I've been saving them to read in his absence."

"And will you marry immediately upon his return?"

"'Tis the plan. On Indigo Island by his new sea chaplain."

"Speaking of sea chaplains, Nathaniel Autrey is coming to our holiday party."

"Oh? Is he well?"

"How blandly you ask about him. You'd rather marry a privateer and reside on an all but deserted island when you could live but a stone's throw from your sister at Mount Autrey."

"I would indeed."

Their conversation paused as a tea tray was brought. Esmée abandoned her embroidery, the room's drafts calling for a steaming cup. She poured and added sugar and cream to Eliza's, knowing just how she liked it.

"How goes it on the island?" Eliza took a sip. "You're the talk of the Tidewater, what with your sudden betrothal and being appointed lightkeeper."

"I can only imagine the tittle-tattle," Esmée said. "Keeping the light is all I'd hoped it would be, as is life on the island. Serene and simple and beautiful, even in winter."

"No sand fleas, at least, since 'tis cold." Dulcet jumped from Eliza's lap, jarring her cup. "Father said he can see the light from the townhouse's rooftop in York."

"My hope is to help a great many at sea, to shed light—and hope—in a storm or some such calamity. And return Henri to me."

Lord, let it be.

CHAPTER *forty-eight*

Lucy sat across from Esmée in the Cheverton coach, the liveried coachman and postilion as extravagant as the silver foot warmers at their feet.

"D'ye reckon Alice will take the work, Miss Shaw?" Lucy asked as the coach took a sharp corner. "'Twould be far better than the almshouse. Ever since I got shed of it I feel free as a lark."

"You're such a help to me, Lucy. I pray Alice can come to Williamsburg. 'Twould be a better arrangement for her and baby Alden, at least till her husband returns."

"I suppose a soldier in the backcountry is no better than a jack at sea."

Esmée raised a brow. "By jack, do you mean Cyprian?"

Lucy's chuckle was followed by a flush, her cheeks red as June's roses. "'Tis a terrible tussle to not think of him, Miss Shaw."

"A terribly delightful tussle." Esmée smiled as the coach lurched to a stop before the almshouse entrance. The buildings seemed less stark covered in snow, but the French encampment was widening, dense smoke hazing the air from countless fires.

They alighted and were promptly shown to the trustee's office.

Esmée sat down in an unfamiliar Windsor chair, eyes drawn to the new window curtains and other amenities. Henri's doing? Lucy remained standing by the door.

"What brings you out on such a frigid day, Miss Shaw?" The trustee's condescending manner toward almshouse residents turned to deference in her presence.

"I've come to speak with Alice Reed about a position in Williamsburg with my sister."

"Ah, Lady Drysdale? A timely arrangement." He looked to her purse. "'Tis unusual for you to visit empty-handed, Miss Shaw."

Did he expect a bribe? "Surely your recent windfall from an especially generous patron makes anything I might bring a mere pittance."

His eyes showed surprise, but he merely cleared his throat and called to an assistant in the corridor. "Summon Alice Reed."

Alice appeared in minutes, overjoyed to see Lucy. They embraced, and Esmée laid out Eliza's offer as best she could.

"A wet nurse, Miss Shaw? In Lord and Lady Drysdale's townhouse?" Wonderment softened her wan face. "How can I say nay?"

"You'll have bed and board, of course, generous wages, and company. A dozen servants are in Lord and Lady Drysdale's employ." Esmée paused. She mustn't paint too rosy a picture, given Eliza's moods and whims. "My sister can be temperamental at times, and you'd have the care and feeding of two babies night and day till weaning."

"I think my Johnny would be pleased with it, till he's done with his soldiering. And I get to see my dear friend besides." She looked to Lucy, who wore a wide smile. "Aye, then, and as soon as possible."

Relieved, Esmée gestured to the door. "'Tis snowing again. Best accompany us right away. Lucy can help collect your belongings and your sweet babe."

"Oh aye, Miss Grove is minding him till my meeting with ye is o'er."

"Please give her my regards." Esmée stood and glanced at the clock. "If we leave soon, we'll be in time for supper. You can settle in your dormer chamber across from Lucy's own."

Lucy was already unpinning the scarlet *P* on Alice's sleeve that marked her as a ward of the parish. Esmée felt a qualm for all who remained, but at least they were sheltered and fed, not freezing in some forgotten alley.

In a quarter of an hour they were underway, Lucy and Alice's excited chatter filling the coach to the brim. Esmée held Alden, now asleep and bundled in a woolen blanket smelling of lanolin. As was her habit upon leaving, Esmée looked back at the almshouse and said a prayer for those who stayed behind.

A lone figure in a worn matchcoat and hat stood by the woodpile, watching them. Jago Wherry. Was he remembering rowing her to the island?

He did not raise a hand in farewell.

CHAPTER *forty-nine*

Father's earnest prayer echoed in the townhouse dining room on Christmas Day. Only the snap and pop of the fire and the press of wind against the windowpanes intruded on the stillness.

"God, which makest us glad with the yearly remembrance of the birth of Thy only Son Jesus Christ, grant that as we joyfully receive Him for our Redeemer, so we may with sure confidence behold Him, when He shall come to be our judge, who liveth and reigneth. Bless this food to our bodies, and be with those who are apart from this table and go down to the sea in ships, that do business in great waters. Bringeth them unto their desired haven, we pray. Amen."

Esmée's family echoed, "Amen."

Esmée felt a new tenderness toward her father for including the 107th Psalm. She'd read the Scripture over and over again, imprinting the holy words on her mind and heart. Doing so seemed to keep Henri close as she prayed those verses to the Almighty.

"A bountiful feast," Quinn was saying, presiding over the Christmas goose and roast beef with a look of satisfaction. "I've promised the kitchen servants a holiday after Epiphany, as they've worked so diligently of late."

The entire household had gone to bed and then awoken to the traditional "shooting in the Christmas" as boys about town fired their guns in celebration of the holiday. A few random pops could still be heard, reminding Esmée of the time she and Henri had begun to find their way back to each other the night of the illuminations on Palace Green.

"I'm hungry as a horse," Eliza said as dishes were passed. "This babe must be a boy, as he tumbles like an acrobat and swells my appetite."

"You'll be well fortified for our guests later today, then," Quinn replied, the dark half-moons beneath his eyes telling that he was getting as little sleep as his wife. "Not much company, just a few of our closest friends. I don't want to overtire you."

"Esmée is going to play the harpsichord on my behalf." Eliza seemed more her vibrant self. "I shall do my best lying on the sofa and conversing. But how I wish I were up for a little dancing!"

"Next season you will be." Father took both beef and goose, heavily layering them with gravy. "Think of what a year will bring. A wedding. A grandchild—perhaps two." He winked at Esmée. "I want this table bursting with them. Your mother would have been so delighted."

"Dear Mama. How she loved the Christmas season." Eliza raised her fork. "I take care to hang mistletoe in the hall for her every season. Did you notice, Father?"

"I did indeed. A thoughtful gesture. Perhaps your mother is even now looking down from heaven." His eyes misted in a rare display of emotion. "I miss her presence especially during the holidays. As I'm sure Esmée is missing Henri."

"God bless the *Intrepid*'s captain and crew," Quinn said between forkfuls. "How *does* one spend Christmas aboard ship?"

"With as much respect to the vessel as possible," Father replied. "An extra ration of rum, perhaps, for midshipmen, and the best Bordeaux claret for the officers."

Eliza eyed Esmée as she plied her fork with gusto. Was Eliza remembering the Christmases spent without Father?

"You were home for Mama's last Christmases, thankfully." Esmée smiled at him, wondering if Henri would miss the sea as Father did. "And you shall be present for those of your grandchildren."

"A toast to Christmases past and present." Quinn raised his glass, the crystal winking in the candlelight. "And our child, to be born in the new year."

They toasted, Eliza resting a hand on her waist and giving a slight wince. Was she still feeling early pangs?

"Tell me again the names you've chosen," Father said as a maid refilled his Madeira.

"In the unfortunate event it's a she," Eliza said, "we'll call her Ruenna after Quinn's mother, who is regrettably still in England on account of this fracas with the French."

Quinn nodded. "My parents are extremely pleased. As for a boy, 'twill be Philip after Grandfather Shaw."

"Not Barnabas?" Esmée teased. "After our very own papa?"

Eliza grimaced. "I care for that forename as little as I do Mama's."

"Well, my parents liked Barnabas, at least." Father studied his youngest daughter, merriment lightening his usually stern features. "So 'tis Ruenna and Philip. Splendid, both of them."

Eliza looked contrite. "I don't mean to offend you, Father."

He winked. "Is it too much to hope for twins?"

"Pish!" Eliza all but threw her napkin at him. "I'm thankful the Almighty gives most of us one infant at a time."

A wail erupted from the upper floors, drawing every eye to the high ceiling. "Good practice for what's to come," Esmée said of little Alden. "Though I must say he's a remarkably docile baby. And Alice can be a great help to you should you have questions."

"Any news of Alice's husband?" Father inquired.

"A letter of late has him at Fort Edward. But with the equipping of many frontier forts, that may soon change." Esmée didn't know if the missive brought more relief or concern. "He's been ill of late, as have many of the men, under winter camp conditions."

Quinn looked up from his plate. "I've heard there are to be no discharges and no more than two days' furlough granted them, which is of no use, given they are so far away on the frontier."

"Understandable since the frontier is beset with fighting," Father replied, taking another helping of beef. "There's a council of war occurring in New York with many colonial governors as we speak."

The men began debating Virginia's next move under the appointment of Colonel Washington as commander of the Virginia regiment. Good news, that. Washington was a very eligible bachelor, and rumors of his courting different belles abounded, but in truth, being a military man, he had little time for romance.

Esmée sipped her peach brandy and eyed the mincemeat tarts and plum pudding, trying to content herself in the moment, wondering what Henri was doing that very instant.

Thinking of her as she was him?

The holiday party commenced. Esmée nearly struck a wrong note at the harpsichord when Nathaniel Autrey entered the parlor. She was never sure of him, knowing him only slightly. Most men would have been offended by her refusal, but the sea chaplain seemed made of sterner stuff.

Esmée played on as a dozen guests chatted and toasted and laughed. Half an hour passed, and she cast Eliza a beseeching look. Her sister held court from the sofa she sat upon, finally giving a nod for the music to end. Eliza had confided that these select friends happened to be among Henri's foremost supporters. That alone cheered Esmée. A shame the captain couldn't be here among the very people who admired and espoused him.

When she arose from the bench to seek a quiet corner, Chaplain Autrey approached, bringing her a cup of punch. The thoughtful gesture touched her. Had he come alone? Or perhaps he'd needed a respite from the company of his doting aunts? Before she could cast about for an answer, he gave a small bow.

"Merry Christmas, Miss Shaw."

She thanked him and took a sip. "Merry Christmas to you. How goes it at Mount Autrey with your aunts?"

"A far cry from my seafaring days, but I've no complaint. How is it on Indigo Island without a chocolate shop to be had?"

"The lighthouse is an admirable trade. 'Twould seem we've exchanged places. You here and I there."

His gray eyes held hers for a decorous second. "And when is Captain Lennox due to return?"

"I cannot say." A chill settled round her heart. "His orders are secret."

"I wish him well. There's no worthier captain to be had on land or sea." His thoughtful reply bespoke many sailings and circumstances unknown to her. "I wish you both well."

"Your kindness is much appreciated."

"I've been meaning to return to the island. I've a debt to settle there with one of the crew. Soon the spring planting will be upon us and I'll not be able to get away."

"Perhaps Captain Lennox will be on hand to greet you then."

Quinn approached, flushed and garrulous. "My friend! How good of you to come on such a blustery day. I trust you and your kin at Mount Autrey are all well?"

As the men fell into easy conversation, Esmée finished her punch. Looking toward the door the servants used, she said, "If you gentlemen will excuse me, I have an errand elsewhere."

Belowstairs, the Chevertons' townhouse staff was making merry. Esmée could hear their hubbub before she'd made her way to a rabbit's warren of rooms. A butler, two footmen, and half a dozen maids, including all the kitchen staff save the French cook, were gathered around a large table where they took their meals. Piled high in the center were hot cross buns and a half-drunk bowl of punch.

Suspended from the ceiling was a string with a stick bearing an apple at one end and a candle at the other. Bold souls tried to bite into the fruit without being burned, much to the amusement of onlookers.

At Esmée's approach, the men stopped their game and the women fell silent. 'Twas rare for one of the family to make an appearance.

'Twas even unwanted ofttimes. But with spirits flowing freely and a mood of goodwill prevailing, the butler brought her a chair.

"I shan't keep you from your snap-apple long," she told them, setting a basket on the table. "In the spirit of Christmas, I've brought gifts. We are very thankful for the hospitality of this house."

"I daresay 'tis Shaw's chocolate," one of the maids called out, her words meeting with muted laughter.

Esmée began dispensing small tokens of appreciation that Eliza and Quinn had chosen with care and she and Father had added to. Small sacks of cocoa, clove-studded oranges, gloves, pockets, penknives, coins, pins, and lace.

Alice sat near the hearth, Alden asleep in her arms, Lucy beside her. They were smiling as the gifts went round. A sense of fullness stole over Esmée. Mama seemed especially near at such times. She sensed to her bones that Eleanor Shaw would have enjoyed this firelit moment. Had she not said, "At Christmas be merry, and thank God of all, and feast thy poor neighbors, the great with the small"?

Alice exclaimed over the wee bonnet and gown for Alden, while Lucy held up a length of lace for them both in the firelight's glow.

"Is it true, Miss Shaw?" one of the footmen said. "That yer to marry Captain Lennox and keep the light?"

"Ye prattling ingrate!" the housekeeper snapped, appearing in the doorway, her mobcap the largest thing about her. She wiped her hands on her soiled apron. "'Tis no more concern of yers than the garden snake."

With a smile, Esmée lifted the housekeeper's gift from the table and handed it to her, then made her way to the door. "A merry Christmastide to you all!"

CHAPTER *fifty*

Their return to Indigo Island was delayed by rough weather. Finally, after two days waiting in York, a small sloop took them across the expanse of churlish water, leaving both Esmée and Lucy a bit green by the time they reached shore. Still, after all the feasting and fuss of town, Esmée felt a rush of elation upon returning.

Treading carefully on snow-slick rocks and steps, they reached the snow-covered cottage. Esmée threw open the door, wanting to shout, "Huzzah!" Cold as it was, it now felt like home, a place of happy memories. Lucy's cat, Tibby, greeted them with a yowl before curling up contentedly at their feet.

She and Lucy spent the rest of the day by the blazing hearth, drinking tea and planning their next tasks. The relief lightkeeper took leave by the vessel that had delivered them, promising to return again, weather permitting.

Esmée's work resumed at twilight. Head and heart full of what Henri had taught her, she climbed the steep tower steps alone. The relief keeper had cleaned the top thoroughly, even filled the compass lamps with oil, so she faced out to sea with a view unmarred by the smoke and fumes that quickly besmirched the glass. As far as she could see, silvery water flecked with foam rolled toward her in an incoming tide. She leaned forward, feeling like the figurehead on Henri's ship, penetrating the gathering shadows.

Oh, Henri, where are you in the deep?

A fragment of a Psalm quickly followed the lonesome question.

He maketh the storm a calm, so that the waves thereof are still.

Father had nearly lost his life in storms at sea. Henri had told her to expect shipwreck survivors—even lost souls—to wash up on shore during her tenure as lightkeeper.

Lord, prepare me for hard, heartbreaking things.

Since childhood she'd been haunted by the fate of the Boston lightkeeper. Upon returning to the island after church, he and his family had drowned when their boat capsized. Father had taken her to Boston's North Burying Ground, where the Worthylakes' triple headstone stood. Too much, perhaps, for a small girl to take in. She'd never forgotten.

"We'll build a chapel here," Henri had told her the day they'd looked at the boundary stones. "No crossing needlessly to Grace Church with all its risks and implications. Mayhap someday we'll even have an island parson."

Recalling it now, she began lighting the oil blazes, the fishy smell making her breath shallow. Each light flared, a small beacon of hope. Tallow candles, set on benches nearest the glass, remained unlit, saved for the stormiest weather when added illumination was needed. With the wicks trimmed, the oil would burn twelve hours and last through the night. All glowed gold, the windows agleam. By morn, all would beg for cleaning.

Though the wind that drove the waves beat upon the tower, nary a draft was felt. Below, the British flag was fully unfurled, its colors striking even in the twilight. She moved to a small desk where the logbook lay open, a quill and inkpot near at hand. The assistant keeper's script was small and tightly worded. She paged back to Henri's scrolling words, a beat of longing in her breast. He'd recorded the weather and wind direction, ships passing, and oil used.

Taking up the quill, she made her own entry.

8th January 1756. Northeast wind fresh.

She set down her quill and bent her head in prayer before the smoke and fumes hastened her down the steps. Taking a final look around the lit tower, she remembered Lucy had supper waiting.

Esmée smiled in anticipation as she approached the kitchen. "You spoil me." Bowls of thick barley stew with bread and butter graced the table, even a plate of molasses cookies. "I prefer molasses to the ever-popular jumbles."

"I'll make jumbles next, though they'll lack orange glaze." Lucy wrinkled her nose as she poured them both cider. "Nary an orange to be had."

"Perhaps the captain will return with citrus. He's partial to it."

Lucy sighed. "D'ye wonder night and day what they're about?"

"Captain and crew, you mean?" At Lucy's aye, Esmée nodded. "All the time. I pray continually for their safety and a speedy return to us."

"How many jacks are left on the island at Mistress Saltonstall's?"

"Half a dozen." Esmée buttered her bread. "Three injured and three able-bodied. The latter are to check on us daily, more so in foul weather."

"'Twill be good to have men about just in case." Lucy ate a few bites, her mind clearly on other matters. "Ye must think of yer dear sister too, soon to be in childbed."

"Any day now. Nor can I forget Alice and little Alden." Was Alice adjusting to town life? Rather, was Eliza patient and kind as her mistress? "Father promised to send word when the baby comes."

"I do hope 'tis a son." Lucy drew a spoon through her stew. "Lady Drysdale has her heart set on it."

Too much so. This was Esmée's worry. As for herself, she had no preference. She would be an aunt, at last. "Ruenna or Philip it shall be."

"Bonny names, both. Fit for a child with a silver rattle."

A silver rattle and an entire nursery overflowing with London-imported toys suited for a growing boy. Carved wooden soldiers and horses but no dolls. Balls and peg games but no miniature tea sets.

"I hope to have a babe o' my own someday." Lucy grew wistful.

"Now that I'm away from the almshouse I might stand a better chance. Is it wrong, d'ye think, to pray for a husband? Does the Almighty care about such?"

"Indeed He does." Esmée gave a reassuring smile. "Remember Adam and Eve? 'Twas not good for man to be alone, and so God made a helpmeet."

"Glad I am of it, but I want to see ye wed first. Ye've waited so long and now have to wait longer still." A smile suffused Lucy's pockmarked features. "I suppose I'll soon be calling ye Mistress Lennox."

Yawning, Esmée stoked her bedchamber fire, then drew a chair nearer the heat and light of the hearth. A small leather sea chest, painted blue with flower medallions, was at her feet. She lifted the lid, releasing the scent of ambergris. Had Henri sealed his letters with perfumed sealing wax? The French were noted for such.

Her heart did a little dance as she bent nearer, breathing in the unique scent. Mounds of letters, stark white against the red seals made with Henri's signet ring, were a testament of his missing her. Each bore her name on the outside, penned in his unmistakable hand. She'd savored a dozen or so, each like the richest dessert.

She reached down and picked up an unopened one. Brought it close and breathed it in before breaking the brittle, fragrant seal.

19th April 1749

Dearest Esmée,

Four years. We have not spoken nor seen each other, yet you still seem nearer to me than the sea I sail upon. For all I know you have chosen another who, I am certain, is not a mariner. No matter our past, I choose to remember the good, for there was much of it in hindsight, if not the misspent words between us at the last . . .

CHAPTER *fifty-one*

Esmée stood before the looking glass of her cottage bedchamber, donning her cape before venturing out. Lucy was busy making bread in the kitchen, the earthy yeast scent promising a fresh loaf for supper.

"Yer going for a walk, mistress?" she called, waving a flour-covered hand.

"The sun calls for it after so much dreary weather. But our rain barrels are full at least," Esmée replied. "I shan't be long. I've letters to write and embroidery to finish."

Bidding her goodbye, Esmée stepped from the shuttered cottage into bright noon sunlight. The snow had melted as January progressed, the wind banished with it. She sensed spring. Or was it only her woolgathering about her coming wedding?

With a last look at the lighthouse, she turned her back on it and began a slow walk to the beach. The tide was out, the water so flat it looked like a painted blue floor. She breathed in the salt air, thankful the time they'd been back on the island had seen no tempests nor foundering ships.

Her thoughts skipped forward, drawing her to the boundary stones. They were just as she and Henri had left them. She walked the perimeter now, envisioning the parlor and hall, the staircase leading to bedchambers and the upper portico. They'd decided the most basic details. Potomac River sandstone. Gambrel roof. Milk-paint walls. Balustraded verandas like those Henri favored in the Caribbean that tempered summer's heat.

She took in the view they'd have from the front of the finished house. A lone sloop sailed into her line of sight, relying on the current instead of the wind and heading toward York. She missed town not a whit. Solitude suited her just as society suited Eliza.

She walked back onto the beach, eyes on the sand, the smallest of breezes stirring her petticoats. Father always said the best shelling happened at low tide after a storm. The tide was now turning, the sea coming a little closer. Spying something purple, she bent and shook the sand from a pansy shell, as Mama called them—or mermaid coins, said Father. It was round and white with a petal design on top. Sadly, Eliza had never shared her love of shelling.

Esmée walked in the direction of her cottage, wishing it were warm enough to remove her shoes. For a time she forgot all about winter, lost in the pleasure of the beach. A few shells later, she all but ran back home, as carefree as a child. Into the parlor she went, the warmth of the hearth nearly suffocating after her outing. Three loaves of bread sat on the kitchen table. Had she been away so long?

Lucy's expectant face greeted her, a dab of flour on her chin. "What have ye there, Miss Shaw?"

"Treasures of the deep." Esmée held out a conch shell, pink and glossy. "If you place it to your ear you can hear the sea."

Lucy did so, eyes wide. "I do, aye!"

Esmée held up another shell. "Look at this scallop, orange as a persimmon."

"The mantel looks magical with so many shells." Lucy set the conch, the largest of them all, on one end. "Whilst ye were away, two of Captain Lennox's crew rowed here from the tavern. The peg-legged Tomkins and an African."

"I'm sorry I missed them," Esmée replied, removing her cape. "Is all well on the island's opposite end?"

"Tomkins said his old bones foretell a tempest."

"A tempest?" Seasoned mariners were often able to predict the weather. Esmée was doubly glad for her beachcombing ahead of rough seas. "Two of the most able-bodied men will be quartering in the captain's cottage come any storms. Captain's orders."

"A tempest I can do without," Lucy exclaimed. "D'ye recall the last? 'Twas when I first came to the almshouse. Hail the size of turkey eggs!"

"I recall a massive sandbar lay in the Chesapeake when there'd been naught before. A great many ships ran aground. Did the crew say what needs to be done in preparation?"

"Batten down everything outside we can. Bring in more firewood to keep it dry. Secure the poultry and such." Lucy bent and added another log to the hearth's fire. "I do fret about our men at sea. What's to become o' them in a storm?"

"We shall keep praying for them." What more could they do? "One of my favorite biblical stories is Jesus calming the wind and the waves."

"Can ye read it to me tonight, Miss Shaw? After ye mind the light?"

"A lovely plan. Count on it."

CHAPTER *fifty-two*

Esmée sat by the parlor window embroidering, carefully alternating between stem stitch and satin stitch, tiny leaves and vines unfolding before her unwavering eye in different hues of brown and green. Dear Mama had taught her well. Lucy's exclamation was proof.

"I've ne'er seen the like, Miss Shaw. And so fetching a fabric!"

"'Tis silk damask. I'm flowering a waistcoat for the wedding."

"The captain'll make a handsome groom, he will." Smiling, Lucy pulled up a chair and took out her own handwork. "I'm knitting more stockings. Seems like I'm ne'er warm enough even with the fire blazing night and day."

"There's a chill on the island with the wind coming from all directions."

A bob of her capped head led to a grimace. "I keep pondering what's been said about a tempest. Best prepare for such by dressing warmly, aye."

"Thankfully, all is well today. A mild south wind. Clear skies." Esmée looked up from her work to gaze through the glass. The lighthouse seemed to watch over them, casting a long shadow in the sun. "You should come up in the light on a starry night."

"Yer a brave soul climbing all those steps." Lucy busied herself with her needle. "A bit like a jack-tar climbing aloft to the lookout."

"Surely iron steps are better than a rope ladder."

Lucy chuckled. "Those jacks have a bit o' Hermes in them, they do, monkeying to the top."

"How *is* the mischievous creature, I wonder?"

"Livelier than a lamb in spring, no doubt." Lucy's thin frame shook with mirth. "He's missing Mistress Saltonstall by now. Or Cyprian, who had care of him till sailing."

Esmée plied a few more emerald-green stitches, finishing a leaf. She startled when Lucy rose abruptly from the table, jarring it and bringing their peaceful interlude to an end.

"By Jove . . . Is that yer father, Miss Shaw?"

Esmée looked again to the window as a small vessel drew up alongside the pier. Two jacks were tying up Father's Bermuda sloop, favored for its agility and speed. Had he news of Eliza?

Abandoning her embroidery, Esmée grabbed her cape hanging near the door. Lucy was on her heels, the cold air seeded with questions. By the time they reached the water, her father was helping a caped woman onto the main deck from the stern cabin below. Alice? An infant's cries shattered the stillness, startling a charm of finches in the near beach grass.

Esmée's insides turned to ice. With Father's help, Alice—her arms full of two bundles—stepped onto the pier. Her face was pale as frost, one arm jostling a crying babe. Father's strained face only added to Esmée's angst as he took one of the infants. She'd expected him at some point but not with babies. Nor Alice.

"Father, what has happened?" Esmée's voice sounded overloud. A bit breathless.

He simply stared back at her, unsmiling. When Lucy took one infant the blanket fell away, and they saw it was Alden. His fat fists punched the air and his round face was puckered, but he gave no cry.

While Alice and Lucy hastened to the cottage with the babies, Father came to a standstill on the dock. "Your sister, racked from a hard birth, lies gravely ill with the pox. One of the kitchen maids in their employ has died of it. Now 'tis spreading through Williamsburg like fire and has reached York. Quinn is also ill, though not as ill as Eliza. He begged me to bring the babe to you straightaway for safekeeping. You know how hard the pox is on children."

Dismay nearly stole all speech. "Girl or boy?"

"A girl." His eyes glittered. "Your niece, Ruenna Cheverton."

Taking his arm, Esmée kissed his unshaven cheek as she fought back tears. "What a time you've had. Alice looks exhausted too, though I'm glad to see her standing. She survived the pox once upon a time, as her scarring shows."

"As have you and I, thanks be to God." His voice was rough with emotion. "You could have picked no better wet nurse, nor could the Almighty have provided one."

"Another praise, especially now."

He raised his eyes to the lighthouse. "If ever a structure seemed a beacon, a symbol of hope, 'tis Lennox's light on this day particularly."

"Come in by the fire and we'll get everything settled, the babies included. You must stay the night. Henri's cottage is readied for any visitors." Her words came in a rush as one thought tripped over another. "Are you hungry, Father? Lucy can serve tea and bread till supper . . ."

"Less than a sennight old and what a hard start you've had." Esmée leaned over the makeshift cradle, a dresser drawer layered with linens and blankets, and stared into the face of her newborn niece. "You are a beauty like your mama, though I do believe you have your father's mouth and brow."

Ruenna, quiet now after a feeding, blinked up at her as Esmée scoured her porcelain skin for any sign of the dread disease. The first flush of fever. An early rash. Father had said the babe was removed immediately from Eliza's arms at birth and placed in Alice's, a quick-witted act that might well have saved her.

But what of Eliza?

Taking Ruenna in her arms, Esmée marveled at how light she was, more like a doll. Were all newborns so tiny? Alden seemed like a giant at a few months older. Lord willing, he would be spared any illness, though time would tell. Thankfully, Alice had a healthy supply of milk for them both and seemed glad to be away from the townhouse and its shadows.

Esmée carried her niece into the parlor and sat down by her father near the hearth while Alice and Lucy visited in the kitchen, their low voices threaded with relief and joy at being together again.

Father took a sip of tea, finally settling down after his arrival an hour earlier. "I'd quite forgotten how taxing town is when a plague is set upon it. Since there is no pesthouse in all Virginia, the governor's council has decreed a fine of two pounds sterling to be paid for those housing any pox."

"How are your indentures?"

"Keeping to their quarters as best they can. I've closed Shaw's Chocolate and the coffeehouse till this passes by."

"You'll be returning to Williamsburg, I take it, till Eliza recovers?"

"As soon as possible. Heaven knows what awaits me when I do. Your sister is that ill."

She could only imagine the bustling capital now at a standstill. "Have you heard anything of the almshouse?"

"Supposedly the pox started amongst the French refugees, though it might be a malicious rumor."

Not all the specie in the captain's bequest could stave off smallpox. She bit her lip to stay a sigh and studied the baby in her arms. Reaching down, she released the chatelaine from her waist with her free hand and dangled the tiny silver lighthouse in the baby's line of vision. Though she was too young to grasp much of her surroundings, Ruenna's blue eyes fastened on it fleetingly.

"I know nothing about infants," Esmée lamented, returning the chatelaine to her waist. "All I can offer are my arms and a lullaby or two."

"That and feeding are about all a babe warrants aside from sleep." He leaned nearer, voice softening. "She's a beauty. Her father is quite smitten with her."

"Poor Quinn. Glad I am the physic and apothecary are near and his case is slight, if there is such a thing."

"He may well be on his feet by my return. He's always been hale and hearty." Father set his teacup aside. "I daren't say it, but if the babe sickens . . ."

Lord, nay. With no physic on the island . . .

"Oh, Father. Let's not think of such. We'll pray against it." She brought her niece nearer, marveling at her tiny lashes now closed in sleep, the peach hue of her skin. "She's safe as she can be right here. Please tell Quinn I shan't let her out of my sight except when I mind the light."

"How *is* the light?"

She smiled, wanting to reassure him. "I'm settling into a routine. At night when I do lie down to sleep, the light is so bright I wake up at once if it goes out, as it once did when the oil grew cold."

"Have you had to fire the fog cannon?"

"Twice. One of Henri's crew comes from the island's opposite end if warranted to perform that duty."

"Ah, Henri." He stared into the fire, seemingly far away, that wistful cast to his features telling.

Was he thinking of his own command? The days he spent far from hearth and home? His longing for the sea was palpable.

"If only we had the capability of knowing just where he was and when he'd return," Father confessed. "'Tis a risky mission. The future of the colonies might well depend on it."

"Perhaps he's spared the pox. I cannot recall if he's already had it." The possibility he had not sent a new terror through her. But surely all those ports, all those peoples, had made him immune already.

Lord, please, hedge him from harm, and all his crew.

Haunted, she kissed the baby's velvety brow as her initial shock faded over the unexpected arrival. There was little she could do about Henri. Or Eliza and Quinn. Providence had given Ruenna to her keeping, and she'd do her best to love and protect her in the meantime.

CHAPTER *fifty-three*

Father left at dawn. He bid his first grandchild goodbye stoically, if reluctantly, before returning the sloop to York. Esmée wondered if he would ever see Ruenna again. If the babe sickened and died in her care, mightn't Quinn and Eliza blame her?

At least the wind and weather were favorable this morn, hastening his departure. Esmée stood on the pier and waved, a sinking feeling inside her. If ever she'd missed Father's strengthening presence, 'twas now.

She returned to a cottage lusty with the cries of both babies. Hurrying inside, she took Alden and amused him with her chatelaine while Alice fed Ruenna. As she listened to Alice recount Eliza's travail, the room grew still.

"'Twas dreadful, Miss Shaw." Alice's face was drawn with worry. "Lady Drysdale had such a time of it, laboring nigh on two days. The physic was called in at the first pains, then the midwife at the last, who said the babe had not yet fallen down . . ."

'Twas all Esmée could do to sit and listen to the details of her sister's travail. Eliza was not long-suffering in nature, yet she'd endured childbirth only to sicken with smallpox. Now, weakened from the birth as she was, would she even survive?

"Lady Drysdale's lying-in should have been far easier." Tears came to Alice's eyes as she finished feeding Ruenna. "It grieved me to see her babe whisked away into my keeping so soon."

"Merciful days," Lucy murmured in sympathy, poking at a gammon roasting on a spit. "How did her ladyship come by the pox?"

Alice's slim shoulders lifted. "Lord Drysdale suspected a kitchen maid brought it into the house. Every morn we were all summoned to Lady Drysdale's chamber to get our orders for the day, ye see. The poor maid was always there too, up till she sickened and died. But every house in Williamsburg seemed to have someone down with it, so who can say how it began?"

"We're thankful to have you on the island if not in the townhouse," Esmée reassured her. "And 'tis my job to make sure you're eating bountifully and resting."

Alice smiled a bit wearily. "My Alden doesn't seem to mind sharing, though it's a bit tricky minding two babes when both fuss to be fed."

They traded infants. Alden was awake and active, Ruenna asleep, her rosebud mouth white with dried milk.

"Have you enough clouts?" Lucy asked, moving from hearth to table.

"Admiral Shaw brought as many things as the coach and then the sloop could hold." Alice looked toward Esmée's bedchamber, where two trunks rested. "A shame we couldn't have carried away the babe's beautiful cradle with its silk hangings. A humble drawer seems sorely lacking."

"Thankfully, the babe doesn't mind a whit." Esmée settled back, wishing for a rocking chair. She was growing used to the feel of Ruenna in her arms, no longer on eggshells fearing she might drop her. That this was Eliza's child hadn't quite taken hold, not when she saw more of Quinn in her tiny features.

"She's a quiet little miss," Lucy remarked, reaching down to stroke Tibby's back.

"Glad I am of it when Alden is nothing of the sort," Alice mused, kissing him on the brow. "Right out of the womb he fussed. I do wonder though . . ."

Esmée looked up. Alice's hazel eyes held a timid question.

"D'ye think Miss Ruenna may have a touch of the pox? I fear for both babes. The pox steals away the young and old especially."

"I pray not." Feeling Ruenna's forehead, Esmée breathed another silent prayer. 'Twas trying enough worrying about Eliza and Quinn. And all of Virginia. What if one or both babies came down with the disease? She looked at Lucy quietly peeling potatoes. Had Lucy had the pox?

"I'm as like as the babies to come down with it." With a little moan, Lucy continued her simple task. "I've had other distempers but not the pox."

"You'll likely be well here on the island," Esmée sought to reassure her. "But if there's the first touch of fever . . ."

Lucy gave a bob of her fair head and set the potatoes to boiling. The aroma of roasting meat filled the kitchen, following Esmée out to the parlor as she moved to a window, Ruenna still in her arms. The gray landscape turned the lighthouse a starker white. Beyond it were two merchant vessels, a weighty presence in the water but toy-sized at such a distance.

Ruenna stirred and made a face. Despite feeling overwhelmed, Esmée chuckled then wrinkled her nose as an unmistakable odor overcame the more palatable aroma from the kitchen.

"I see you're going to cause me a great deal of fuss and bother during your stay," she said softly, moving toward the bedchamber. "Your grandfather was wise to bring a great many clouts."

Ruenna opened her eyes at the sound of Esmée's soft voice. She smiled. Or was it only indigestion? Despite the odor, Esmée's heart melted.

CHAPTER *fifty-four*

29th January 1756. Cold day. Heavy NW gale toward night.

Esmée's light was snuffed thrice as she took a tin lantern up to the waiting lamps. Back to the cottage she went to kindle it again at the hearth's fire. Lucy and Alice, babies in arms, looked on, alarm in their eyes. The wind, steadily rising throughout the afternoon, had a particularly sharp, unfriendly feel. It moaned as it whipped round the cottage's corners and gabled ends, pressing against the windowpanes with such force Esmée feared they might shatter.

"First fog and now this," Lucy said before Esmée slipped back into the twilight.

Since early morn, passing ships had fired their cannons, and then the island's fog cannon answered with a sulfurous blast. The noise woke the babies and fretted Alice and Lucy. Even Esmée wanted to cover her ears. But at least she didn't have to man the cannon. Two of Henri's ablest crew, kept from sailing by a recurrent malarial fever, took on the chore without complaint.

Now at dusk, another boom sounded as the wind whipped Esmée's cape and petticoats, snatching off her hood as she made for the tower. With all her might, she slammed the door shut, preserving the lantern's light. Up the spiraling stairs she climbed, thankful for five-foot-thick stone walls, though she still heard the wind's wailing.

Was the wind worsening?

She hung the lantern from a hook and paused to look out on the surly Atlantic. A briny mist covered the glass, but it in no way dimmed her view of the blue-gray swells tipped a frothy white. The surf was encroaching where it had never been during her tenure as keeper, splashing over rocks and through sandy openings she'd thought impenetrable, closing in on the very foundation of the lighthouse.

Her stomach quavered as if pitched by the mounting waves. With a move so brisk it rattled her chatelaine, she began to light the lamps, praying they'd stay on, hoping they'd provide some sense of direction and bearing to any needy ship and keep them out of shoal waters. 'Twas her first storm as keeper. Would she weather it?

Where was Henri in this tempest?

She shut her eyes, caught between a prayer and a sigh. Oh, to have him by her side, capable and uncomplaining, not out on a vessel whose masts might be snapped by the wind's force and founder.

"Captain Lennox is the same in rough weather as if the seas were standing still," his quartermaster had once said in her hearing. "Dead calm."

She didn't doubt it. She wished for a mite of that composure. Her heart seemed to skip beats as she studied the waves, her breathing shallow. A motion below caught her eye, and she spied the two of Henri's crew who'd been manning the cannon. One made his way to the lighthouse while the other stood on the rocks and faced the surf. His bald head was covered with a brown Monmouth cap, a button on top. His hoary hand clutched it to his head lest the wind snatch it like her cape hood. He faced the sea as if to stand down the storm.

Chary, she returned her attention to the waves. As she hadn't heard any tread of steps on the stair, she started when Cosmos, one of Henri's ablest Scotsmen, appeared.

"Pardon, Miss Shaw." His gruff manner made his apology almost amusing. He came to stand beside her, his expression unreadable.

Reaching for the brass spyglass, he grunted his dismay. "A league or so distant is a Guineaman with her foremast cut away. Likely heavy laden with Africans."

"A slaver, then." The very word was bitter on her tongue even as compassion rent her heart. Who knew how many men, women, and children were aboard that vessel, taken by force. She'd once seen a child's shackles lying near the York wharves. Considered the most valuable cargo, children were stashed in a slaver's smallest spaces.

"The lot o' them are better off at the bottom o' the deep than in chains," he said. "The crew daren't launch their longboat even to save themselves. That she's lying bow to sea might keep 'er from breaking up."

Shaken, Esmée turned away from the struggle. Two of the lights had gone out. She rekindled them, fighting a swelling dismay as the wind lashed the tower with renewed force. It had been constructed with a bit of sway for hurricanes. Would it hold?

In a quarter of an hour the Guineaman was lost from view, the night thick and black as tar. Cosmos was still on watch, spyglass in hand.

Esmée nearly started again when he said, "Best return to the cottage and ready for worse."

"Worse?"

"The wind's mounting, the waves with it. There's nae telling what the storm's tide will do." His Scots burr was so thick she stumbled over his words. He raised the spyglass again. "At best, the Guineaman will run aground. At worst, she'll founder."

She looked out again as darkness pressed nearer. "God help them, then."

He looked straight at her. "If the hurricane doesna abate, the surf will be o'er this part of the island, washing into the cottage and even the bottom o' the lighthouse. Ye've got two bairns below, aye? Best bring them to the tower out o' the worst o' it."

She nodded, wasting no time in heading for the stair. But was it wise to bring the babies into the wintry blast? Had she no choice? The fumes from the pan lamps alone were an abomination.

She fought her way to the cottage, pushed and shoved all the way. Once inside, she found Lucy and Alice huddled by the hearth's fire, the babies swaddled and sleeping between them.

"Ye look tuckered out, Miss Shaw." Lucy stood as if wanting to help in some way. "I feared the wind would blow ye into the water."

"It nearly did." Gathering her wayward hair into a knot, Esmée secured it with the few remaining pins. "I come with hard news. Cosmos believes the water will soon rise and reach the cottage. 'Tis best if we all go to the tower."

Lucy shuddered. "Up those stairs to sit at the top with the light?"

"I'm afraid so. When the storm tide surges, we don't want to be here below."

"But, mistress, I'm nigh terrified o' heights. And what if the tower should fall into a heap o' rubble? Would we not be safer right here?"

Esmée's encouraging smile felt feeble. "Warmer but not safer, sadly." She began to move what she could atop tables and shelves. "Wrap yourselves in your warmest garments. I'll take Ruenna and lead you there."

She leaned over the baby's drawer bed, hating having to disturb her. Ruenna slept on peacefully, unaware of the danger. As Esmée picked her up, she marveled what a sennight's change could bring. Ruenna felt heavier, with no sign of the scourge that plagued her parents. Her prayers for both Quinn and Eliza seemed unending, her thankfulness that their daughter was out of harm's way ongoing, and now this . . .

She held Ruenna close against her bodice, her cape shielding them, head down in the wind and rain. Sand and shells stung her face and neck as she hastened to the lighthouse door, Alice and Lucy following with Alden. Cosmos was still in the light tower while the other crewman stayed on the ground, boarding up the cottage's windows and hammering with all his might.

Finally in the tower, Esmée tried to reassure Lucy, who stared at Cosmos and the lit pan lamps with trepidation. They'd begun to smoke badly, sending black tendrils into the air around them.

"You'll need these to cover your nose and mouth," Esmée told them, taking clean handkerchiefs from her pocket. She was glad for the benches where they could huddle together for warmth. Still holding Ruenna, she looked toward Cosmos, who was standing stalwart at the glass but likely couldn't see in the pitch blackness beyond.

"The Guineaman's closer," he said at a near shout above the wind's fury.

Ruenna began to stir, and Esmée took a seat, rocking her as best she could. In minutes Alden began to howl, the tense sound reverberating in the closed space and boxing their ears. No matter what Alice did, naught would quiet him. Soon Ruenna joined in, sending Cosmos down the stairs and out into the storm, whether from the noise or another matter Esmée knew not.

In the ghostly, flickering light, Lucy's face was drawn. Dear, steadfast Lucy who never complained but accepted her lot whatever befell her. Conversation was pointless with the din within and without. Another windy blast had Esmée trimming and relighting wicks, nearly overcome with smoke. Alice was crying quietly and trying to nurse Alden while Lucy soothed Ruenna as best she could.

Hands trembling, Esmée prayed, her words lost to the wind.

CHAPTER

fifty-five

As daybreak crept over the unsettled but vastly improved sea, Esmée felt alone in the tower. Alice and Lucy were half-asleep, huddled with the babies on benches. Cosmos and the other crewman were below. Just where, she didn't know. She stood at the glass and looked east, hoping for a flicker of sunrise, anything to temper the somber silver of water and sky. But she needed no sunrise to see the wreckage below.

Downed trees. Rocks and sand where there had been none before. The cottages stood stalwart though missing shingles. Her gaze trailed to the storm-scrubbed beach. Pressing her face nearer the glass till it fogged beneath her breath, she spied the two crewmen on the sand, paying attention to what seemed to be the hull of a ship, or what was left of it.

Nearly tiptoeing past the women and sleeping babies, Esmée descended the stairs, an eerie calm greeting her as she opened the door. Lungs and head clearing, she stepped outside. On the beach, shells and sea urchins amassed with tangles of seaweed. The air held a just-washed smell, briny and clean, but at her feet was wreckage. Soon she traversed shattered glass, trying to take in all she saw from the shipwreck.

Broken bottles. An intact green hourglass. A small chest. Rigging and wood. Coins. Even a tortoiseshell comb and buckled shoe. An apothecary's cup. She moved in the opposite direction of the men, along the south shore of the beach, her senses assaulted by the devastation. At least the wind and waves were spent, no longer a roar but a worn-out sigh.

"Miss Shaw." Cosmos stood behind her. "I urge ye to go inside. Captain Lennox would say the same."

She looked at him. He had been up all night like she, his bewhiskered face and bloodshot eyes holding a warning. True, Henri would not want her on the beach. She needed to return to the tower and tell the women to take the babies to the cottage.

"If ye've ne'er seen bodies wash ashore, I'd spare ye the horror."

She flinched. "From the Guineaman, I suppose."

"Aye. Expect it for days. Best keep to yer hearth's fire."

Nodding and heartsick, she turned back toward the cottage and lighthouse.

Though the cottage had been spared the storm tide, waves had licked the doorstep, leaving the wood frame wet. The brine seemed to penetrate the damp, cold interior but was quickly remedied by robust fires in the hearths. Lucy and Alice went about their tasks singing, the babies alert and content despite so long a night. Even Tibby seemed to have weathered the worst of it though was thoroughly soaked.

Changing into fresh garments, including a warm, quilted petticoat, Esmée looked at the bed longingly. For now, all she wanted was breakfast by the fire and a long cuddle with her niece.

Holding Alden on one hip, Alice stood by the kitchen window, shoulders bent, chewing on her lip as was her custom when worried. As Esmée entered, Lucy smiled wanly, taking the steaming teakettle to the table. Toast and quince preserves awaited.

"Come, the both of you, and breakfast with me," Esmée said.

They sat and Esmée said a prayer, her words laden with thankfulness and relief even as guilt rushed in that she had the luxury of breakfast with the wreck of the Guineaman beyond their door. But she didn't want to weight anyone else's spirits, so she struck a brighter tone.

A half-smile softened Alice's girlish features. "Yer a world apart from Lady Drysdale, Miss Shaw."

"Supping with the help, you mean?" Esmée looked at Ruenna, who flailed a wee hand, the dimples in her cheeks more apparent. "I daren't think what my dear sister would do if she found her firstborn in a dresser drawer."

They laughed, and Lucy said, "Is it true the ship's carpenter who stayed behind is making Miss Ruenna a proper cradle?"

"He said so, though I'm not sure how long she'll stay."

"We've a great many questions that beg answers," Alice said softly. "My mind is on the frontier and how my husband is faring fighting Indians and French."

Giving a rare sigh, Lucy poured the tea. "My thoughts are far out to sea."

"As are mine." Esmée spread her toast with the preserves before biting into the buttery goodness.

"'Tis the not knowing that nettles me. Forever wondering how they're faring out in the deep. And there's those in town with the pox besides—yer dear sister and husband. I wonder about the almshouse too." Lucy looked at Esmée entreatingly as Alice left the room at Alden's fussing. "I wish I could be more like ye, drawing comfort from Scripture, reading the holy words for myself."

Esmée set down her cup. The Bible lay open on the table, the twenty-third Psalm marked with a length of silk ribbon. Why had she not thought of it sooner? A bit shamefaced, she said, "I could teach you."

"I've tried to content myself with listening to ye read aloud." Dismay shadowed Lucy's features. "I'm too daft to learn, my pa always told me."

"Daft? Nay. If you want to learn, you will. We shall buy a Bible for both of you from the booksellers next time we're in York."

Lucy's shocked expression underscored the rarity of such a luxury.

"In the meantime, you can learn your letters. I've no slate, but we have paper. You can practice writing your name too."

"But what of my chores, Miss Shaw? And now with Alice and both babies . . ." Hope faded to confusion. "Is there time enough?"

"We'll make time. The three of us can manage better together. Alice can even join us if she'd like." Esmée looked toward Alice, who sat nursing Alden in the parlor. Her fair head was bent over her babe, eyes closed in weariness. "Though at present perhaps 'tis enough to be a mother."

"Alice can read but cannot write. She wants to answer her husband's letters in the worst way, but . . ."

"I can help her till she learns to pen her own letters." Finishing her tea, Esmée reached for Ruenna. She wore a soft linen gown embellished with ribbon and lace, the sewing exceptionally well-done.

"No sign of the pox, I pray." Lucy looked as distressed as Esmée had ever seen her. "It strikes fast, it does. Took my brother and mother straightaway." 'Twas the first time she'd ever spoken of it, tears close.

Esmée reached out and squeezed her hand. "Oh, Lucy. I cannot imagine. I'm more sorry than I can say."

Lucy blinked, digging in her pocket for a handkerchief. "I pray this wee one will thrive and reunite with her parents soon. 'Tis a grave task ye've been given."

Esmée felt that in spades. She kissed the bottom of Ruenna's tiny foot as she lay in her lap, then marveled as the baby grabbed hold of the finger where Henri's posy ring rested. Forgetting herself, Esmée made over her as if she were her own, singing an old French lullaby that was a favorite of her mother's.

"Frère Jacques, Frère Jacques, Dormez-vous? Dormez-vous? Sonnez les matines. Sonnez les matines. Ding, ding, dong."

CHAPTER
fifty-six

The next sennight found Esmée standing by the graves of those who'd washed ashore after the storm. Six men, two women, and one child. Their final resting places were hastily dug, but the memory of the foundering Guineaman lingered long. Who knew what suffering had taken place that fatal night? The cries for mercy or attempts to be saved? Not even the lighthouse had aided them.

She bent and laid the silk flowers she'd made atop the sandy mounds. None other could be had in the barrenness of winter. Suddenly the island—home to her renewed courtship and future dreams—held a forlorn, wretched feel. Gray skies glowered, adding to her melancholy. That and no word of Eliza or anyone else left her at loose ends. Bending her head, she pondered the lost souls at her feet. And Henri, wherever he happened to be.

The graves were near the buried cache Henri had shown her. She looked toward the sheltering pines that marked it just a stone's throw away. Unseen treasure. But what did it matter if those who meant most were missing? Coin was cold comfort. True, it provided shelter and sustenance, but not family or fulfillment.

She turned away, the pleasant memory of shelling on the beach tattered beside the wreckage washing up. All she wanted at present was the hearth's fire and Ruenna in her arms. And her questions answered.

How was Eliza? Had Quinn recovered fully? She wondered about Father—how he was faring with Virginia all but shut down? Such outbreaks lasted for months and oft returned with a vengeance.

And Henri. Always Henri. Would this new voyage rekindle his love for the sea? Or was it as he said, that those days would soon be behind him?

She cut into the woods on the path that led to their future home. The ground was still soggy, and occasionally she veered round a fallen tree or branch. Before she reached the boundary stones she heard voices—the sound of labor and shouted directions. Coming into the clearing, she stopped beneath an oak, content to watch the work. One of Henri's crew waved at her.

She came closer, noting they'd built a partial wall. The kitchen garden enclosure? A little trill of delight lifted her melancholy.

Cosmos greeted her, wiping his hands on his leather apron. "We're at work with rock remaining from the lighthouse."

"'Tis a handsome wall that breaks the sea wind."

"We mean to finish that and a smokehouse and such before the captain's return, or toil till we've run out of stone."

"I long for spring and the first supply ship." She looked to the beach warily. She nearly couldn't broach the subject. "Have any more . . ."

He gave a yank to his Monmouth cap. "No more to bury, Miss Shaw. But that doesn't mean we're done. If another storm blows in . . ."

"I understand. You've all been such a mainstay. Captain Lennox will reward you handsomely for it."

"He's a generous man, the captain. If ye have need of anything, we're at your service."

She thanked him, and he returned to work whistling, further lightening her mood. She hastened back to the cottage, where she shuttered dark thoughts and spent an hour planning her garden and taking stock of the seed packets Kitty had given her, mostly flowers and herbs. 'Twas February and Candlemas, the month that required the attention of a gardener more than any other. What had Mama said? *If Candlemas day be fair and bright, winter will have another flight; but if it be dark with clouds and rain, winter is gone and will not come again.*

Weather permitting, she'd prepare her ground and sow salad herbs, mainly Silesia and imperial lettuces, by month's end. But the garden wall needed finishing before she set to work.

A cry arose from the drawer bed. Abandoning her seed, Esmée picked up Ruenna, who quieted at her touch. Recently fed, she couldn't possibly be hungry again. Finding the room cold, Esmée sought the warmth of the parlor and sat near the hearth, a sliver of trepidation accompanying what had become her usual routine. Gently she pulled back the baby's swaddling, searching for any worrisome sign.

Relieved, she placed Ruenna against her chest and shoulder, the warm bulk of her honey-sweet. All that Eliza was missing tugged at her. Each day brought telling changes to a child so young. Though the babe had been here but a fortnight, she was plumper and less wrinkled. Even her dark hair was curling at her crown.

Alice came into the parlor cradling Alden, smiling at them. "Ye've taken to Miss Ruenna like she's yer own."

"You set a worthy example," Esmée replied as Alice took a seat opposite, turning Alden around on her lap to face the fire. "His father would be proud."

"Aye, Johnny would be, as the imp looks just like him." Alice kissed the top of Alden's russet head. "I thank ye again for helping me pen a letter."

"Once Father returns we shall post it." Esmée took Ruenna's silver rattle from a basket and handed it to Alden. He shook it in his fat fist before bringing it to his mouth, the tiny bells tinkling.

"He's about to sprout a tooth. I can feel it on his gum." Alice settled back and looked to the kitchen, her thin frame less bony than before. "Lucy is determined to fatten me. She's baking ratafia cakes right now."

"I thought I smelled orange flower water." Esmée breathed in the delightful aroma coming from the bake oven. "We shall have a pleasant tea party, we three. Celebrate being here safe and sound together."

Alice nodded, gaze falling to her son. "If not for the island—and you and your father—where would we be? My own babe might have sickened and died. Here, away from the scourge, we're blessed indeed."

"D'ye think Alice will be here for a while yet, Miss Shaw?" Lucy called from the kitchen.

"At least till my sister has recovered and the smallpox fades." Esmée kissed Ruenna's soft brow. "My father should bring us news soon, I hope."

Alice looked toward a window. "The weather has settled, God be praised."

"We've much to be thankful for," Esmée replied. "Ratafia cakes. Healthy babes. Spring planting. The *Intrepid*'s return."

"I hope I'm here to see ye and the captain wed." Alice's smile broadened. "Lucy is sweet on one of the crew, aye? We might see two weddings come spring . . . and more babes the next."

Such happy talk pushed back every dark thought, at least for the present.

CHAPTER *fifty-seven*

After Candlemas, the weather brightened. Nights were clear and cool, the stars so brilliant Esmée stayed longer in the lighthouse. By day, the sun beckoned her outdoors, though shelling had lost its allure, the memory of the wrecked Guineaman too fresh. But at least no wind frothed the water into a tempest. Some days the sea merely rippled and shone like blue silk.

The garden's stone fence was finished, so she trod the pine path to her future home, reveling in the enclosure warmed by winter's sun. Here she turned the sandy soil with spade and hoe, uprooting stubborn weeds in such a way Eliza would deem her a field hand. Her gloves protected her from the worst blisters, and soon she'd made a solid start. No seed planted yet, but still she rejoiced in what was to come as she returned to the cottage for tea.

Washing up, she sat down at the table, only to rise again as a knock sounded and Lucy went to answer. There on the threshold stood Henri's ancient ship's carpenter, toting a cradle mounted on rockers. He set it before the parlor fire, and Esmée brought linens, anxious to settle Ruenna in her new bed, as she would soon outgrow the dresser drawer.

"You've outdone yourself," Esmée told him, admiring the smooth pine and expertly carved crowns and anchors that embellished it, even the hood meant to keep away drafts. "'Tis a cradle fit for a nobleman's daughter."

"Not to mention the admiral's granddaughter." Hat in hand, he smiled, his grizzled face shining with pride in a job enjoyed.

"Father will be pleased. I expect him any day now."

"I'll start work on the second bed for Master Alden." He left, several tea cakes in hand.

The women returned to the hearth's warmth, Esmée enjoying her hyson while rocking the cradle with her foot. Soon Ruenna was fast asleep, snug as she could be within the bed's high, cushioned sides.

"A wee fairy she is." Lucy passed a plate of currant cakes before sitting down and pouring herself a cup of tea. "Almost a month old, aye?"

Esmée looked at the calendar pinned to the far wall, its numerals in boldface. "Three weeks as of yesterday."

Again her thoughts turned to Eliza and Quinn. Nary a word had come from Williamsburg. She'd expected Father before now. As for Henri, he'd been gone two months. Yet any day now she might see those linen sails she missed bearing down on the island. She turned toward the window in anticipation, expectation fragile as a spring flower inside her.

Sails were indeed in her line of sight. Two sails signifying a much smaller vessel than the *Intrepid*. Esmée set aside her tea, foot ceasing to rock Ruenna.

Father? At last. Did he bring good news?

She was out the door without her cape, so anxious was she to see him, only to turn around and ascertain Ruenna was still asleep and not too near the unattended hearth.

While Lucy and Alice hovered near the open door, Esmée hurried down the path to the pier. Paying scant attention to the deckhands aboard the sloop, she focused on her father. His back to her, he stood by the companionway, where a cloaked figure was emerging. Eliza?

In all black.

Eliza never wore black. She hated black. All the implications came crashing down as Father helped her onto shore. Eliza was in mourning.

Esmée's stomach flipped. By the time she reached them, another realization nearly had her casting up her accounts and left little time to hide her horror. Eliza had stepped onto the pier and looked straight at her, her face masked by a black veil. Just then the wind caught it and exposed once-smooth skin now horribly pitted, her very eyes inflamed. Some pox victims went blind . . .

Lord, I cannot bear it.

Eliza's veil settled back in place. Coming alongside her, Esmée took her arm while Father supported her on the other side. Questions Esmée couldn't ask sat like gravel in her mouth.

The cottage door stood open, but Lucy and Alice had vanished. Helping Eliza inside, Esmée and her father led her to a fireside chair, Ruenna near in her new cradle.

"I'll have Lucy bring you both tea." Hardly aware of what she said or did, Esmée removed her sister's wraps while a clatter went up in the kitchen.

Father kept on his greatcoat, his expression causing Esmée's heart to wrench harder. He looked down at Eliza, who stared vacantly into the fire. This was not her beloved, vibrant sister. This was a shell of Eliza, a fragile, miserable echo.

"Father . . ." Esmée looked at him imploringly, hands spread. Was Eliza listening? "What of Quinn?" Esmée whispered.

He swallowed with difficulty and hung his cape from a wall peg. "Though he seemed to rally, by the time I returned from bringing the baby to you, he was gone."

Gone. Such a small word for such enormous loss. It left her breathless. Quinn—an integral part of Williamsburg, from the House of Burgesses and governor's council to titled peer and attentive host, the pride of their very lives—now lay in the Bruton Parish graveyard. His absence tore a hole in everything they knew. Now Ruenna had no father, only a sickly, grieving mother. Death was never far, but never had it felt so personal since Mama's passing.

Numbly she watched as Lucy brought tea. Eliza said nary a word. Father took the chair beside her while Ruenna slept without stirring at one end of the hearth. Esmée felt hapless and uncertain, words of sympathy catching in her throat. Circling behind her father and Eliza, she took the empty chair by her sister, who was accepting a cup of tea from Lucy's hands.

"Despite everything, I'm glad you're here," Esmée began quietly once Lucy had retreated to the kitchen. She looked to the cradle. Ruenna wore the lace and linen gown she'd come to the island in, a matching cap on her head, the strings tied loosely beneath her chin. "Your daughter is well, thankfully. She has a felicitous disposition and cries little. She—"

"Looks just like her father." Eliza set down her cup with a clatter.

Esmée glanced at their father in a silent plea. He regarded his granddaughter with bloodshot eyes as if he'd not slept in a fortnight. What a time they'd had since they last parted. Esmée couldn't imagine the tears and the turmoil.

Drying her eyes, Eliza returned to her tea with a visibly set jaw, a handkerchief fisted in one hand. She did not raise her veil or look Ruenna's way again.

CHAPTER *fifty-eight*

Father and Eliza took Henri's quarters with its two bedchambers and larger parlor. Eliza made it quite clear Ruenna was to stay behind.

"I cannot have the care of an infant when my heart is broken. Not yet." She'd faced Esmée, the old fire in her eyes a mere flicker. "Perhaps not ever."

With that she'd hastened to Henri's cottage, Father in her wake. Esmée sensed Lucy's and Alice's unspoken relief when the decision was made.

In the ensuing days, Eliza was rarely seen, sleeping the hours away, trying to recover her health—or lose herself in slumber. Lucy would deliver their meals only to return posthaste. The easy amiability Esmée had once shared with her and Alice was now fraught with profound sadness. Even the weather grew stormy, washing more bodies from the Guineaman ashore.

Inking a quill, Esmée penned her uppermost hope during one of their lessons. "This too shall pass."

She wrote it in her light, scrolling hand, Lucy and Alice following with their own quills and paper. Esmée felt a glimmer of hope when

Alice suggested they write down what they were most thankful for, a challenging task amid their sadness. But quickly their gratitude was spelled out.

Birdsong. Cats. The Bible. Hyson tea. Warm bread. Jam. Companionship. Laughter. Firelight and starlight. The coming spring. Heaven.

That night, Esmée lingered in the tower, looking out on the vastness of the water and willing Henri back to her. Ensconced on high, she seemed to rise above the worries of the moment. She pulled another old letter she'd gotten from the sea chest out of her pocket.

7th June 1749

Dear Esmée,

Since we passed the island of Barbados we have had continuous contrary winds. We therefore mostly sailed with set sails and double-reefed topsails.

I have not written in some time. I have realized these letters, which you will likely never read, have instead become necessary to me. Somehow the simple stroke of writing your name brings you nearer despite the miles and circumstances that separate us. Though coastal Virginia fades in memory the longer I'm away, you remain steadfast. I see your eyes in the green of a Montserrat forest, your dark hair reflected in the black-sand beaches, your comely form in the wending hills and valleys of these lush islands. You once said I am all rigging and sails, not a whit romantic. Let this be proof I am not that which you claimed, not soulless but soulful, and still besotted.

She could almost hear him speaking, his penned words reflective of his voice. Longing swam through her in a giddy rush. All the years lost to them still stung like a sea urchin, but she sensed Henri was on his way back to her. Or so she hoped. Eliza had no such silver lining.

Setting aside his letter yellowed with age, she took out a blank sheet of new paper and inked her goose quill.

Dear Henri,

Words cannot express the depth of my missing you. Each day feels a year, each minute hours. Yet I am proud of your service to the colonies and am confident your mission will be a success.

All that has happened since you sailed breaks my heart. I cannot even commit my feelings to paper without spotting the page. Smallpox is making a misery of Virginia once again. Father and I are spared, as we have mild scars to show for it from years past. But dear Eliza has lost Quinn and is even now on the island with me, a scarred widow. Father is with us. I fear he is afraid to leave Eliza as if she might die of grief. I know not what to say nor how to comfort her. She has no interest in her newborn daughter. I pray to help her but cannot see my way clear.

Another heartache is that a ship foundered in a tempest a sennight or so ago . . .

The candle flickered, a glaze of gold before her tear-filled eyes. Her quill dropped and spattered ink. She laid her head against the table, another prayer rising in her heart.

Lord, help me help Eliza.

On the Sabbath, Esmée walked with her father on the beach. The tide was out, the sun making a blinding blue of the water. Signs of spring were taking hold, not only beach grass but a lone spot of color here and there poking out amid marshland and forest.

"I miss Grace Church," Esmée confessed, her arm tucked in his. "It seems strange on the Lord's Day to be absent."

"Sabbath services are suspended till the pox subsides." He bent to examine a piece of sea glass. "Henri told me he might build a chapel here, though he would be hard-pressed to find a clergyman to live on the island. 'Twould be an exceedingly small flock."

Esmée lifted her head to the sea breeze, trying to imagine it. She'd just shown Father the finished garden wall and boundaries of their future home. His approval meant the world to her. He'd also asked to see the graves. She bit her lip when tempted to tell him about the buried treasure.

"Has Mistress Saltonstall returned yet?" He was looking toward the Flask and Sword, whose twin chimneys could be seen puffing smoke.

"Not yet."

"Do you mind if your sister stays on with you for a time?"

Esmée hid her dismay. The sinking inside her turned to shame. She'd never been sure of Eliza even at her best, and now . . . "I thought perhaps she might want to return to the townhouse and the comforts of town."

"Your sister doesn't know if she's afoot or on horseback at present. In her grief she's incapable of any decision making, however small." His lined face seemed more so since Quinn's death, his periwig hiding the silver of his hair. "I was thinking your company might do her good. At the very least she needs to be near Ruenna."

The ache in Esmée's breast swelled. "But Eliza refuses to have anything to do with her."

"Give her time. Grief is a hard taskmaster." He pressed her gloved hand with his own. "Let us speak of more hopeful things. No doubt you are ever on the lookout for your captain. He's been cruising for some time now."

Her half-smile ended in a sigh. "Over two months, in fact."

"Which will soon have an end." His expression lightened. "I look forward to a wedding immensely."

"A wartime wedding, I fear."

"Aye. France is vying for empire not only in America but in Africa, India, and the Caribbean. 'Tis time to see it end. But it shan't end without another war."

"Which means Henri will be expected to sail again."

"Few are better qualified than he."

She digested this confirmation like a sour apple. Of course Henri would be expected at sea with war declared. As a captain's wife, she'd best get used to that. His talk of becoming a landsman was hopeful but unrealistic given colonial politics. Although Henri was no puppet, Dinwiddie was as intractable as a Scottish bulldog.

She finally said, "The governor and his family are well?"

"Dinwiddie's been ill for some time with something other than the pox. And as harried by contentions at the College of William and Mary and amongst the burgesses as by the French and their Indian allies."

"I feel for him."

Her father reached a hand into his weskit and consulted his timepiece. "Let us go have tea with Eliza—or attempt to, shall we?"

Tea no longer held the appeal it once did, but Esmée forged ahead. She must help rally her sister, and even their beleaguered father. "Of course. Lucy has made her favorite lemon cheese tarts. Hopefully that will help cheer her. And I'll open my best tea."

CHAPTER *fifty-nine*

The lemon cheese tarts were brought alongside Esmée's tea chest, but would Eliza rouse herself and join them? Ensconced in Henri's parlor, Esmée promptly forgot the matter at hand. Wherever she looked seemed to whisper her beloved's name. There over the mantel was one of Henri's swords with its silken knot, beneath a map of the world. A handsome pipe and silver tobacco box rested on a near table. His upholstered chair, a rich blue brocade with a nautical theme, suited Father well. All carried Henri's distinctive style, his scent. She couldn't get enough of it.

In the other room Eliza could be heard readying herself. Without her maidservant it took considerable time. Father had said she had sickened as well and would hopefully recover. Till Eliza's return, the servants were being cared for by a physic and apothecary.

Esmée looked at the tea service that had been her mother's, artfully arranged on a silver tray. Lucy had brought it over before returning to their cottage, sending Esmée a sympathetic look. Alice carried Ruenna. Wide awake, she made cooing sounds from her basket and flailed her tiny limbs. Esmée couldn't resist leaning over and stroking her dimpled cheek, smiling down at her as she wished Eliza would do.

"I fear I have the look of an unmade bed." Eliza appeared, her unwashed hair in tangles and only half pinned up, sultana wrinkled, eyes red. "And I have no appetite."

"At least try a lemon cheese tart," Esmée coaxed. "Lucy made them with you in mind."

"I prefer a peck of toast." Eliza's gaze swept the tea table and landed on Ruenna. "Why is the child here? She should be by Alice's side."

Father patted the chair beside him. "We are family, Ruenna included."

Eliza sat with a frown. "She is so lively it tires me."

Grasping the handle of the teapot, Esmée bit back a hasty retort and poured her sister the first cup. "My chest of congou is nearly empty. Bohea it shall be for future teas."

"Such an infernal tax on tea, no wonder 'tis smuggled so," Father said, sipping from his saucer. "Lucy brews a perfect pot. She seems a hand at many tasks."

Esmée poured herself a cup. "I couldn't ask for better company—"

Eliza's unladylike snort clipped her words. "Really, Sister, to say a mere almshouse maid is good company borders on the ridiculous."

Father looked at his youngest daughter, his voice even. "Grief does not excuse insolence nor arrogance, Eliza. Not even Quinn would conscience that."

Her chin trembled. "And would you add to my grief with your untimely rebuke?"

"I am merely trying to return you to the world of the living." To his credit, he reined Eliza in as forthrightly as an admiral would a truant officer. "As your father, I would not see you inflict more suffering on yourself or others any longer. True, you are bereaved. Others are as well, myself included. True, you are scarred, but many are buried. As your mother oft said, the best of all healers is cheer."

Chastened, Eliza took a tart. At Ruenna's sudden cry, she started, a pained expression on her unveiled face.

Setting her cup down, Esmée reached for the baby, who smiled so wide her pink gums appeared. The tension in the room, which had been tempered by Father's wise words, ratcheted higher.

Ruenna was the image of Quinn. Dear Quinn. If not for him and his unwitting dinner invitation to Henri in the fall, Esmée might not be betrothed. How much she owed her brother-in-law. The latent realization left her wishing she'd thanked him before it was too late.

"She's a charming child, well content and getting plumper by the day," Father remarked. "Best enjoy her at every stage, as the first year flies away all too soon. Soon she'll be toddling about in a pudding cap."

Eliza jabbed her untouched tart with a finger. "I daren't think of the future. 'Tis too bleak."

"Bleak, my dear?"

"What have I?"

"Need I remind you that you are now one of the wealthiest widows in the colonies, not impoverished like so many?"

She brought her fist down on the table, rattling the china. "Would that I had Quinn and be destitute!"

A sullen silence fell. Esmée hardly tasted the delicious tart. Holding Ruenna in one arm, she resumed drinking her tea with her free hand, careful not to spill any.

Eliza continued undaunted. "I cannot imagine dancing or walking about or playing the harpsichord or anything I used to enjoy. Not without Quinn. He was so many things to me. Husband, confidant, advisor, a bulwark in every storm."

Father nodded gravely. "We will sorely miss him. Have you given any thought to returning to Williamsburg?"

"Nay." Eliza darted another look at Ruenna. "But this rusticated island is not the place for me either."

"You are always welcome to reside at our York residence. Your rooms are much as you left them."

Eliza added more sugar to her cup. "You are generous, Father, but I am foul company at present."

"You'll be in mourning, of course, wherever you go."

"A year at the outset." She shook her head in distaste. "I suppose this calls for a visit to the mantuamaker and milliner, as I'll be clad in black bombazine for an eternity. Not to mention we must blacken the townhouse. Coaches and chairs are to be covered in black cloth, and all the servants must wear shoulder knots of black silk ribbon. Even Ruenna shall be in all black."

At this Esmée nearly protested, but 'twas the custom, after all. Ruenna, thankfully, had not the slightest inkling what she wore. Esmée raised her eyes to Eliza, schooling the shock she always felt at her appearance.

"Being the bluestocking you are, I suppose you shan't postpone your wedding." Eliza's gaze held a challenge. "What say you, Sister?"

As Esmée finished swallowing a bite of tart, Father answered with vehemence, "Most certainly not. She and the captain have waited ten years and shan't delay a moment longer. I mean no disrespect to Quinn, but age and experience have taught me that some matters are best seized at once despite forms and customs."

"'Gather ye rosebuds while ye may, Old Time is still a-flying; and this same flower that smiles today tomorrow will be dying.'" Eliza quoted the old poem dry-eyed but with a bitter taint to her tone.

Ruenna gave another cry, and Esmée set down her cup and shifted the babe to her shoulder. "Shush, poppet."

"Does she need to nurse?" Eliza asked, eyes dark.

"'Tis not her hungry cry. She just had a feeding before Alice brought her over. Here, why don't you hold her?" Esmée made a motion to pass the baby to her, but Eliza held up her hands in protest.

"She would cry louder at my ravaged face." Chin trembling again, Eliza looked at her untouched tea. "Besides, you and Alice are the ones she needs. And once Alice weans her, she shall be in a nurse's care. 'Tis as it should be. Infants tire me so."

"Sister, please reconsider." Esmée returned Ruenna to her shoulder. "She needs her mother most of all, not a nurse."

Father tapped his fingers atop his chair arm, eyes on Eliza. "I must leave tomorrow. You'll have till then to decide whether you wish to remain here on the island or return to the mainland."

CHAPTER *sixty*

Twas a shimmering twilight when Esmée lit the pan lamps. She took up her quill and wrote in the logbook.

9th February 1756. Sea calm. Mild southwest wind. Lamp oil low.

Just that morn, two of Henri's crew who'd weathered pox in the past had returned with Father to York for supplies. She had enough oil for another sennight, or so she hoped. At least till their reappearance. She chided herself for letting supplies get so low.

Standing by the glass, Esmée looked down on Henri's cottage, where Eliza had chosen to stay on for an indefinite amount of time. Light rimmed the windows, making Esmée wonder what her sister did in Father's absence. His steadying presence was missed, especially where her sister was concerned.

Eliza's choice to stay surprised them all. She did not remain out of love for the island. A rustic outpost, she called it. She simply wanted to avoid the scrutiny of Williamsburg and York and so hid here, Esmée sensed, her grief over her pockmarked skin seemingly as great as her grief over Quinn. And there seemed no way to assuage it.

Lord, what would You have me do for my sister?

At a loss, she sat down and looked out the glass at a passing sloop. Lately her heart had ceased to catch over every ship, as if her hopes were fraying. Still, she stared at the handsome vessel till its lofty sails were swallowed up by darkness and seemed no more substantial than a moth's wings.

A half hour more and the tower shone bright as a lantern in the gathering darkness. Once the watery view was lost to her, she checked the lamps again, trimming wicks as needed.

"Miss Shaw."

The low voice nearly made her drop her candle. She spun, gaze fastening on a shadowed figure at the top of the stairs.

Jago Wherry?

He was heavily bewhiskered, his hat pulled low. His right hand clutched a pistol. A chill passed through her. She had no weapon here in the tower, only a flintlock pistol in the cottage.

"Why have you come?" she asked, her voice sounding stronger and more well-intentioned than she felt.

He took a step toward her, and she took a step back, bumping the desk behind her. "I've a need only ye can remedy."

"Speak plainly, sir." Her voice seemed to echo. "I must return to my cottage lest others come looking for me."

For the first time Esmée silently bemoaned Henri's crew at the island's opposite end.

"Not till ye hear what I'm after." Wherry stood betwixt her and the stairs. Caressing the weapon with his thumb, he smiled thinly. "I ken ye have knowledge of prizes secreted here on the island. And ye'll not be rid of me till ye show me just where."

How did he know? A sourness closed her throat. And what would he do if she didn't do as he bid? "Captain Lennox is due any day. If he finds you here wanting to steal from him, I shudder to think what your punishment will be."

Something inexplicable passed over his tight features. The reek of rum threaded the cold air. He'd been drinking, not enough to dull his wits or his limbs, but enough to make him dangerously reckless.

"Ye'll meet me at first light—alone—and take me to where the cache is buried."

She pondered this and her way out of it. Wherry was a canny man. She doubted he was alone in his nefarious dealings. "You're making a terrible mistake coming here and asking me such."

A low laugh. "I've half a dozen rogues and cutthroats in a near cove who consider it a handsome plan, not to mention some well-placed gents in Williamsburg. Beware my mates near at hand. When they're liquored they're prone to mischief. I'd hate to see them make sport with the other three women who keep ye company. Two babes wouldn't stand in the way."

"How dare you—"

"Oh, I dare, make no mistake. Weary o' the almshouse as I am, 'tis time to move on with coin in my pocket and that o' my companions."

Her stomach churned as her mind whirled. How to rid herself of him and his fellows was uppermost, but how to do it with so few of the crew near . . .

"I was leaving the French camp when I saw the captain leave the almshouse one night under cover o' darkness. No one said a word, but afterwards we were all the better for it." He spat a stream of tobacco on the pristine floor. "Everyone knows he's a prize master. Stands to reason he'd hardly miss what's cached right here. Word is he's after the French as we speak, taking more still. Needs be we poor folk have our day."

Esmée shook her head. "I cannot share what is not mine to give."

He all but lunged at her, grabbing her arm and pressing the pistol's cold steel against her temple. "Make no attempt to gain help at the Flask and Sword. We've timed our coming with care. Meet me at daybreak on the path that leads to the south beach. Come alone. If ye play me false ye'll not return to the light."

"Are ye all right, Miss Shaw?" Alice's voice penetrated Esmée's panic as she removed her cape at the door of the cottage.

A baby's cry spared her an answer. Alice moved toward Ruenna in her cradle near the hearth, giving Esmée a moment to gather her wits.

"All well here?" Esmée asked, crossing to the window to take another look at the light.

Jago Wherry had vanished as quickly as he'd come, making her wish their meeting was a bad dream. Her every nerve stretched taut, her stomach roiling. But for the moment Alice was holding Ruenna out to her with a slightly exasperated smile.

"The babe is fat as butter," she said as Esmée took Ruenna in her arms. "And she's been fed, so I don't know why she's cross."

Did the baby have a bit of Eliza's temper? Ruenna's blue eyes were awash with tears, her tiny fists bunched. She wailed as if she'd been pricked with a pin. Esmée made certain that wasn't the case, then cradled her closer, wanting to protect her at all costs.

Alice took Alden from his new cradle, his crying giving way to hiccups. "Just when we got the babes quieted for you, up they pop!"

Esmée took a steadying breath. "Have you seen my sister?"

Alice shook her head. "Lucy served her supper in the captain's cottage a half hour ago."

Taking a chair, Esmée studied the babe's delicate but flushed features, wishing Eliza would come in and console her. As it was, she was so distracted she could give little comfort.

"Would ye like a cup of chocolate, Miss Shaw?" Lucy came from the kitchen, all concern, as Alice excused herself to change Alden. "'Tis so chill in the lighthouse. Your cheeks are red as roses."

"Please," Esmée replied absently, though her supper sat uneasily, her head a-hammer. How would she manage the rich drink?

She studied Lucy's comely form as she went to the kitchen. Wherry had threatened harm to not only her but the women with her. How many of his fellows were with him? Were they even now watching the cottage?

Lucy returned, cocoa in hand. "Has any crew come from the Flask and Sword?"

"I haven't any idea." Esmée looked at her, startled. "Why do you ask?"

Lucy darted a look at the kitchen. "I spied a man coming out of the light. He had a familiar look about him."

An odd relief overrode Esmée's panic. "I'll not dissemble." She lowered her voice as Ruenna squirmed in her arms. "We are in a predicament. Jago Wherry has come seeking prizes."

"Wherry?" Lucy's alarmed words raised the gooseflesh on Esmée's arms. "Surely the old sot's bluffing?"

They stared at each other. Esmée couldn't risk their safety and oppose him. But neither could she betray Henri's trust and forgo the cache, though she was certain he would say it mattered little compared to their lives.

"I suppose Wherry's brought his cronies?" Lucy's eyes narrowed. "From the back alleys of York and the track, most likely. 'Tis spirits that embolden them to act so rashly and defy the captain, likely."

"Please, say nothing to Alice." Esmée heard her singing to Alden. "Pray for our protection and deliverance."

"God help us . . ." Lucy's usual paleness leached whiter. "There's the babes to think of—and her ladyship, who seems half-barmy, if ye pardon my saying so."

This was another of Esmée's fears, that her sister's disordered mind would refuse to right itself. No doubt the Eliza of old would rise to the challenge of outwitting Wherry if she got wind of his schemes. Or if she knew Henri's treasure was pinpointed on a map beneath the very floorboards of the cottage she now occupied.

Esmée's reply died in her throat when Alice reappeared with a smile, obviously none the wiser.

As cups were filled and the fire crackled and Ruenna finally began to settle, Esmée's mind spun. Might she lead Wherry to a false location and let him dig? Say the treasure had been taken when he turned up emptyhanded? But then what? If he became angry . . . if he knew she'd misled him . . .

Lord, a way of escape, please.

CHAPTER *sixty-one*

The cold dawn added to Esmée's angst. Rain threatened, the sea churlish. Sleepless and sharp-tempered, she walked the path to Wherry's appointed meeting place with leaden feet. Though she'd considered avoiding him, she sensed he would appear at the cottage and thereby place the other women in more danger. So she slipped out, telling Lucy to lock the door after her and not unlock it till she returned.

Her silent prayers seemed to rise no farther than the clouds hanging above her head. When she spied Wherry waiting among the cover of pines, her chest tightened till she couldn't breathe. Yet she held to the Scripture that had come to her in the night, just as she clutched the captain's pistol hidden in her pocket.

The wicked plotteth against the just, and gnasheth upon him with his teeth. The Lord shall laugh at him: for he seeth that his day is coming.

She certainly felt gnashed upon. Then Wherry was at her back with what she assumed was a primed, loaded weapon and a shovel. He spoke little, his bloodshot gaze and shambling gait unnerving her further. When they passed the copse of trees where Henri had carefully stored his cache, she felt a momentary qualm. Should she just give Wherry what he wanted? *Nay*, came a bone-deep conviction. She led him on down the path as far from the women and infants as possible.

"Hasten your steps, Miss Shaw." The gravelly voice was thick with drink. "I've no time to waste."

A sharp jab to the small of her back stole the last of her composure. She whirled on him, legs atremble beneath her quilted petticoats. His surprise flared as she thrust her own pistol in his leering face.

"Shall we have it out betwixt us first?" Her voice shook with heat. "I'm done with your threatening and demands."

"A foolish move." Their pistols were pointed at each other, only his hand was steadier. "My men are trailing us. If I say the word, ye'll have more than me to reckon with."

Could she believe him? She'd neither seen nor sensed anyone else. In the trice of her ruminating, he wrested the gun from her grasp, twisting her wrist and fueling her ire.

"Thou art unfit for any place but hell." She spat out the Shakespearean slur even as she prayed for deliverance.

On they went, two weapons now trained upon her. She stopped atop a dune. The storm surge had swept this side of the island, doing far more damage than to their own rocky point. When she gestured to a patch of sandy ground, he tossed aside the weapons and began digging, a mistrustful eye upon her.

Wrist aching, she watched him, standing well apart from his feverish work. At a gull's hollow cry, she scanned the surrounding brush and trees, searching, sifting. Wherry would soon tire of his fruitless search and turn on her.

Should she run?

Sleeplessness burned her eyes and left her cumbersome. A flicker of movement in the trees sent another tremor of alarm through her. His cronies? *Someone* was there, crouched just beyond a tangle of seagrass.

Wherry threw down his shovel in disgust, a great mound of sand the proof he'd been digging for naught. "Ye've fooled me, and there's but one fix for it." Taking up the pistols, he waved her on to walk in front of him again. "Mayhap yer of more value to me than buried treasure. What would yer admiral father give, I wonder, to see ye safely returned?"

In minutes they were alongshore in the island's smallest, most private cove, perfect for a hideout. Esmée stared at a sleek jolly manned by half a dozen crew. So Wherry hadn't lied to her. The men watched their approach, their wariness turning to outright disgust at seeing them emptyhanded. Had they truly expected chests of specie?

Esmée slowed her pace, only to be shoved from behind by Wherry, both pistols waving as he unleashed a string of epithets fit for the basest waterfront tavern. Another man grunted a few words to him from the jolly as they readied to push off.

With her aboard.

The realization ricocheted around her head but gave no motion to her leaden feet. She was shaking now, and another shove from Wherry left her stumbling in the sand. Rain began pelting down, a grumble of thunder overhead. Where would they take her? What demands would they make of her father?

Oh, heavenly Father, help me!

One buckled shoe came off in deep sand, and she bent to right it. At that moment, an ear-splitting crack sounded. Something whistled past her head, jarring her with its nearness. Wherry's pained howl stirred her to action. Grabbing up her skirts, she abandoned her shoe and started toward the nearest trees.

Another gunshot came, this one aimed at the shallop. A third shot sent a man overboard with a splash. Wherry's crew scrambled in all directions to take cover even as they put out to sea. Dangerously light-headed, Esmée looked on from where she crouched behind a thick pine. Wherry got to his feet, scarlet streaming in wide ribbons down his shirtfront. Another shot took off the club of his queued hair. He weaved atop the sand, taking a few staggering steps toward the jolly before collapsing on the beach.

Who had been the answer to her prayer?

Spent gunpowder burnt Esmée's nostrils as it carried on the damp air. An answering shot from the jolly hit a near tree, splintering the bark. The vessel withdrew into choppy water, minus two men.

"Miss Shaw!" A vaguely familiar voice bade her turn round even as the rustle of brush announced a man's approach.

Nathaniel Autrey? He stepped free of the beach grass, staring at her as if to ascertain she was unhurt.

She put a hand to her throat. "I've never been gladder to see someone!"

"Would you had said such upon my pursuit of you." His wry smile further reassured her as much as the smoking weapon in his right hand.

With a choked laugh, she stood on unsteady legs as he helped her to her feet. "You are unscathed, I hope, but understandably shaken." At her nod, his attention returned to the beach where Wherry lay. "God forgive me, but I could see no other way to aid you but take him down. Clearly his intent was to do you harm."

"He was bent on mischief. He threatened to harm the women and children." She leaned against the pine's trunk, winded. "However did you happen to be here at such a remarkable time?"

"Uncanny indeed. The Almighty gets all the credit. I was merely intent on paying a debt, the one I mentioned when I last saw you in the Drysdales' parlor over Christmas." He returned his gun to its holder beneath his frock coat. "I came over with the crew you sent to the mainland for lamp oil. And I bring good news from a trusted source. Captain Lennox's return is imminent, so I hoped to see him again as well."

Esmée's spirits took wing at the latter. *Henri home. Henri here.* 'Twas he who'm she'd be most glad to see when all was said and done.

Footsteps turned her on edge again till Cosmos and another crew member appeared.

"We heard the commotion from the tavern." Cosmos regarded them, alarm stitched into his bewhiskered face beneath his Monmouth cap. "We came as quick as we could."

"Which ain't quick enough given the state I'm in," the florid-faced master's mate muttered in apology as he rubbed his gout-stricken leg. "Needs be we see to burying the bilge-swilling blackguard. Or take 'im out in the captain's jolly at high tide."

All eyes turned to Wherry, who was clearly dead. Esmée's stomach twisted, and she swallowed hard even as Nathaniel took her elbow. "I'll return you to your end of the island," he said. "And I shall stay till the remaining crew at the Flask and Sword—or Captain Lennox—return."

CHAPTER *sixty-two*

"You must stay on in the captain's cottage," Esmée told Nathaniel as they walked the path toward the lighthouse, far calmer than when he'd found her on the beach. "But first I must remove my dear sister."

"I suppose it can't be helped," he remarked, hat in hand. "I heard Lord Drysdale has been buried. A better man I've not found in all Virginia."

"Truly. We miss him sorely." Tears threatened at Quinn's mention, but she blinked them back. "Having you near will be a great relief to us all. But will it tax your aunts having you away? Mount Autrey needs you, surely."

"Mount Autrey and my aunts survived a great many years without me, including the pox. A few days or even a fortnight or longer won't change that." He looked toward the cottage in question. "Though I am loath to displace her ladyship."

"Think no more of it, please. We shall all be glad of your presence."

"I'll wait here by the pier then," he told her.

Esmée found Eliza sitting by the hearth's fire in her sultana, not abed as she so often was but still marked by the same forlorn expression. The remaining sores on her face were fading, but the scarring would remain. Near at hand was a Madeira bottle and cup. With a tick of alarm Esmée saw that it was half-empty.

"I'm happy to see you up." Esmée's voice sounded as washed-out as all the rest of her. "We've just come through a calamity, which I'll soon explain. For now, Chaplain Autrey is standing out in the cold and needs to lodge here in the captain's quarters while you return to us."

"Return? There's hardly room!"

"We've trundle beds in a pinch."

Eliza jumped to her feet. At once her hands flew to her face, revealing the gist of her thoughts. "But I cannot be seen. He will—I look a fright. I am not the woman he remembers."

"You are far more than your appearance, Sister." Esmée's words were soft. "He knows you're grieving and is thoughtfully waiting by the water till we move you."

Eliza hurried across the room and reached for her veiled bonnet and her cape. "I have no wish to exchange words with him so shall rush past straightaway."

"I'll have Lucy bring your belongings over then." Esmée took a poker, built up the fire, and added another log before following her.

In a quarter of an hour, the exchange was made, the former sea chaplain ensconced by his own fire with a book from the captain's library: *Travels into Several Remote Nations of the World.*

"Promise me you won't invite him to supper." Eliza was more animated than Esmée had recently seen her. "Though the chaplain was a friend to Quinn, I fear facing him would simply magnify my grief."

"You grieve more than a husband." Esmée saw past the ruse to the real heart of the matter. "You grieve your health." *And your beauty.*

Tears sprang to Eliza's eyes. They were alone in the parlor, Lucy and Alice in the kitchen with Alden amid a cacophony of crockery and cooing. Wherever Eliza was, they went elsewhere, not daring to trespass on her quicksilver moods. Ruenna slept in her cradle near the hearth, oblivious to her mother's angst.

"Tell me, Sister." Eliza's voice held a rare fragility. "Why is it the pox left you only lightly scarred but disfigured me completely? I feel naught but an abomination."

"The pox did not touch your soul," Esmée returned quietly. "Nor your spirit. Not unless you let it."

Eliza's chin firmed. "You evade the question."

"I was but a child when the pox struck—and lightly at that. I cannot say why it affected you differently as a woman."

"So you agree I am unsightly and unfit for company."

"I said nothing of the sort." Esmée gestured to a chair. Exhausted, she took the one opposite and said as much to herself as to Eliza, "Please sit and becalm yourself."

Eliza sat, shoulders hunched, her filmy veil hiding her features. "I recall a sermon Reverend Dawson gave before Quinn was taken from me, about prosperous worldlings being an affront to God. Do you think my pride—counting the world my darling—brought me low?"

"I have no cause to throw stones, Sister, not when my own ruinous vanity nearly cost me a future with Henri." This was said with such conviction Eliza fell silent. Esmée looked at her earnestly. "Please remove your bonnet so I can see your still-lovely face."

Though she could not see her sister's withering look, she felt it.

"One miracle at a time," Eliza retorted. "Is it not enough I am not abed but in a chair?"

"Would you care for tea?"

"Tea? Bah! Brandy is what I need."

"I have none," Esmée replied. She would not volunteer Henri's supply.

"Even arrack punch will do."

The smell of Madeira hung heavily about Eliza. "How will you explain to Captain Lennox your emptying his cellar?" Esmée asked.

This brought a momentary hush. "Spirits help temper my grief."

Esmée shook her head. "The Almighty is a far better tonic and leaves you with no headache after or any apologizing to do."

Eliza pulled off both bonnet and veil, revealing a tumbling mass of curls. "Is that Ruenna fussing?"

Esmée had hardly noticed, given their heated exchange. Stifling the urge to reach for Ruenna, she waited. Ruenna's cries grew more shrill. Alice appeared from the kitchen, but Esmée stilled her with a slight shake of her head. Casting Esmée a murderous look, Eliza got up and walked stiffly to the cradle.

Esmée held her breath. *Lord, be in this moment, please.*

"You mean to make a mother of me." Eliza picked Ruenna up and held her at arm's length. Alarmingly so.

Esmée had to lace her hands in her lap to keep from taking the babe. "Be at your ease. Ruenna loves to be held, talked to, and sung to."

Eliza cradled her awkwardly. "I am fresh out of lullabies."

"Remember the one Mama used to sing? 'Over the Hills and Far Away'?"

A softening touched Eliza's ravaged face. Esmée began to hum, focusing her gaze on the lighthouse beyond the window. In seconds Eliza began humming along with her, then gave way to song. Ruenna looked at her mother, quieting at the sound of her singing voice, which had always been lovely.

Spying a single tear coursing down Eliza's cheek, Esmée, worn to a thread by the morning's events, was nearly undone. The tear trailed to Eliza's chin, fell, and spotted the baby's linen gown.

They moved on to another lullaby, "Cradle Song," and for a few fleeting moments it seemed their beloved mother drew near.

And then, just as abruptly, Eliza swiped another tear away, the tender moment banished. "Why has Nathaniel Autrey come?"

Esmée took a breath, and the story poured forth.

Eliza, for a few rapt minutes, forgot her own misery. "That odious Wherry? From the almshouse? How fortuitous he was dispatched by the sea chaplain. I shudder to think what Captain Lennox would have done to him."

"Praise God we are safe." Esmée moistened dry lips and imagined Henri's reaction. "Now if the captain would return . . ."

Ruenna squirmed and gave a little cry, shattering Eliza's composure. She held the baby out to Esmée with a stony expression that signified she was done. Esmée took her niece, wanting nothing more than to retreat to her bedchamber and sleep till the lighthouse needed tending.

"I do wonder how Father is faring." Esmée placed Ruenna on her shoulder, patting the baby's back. In such times she missed Father fiercely.

"I suppose he'll soon return and want to take me back to the mainland. But I have no desire to return to Williamsburg. Not yet."

"You are always welcome here." Weary as Eliza made her, she was her beloved sister, after all. "I shouldn't want you to return to the townhouse till you and Ruenna are ready."

Eliza toyed with the bonnet in her lap. "Though I once called your island rustic, I rather like the seclusion. At least in my grief. And I must admit you are handling it quite well, despite having a nurse and two babies thrust upon you, not to mention an ill-tempered sister."

Well seemed an overstatement. Esmée withheld a sigh. *It is well with my soul, at least.*

A light footfall announced Lucy. "Are ye ready for dinner, milady? Miss Shaw?"

Eliza gave a curt nod, meeting Esmée's eyes with resignation, not refusal.

"Let's dine here by the fire, just the two of us." Esmée smiled at Eliza and then Lucy. "We'll invite Nathaniel Autrey to join us on the morrow."

"Very well, Miss Shaw. I'll take his victuals to him in the captain's quarters posthaste."

CHAPTER sixty-three

Taking comfort from the light shining from Henri's cottage and the slim silhouette in a front window as Nathaniel smoked a pipe, Esmée returned to her lighthouse duties at twilight, the pistol Wherry had wrested from her in one hand, a lanthorn in the other. Though he was no longer a threat, his dark presence still seemed to linger. At the foot of the tower steps, she bent her head and thanked God again for His protection and blessing.

And Lord, lest I petition Thee to death, please hasten Henri's safe return and the healing of Eliza's torn heart.

Slowly she climbed the steps, glad to resume what she found to be a tranquil routine, and lit the lamps. She stayed on for a half hour to make sure they were burning properly, intending to return twice between eight o'clock and sunrise.

Taking up a quill, she wrote in the logbook.

10th February 1756. Cloudy, wind moderate, seas calm. Lamp oil abundant.

Would Henri return and find her on watch? Darkness was falling on the water, the inky night meeting the inky deep. How she missed the sunrises and sunsets on clear days. Not the bitterness of January and February. March held a whisper of warmth that heralded kinder weather.

A white sail caught her eye if not her heart. 'Twas a merchant vessel, gliding through the water like a swan, headed toward York or Norfolk or some other Virginia port. Something akin to a physical ache rent her heart. She'd gone through Henri's trunkful of letters twice, setting aside the most romantic. The scent of the French wax was fading. Other than his penned words, what did she have? Memories. Closing her eyes, she recalled a beloved one of years before from another lofty vantage point.

Henri had come to their townhouse to see her father, who wasn't yet home. With her mother and Mrs. Mabrey busy elsewhere, Esmée had shown him to her father's study, offering him refreshments and exchanging light banter, much to the amusement of the giggling housemaids behind the nearest door.

So heady was his company she felt flirtatious. Somewhat bold. Rather than leave him alone to wait for her father, she gestured to the ship's ladder at the middle of the west wall. "Would you enjoy a nighttime view of the harbor?"

His attention swiveled from her to the hatch in the ceiling. "Going up-scuttle?"

"'Tis the best observation point in all York," she replied as his eyes met hers again. "I much prefer it to dousing chimney fires."

Smiling, he looked to her petticoats, raising a silent question.

"Never mind my skirts. As Father says, labor like a captain, play like a pirate." At his chuckle she took a step toward the ladder. "You lead and I'll follow."

He did not hesitate. He climbed up the ladder, then pushed open the hatch as if he'd crafted it before reaching out a hand for her. She gathered up her petticoats in one fist while his firm hand pulled her upward.

Into the warm, velvety night they went, trading the study's leathery, smoky scent for the gambrel roof. In winter, the view was clouded by chimney smoke, but in summer, little marred the breathtaking seascape, countless stars bespangling the sky above and ship's lanthorns lighting the water below, softening countless hulls and spars.

Henri stood beside her, not letting go of her hand. Her heart beat like a drum at the pressure of his callused fingers. Moonlight silvered the rooftop, and the narrow walk between chimneys was enclosed with an ornate iron balustrade.

He pointed across the York River toward Gloucester Point. "Over there lies the *Relentless*."

She'd heard he was friends with Captain Perrin, who owned a plantation at the point, his private waterfront far less crowded than York's. "Are you a guest at Little England then?"

"Tonight, aye." He turned toward her with a slight smile, the night wind ruffling his dark hair and the tails of his frock coat. "The hospitality of the Perrins is only exceeded by that of the Shaws."

"High praise, given my father isn't at home." Her flirtatious banter seemed more invitation. Was he as delighted as she was that the admiral was away?

He reached for her other hand. Together they stood facing each other, fingers entwined. The still, starlit moment begged for intimacy. Her racing pulse was no match for the butterflies swarming her middle. Even in the dark she sensed his intent. She went willingly into his embrace as she would never have done by day in full view of all York.

The touch of his lips was surprisingly soft, given the strength of his arms. They enfolded her, drawing her against his chest. His mouth grazed her cheek . . . her hair . . . her lips. Then and there she lost her heart to him and felt a little thrill that no man had kissed her or held her till this. The moment had held a sweet purity she'd never forgotten.

She blinked and opened her eyes, the present darkness rushing in, the glass turning slightly smoky. But in her heart she was still up-scuttle with her handsome captain, the taste of his kisses all the sweeter in hindsight.

CHAPTER sixty-four

You cannot possibly expect me to sit at table with Nathaniel Autrey and dine." Eliza's folded arms underscored her resistance. "Not even if he acts as our valiant protector for the time being."

"'Tis a courtesy we should extend," Esmée returned, setting a small vase of paper flowers on the table. "'Twill be good for us as well as him."

"*Good?* Rather, embarrassing. Mortifying." Eliza was near tears. "No doubt he will look upon me in revulsion."

"I am sure he will not. He's an experienced seaman and chaplain, remember, who is no stranger to suffering, having seen countless ports of call." Esmée spoke patiently but privately wearied of the ongoing battle with her sister. "You cannot spend the rest of your life shamed by your skin."

"How easy it is for you to say! The pox and my scars will always be an unwelcome reminder of the winter Quinn was taken from me. Of the beautiful life we lived before tragedy struck." Eliza raised her hands to her once smooth face. "Would that I could wear a veil from now till the day I die."

A knock spared them further conversation but led to the excruciating moment Eliza dreaded. Looking near bolting, she tensed as Esmée placed a reassuring hand on her shoulder. Esmée leaned down and kissed her sister's ravaged cheek as Lucy let the chaplain in.

To his credit, Nathaniel Autrey made a splendid supper companion, warming their ears with tales of his escapades sailing around the globe. Even Eliza seemed to forget herself for a time as she listened.

"How long will you stay on here?" Eliza asked as Lucy served apple tart for dessert.

"Till you've no more need of me," he said. "The captain's cottage is quite comfortable till I return to Mount Autrey."

"At least you are spared the mainland's plague," Eliza murmured, eyes downcast.

"I've already had the pox." His answer brought Eliza's head up. "But my scarring isn't as visible as it once was. The salt air and sun have been a blessed tonic."

Apparently forgetting herself, Eliza made a brazen study of his face. Esmée flushed at her sister's scrutiny. But Nathaniel simply enjoyed his dessert as if unaware of it, his easy manner a godsend.

Eliza's gaze returned to her. "I suppose Captain Lennox has weathered the pox too."

Esmée felt a renewed beat of alarm. Had he? Their ten-year separation yawned wide. She remembered no scars on his person. Esmée raised her shoulders, then looked to Nathaniel and saw uncertainty in his eyes.

"We shall pray to that end," he said quietly.

Excusing herself, Esmée went into her bedchamber, where a just-awakened Ruenna began to coo. Playing the doting aunt, Esmée brought her to the table. Tonight Ruenna was all smiles, looking about with lively blue eyes, rosebud mouth pursed.

"A veritable cherub," Nathaniel said with a chuckle.

"She is indeed." Esmée smiled, sitting the baby on her lap. "Soon she shall find her feet and run away from us."

They chatted a few minutes more till the conversation dwindled and Eliza stifled a yawn.

"I believe a turn on the beach will do me good after so fine a meal. If you ladies will excuse me . . ." Nathaniel gave a slight bow and bid them good night.

Esmée passed Ruenna to Eliza and retreated to the lighthouse. Looking down from her lofty perch, she observed the sea chaplain walking in the delicate twilight before returning to his lodgings, where he took up his usual pipe. He wasn't Henri, but his presence seemed to bring comfort, a sort of peace to their uncertainty and grief.

For now, 'twas enough.

CHAPTER *sixty-five*

A fortnight passed. Esmée studied her calendar as signs of spring grew brighter and daylight stretched, enlivening all the nooks and crannies of the island as it slowly returned to life. Time's passage was made more memorable as Eliza began walking the beach with Nathaniel, her head covered in her usual veil and bonnet. In fair weather they could be seen deep in conversation as they walked back and forth, retracing their steps on the sand in full view of the cottages and lighthouse.

"What d'ye ken they're about?" Lucy asked one day, returning from outside with an apron full of eggs.

"Taking the air and grieving," Alice replied. "The chaplain with one of his ailing sheep."

From the bedchamber where she sat at her desk, Esmée listened, hope rising. Though she'd tried in vain to help her sister, comfort had finally come from someone else. A rush of thankfulness aided her writing an overdue letter.

Dear Father,

'Tis almost March and we are glad of the coming spring. Eliza shows some signs of improving, reckoning with her loss inwardly if

not outwardly, though still making much of her scarring. Thankfully, God has sent us deliverance twice in the form of sea chaplain Autrey. If not for him, I would be writing you an entirely different letter. He will return to Mount Autrey once Henri arrives—any day now—bringing you this letter when he does, as well as more news that I shan't belabor here. I confess my impatience knows no bounds where Henri is concerned, though I do find tending the light satisfying if lonesome without him by my side.

I trust you are well. I pray for you and the indentures as well as our friends in York, especially the almshouse. Lord willing, this scourge will soon pass.

The next day, Nathaniel went to the island's opposite end to visit with former crew. Lucy and Alice busied themselves with their handwork in the sunlight beneath the cottage's eave, leaving Esmée alone with Eliza and the sleeping babies inside.

Eliza sat staring into the fire while Esmée stitched clouts. Her stomach rumbled in anticipation of supper, which promised game pie if the kitchen smells were any indication. The ensuing silence was tedious, and she almost wished the babies would awaken, the only sound the loud ticking of the mantel clock.

Whereas once she and Eliza had shared nearly everything growing up as sisters, Esmée felt a widening chasm between them. Did Eliza envy her future happiness? She daren't mention Henri and his homecoming. Like salt in a wound it was, adding to her sister's misery.

Eliza straightened her slumped shoulders, gaze never leaving the fire. "Those for whom God has mercy in store He first brings into a wilderness."

Esmée's needle stilled.

"Chaplain Autrey told me such." Eliza cleared her throat. "I pray my wilderness is not too long nor too grievous. And that I learn my lessons well lest I repeat them."

Another stitch and Esmée said, "God's mercy is great and comes to you, perhaps, in an island's refuge and a chaplain who's no stranger to the pox."

The fire snapped, sending a stray spark onto Eliza's skirt hem. She seemed to give no notice, though it left a small black spot. "Do you recall Mama's favorite verses?"

"Mama had many beloved verses. Which do you speak of?"

"'Favour is deceitful, and beauty is vain: but a woman that feareth the LORD, she shall be praised.' That is what comes to me at night when I cannot sleep, though I gave little thought to it before."

"Heaven itself is speaking to you then." Esmée rethreaded her needle. "'Strength and honour are her clothing; and she shall rejoice in time to come.' Notice it has nothing to do with how one looks."

"True, as does this—'the ornament of a meek and quiet spirit,' which is precious to God. Not outward adorning of hair and gold and dress." She sighed. "I am all about adornment."

"There is nothing wrong with being pretty. Being at your best." Esmée was moved by the distress in her sister's voice. "'Tis wrong to make a god of it. To usurp the place of the Almighty Himself with trifling matters."

"Which I have done. In spades."

"There are none of us righteous, not one."

"But there are some, like Quinn, who act righteously. Or attempt to live by what Scripture teaches." Eliza's voice shook. "Yet he was taken."

Quinn had been, in hindsight, having a soul awakening all his own. But before any of them realized what was happening, he was gone. Might his untimely death be of more consequence than his life?

Eliza took a handkerchief from her pocket, her husband's initials embroidered in blue thread. "Chaplain Autrey says there are those God loves so much He calls them home early."

Touched, Esmée paused. Had she not clung to one such Scripture in light of Mama's passing? "'Precious in the sight of the LORD is the death of His saints.'"

Eliza firmed her trembling chin. "Then I am glad Quinn was taken and not me. For I am no saint, nor am I at all sure of my standing with the Almighty. Perhaps that is His first severe mercy to me."

CHAPTER
sixty-six

The next day dawned uncommonly warm. Midmorning, Esmée left the cottage as the sun climbed in what Henri called a lapis lazuli sky. Eliza was walking the beach again, this time alone. Nathaniel sat beneath the eave of the captain's cottage, reading. Lucy was gathering wood for the cookfire, and Alice was inside the cottage, nursing the babies. 'Twas a fine time to slip away. The shadow she'd felt with Jago Wherry had finally passed.

The cove she sought was not far, sunlight shimmering on sand and sea with such blinding force Esmée narrowed her eyes beneath her straw hat. Henri had taken her here and told her it was the prettiest place on the island. She sat down on a piece of driftwood and removed her shoes and stockings.

Clenching her teeth, she waded into the cold water, foam rushing around her bare ankles. Once she and Eliza had chased the waves as children, running out onto the sand as far as they dared, then returning to shore before the water would break around them. Bunching up her skirts with her hands, she left sandy footprints as she followed the retreating sea, only to outrun it as it turned on a wave and rushed back to shore.

Next time I shall bring Eliza.

How carefree the sun made her. She felt like a girl again, enchanted with the water in all its sparkling liveliness. Again and again she raced the waves as the tide turned, casting off the lethargy of a long winter. Breathless and exhilarated and wet to the knees, she ventured forth again, only to stop completely and inexplicably. Transfixed, she turned toward the pines that clustered at her back.

Esmée.

Had she heard her name? The roar of the surf behind her snatched the word away, but as her gaze traveled up a sandy dune, her heart lurched. A man strode toward her, navigating the uneven ground with sure, swift steps.

Henri. Running. At long last.

All thought of the ocean left her head. A wave rushed her from behind, buckling her knees with its foamy force, knocking her down and taking her under. Choking on water, she felt her soaked petticoats pull at her even as her bare feet and fingers raked over sand and sharp shells and pebbles.

"Esmée!"

She stumbled, all the wind knocked out of her, and then hard hands encircled her waist, pulling her free of the surf. Henri lifted her and swiftly carried her to safety. He sat down hard on dry sand, sheltering her in his arms. She was a bedraggled mess, coughing up water, her heart leaping with joy.

He was smiling, his chest shaking with mirth as he smoothed back the tangled mass of her hair with one hand, his words warm on her cheek. "Comeliest mermaid I've ever seen, right here on my very own island."

She shut her eyes, swallowing down another sputter, and rested her head against his damp linen shirt. His heartbeat thumped as loud as her own. She felt she might burst with happiness.

"So much has happened." Her words came breathless, her nose stinging from salt water. "I hardly know where to begin. But all that matters now is that you're here, safe and sound."

"I wanted to surprise you." He held her closer, kissing her finger where the posy ring rested. His own signet ring caught the sun flashing in its fiery climb to noon. "The *Intrepid* is anchored off the south side of the island. We docked at York briefly before coming here. Long enough to see your father and finish business with colonial authorities."

"Did you meet with success?" Her hopes hung on the word. Success and then retirement, at least from the naval world. 'Twas her highest hope.

"Aye, aside from half a dozen men lost."

"I'm so sorry."

"As am I." His voice dropped, then rebounded. "Our prizes include a French naval ship carrying war materials to Canadian militia, as well as a troop ship. Our greatest coup was capturing a French commander and his officers, including a copy of their war plans. These we delivered to Williamsburg to the governor's care."

Bold operations, all. She couldn't imagine the danger and complexities of overtaking war ships. "How is Father?"

"Glad to see us in port. Anxious about you and Eliza."

She nodded, her eyes on the roiling surf. "You heard about Quinn, then, and the baby and Eliza's being here."

"Your father told me. I cannot convey my shock and sorrow. But what most concerns me is you." His lips brushed her brow. "How you're faring with so much strife and then keeping the light too."

She raised a hand to his deeply tanned cheek, her own condition the least of her worries. The fatigue in his eyes . . . the loose folds of his shirt. His blue coat lay on the sand. He'd abandoned it coming after her. "You've lost a stone or so, to my eye. And you look exhausted."

"War wears one down." His smile was thin. "But with your company and care, I'll be in prime shape in no time."

She pushed herself to her feet, the sharp wind reminding her it was not yet spring. He stood too, retrieving her hat while she put on her stockings and shoes. Her skirts dragged on the sand as they left the beach hand in hand. Unable to contain herself, she turned to him, caught in a warm ray of sunlight, the fragrant pines ringing them.

"I cannot believe you've returned at last." Her hands were pressed to his chest. "I shan't believe it till you kiss me. Soundly."

He smiled as his arms went round her, undeterred by how damp she was. She shivered, more from pleasure than the chill. She leaned into him, seeking his beloved scent, his strength. His mouth was warm and insistent against her own, next trailing down her neck and the bare hollow of her shoulder till her very being stood on tiptoe.

"I've dreamed of this moment day and night away from you," Henri said. "It drove me half-mad."

"Kiss me again," she said, wanting to squeeze the last drop of joy from every hard-won moment.

"Have done with kissing. Marry me, Esmée." A flicker of uncertainty darkened his eyes. "If you're indeed sure of anchoring yourself to a man with salt water in his blood."

She threw her arms around his neck, determined to remove all doubt. "Let this be my answer." Pressing her lips to his, she kissed him with an abandon that brought them not simply body to body but soul to soul. The beach seemed to spin and fade, her awareness of him so complete it chased all else from consciousness. He kissed her back with equal fervor, and time came to a blessed standstill.

Breathless, he said, "Let us wed at once, then."

She smiled up at him, the sun in her eyes. "Nathaniel Autrey is on hand. He can have the honor."

"Ned?" Surprise enlivened his weary features. "Here?"

They began walking again, Esmée spilling out the whole story. "What's more, his coming seems to have helped revive Eliza."

"He understands loss. His own beloved died some time ago."

"The Almighty sent him as surely as you're standing here. I was at my wit's end about Wherry and then at my wit's end about Eliza. I still worry about her and Ruenna—"

"Ruenna?"

"Her wee daughter. She's the sweetest, prettiest babe."

The lighthouse was visible now, the sun striking the glass of the tower. He stopped for a moment, taking it in. She searched his face, seeking reassurance he was safe from the pox. Aside from faint, sun-weathered lines, his skin was smooth, no telltale marks of any scourge evident, past or present.

He brought her hand to his lips and kissed her fingers. "I've much to tell you, *ma belle*, but first a bath and a hot meal are in order."

CHAPTER

sixty-seven

Soon a bowl of hearty stew and crusty bread restored Henri. He and Ned had talked at length in his cottage while the women kept to theirs, preparing supper and minding the children. Lucy did slip out to reunite with Cyprian, who'd walked from the Flask and Sword, a gift of oranges and lemons in hand.

To Henri's surprise, a veiled Eliza had presented Ruenna to him with pride in her voice upon his return to the lightkeeper's cottage. Esmée wasn't far, arranging a table for four in advance of an early supper and minding the light. A linen cloth was laid, anchored by a pitcher of dried flowers, not the seaside goldenrod and sweet everlasting of summer.

Would Eliza join them?

He could sense Esmée's concern. Though he wished it could be just the two of them, he was grateful for Ned's engaging presence and Eliza's sincere if subdued welcome.

He stood by the hearth, adjusting to life outside wooden walls. After so many wintry weeks at sea, he couldn't seem to get warm.

Esmée lit the candles at table. She'd lost the look of a mermaid and drew his eye like solid ground for a drowning man, her figure in floral chintz a veritable garden, her curled hair beribboned.

She turned toward him with a smile. "Are you hungry, Captain Lennox?"

"Aye, for more than supper." He winked as Ned came into the cottage, accompanied by Eliza, her head down.

How proud she'd once been, the belle of any function, charming everyone near and far. Now he schooled his dismay to see her unveiled, her once flawless complexion a dim memory. Quinn's absence was especially felt, for he'd never been far from her side. It doubled Henri's intent to marry as soon as possible. Tomorrow was never promised. All they had was the enviable present.

"What news do you bring from the mainland?" Ned asked after saying grace.

"Very little." Henri took up a knife to carve the chicken and chose his words as carefully as he could before a newly bereaved widow. "April's legislative session has been postponed. Many shops remain closed in York and in Williamsburg as well."

Eliza raised her gaze. "Did Father say when he'd return to the island?"

Henri shook his head. "Till he does, he feels you and your daughter are safer right here."

"Wise of him." Esmée passed a basket of bread. "Eliza is welcome to stay as long as she likes. Besides, we'll have one less in our cottage soon."

"Which begs the question"—Ned smiled as he buttered his bread—"when will your nuptials be, and where?"

Esmée glanced at the window where clouds gathered, as if contemplating wedding on the beach. Next she looked to Henri as he finished with his carving.

"On the morrow." He didn't look back at Ned till she nodded in agreement. "The license to wed is in my pocket. We've only need of you to officiate before you return to Mount Autrey."

"My pleasure. I can think of no better sendoff," Ned told them.

"You've been good to stay on the last fortnight." Though Eliza's voice was calm, Henri detected a beat of dismay beneath. "I shall remember all your counsel."

"Keep close the Bible I gave you." Ned's features softened as he forked a first bite. "Within its pages you'll soon have need of little else."

Talk turned to the light, the last storm, and the moment the *Intrepid* overtook the French fleet. Esmée seemed on tenterhooks as Henri recounted the details.

"Your mission is finished then, at least for now," Ned said. "Virginia is never long satisfied."

"Our success has only intensified colonial officials' desire for further cruises, aye. Immediate ones." He could feel Esmée's eyes on him, the dismay his words wrought. "But we'll wed and have our honeymoon before any more pressures come to bear."

"A honeymoon at a pox-ridden time while tethered to a lighthouse is quite a feat." Eliza's voice held a touch of asperity. "I fear Virginia is still riven with the scourge."

Esmée reached for the saltcellar. "With things as they are, perhaps remaining here on the island seems best."

Warmth filled Henri's chest. "Given I've been away, the island is idyllic . . . and this meal likewise."

Smiling, Lucy murmured her thanks as she replenished their cups. The clink of utensils against pewter plates and the snap of the fire were the only sounds for several minutes. But it was a jubilant silence, lending to Henri's profound contentment to be home.

Ned eyed him with amusement. "Is it true Mistress Saltonstall is back on the island and has reopened the Flask and Sword?"

"She returned just yesterday, aye," Henri confirmed. "Hermes is beside himself."

"She's likely at her wit's end managing a full crew from the *Intrepid*, with no one wanting shore leave." Ned regarded him with a canny eye. "You look well, Captain. And what of your men? No maladies on board?"

Henri took another bite of chicken. "None, God be thanked. No scurvy either due to a short cruise."

"How long were you in port?" Ned persisted.

Long enough to catch the pox.

Was that what Esmée was thinking? He saw the joyous light in her eyes dim.

"Two days," he replied. "I suffered the pox soon after my impressment in the Royal Navy, if you're wondering. And it doesn't strike twice."

Esmée was regarding him over the rim of her glass with stark relief.

He smiled at her, knowing she'd be pleased at what had delayed him on the mainland. "I'm happy to say my time in York was more pleasure than politics. While there I spoke with stonemasons and ordered materials to begin building within a fortnight."

"Glad news indeed." Esmée's delight washed over him like a warm wave. "Your crew who remained behind have made a sturdy garden wall in your absence. I've even begun a small kitchen garden."

"How long will the house construction take?" Ned asked.

"Excavation of the cellar needs to happen first, then hauling the stone since it's not quarried here." Henri took a drink. "The double-pile plan and open staircase will take time, but I hope to see us at home there by winter."

As the men finished supper and moved nearer the hearth to continue their conversation, Esmée turned her attention to Eliza. The absence of a veil was no small matter. Though heavily powdered to cover the worst of the scarring and far quieter than before, Eliza seemed to have made a breakthrough of some sort.

"You seem better tonight, Sister." Esmée's voice was low, hardly heard over the men's robust conversation. She longed to draw Eliza out but always felt she walked a precarious line. "I'd like to see the Bible Nathaniel gave you. 'Tis kind of him."

"He said 'twas the least he could do, as Quinn and I were so hospitable to him upon his coming to Williamsburg and assuming his place at Mount Autrey. He's also indebted to us for introducing him to Quinn's cousin Elinor. They plan to wed next summer."

Elinor. Esmée had all but forgotten. The tears in Eliza's eyes spiked her alarm. Might she be too attached to the sea chaplain?

"I am happy for them." Eliza paused at the men's rumble of laughter over some matter. "I asked him what drew him to her as she is so plain. Of course, I did not say she was plain, though I've long thought it. And do you know what he told me?"

Held by her sister's shimmering eyes, Esmée waited.

"He said she has an inner beauty that can never be marred by age or disease, a gentle and quiet spirit of great price in God's sight. She is radiant to him, he told me. *Radiant.* And that, unquestionably, is far better than being beautiful."

"They are well suited, then. Both of them devout."

Eliza nodded and brought her serviette to her lips. "All this makes me wonder about my future." Her calm voice belied the emotion beneath. "My outward beauty is gone. I've done little to cultivate unfading beauty . . . or radiance."

"'Tis never too late. Spiritual beauty is something we should all aspire to." Esmée herself was convicted, her thoughts leaping ahead. "Perhaps 'twould be wise to cultivate Elinor's company once she becomes Mistress Autrey."

"Perhaps." Eliza looked at her hand, where the ruby ring Quinn had given her rested. "Given time, will any man want me?"

"The right man will." The words were out of Esmée's mouth before she'd given them thought, and they now became a silent prayer.

Eliza's eyes held doubt. "As for a second husband, the very thought sickens me. For now I need to consider returning to the townhouse and sorting through Quinn's belongings, his study, and his many papers. He was in some sort of a quandary before he fell ill. Some matter concerning the governor's council, other burgesses, and such . . ." Her voice trailed off, and she put a hand to her brow. "I feel a headache coming on."

Excusing herself, Eliza left the cottage. From where he stood by the hearth, Henri gave Esmée a concerned glance, but her smile offset it.

"So tomorrow is your wedding day." Nathaniel looked nonplussed about Eliza's abrupt departure. "Are you going to observe custom and marry in the morn? Or do you need more time?"

"Time enough to give Mistress Saltonstall leave to concoct a bride's cake," Henri said. "I promised her."

Had he? Amused, Esmée discarded her notion of a small affair.

Nathaniel chuckled. "Your crew will want to be on hand, of course, for the frolic after. But what of the admiral?"

"Father knew he wouldn't be here, given the timing and circumstances," Esmée told him, regretful but resigned. "But he'll be happy to hear you married us."

With a knowing smile, Nathaniel reached for his wool coat hanging by the door. "If you'll excuse me, I'll hie to the Flask and Sword and alert Mistress Saltonstall that her services are needed. You won't mind being left alone, I daresay."

"Nay," Henri said emphatically, to Esmée's delight. Clearly, wedding cake was the last thing on his mind.

CHAPTER
sixty-eight

The bride's cake was hurriedly baked, a plump confection stuffed with dried fruit, spirits, and nutmeats. The punch was enlivened with citrus brought off the *Intrepid* and poured into an ornate silver bowl. Mistress Saltonstall was pleased to host the wedding reception at her ordinary and would try to keep Hermes calm amid all the fuss, Lucy told Esmée as she returned from helping at the tavern the next morn.

"Will the whole crew be at the nuptials, Miss Shaw?"

"Nay, only the festivities after."

"Glad I am to be part of it." Lucy's eyes misted. "Ye look like a bride. But more than that, ye look happy. Happier than I've ever seen ye."

"That I am," Esmée replied, embracing her.

Though the morning was one of fog and bluster, a gentle wind banished the clouds by midafternoon. Esmée left the cottage, followed by Eliza and Lucy. Alice remained inside by a window, minding the babies as the women walked down the beach to where Henri waited.

Esmée kept her eyes on Henri, struck by how commanding he was even away from the ship. The look that graced his face when he saw her made her teary-eyed. He loved her. There could be no doubt. Why had she ever wondered?

Joining hands, Esmée and her groom stood on the stretch of sand before their house site, the sun fickle but warm upon their shoulders. Clad in her best lavender silk dress, lace cascading from her sleeves and pearls about her neck, she looked up at Henri, who was resplendent in black breeches and a fawn-colored coat. Freshly shaved, his hair trimmed and queued, and hinting of castile soap, he left her weak-kneed.

Eliza was somber in her black taffeta gown and hat, her veil swaying with the wind. She and Henri's sailing master, Tarbonde, stood as witnesses. The festive mood turned hallowed as Nathaniel read the age-old marriage rites, a Bible open in one hand. Though Esmée missed Father fiercely, not even his absence dimmed her happiness.

Henri looked down at her, his eyes conveying what he did not say. Did he sense her unspoken thoughts?

My love, you have my heart, my whole heart, from this day forward. There's been none but you, nor will there ever be, come what may. You are the Almighty's choice for me.

"You may kiss your bride, Captain Lennox," Nathaniel said at last.

Not one kiss but two sealed their vows, promising a night of bliss to come. The sun shone down as they began a walk to the Flask and Sword, determined to return by dusk to mind the light. Esmée looked forward to climbing the tower steps with Henri alongside. For now they led the small wedding party, though Eliza returned to the cottage to remain behind with Alice and the babies.

The fiddling could be heard from quite a distance. Esmée's anticipation quickened, though what she wanted was to be alone with her groom. But she wouldn't deny the crew their enjoyment of their captain in his newly married state. They went up the tavern's wooden steps into the taproom, where tables and chairs had been pushed back along the walls to allow for dancing. Huzzahs erupted at the sight of them. Hermes scampered hither and yon, not screeching but clearly excited by all the fuss.

Esmée's eyes went to the bride's cake and punch bowl, as she'd hardly eaten that morn. But such was forgotten as Henri led her out for the first dance. Lady Mary Menzies's Reel. There were no finely stepped minuets here. Just wild, happy romps where an abundance of men joined arms in a ring and cavorted around the two of them.

A sea breeze kept them cool, wafting in through wide-open windows. Cake was consumed and punch downed as the sun slipped west in a haze of pink and cream. With a look at the watch he kept in his pocket, Henri winked at her, signaling it was time to make their escape. And escape they did, just the two of them, while the merriment continued unabated.

"If only I could return you to our house and not our cottage," Henri said as they skirted the site.

She squeezed his hand. Lucy had helped her move all her belongings to Henri's that morning. "But your—*our*—cottage is quite cozy."

"Aye, that it is." His grin told her he minded not a whit. "The night is just beginning. Time enough to light the tower, then kindle our own fire."

She flushed, warmth drenching her. At the top of a sand dune they turned and took in the sunset, now little more than layered rose ribbons on the horizon.

He brought her hand to his lips. "Not long ago I was smelling black powder and dodging bullet lead. All this seems more mirage, Mistress Lennox."

"I pray the mirage never ends, Captain, and 'twill be smooth seas for us in the years to come."

He looked down at her, gathering her hands in his. "Now seems a good time to tell you I won't be returning to sea. I've told the governor the same. My maritime career is finished."

Finished. And said with such finality. "Are you . . . sure?"

"Without a doubt. My future is you. Our children. Indigo Island. And something tells me you'll not voice a single objection, *ma belle*."

Laughing, she snaked her arms around his neck as he swept her off her feet into his arms and walked toward the lighthouse standing stalwart in the distance.

CHAPTER *sixty-nine*

Esmée opened her eyes to a rooster's crowing. Lying quietly, she pondered yesterday's events with a thankful heart, Henri's bulk warm and disheveled beside her. His boots stood near the bed along with his queue ribbon and her lavender gown. Raising a hand, she admired her posy ring, feeling every inch married. Would that they could stay abed all day. But life continued all around them, the sun streaming across the coverlet and rousing them to greet the day.

She must check in on the women and babies first thing. Eliza had mentioned leaving soon, perhaps with Nathaniel on the morrow. The jolly would return them to York. Would Alice and Ruenna leave too? If so, 'twould just be her and Henri here on their end of the island and Lucy in the adjoining cottage. Construction would soon begin. Esmée could plant the remainder of their garden and welcome summer when it came.

The rooster's renewed crowing brought Henri round. He blinked, eyes half-shuttered against the sun. And then he got his bearings, rolling toward her and tickling her without mercy.

She laughed till the tears came, her words breathless. "Stop, Husband, lest we bring all the islanders to our door!"

"Nay, *ma chérie*. We are honeymooning. They wouldn't dare."

To escape him, she rolled away and hung her feet over the side of the feather mattress. "I must see to your breakfast like I've dreamed of doing for years. Hot chocolate and toast for you to start."

He reached for her again, but she eluded him, dressing hastily in the silk gown she'd discarded. She wouldn't return to her workaday clothes just yet. Peering in his shaving mirror, she wound up her hair as best she could, secured it with pins, and topped it with a lace cap, aware he watched her every move.

He pushed himself up on one elbow. "You're blushing. It becomes you."

She blew him a kiss as she started for the kitchen, her stomach a-rumble. The cottage was chill. The hearth's fires had gone out in the night. She stirred the kitchen coals with a poker, then went in search of wood. And drew up short just past the threshold.

An unfamiliar boat, a sloop she did not recognize, was docking at the pier. Wariness needled her. One man in particular drew her notice. Was that the Williamsburg sheriff? His grim expression soured the high mood from their wedding day.

It was then she heard a feminine shout.

Eliza?

Her sister's voice crested before Eliza spun on her heel and returned to her cottage with an emphatic slamming of the door. Hard enough to make the dishes rattle, surely.

Esmée returned inside posthaste. "Henri," she called.

"I'm nearly dressed," he replied from the bedchamber.

"I fear we have company."

He entered the parlor but drew up short at the window. His face showed no surprise or alarm, though her own heart ticked like a wayward clock. When he stepped outside, she followed, standing with him to watch the men on board disembark.

"Go inside and I'll join you shortly." His low tone brooked no questions. No argument.

She pulled her attention from the sheriff to Henri's now guarded face. "All right."

Head down, she took the shell path to her former cottage. Eliza stood looking out the window. As soon as Esmée let herself in, Eliza whirled on her.

"Why is that blackguard Osborn here with his minion magistrates?" Eliza's eyes lit with cold fire. "They were skulking for half an hour before landing."

At her outburst, Alice and Lucy scurried to the kitchen, babes in arms.

Esmée joined Eliza at the window. "I sense their coming bodes ill."

"It can't be about Father or they'd have told me when I confronted them." Eliza crossed her arms. "I shouted at them in most unladylike fashion when they docked. Asked their intent. They said they came seeking the captain."

Esmée's stomach clenched. Had Henri hidden something from her?

Eliza remained at the window, her expression a picture of disgust. The sun climbed higher, calling out the tense expressions of the men deep in conversation. Lucy and Alice were speaking in low tones in the kitchen.

Esmée kept on her cloak and went to the fire, chilled by more than the cold morn.

"My, how stern the sheriff looks. I've rarely seen him sober." Eliza sniffed. "Well, the captain shall soon send them packing, I've no doubt."

But the men remained through toast and tea and the babies' next feeding. Eliza paced while Esmée dandled Ruenna in her lap, trying to pray her way through the untimely interruption.

"At last, they're leaving." Eliza released a pent-up breath and joined Esmée at the hearth.

In moments, a knock at the door signaled Henri. "No need to look *contrarie*," he said, eyes on Esmée. But she knew that look. He said no more, but she sensed he was withholding something so as not to alarm them. Or waiting to be alone with her before he enlightened her further. "The men are on their way back to the mainland."

To her amazement, Eliza did not question him further. If she had, he might not have heard her, for Ruenna began crying her loudest and Alice hurried in, intent on helping.

"You two are on your honeymoon," Eliza said, unsmiling. "No need to stay here a moment longer."

Esmée soon left the cottage with Henri, looking over her shoulder to see the unwelcome boat moving slowly west toward the mainland.

CHAPTER
seventy

This was not how she'd envisioned her honeymoon. The knot of disappointment inside Esmée widened to alarm as she stepped from the *Relentless*'s jolly onto the York dock with the help of Henri's firm hand. Eliza stepped out after them, her veiled hat aflutter. Lucy and Alice had remained behind on the island with the babies. They couldn't risk returning them to York with smallpox still a menace.

Esmée cast a look down Water Street to where the sign *Shaw's Chocolate* swung in the early March wind. The town seemed fractious today, the taint of tar and brine and fishmongers curling Esmée's nose under a leaden sky. The weather had kept them from returning yesterday, the wind contrary, the waves high.

A carriage took them up the hill to the Shaw townhouse. Patches of green burst through the gloom along with the first of spring's blooms, pear trees and daffodils foremost. So focused was Esmée on her inner turmoil that the colors seemed muted, a shadow of themselves. Few folks were about, lending to her worry the smallpox was far from over.

Esmée turned her postponed plans over in her mind as she would soil with a garden spade. She should be sowing sweet marjoram and hyssop and thyme in their kitchen garden and expecting the laborers to arrive with the building stones for their home. But instead they were headed to Williamsburg because her new husband had been accused of something nefarious.

Father was not at home, nor was he expecting them. Mrs. Mabrey greeted them and made them comfortable in the parlor. Henri wanted to wait and inform Father that they were en route to the capital.

Eliza seemed to turn inward, saying little, her expression a mystery beneath her veil. She wasn't wanting to return to the Williamsburg townhouse, to the place where she'd known such happiness with Quinn. She'd confided this when Henri had told them he must meet with authorities in Williamsburg. But at the last Eliza decided to accompany them. Perhaps putting off the inevitable somehow made it more painful as a widow.

Esmée, seated near the fire with Eliza, kept her eyes on Henri, who stood looking out a draped window. When the front door opened and shut with a familiar thud, she knew Father was finally home.

"Company—the very best kind." He came in, his pleasant expression somewhat guarded as he set aside his hat and walking stick.

They greeted him, and Henri spoke with a composed ease that made him all the more irresistible to Esmée. "First the good news. Your daughter and I are now wed as of day before yesterday, and your granddaughter is well and remains safely on the island with her nurse."

"My felicitations can wait. What, pray tell, is the bad news?" He looked in concern at his daughters. "My study might be best suited for such."

He and Henri passed through the adjoining door to the room in question, their voices a dull monotone once the door was closed.

"What mischief has led to this?" Eliza's sharp question unnerved Esmée further.

"I know little except that the sheriff and his men were sent by unnamed officials to summon Henri to the governor's chambers."

They fell silent as their father's voice grew more strident. Though she couldn't make out the words, she knew he was as confounded and disbelieving as she. Tea was served, and they made small talk with Mrs. Mabrey, who inquired about Ruenna.

The thoughtful question hung on the air. Eliza said nothing for several uncomfortable seconds, leaving Esmée to answer. "She's as bonny a babe as ever drew breath. Tiny but healthy and very fond of being held."

Did Eliza miss her? Esmée certainly did.

When Mrs. Mabrey excused herself, Eliza turned to Esmée in exasperation. "You think I'm a terrible mother, don't you?"

"Nay," Esmée replied calmly, countering her sister's sudden mood. "I think you're a grieving one."

Eliza set down her cup with a rattle. "The truth is I absolutely abhor returning to town. Even sitting here having tea and fielding questions, however well placed, is excruciating."

"Would you rather have remained on the island?"

"I have no choice but to return and try to get on with life as best I can. But I shan't resume any society, I assure you. Not looking like this." Her voice shook with emotion. "Thankfully, I am a woman of means and can shut the world out if I want to."

"I hope you do not, for your daughter's sake." Esmée would waste no words on behalf of Ruenna. "Quinn would have wanted you to live life to the fullest. 'Tis one of the reasons he married you. Your zest and—"

"All that has passed, along with my beauty. I am a shell of what I was, and you know it." She reached into her purse, withdrew a vial of hartshorn, and waved it beneath her veil, lapsing into sullen silence.

Soon Esmée and Henri were in Williamsburg, ensconced in Eliza's best guest bedchamber, and then Henri was on his way to the governor's palace. The townhouse had a forlorn feel. Quinn loomed large in memory, as he had in life. Reminders of him were everywhere. Most of the servants had been dismissed. Few remained to keep the elegant house, further adding to the echoing rooms.

True to her word, Eliza withdrew to her second-floor bedchamber. Esmée heard her door shut with vehemence from down the hall. The silence soon gave way to weeping. Should she go and offer comfort?

Uncertainty kept her from it. Eliza needed to grieve. Esmée sent another prayer heavenward, and the house quieted again.

Standing by a tall window, Esmée overlooked the townhouse garden with its lovely fountain and sundial and bricked paths. The paling fence kept out deer and other marauding creatures. One busy gardener remained to tend to spring's showiest flowers. All was as lovely as ever, yet everything had changed.

She sought a window seat and a book. But Eliza was not a reader, and Esmée daren't go downstairs to Quinn's study. Instead she began pacing back and forth upon the Turkish carpet, wishing it weren't a glaring red but a soothing blue. A low fire burned in the grate, but she longed to open a window. A clap of thunder scuttled her plan and sent her back to the hearth and a comfortable chair. Eliza's Angora cat sauntered in, leaping into Esmée's lap and purring fitfully.

Esmée missed the cottage's simplicity. The babies' noises. The teakettle's singing. Alice and Lucy's good-natured chatter. Henri's abode was richly masculine, and she missed that too. His sea chest rested near the door, and she fixed her eye on it, willing him back, craving the low timbre of his voice and his kiss.

Supper arrived on a tray. The French chef was still in the kitchen, thankfully. Loin of veal, salad, crusty bread, a dish of early strawberries and cream. She had little appetite but partook with a listening ear for Henri's return. Within minutes she was rewarded as the hall clock below chimed seven and the butler opened the front door.

Up the stairs her bridegroom came, slowly, without the usual spring in his step. She set down her fork and brought the serviette to her lips, ready to greet him when he came through the doorway.

Her smile slipped past her trepidation. "Welcome home, Husband."

Even if it was not their home. Nor their desire to be here.

A flicker of joy lightened his solemnity. "Home is wherever you are, aye." He shrugged off his greatcoat and laid it over the back of a chair. He was wearing his wedding suit, the finest clothes he had. As was his custom, he went to the washbasin.

"I'll have your supper sent up," she told him, pulling on a bell cord.

With a nod, he took the seat opposite her, but she sensed he was in no more of a mood to eat than she.

When she sat back down, he reached for her hand. "This isn't the sort of news I wanted to bring you, especially so soon after our wedding."

Their joyous joining on the beach seemed a lifetime ago. Had it only been two days?

She squeezed his hand. "I've sat here and wondered what would take you away from me for hours on end, and at last I shall have it."

"I met with Governor Dinwiddie first and then his council. It appears certain charges have been brought against me. One of them is spy—"

"Spy?" She spat the hated word out in disbelief.

"For the French. Also, it seems some planters—burgesses—have banded together with the intent of seeking revenge for my liberating the *Swallow* and its Africans all those years ago. They believe I remain a threat to plantation owners and Virginia's economy, not to mention other slaveholding colonies, with my crew of black jacks and my stance on slavery. They accuse me of enticing their Africans to run away and fomenting discontent for untold freedoms and that sort of nonsense."

She sat back, her stomach giving way. "Nonsense is the kindest word for it. 'Tis outrageous—laughable."

Henri cleared his throat and said evenly, "There are men powerfully placed who have aligned themselves against me."

"But there must be just as many honorable men for you who would call this matter mutinous and seek to end it."

"Perhaps." He released her hand and sat back, expression weary. "For now I am under house arrest here at Lord—*Lady* Drysdale's."

She felt she'd been struck in the face. House arrest? If only Quinn were here. Quinn would set matters aright. Quinn had been one of those men powerfully placed.

What other allies did Henri have?

CHAPTER *seventy-one*

For the first time since leaving it, Esmée missed the chocolate shop. There was simply little to do at the townhouse besides a great deal of hand-wringing. She couldn't even fiddle with her chatelaine as she was wont to do, since she'd left it on the island. Most of Williamsburg remained shuttered, though the smallpox was said to be abating. Henri was in his third day of meetings at the palace, which left her on tenterhooks. With Eliza hiding in her bedchamber and sinking further into despondency, Esmée summoned a plan and knocked lightly on the bedchamber door. No answer. Gently she jiggled the doorknob. Locked.

Her voice was quiet but aggrieved. "Eliza, please let me in."

A groggy reply. Had Eliza been imbibing again? Or merely sleeping?

"Please open the door. I'm concerned about you and need to discuss what is happening with Henri."

Slow footsteps and then the door opened a crack. Eliza stared back at her, eyes swollen and bloodshot, hair in a frayed braid that dangled over one shoulder to her waist. Her sultana was stained. Wine, likely. Esmée spied an uncorked bottle near the bed.

Esmée pushed past her and threw open a window sash. The March wind roared in, stirring the drapes and cleansing the air. "I've sent for tea." She began arranging two chairs near the open window, then lifted the tea table and placed it there.

"My, Sister." Arms crossed, Eliza regarded her with grim amusement. "You're a veritable whirlwind when you want to be."

"Cook has been asking what you are hungry for."

"A pity, as I have no appetite."

"Would that you could say that about the wine instead." Lifting a dark green bottle, Esmée saw that it was French champagne. "Must I run your household for you and lock the wine cellar?"

With a derisive snort, Eliza collapsed into a chair. She toyed with the fringe of her sash, eyes down, as Esmée took a seat opposite her.

"You need to know what is happening all around you," Esmée began, needing an ally. "Henri has been placed under house arrest at your very residence." The ugly words even tasted bitter. "He's at the palace presently, enduring who knows what as we speak."

Eliza studied her through narrowed, incredulous eyes. "The same captain who only recently chased down an entire French fleet on behalf of Virginia's colonial government?" The cold irony in her tone fueled Esmée's ire. "And came away with countless sealed documents and high-placed prisoners of war, not to mention enemy ships?"

"At the moment all seem to have forgotten that. Henri says little to me about the proceedings. But I believe the word *spy* was mentioned."

"Spy? What blather!" Eliza sat up straight. "I recall hearing some hullabaloo about his championing of blacks when he returned to Virginia last fall. Several burgesses—most of them planters—were quibbling about his signing on black jacks as crew, thereby fomenting discontent among plantation slaves who wish to gain their freedom by sea."

"There are many black jacks, free and runaways, from all the colonies, even England."

"True, but England has no plantations or slave labor like America. And slave owners fear giving Africans *any* liberties lest it threaten

Virginia's very foundation . . ." Eliza's voice faded as tea was brought. "Close the door after you, Rose," she told the servant.

Esmée waited, hands folded in her lap, for her sister to serve. Eliza did so reluctantly. Taking up the silver teapot with an unsteady hand, she sloshed rather than poured tea into Esmée's cup.

"As we were saying," Esmée continued, wondering what else Eliza recalled, "matters have obviously come to a boil. But till now I knew nothing of it."

"Quinn certainly did—" At the mention of his name, Eliza broke off for an emotional moment before continuing. "He made mention to me of it when Henri left on his cruise. He said he was going to put down any trouble regarding it, and so I've thought little of it since."

Esmée stared at the plate of untouched pastries. She knew Henri had enemies, but as he'd been away for years till recently, she'd thought the animosity had died down. "Do you know who is involved? Did Quinn mention them by name?"

Eliza rattled off enough names to chill Esmée's blood. "The prosperous planters stand to lose the most if slavery is challenged. They have the governor's ear, of course. Two of the troublemakers are related to him by marriage." A shrewd glint shone in her eyes. "And I do wonder if a few of them weren't in cahoots with Jago Wherry. Two of Henri's opponents are in horrendous debt and could benefit from any and all prizes."

Stunned, Esmée sipped her tea without tasting it as her mind flooded with what she knew of maritime criminals and vice-admiralty courts. Though Eliza tried a pastry, she soon gave it up and left her tea unfinished, pleading a headache and saying she wanted to sleep.

Unable to stand the confines of the townhouse and wanting to be free of the house's black trappings that bespoke Quinn's passing at every turn, Esmée put on her cape and escaped into the windy spring afternoon. Sun broke through amassing clouds with a feeble light, illuminating gardens hemmed in by tidy fences and the few passersby traversing the cobblestone streets. She walked toward the governor's palace, her eyes roaming the building's brick face. Somewhere inside was Henri.

Eliza's confession threatened the small peace Esmée had held on to since they'd arrived in Williamsburg. Henri was careful with what he told her. She sensed his holding back, and it frightened her. She longed to ask him detailed questions but felt it only added to the trial before him. She'd not grill him as officials were doing behind closed doors. Her task was to stand by him. Love him. Pray for him.

Lord, please end this. Let truth prevail.

She bypassed the palace and turned right, continuing on in the windy afternoon. So sunk in her own private thoughts was she that she hardly heard a coach roll to a stop across the lonesome stretch of road.

"Daughter, what on earth are you doing on the outskirts of town?" Her father's concerned voice returned her to the present. "Join me in the coach. A storm is brewing."

Indeed, a storm within and without. Esmée looked at the sky, startled she'd walked so far so mindlessly. She'd passed the gaol with its forlorn sounds and smells, the courtyard overfull of the indigent and derelict. The usual pang of sympathy she always felt eluded her completely. She seemed as wooden as a ship's figurehead.

The postilion opened the door, and she settled opposite her father, escaping a lightning-lit landscape. "Why have you come?"

"I heard news—ill news—that the governor is being pressured by certain officials, mainly planters, who've invented charges against the captain. Henri may well be sent to Marshalsea in London for trial at the admiralty court there, thus relieving Virginia of responsibility—"

"*Marshalsea?*" The word was more epithet. Esmée stared at him, lips parted from the most grievous shock yet. "The place of pirates and rogues?"

"That or Newgate. But I'm hoping it's hearsay, and I've come to find out."

Her father never minced words, but for once she wished he would. She could only sit, stunned, as the coach picked up its pace and headed toward the heart of Williamsburg. Her heart seemed to keep time with the horse's hooves, her thoughts somersaulting over themselves in dismal abandon.

"How is your dear sister?" Father asked.

She barely heard his query. Her breath came short, her words scattered. "Eliza . . . she seems to have worsened back at the townhouse. She's begun to go through Quinn's belongings, his study and papers. I've offered to help, but . . . Eliza refused me outright. We visited his gravesite yesterday. Left flowers."

He nodded soberly as the coach turned down Nassau Street. Her gaze returned to the palace as she alighted from the coach. What if Henri wouldn't be coming back to the townhouse? What if he was immediately taken to a port and shipped to England? Hot tears blurred her vision. 'Twas all she could do not to go to pieces in front of her father.

"I'll see how Eliza is before I go to the palace and learn what's afoot," Father said.

They entered together, the butler taking their wraps. No supper smells. No other servants at hand.

"Lady Drysdale is upstairs in her rooms," the butler told them.

Father mounted the steps slowly as if pondering what to say to his youngest daughter once he knocked on the door. If ever Mama was needed, 'twas now.

Esmée passed into the guest chamber and shut the door. Her Bible lay open on the table, a silk ribbon marking the passage she'd been reading before her walk.

The scrap of Psalm was impressed on her heart, a promise to prevent her from falling apart.

In the day of my calamity, the Lord was my stay.

CHAPTER *seventy-two*

"I've never seen Dinwiddie in such a quandary." Father returned from a private meeting with the governor and shook his graying head. "His own ill health is forcing a speedy end to the matter, either here or on English soil."

"Ill health be hanged!" Esmée exclaimed as he removed his hat. "Is there no one in all Virginia who supports my husband?" The exasperated words were tempered by grief. "Oh, that Quinn were here. Then all would be well."

She paced before the parlor hearth as the butler opened the front door to admit Henri himself. He joined them, his slight smile not at all reassuring, though his embrace was warm and heartfelt despite all that was against them.

He took a chair opposite Father by the hearth while Esmée settled on the stool beside him. A maid who had recovered from the pox brought steaming flip and announced supper would be served as soon as they wished. Eliza would not be joining them, pleading a headache. During the time they'd all been at the townhouse, she'd supped with them but once. Esmée had seen the light on in Quinn's study the last two nights. Was her sister unable to sleep and sorting through his things instead?

"How are you holding up under all the scrutiny?" Father asked Henri quietly.

"Well enough." Henri's weary eyes declared otherwise. "I'm most concerned about my crew—the Africans—who've been brought in for questioning. Though freemen, they risk being captured and sold into slavery the longer they're ashore. 'Tis a tenuous business."

"Indeed." Father heaved a sigh. "Dinwiddie and his council seem at sixes and sevens about the entire matter. I've yet to hear any formal charges against you. 'Tis a secretive business as well. The newspapers are printing all manner of false drivel, but most of it is in your favor."

"There are some who feel I'm more pirate than privateer, and no amount of argument or proof will convince them otherwise. And there are those who covet the prizes we've brought in."

"It all smacks of treachery and greed to me." Father stared into his steaming cup. "What of this about banning any outsiders—any spectators—from the proceedings on Friday?"

Henri lifted his shoulders in a shrug. "A precautionary measure, perhaps, as such matters always generate too much interest. But I'm going to request my crew be there. And you and Esmée, of course."

"If they deny you, 'twill be a means of furthering their dark deeds when exposing them to light could end the matter entirely." Esmée's heated remarks drew both men's attention. "I for one will be there. And on the very front row."

"I detect some of your sister's spirit in you," her father said, a beat of sadness in his tone. "Or what once was."

"She's no better?" Henri asked, holding Esmée's gaze.

She reached for his hand. How like him to deflect this serious business and ask about someone else. "She keeps to her rooms by day and Quinn's study by night. I've instructed the servants to serve her no more spirits other than medicinal tonics. She's as yet unable or unwilling to dine with us."

Sympathy shone in his eyes. Grief was a hard season, singular and unpredictable.

A slight commotion in the foyer drew Esmée's eye. When the butler announced Nathaniel Autrey, Henri got to his feet. The men embraced, emotion on both their weathered faces.

"Pardon the interruption, but I wanted to see the captain." Nathaniel took a near chair. "And inquire about Lady Drysdale."

Tears came to Esmée's eyes. Henri had few friends on land, away as he'd been. Quinn had been one of them, and now Nathaniel remained. Ned, Henri called him. His steadfast friend. "You're a most welcome interruption," she said.

"I second that." Henri leaned back in his chair, his reflective mood of moments before shifting. "Stay on for supper, at least."

The parlor air was laden with the smell of roast beef, and through the open door Esmée saw a maid setting the dining room table. Ned and Henri fell into conversation with her father while she excused herself and went upstairs to Eliza's bedchamber.

Not wanting to wake her sister, Esmée cracked open the door. Eliza sat before her dressing table, combing her waist-length hair. Freshly washed, it pillowed about her slim shoulders as it dried, the candlelight calling out every russet highlight.

Esmée entered, shutting the door behind her. "Nathaniel Autrey is here. I thought you might want to see him."

"Chaplain Autrey?"

"He's staying for supper. I hoped you would join us."

Setting her brush aside, Eliza leaned nearer the looking glass. Pots of powder and rouge lay open as if she'd been about to cover her scars. With a shudder, she turned away from her reflection and looked at Esmée seated next to her. "I have no heart for it."

"Please." Esmée was rarely so entreating where Eliza was concerned. "It might well be the last time we are all together."

Eliza's gaze sharpened. "Because Henri might be transported to England, you mean."

Esmée nodded, her whole world upside down. "There's Father besides. He's aged so much of late. Quinn's death has taught me we must never take each other for granted. Ever."

"A lesson I learned too late." Frowning, Eliza reached for some

Hungary water to rub on her temples. "Betimes I think these headaches will crack my skull."

Esmée breathed in the rosemary-mint scent. "The physic will be here tomorrow."

"Why? No physic has the remedy for what ails me."

Esmée's gaze traveled from the rumpled bed to the bedside table, where a book lay open. A Bible. The one Ned had given her?

"I am missing my wee daughter."

Eliza's surprising admission returned Esmée's attention to her. How could she not miss her own flesh and blood? Yet not once had she mentioned Ruenna since they'd returned to Williamsburg.

"If I am seldom around her, she'll never think of me as her mother. I want Father to bring her to me as soon as it's safe to do so. Besides, I've been reading the papers." She gestured to the copies of the *Virginia Gazette* littering the plank floor. "The pox seems to be abating, according to the medical men. Alice must return too."

"Of course. Father and I would be overjoyed." A glimmer of light broke through the darkness. Esmée smiled, her first in days. "I'm sure Ruenna will be much changed even in the short time you've been apart."

"No doubt." Eliza picked at a stray thread on her sultana. "For now, I want you to give serious thought to living here with me if the worst happens."

The worst? Esmée's mind raced. Henri transported, hanged from the gallows, or perhaps drawn and quartered. A wave of nausea washed through her.

With a grimace, Eliza focused on a window that overlooked Palace Green. "I suppose the matter is to be decided day after tomorrow."

Esmée nodded. "Despite your gracious invitation, I cannot stay on here in Williamsburg. If Henri is to be transported, I will go with him to England."

Eliza turned back to her. Something rare passed over her sister's ravaged features. Fear. But instead of mounting a protest, Eliza seemed to withdraw once again, the pain in her head reflected in her glassy eyes. "Please give my regards to the company. I cannot possibly endure supper."

Heartsick, Esmée stood and leaned in, kissing her sister's once smooth cheek.

Lord, be my stay.

CHAPTER
seventy-three

The governor's chambers were cold, the seats hard. Sunlight speared through the closed shutters, arrows of light across the polished floor. Nine o'clock. Esmée and her father were the first to arrive, Ned with them. As they sat near the front, Esmée saw the sea chaplain's lips moving as if in silent prayer.

Dinwiddie had yet to appear. One by one the governor's council members came in, all bewigged and powdered, some undeniably pompous, all eyes down. She knew of these men. Many of them were the most powerful in the colony, with wealth and connections that wove an impenetrable web, placing them above the law. Only two gentlemen were above reproach, men of integrity. Quinn's fellow barristers.

Lord Drysdale's usual place was left vacant. The heaviness in the chamber chilled Esmée to the marrow. Henri sat directly in front of them in a Windsor chair. His wide-set shoulders were unbowed, his manner untroubled. A murmur rippled through the room when his crew took seats in the gallery. Esmée was heartened by their presence. Not one of them seemed to be missing, though the black jacks were here at their own peril, their presence sure to infuriate the most prejudiced on the council.

Her father's shoulder pressed against hers, his low murmur reaching her ears. "I spy the printer for the *Virginia Gazette*."

Behind them, the squint-eyed owner had entered the chamber, a printer's devil with him. The word was that Dinwiddie and the council read and censored every word of each edition before circulation to the public. Would what was printed about these proceedings be fact or fancy?

The governor entered. Esmée felt a flicker of dismay. He looked old. Ill. However careworn and grim his countenance, she would not let it chip away at the promise stored in her heart. She laid hold of the memorized Psalm like a woman drowning.

He delivered me from my strong enemy, and from them that hated me: for they were too strong for me. They prevented me in the day of my calamity: but the Lord was my stay. He brought me forth also into a large place: he delivered me, because he delighted in me.

She fisted her hands in her lap. *Thank You, Lord.*

The chamber doors closed. An opening prayer was uttered. A mockery, Esmée thought. She looked at Henri's bowed head once the amen was said. What was rushing through her beloved's thoughts? Had he any inkling what might befall him here?

The governor addressed the chamber, his color high, his voice hoarse. "We are gathered here on this March day to decide the most suitable, expeditious course of action in the case of Captain Henri Lennox—"

A high voice erupted outside the sealed chamber. Some sort of commotion was brewing. A man's voice was cut short by a woman's strident tone. Then the gilded doors swung open, and every eye turned toward the back of the room. In walked Eliza, clad in all black, her step sure if hurried, a ream of papers clutched in both hands. The tap of her heels created a staccato echo in the large chamber. She looked neither to the right nor the left as she strode toward the front, past a great many astonished officials.

The governor stared at her as if trying to come to terms with her unexpected appearance. "Lady Drysdale . . ."

Eliza gave the most perfunctory of curtsies to Dinwiddie, the silk of her sable skirts rustling, before facing the chamber with its now unsettled council members.

One bewigged gentleman shot to his feet, fury staining his features. "I beg of you, madam, to take leave of these proceedings at once. Sheriff! Bailiffs! Escort this—"

"I shan't be silenced," Eliza all but shouted, overriding him. The cold fire in her eyes mirrored the harsh mettle of her tone. "If you force me from these chambers, I shall bring all my powers and my late husband's powers to bear both here and in the halls of parliament, even before the king himself. Do not underestimate me. You shall hear me out."

She stepped onto the raised dais and took the podium. Lifting her chin, she scanned the chamber as if taking stock of each man present. Unveiled—without even a hint of powder—Eliza was a shocking sight.

"As widow to one of the foremost members of the governor's council, I now state my case. My husband's papers are before me. I have studied them at length since his passing. Before his death he compiled copious correspondence and documentation of matters essential to Williamsburg, as befitted his barrister standing." She looked down at the thick ream and took a deep breath. "If you think my husband's concerns and grievances died with him, you are sorely mistaken."

Eliza's gaze traveled to Henri. She gestured to him with a wave of her hand. "Here we have a man who has been named a French spy. A pirate. That he adamantly opposes slavery is crime enough, especially to you mammon-hungry Virginians with your presumptions of supremacy and inhumane trade of human beings. But I digress. My late husband held Captain Henri Lennox in the highest esteem. As a lawyer of prodigious skill, Lord Drysdale could find no taint associated with the captain's character or reputation. In fact, he was the first to recommend him to sail under a letter of marque and reprisal. He would have been appalled at the false accusations that now float about and besmirch this man's honorable name.

"Captain Lennox had no wish to become embroiled in what will undoubtedly become an international war. He was solicited to do so by the governor himself and council members here, who now prove themselves unworthy of the captain's trust." She spoke rapidly and flawlessly, though Esmée saw her hands tremble as she took hold of the podium's sides. "Having accepted so onerous a mission that could easily have led to his own demise, Captain Lennox instead chased down an entire French fleet on behalf of Virginia's colonial government and His Majesty the King and came away with countless sealed documents and high-placed prisoners of war, not to mention enemy ships." Her voice rose a notch. "The same captain who recently gave so many prizes to the parish almshouse that it has no need of funding for the next five years or better."

She held up an accounting book. Quinn had served as vestryman and overseen parish funds. When Eliza stated the bestowed sum, the stilted silence gave way to a shocked murmur.

"Who dares bring a charge against this man?" Again Eliza scanned the overflowing chamber. "I challenge the foremost accuser, Mr. Jeffries. With your fomenting violence and mayhem in your parish's last questionable election, will you cast the first stone?" Her gaze traveled to another man on the first row. "And Mr. Percy, owner of the largest number of slave ships in Virginia, who in the year 1753 killed two Africans in a drunken rage but was never brought to trial? And you, Mr. Taylor, who cries the loudest for liberty against taxes and tyranny yet has recently been discovered embezzling funds from various businesses in town—have you any inkling of true freedom, shackled as you are to enormous personal debt? Lord Drysdale has evidence—witnesses—that prove you were in league with Jago Wherry from the almshouse to further your avaricious purposes. Shall I enlighten the chamber as to how your actions threatened my dear sister and other vulnerable women and children on Indigo Island?" She stared at Taylor till he looked away. "Must I continue, councillors?"

Eliza set the book aside and looked to Quinn's papers. "I also have before me sound evidence regarding a conspiracy involving the murder of a customs inspector a twelvemonth ago that involves your illustrious family, Mr. Calvert. And then there is the matter of Mr. Byrd, who has incited rebellion in his very county with the intent to repeal a new tax. Not to mention Mr. Knox, who has attempted to bribe the Speaker of the House with ten thousand pounds tobacco. Then there is Mr. Burkhardt, who has taken a pen name to publish a scandalous libel on this government and the established church. Such smacks of treason, does it not?"

Esmée did not realize she had been holding her breath till her chest began to ache. Beside her, Father sat stunned. This was the Eliza of old, who seemed to gather momentum with each and every word, driven by a sort of holy zeal.

"Almighty God has a quarrel with you councillors. Has He not said, 'Woe unto you, hypocrites! for ye are like unto whited sepulchres, which indeed appear beautiful outward, but are within full of dead men's bones, and of all uncleanness'? Indeed, which of you will cast the first stone?" She gathered up Quinn's papers. "How dare you accuse Captain Henri Lennox of anything at all."

The entire chamber seemed to hold a collective breath as Eliza left the podium and strode down the aisle to exit through the door she had entered. It closed behind her with a resounding shudder, a proper exclamation point to her heated defense.

Tears gathered in Esmée's eyes, making Henri's back a blur of blue cloth. No one had yet said a word. The silence was ponderous and—could it be?—threaded with an undercurrent of shame, as if the entire assembly had taken a whipping.

Governor Dinwiddie finally stood, his face the scarlet of the redcoated soldiers at his command. He struggled to speak. Taking out a handkerchief, he dabbed at his brow, then looked to the council. "Gentlemen—though I use the term loosely—who among you will now cast the first stone, as Lady Drysdale so eloquently and truthfully put it? Join me in the antechamber at once."

An excruciating silence followed. Esmée fixed her eyes on the podium Eliza had vacated as council members slowly got to their feet and adjourned through a side door. Bending her head, Esmée shut her eyes.

Lord, You alone can deliver us. Not Dinwiddie. Not Eliza. Not even Quinn had he been here. God alone.

Molasses-slow minutes ticked by. Esmée raised her head, eyes on Henri's broad back. He sat stone still, gaze forward. She longed to go to him but daren't leave her seat and cause another commotion. Murmuring began in the chamber around her. What she would give to be a fly on the wall in the antechamber! Beside her, Father and Ned sat as stoically as Henri.

At the stroke of eleven, the governor reappeared. But not the council members.

Dinwiddie inclined his head to Henri. "Captain Lennox, you are hereby dismissed. The council shan't be taking any more of your time with its unwarranted charges and fomenting of libelous gossip. Your exemplary service to the colonies and crown cannot be understated."

Joy sang through Esmée. She shot to her feet with a rustle of her silk skirts, wanting to forsake this cold, accusatory chamber as fast as she could. But not without her beloved. Henri turned toward her, his eyes smiling though his face stayed stoic. Ned grabbed Henri's hand and shook it while Father let out a long, relieved breath.

"This calls for a celebration," Father said. "Let's hasten to the Edinburgh Castle tavern, which has just reopened. A celebratory beefsteak dinner seems in order. Shall we?"

Overcome, Esmée dried her eyes discreetly with a handkerchief. "A shame Eliza can't join us."

Her father nodded as they moved toward the door. "After a stellar performance of which Quinn would have been proud, your sister has earned her rest. But 'twill take me a sennight to recover myself."

Ned grinned and adjusted his cocked hat. "Lady Drysdale's delivery puts most pastors I know to shame. And a great many actors and actresses."

Father led their small procession. "Now seems the time to tell you I'm returning to sea." Catching Esmée's wide-eyed stare, he amended, "It seems the crown is in need of my services now that war with France is to be declared."

They exited the palace into a windy, sun-scented world. Henri picked a blossom from a flowering dogwood on Palace Green and passed it to her. Arm in arm they walked toward Duke of Gloucester

Street, elation in her step as she kept up with his long stride. Her father and Ned went ahead of them, deep in conversation.

"So, Mistress Lennox, what say you about our future?" Henri brought her gloved hand near and kissed it. "Shall we set sail tomorrow for our island? Resume our honeymoon?"

"Tomorrow?" She smiled. "I'm ready to return right now, though Father is intent on a little feasting and we must thank my sister."

"Thanks hardly seems enough," Henri said.

They walked on beneath flowering trees, still stunned by the turn of events. When they reached the tavern, fiddle music spilled from its open windows, joyous and lively, entirely fit for the occasion. While Father and Ned passed inside to seek a table, Henri removed his hat and stood alone with her in the tavern's entry.

"As I told you, I've retired as privateer and government agent." His sea-shaded eyes were as earnest as she'd ever seen them. "My future is yours. Ours. On the island, tending the light."

"God be thanked." She laid a hand on his smoothly shaven cheek, wanting to put distance between them and the mainland as soon as possible. "Let us be away to our island, then. Our future is bright."

Turn the Page for Chapter 1 of Another Captivating Story from Laura Frantz—

Available Now

On the eve of her wedding, Lady Elisabeth Lawson's world is shattered as surely as the fine glass windows of her colonial Williamsburg home. In a town seething with Patriots ready for rebellion, her protection comes from an unlikely source—if she could only protect her heart.

CHAPTER

May 1775

Elisabeth took a breath, breaking an intense hour of concentration. Mindful of the pinch of her stays, she straightened, the ache in her back and shoulders easing. In her apron-clad lap was the round pillow with the new lace she'd worked. Delicate as snowflakes, the intricate design was crafted of imported linen thread, now a good two yards of snowy white. She preferred white to black. All skilled lacemakers knew that working with white was kinder to the eye.

Raising her gaze, she looked out fine English glass onto a world of vivid greens broken by colorful splashes of blossoms. Elisabeth's favorites, butter-yellow roses and pale pink peonies, danced in the wind as it sighed around the townhouse's corners. Nearly summer at last. But not only almost June. 'Twas nearly her wedding day.

"*Oh là là!* What have we here?" Around the bedchamber's corner came a high, musical voice. "Surely a bride does not sew her own laces!"

"Nay, Isabeau. I've not patience enough for that."

"Not for an entire wedding gown, *merci*." The maid rounded the four-poster bed as fast as her girth would allow, holding a pair of clocked stockings. "You have been busy all the forenoon and likely forgot 'tis nearly teatime with the countess. Lady Charlotte surely wants to discuss your betrothal ball. 'Tis rumored Lord and Lady Amberly will be there."

Elisabeth nearly smiled at her maid's flaunting of titles. A humble Huguenot, Isabeau was still as bedazzled by the gentry as the day she'd first landed on Virginia's shores. Elisabeth set aside her lace pillow and watched her maid pull two tea gowns from a large armoire.

"Are you in a blue mood or a yellow one?"

"Yellow," she said. Yellow was Lady Charlotte's favorite color, and Elisabeth sought to cheer her all she could. In turn, the governor's palace served up a lavish tea table that surely rivaled the British king's.

Glancing at the tiny watch pinned to her bodice, Elisabeth left her chair so that Isabeau could undress and redress her.

"'Tis such a lovely day, likely the countess wants a turn in the garden. Do you think her girls will be about?"

"I should hope so. Fresh air and exercise are good for them, though their father oft keeps them inside of late."

Isabeau darted her a fretful look. "On account of the trouble, you mean."

Elisabeth tried not to think of that. "The sun might spoil their complexion, Lady Charlotte says. And she's right, you know. Look at me!" Though faint, the freckles across the bridge of her nose and the top of her cheekbones gave her skin a slightly tarnished look that even ample powder couldn't cover. Her fault for slipping outside with her handwork in the private corner of the garden she was so fond of, forever hatless.

"You are *tres belle*, even speckled," Isabeau said, lacing her stays a bit tighter. "And you've won the most dashing suitor in all Virginia Colony, no?"

"One of them." Elisabeth swallowed hard to keep from saying more on that score too. Her fiancé, Miles Cullen Roth, was many things, but he was not cut of the same cloth as fellow Virginians William Drew and George Rogers Clark and Edmund Randolph.

Isabeau's voice dropped to a whisper. "Though I do wonder about love."

Elisabeth shot a glance at the cracked bedchamber door. Papa always said she gave the servants too much room to talk, but the truth was she preferred plain speaking to the prissy airs of the drawing room. "'Tis a business matter, marriage."

"So says your father." Isabeau frowned her displeasure. "I am a romantic. One must marry for love, no?"

"Is that the way of it in France?"

"*Oui, oui*!" her maid answered.

Though she was an indentured servant, Isabeau did not have a father who orchestrated her every move. Given that, Elisabeth could only guess the gist of Isabeau's thoughts. *I am free. Free to come and go outside of work. Free to marry whom I please.*

And she? Who was Elisabeth Anne Lawson? The reflection in the looking glass told her little. When the history books were printed and gathered dust, what would be said of her?

That she had the fortune—or misfortune—to be the only child of the governor of Virginia Colony, the earl of Stirling? Daughter of a firebrand mother who used ink and quill like a weapon? Possessor of a pedigree and dowry the envy of any colonial belle? Friend and confidante of Lady Dunmore? Wife of Miles Cullen Roth? Mistress of Roth Hall?

End of story.

The scarlet seal on the letter was as unmistakable as the writing hand. Noble Rynallt took it from his housekeeper and retreated to the quiet of Ty Mawr's paneled study. Sitting down in a leather chair, he propped his dusty boots up on the wide windowsill overlooking the James River before breaking the letter's seal.

Time is of the essence. We must take account of our true allies as well as our enemies. You must finagle a way to attend Lord Dunmore's ball 2 June, 1775, at the Palace. 'Tis on behalf of your cousin, after all. Gather any intelligence you can that will aid our cause.

Patrick Henry

'Twas the last of May. Noble had little time to finagle. His cousin was soon to wed Williamsburg's belle, Lady Elisabeth Lawson. He'd given it little thought, had no desire to attend any function at the Governor's Palace, especially one in honor of his nemesis's daughter. Lord Stirling was onto him, onto all the Independence Men, and none of them had received an invitation. But 'twas as Henry said, Noble's cousin was the groom. Surely an invitation was forthcoming or had been overlooked.

Noble frowned, thinking of the stir he'd raise appearing. Lord Stirling was likely to have an apoplectic fit. But if that happened, at least one of the major players barring Virginia Colony's fight for independence would be removed. And his own attendance at the ball would announce he'd finally come out of second mourning.

The unwrinkled copy of the *Virginia Gazette*, smelling of fresh ink and Dutch bond paper, seemed to shout the matrimonial news.

Miles Cullen Roth's future bride, Lady Elisabeth Lawson, an agreeable young Lady of Fortune, will preside at the Governor's ball the 2nd of June, 1775 . . .

The flowery column included details of the much-anticipated event right down to her dowry, naming minutiae even Elisabeth was unaware of. As she turned the paper facedown atop the dressing table, her smile faded. A ticklish business, indeed.

Isabeau, quick to catch her mistress's every mood, murmured, "The beggars! I'd rather it be said you have a sunny disposition and Christian character. Or that you are a smidgen over five feet tall, flaxen haired, and have all your teeth save one. And that one, *Dieu merci*, is a jaw tooth!"

"I *am* Williamsburg's bride," Elisabeth said as her maid pinned her gown together with practiced hands. "The locals feel they can print what they want about me. After all, I was born and bred in this very spot and have been catered to ever since."

"You don't begrudge them their bragging?" Isabeau studied her. "Having the particulars of one's dowry devoured by the masses seems shabby somehow."

"It does seem silly. Everyone knows what everyone else is worth in Williamsburg. There's no need to spell it out."

"Tell that to your dear papa," Isabeau answered with furrowed brow. "He had a footman pass out multiple copies of the *Gazette* this morning like bonbons on Market Square."

Unsurprised, Elisabeth fell silent. Turning, silk skirts swishing, she extended an arm for Isabeau to arrange the beribboned sleeve. Below came the muted sound of horse hooves atop cobblestones.

"Your intended? On time? And in such stormy weather?" Isabeau looked up at her mistress with surprised jade eyes.

Turning toward an open window, Elisabeth listened but now only heard the slur of rain. "Mister Roth promised he'd come. 'Tis all that matters. He didn't say when."

"How long has it been since you've seen him?"

"April," Elisabeth admitted reluctantly, wondering why Isabeau even asked. Her maid well knew, being by her side night and day. Isabeau's pinched expression was a reminder that Miles was not a favorite, no matter his standing in Williamsburg. Elisabeth dug for another excuse. "He's been busy getting Roth Hall ready for us, his letters said."

She felt a twinge at her own words, for his letters had been but two over six months. He sent unnecessary, extravagant gifts instead. Gold earrings in the shape of horseshoes. A bottle-green riding dress. Pineapples, lemons, and limes from his estate's orangery. A London-built carriage. So many presents she soon lost track of them. And not a one had swayed Isabeau's low opinion of him.

Despite his generosity, Elisabeth felt a sense of foreboding for the future. She did not want his gifts. She wanted his presence. If he was like her oft-absent father . . . 'Twas difficult to see clear to what she really hoped for. A happy home. A whole family.

"Your coiffure is *magnifique*, no?" The words were uttered with satisfaction as Isabeau produced a hand mirror for her to better see the lovely twisting of curls falling to her shoulders, the wig dusted a costly powdered pink. Twin ostrich feathers, dyed a deeper rose, plumed near her right ear.

"I don't know." Reaching up, Elisabeth slid free the pins holding the wig in place, displacing the artfully arranged feathers. "Powder is going out of fashion like patch boxes. Tonight I will move forward with fashion."

Her maid's brows arched, but she took the wig and put it on a near stand, where it looked forlorn and deflated. Catching a glimpse of herself in the mirror, Isabeau smoothed a silvered strand of her own charcoal hair into place beneath her cap. At middle age, she was still an attractive woman, as dark as Elisabeth was fair.

"We must make haste, no? But first . . ." Isabeau retrieved the ostrich feathers and refastened them in Elisabeth's hair while her mistress glanced again at the watch lying faceup on her dressing table.

Late.

Miles was nothing if not perpetually late, while she happened to be an on-time sort of person. Fighting frustration, she set down the hand mirror. "I wonder what Mama is doing tonight."

Isabeau looked up, a telling sympathy in her eyes. "Your *mère* will rejoin you when all this talk of tea and taxes blows over, no?"

Elisabeth had no answer. Mama had sailed to England—Bath—months ago. All this talk of tea and taxes had no end.

A soft knock sounded on the door, followed by another maid's muffled voice. "A gentleman to see you, m'lady, in the drawing room."

A gentleman? Not her intended? She smiled wryly. Likely the servants didn't remember Miles.

She went hot, then cold. Miles's visits were so few and far between, he seemed a stranger each time she saw him. Because of it they spent the better part of an hour becoming reacquainted at each meeting. Tonight would be no different. Perhaps they'd recover the time lost to them in the coach.

Isabeau steered her to the stool of her dressing table. With deft hands, she clasped a strand of pearls about Elisabeth's neck. The routine was reassuring. Familiar. Selecting a glass bottle, Elisabeth uncapped it, overwhelmed by the scent of the latest cologne from London. Rose geranium. Again Elisabeth peered at her reflection in the looking glass with a sense of growing unease.

Everything seemed new tonight. Her scent. Her shoes. Her stays. Her gown. She'd never worn such a gown, nor felt so exposed. Despite the creamy lace spilling in profusion about her bare shoulders, the décolletage was decidedly daring. Made of oyster-pink silk, the gown shimmered and called out her every curve. The mantua maker had outdone herself this time. Fit for Queen Charlotte, it was.

Moving to the door, she grasped about for a glimmer of anticipation. "I'd best not keep company waiting."

At this, Isabeau rolled her eyes. "I should like to hear Mister Roth say such!"

Isabeau followed her out, and they passed down a dimly lit hall to a landing graced with an oriole window and upholstered seat. The velvety blackness beyond the shining glass was splashed with rain, not pierced with stars, and the warm air was soaked. This was her prayer place. Isabeau paused for a moment as Elisabeth bent her head briefly before going further.

Then down, down, down the circular steps they went, Isabeau pulling at a stray thread or straightening a fold in the polonaise skirt before reaching the open door of the sitting room, its gaudy gold and scarlet overpowering and oppressive even by candlelight. The colors reminded Elisabeth of red-coated British soldiers. She stepped inside as Isabeau retreated. Her eyes shot to the marble hearth where she expected Miles Roth to be.

"Lady Elisabeth."

She swung round, her skirts sashaying, her head spinning as well. Mercy, her stays were tight. She'd eaten little at tea.

Behind her stood a man, the shadows hiding his features. She put out a hand to steady herself, missing the needed chair back by a good two inches and finding a coat sleeve instead. The gentleman looked down at her and she looked up, finding his dark head just shy of the wispy clouds skittering in blue oils across the ceiling. Whoever he was, he wasn't Miles. Miles was but two inches taller than she.

"Mister . . ."

"Rynallt. Noble Rynallt of Ty Mawr."

What? A recollection returned to her in a rush. Noble Rynallt was a distant cousin of Miles. So distant she had no further inkling of their tie. Quickly she calculated what little she knew of him. Welsh to the bone. Master of a large James River estate. Recently bereft of a sister. A lawyer turned burgess. The Rynallts were known for their horses, were they not? Horse racing? The finest horseflesh in Virginia, if not all the colonies.

She was certain of only one thing.

Noble Rynallt was here because Miles was not.

Surprise mellowed to resignation. She gave a small curtsy. "Mister Rynallt, what an unexpected pleasure."

"Mayhap more surprise."

She hesitated. He was honest, at least. "Is Mister Roth . . ."

"Delayed." He managed to look bemused. And apologetic.

She tried not to stare as rich impressions crowded her senses. A great deal of muscle and broadcloth and sandalwood. The cut of his suit was exceptionally fine, dark but for the deep blue waistcoat embroidered with the bare minimum of silver thread, a creamy stock about his neck. The color of his eyes eluded her, the remainder of his features failing to take root as she dwelt on the word *delayed*.

Dismayed, she anchored herself to the chair at last.

"He asked me to act as your escort till he arrives." He struck a conciliatory tone. "If you'll have me."

He had the grace to sound a bit embarrassed, as well he should. This was, after all, her betrothal ball given by Lord Dunmore at the Governor's Palace, with the cream of all Williamsburg in attendance. And she was coming not with her intended but with a . . . stranger.

Nay, worse. Far worse.

Yet good breeding wouldn't allow a breach of manners. She forced a small smile. "I thank you for the kindness. Will my intended's delay be long?"

"As brief as possible, I should hope," he replied, extending an arm.

No matter who Noble Rynallt was, his polite manner communicated that he had all in hand. Yet it failed to give her the slightest ease.

"As I rode in I noticed your coach waiting," he remarked as he led her down the front steps, past the butler to the mounting block. "I'll ride alongside on my horse."

Behind them the foyer's grandfather clock tolled one too many times. The ball had begun. Lord Dunmore hated latecomers.

They'd be fashionably tardy, at best.

ACKNOWLEDGMENTS

Where do I even begin?

People often ask me how to write a book, and I honestly tell them I don't know. It's a gift. What I do know is that my publisher, Baker Publishing Group, is extraordinary, from editorial to cover design to marketing and sales, and dedicated to bringing the most edifying fiction to readers. I'm always amazed to be part of that extraordinary process, and it's a pleasure to give a shout-out to the people who make my books better.

My agent, Janet Grant, a shining light in the industry. Andrea Doering, with her huge heart for readers. Jessica English, a wordsmith deserving of her name who, with an unswerving eye for detail, helps polish a book till print. The proofreaders, who catch every little error (or most). And my amazing marketing team, headed by Michele Misiak and publicist Karen Steele, to the sales reps and book retailers who give a book a place in a noisy world. And last but not least, Laura Klynstra, senior art director, who captured the mood and essence of *A Heart Adrift* with an exceptional cover.

A shout-out to my dear author friends, especially the irrepressible Pepper Basham, and fellow travelers who continually inspire me and make time spent on our Facebook group page "The Armchair Traveler" so much fun. Please join us!

Last but not least, a book would just sit on the shelf without readers and all those who share their love of reading through social media, reviews, gracious comments, etc. Beautiful bookstagrams especially make my world go round. Heartfelt thanks for your reading time and all else you do!

AUTHOR NOTE

Who would have thought a lifelong love of chocolate would lead to a novel about a chocolatier? But not chocolate as we know it. As has been said, "The past is a foreign country. They do things differently there." And that includes chocolate. Though I am not a chocolate historian, I quickly became intrigued by just how those American colonists developed a taste for cocoa. As so often happened, Benjamin Franklin was ahead of the trend, selling chocolate from his print shop as early as 1735. Even George and Martha Washington drank it as a favorite beverage. If you're wanting to learn more, Colonial Williamsburg is a wonderful resource both on-site and online for chocolate history, and if you crave a taste of historic chocolate, then American Heritage Chocolate might be a good start.

It's such a pleasure to set a novel in the richly historic area of Yorktown, which was once York, Virginia. Though it's hard to imagine what it must have been like in its heyday, one English traveler leaves us with a compelling impression from a letter published in the *London Magazine* in 1764: "Yorktown makes no inconsiderable figure. You perceive a great air of opulence amongst the inhabitants who have, some of them, built themselves houses equal in magnificence to many of our superb ones at St. James, as those of Mr. Lightfoot, Nelson, etc."

Today Yorktown is quieter but surely just as beautiful as it was then. The Hornsby House Inn's gracious hospitality and water views and York's wonderful museums make it come alive. Though Indigo Island is entirely fictitious, there are many islands that exist like it, including the historic Chincoteague with its wild ponies, which inspired me as I wrote this novel.

Ever since I was a child and watched *The Ghost and Mrs. Muir* (there's a novel too!), I've had a fondness for sea captains and an outright fascination for pirates. Of all my research materials, *Black Jacks: African American Seamen in the Age of Sail* by W. Jeffrey Bolster stands out as both compelling and educational, opening a door on a world unknown to many. Privateers such as Captain Henri Lennox played a critical part in the American colonies achieving independence and the formation of the United States Navy—no small feat.

Women lighthouse keepers became increasingly common from the colonial period onward, some serving astonishingly long periods of time and proving entirely capable. *Women Who Kept the Lights: An Illustrated History of Women Lighthouse Keepers* by Mary Louise Clifford was a favorite resource of mine, as was *The Lighthouse Keeper's Daughter* by Hazel Gaynor, a novel based on the life of England's legendary Grace Darling.

I never imagined writing a book about smallpox in the midst of a pandemic, but doing so gave me better insight into the history of disease and made me very thankful for modern medicine. My dear friend Ginger Graham, to whom this book is dedicated, lost her life to COVID-19 as this book neared print, giving me a very personal window on grief in a health crisis. I realized anew that life continues its usual pace even though the hole in your heart is huge. Eternal reunions must be magnificent. I'm so thankful for the hope we have in Christ.

If you've read my other novels, then you know how much I love to tuck children, especially babies, into books. It's fun to think of who or what Ruenna Cheverton might become when she grows up. Maybe she'll have a novel of her own someday. There's no doubt she'll have a fondness for a certain island and chocolate!

If you'd like to stay connected, please visit my website at www.laurafrantz.net, where you can sign up for my seasonal newsletter and find me via social media. And I'd love to have you join us at "The Armchair Traveler," a private Facebook page where we talk tea, travel, and books.

Till next time, happy reading!

Laura Frantz is a Christy Award and INSPY Award winner of thirteen novels, including *Tidewater Bride*, *The Lacemaker*, *The Frontiersman's Daughter*, *Courting Morrow Little*, *The Colonel's Lady*, and *A Bound Heart*. She loves to travel, garden, cook, and be in her office/library. When not at home in Kentucky, she and her husband live in Washington State. Learn more at www.laurafrantz.net.

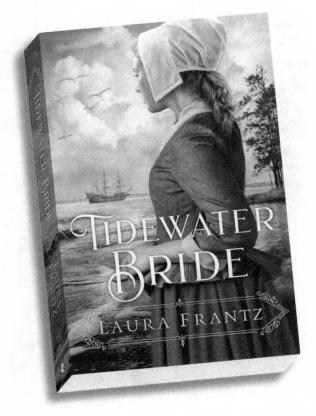

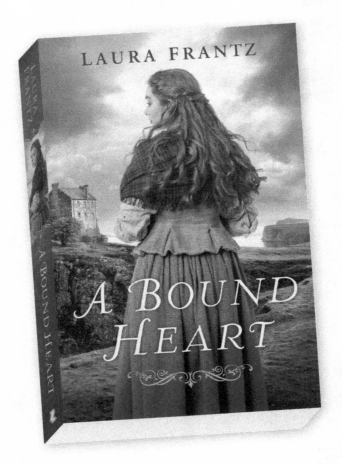

"Peopled with characters as resilient and compelling as the terrain they inhabit, *An Uncommon Woman* is an engaging story that had me up late turning pages."
—Lori Benton, Christy Award–winning author of *The King's Mercy*

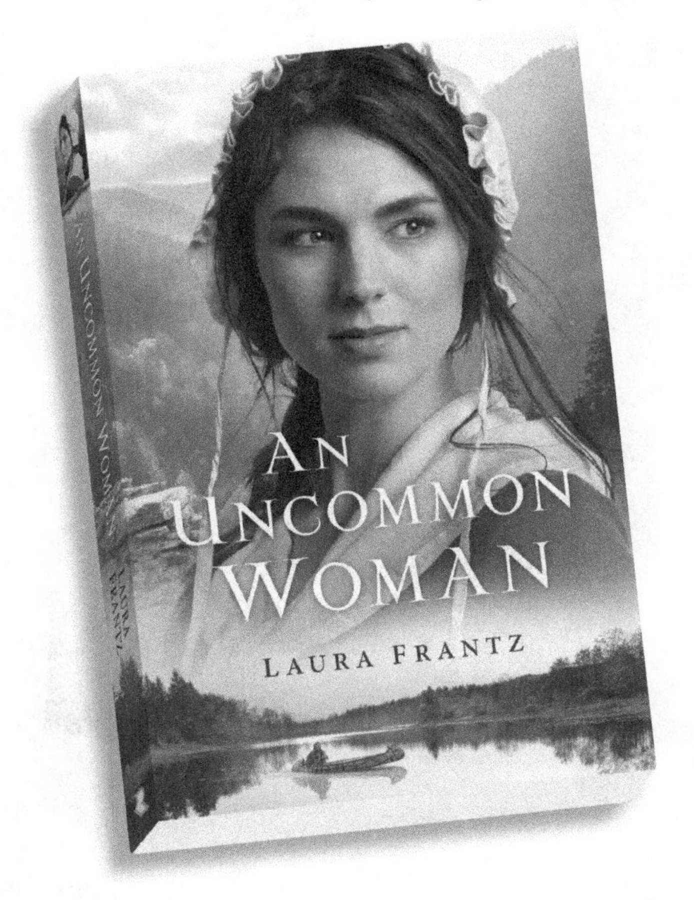

In the borderlands of 1770 western Virginia, there is no place for finer feelings. Charged with keeping the peace with local tribes, a hero of the Seven Years' War is determined to stay free of romantic entanglement—until he meets a frontier maiden who just might be able to change his mind.

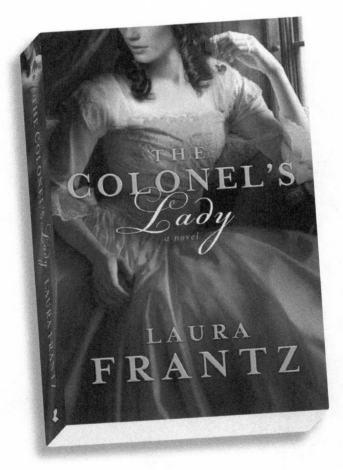

MEET

LAURA FRANTZ

Visit LauraFrantz.net to read
Laura's blog and learn about her books!

Enter to win contests and learn about what Laura is working on now

Tweet with Laura

See what inspired the characters and stories

CPSIA information can be obtained
at www.ICGtesting.com
Printed in the USA
LVHW011948110122
708307LV00002B/196